PRAISE FOR MICHAEL FILLERUP

"Fillerup understands that the world is not black and white, that moral decisions are never obvious, and that yoked to the joys of human life is an irreducible amount of doubt and pain."
—Brian Evenson

"Fillerup tells a spiritually moving story of discovery and rediscovery of faith and love and overcoming the desert of mortality."
—Richard Cracroft

"What Fillerup does is to transform the typical and mundane acts of everyday Mormon life into an art that keeps pace with the hectic and often frantic lifestyle it reveals. … He manages to render lives with compassion and insight with a language that draws attention to the agonies as well as the ecstasies of what it means to be human."
—Pauline Mortensen

"Fillerup is a master of imagery and narrative voices, a writer well worth reading."
—Robert M. Hogge

"Fillerup takes on the easy, bankable clichés, the cross-stitched tole-painted articles of faith and industry, to prod and worry and punish them into stark new metaphors for a precarious earthly estate."
—Neal Chandler

"Fillerup shines most when his characters confront the harshly beautiful desert and intractable worldview of the Navajo, finding their hardest reconciliations within themselves."
—Linda Sillitoe

"Behind the quick prose is a touch of natural sweetness that only a truly moral writer can deliver from the heart."
— Jerry Johnston

"Fillerup's novel is an accurate account of the doubts and fears that wrack our innermost souls—doubts and fears that only love and prayer can overcome."
— Bill McCarron

"Fillerup's stories are often about Mormonism in that direct way that subverts probity with good intention—or would, if the writing were any less wary than his, or any less open to complication, misgiving, ambush. A kind of home teaching, perhaps, but here set forbiddingly far from home. His characters are often profound loners, twice estranged. They find themselves marginalized in a culture—for them—already marginal, where what they do and are is sustained by religious commitment, and religious commitment is imperiled by what they find themselves doing and what, in fact, they have become. Faith, in these stories, is a terrible gift."
— The Association for Mormon Letters

The Year They Gave Women the Priesthood

The Year They Gave Women the Priesthood

AND OTHER STORIES

by

MICHAEL FILLERUP

SIGNATURE BOOKS | 2022 | SALT LAKE CITY

For Rebecca

FIRST EDITION | 2022

LIBRARY OF CONGRESS CATALOGING-IN-PUBLICATION DATA

Names:	Fillerup, Michael, 1953– author.
Title:	The year they gave women the priesthood and other stories / by Michael Fillerup.
Description:	First edition. | Salt Lake City : Signature Books, 2022. | Summary: "In this new collection of short fiction, award-winning author Michael Fillerup explores the shuttered landscapes of Mormon culture where feel-good clichés falter and the faithful are scorched in the refiner's fire. The seventeen stories in Fillerup's new compilation run the gamut in length, style, and voice, but all share an unapologetic authenticity. Whether examining the hypocrisy of sexism, the crucible of forgiveness, or the heartbreak of parenthood, Fillerup leads readers through a labyrinth of emotions but never feeds them to the Minotaur. Light shines at the end of each tortuous tunnel and, to the thoughtful reader, genuine joy"— Provided by publisher.
Identifiers:	LCCN 2021048787 (print) | LCCN 2021048788 (ebook) | ISBN 9781560854456 (paperback) | ISBN 9781560854166 (ebook)
Subjects:	LCSH: Mormons—Fiction. | LCGFT: Short stories.
Classification:	LCC PS3556.I429 Y43 2022 (print) | LCC PS3556.I429 (ebook) | DDC 813/.54—dc23/eng/20211013
	LC record available at https://lccn.loc.gov/2021048787 LC ebook record available at https://lccn.loc.gov/2021048788

CONTENTS

ACKNOWLEDGMENTS

I thank *Dialogue: A Journal of Mormon Thought*, *Sunstone*, Signature Books, Aspen Books, Deseret Book Co., Palmyra Press, and *Flagstaff Live!* for publishing several of the stories, or portions of stories, that appear in this collection: "Ghosts" (in *Once Upon a Christmastime*, Deseret Book, 1997), "How We Do Death" (*Sunstone*, Apr. 1997), "In a Better Country" (*Dialogue*, Spring 2009), "Lost and Found" (in *Christmas for the World*, Aspen Books, 1991; also in *Bright Angels and Familiars: Contemporary Mormon Stories*, Signature Books, 1992, and, in part, in *Go in Beauty*, Palmyra Press, 2005), "Missionary Farewell" (*Sunstone*, July 1997), "Pioneers" (*Dialogue*, Winter 1997), "Selfie" (*Flagstaff Live!*, Mar. 27–Apr. 2, 2014), and "Confession" (*Dialogue*, Spring 2021, under the non de plume Sylvette Wolfe).

None of these stories could have been written without the generous help and support of many friends, teachers, and family members. In particular, I thank: Elouise Bell, for her everlasting friendship and support and for surgically paring and repairing many of the stories; Lavina Fielding Anderson, for her enthusiastic encouragement, editorial finesse, and spot-on recommendations for shoring up several of the stories; Eugene England, for his vision of "a brighter day" and for battering down barriers for so many aspiring Mormon writers; Jay Fox, who introduced me to a panoply of literary gods and lit a spark when I was young and didn't know any better; Richard Cracroft, teacher, mentor, and friend, who many years ago saw some threads of goodness in a sun-bleached blowhard from southern California; my daughter Jessie, who painstakingly read and critiqued almost every story in this collection before it reached publication; my daughter Carrie and her companion, Epimetheus Bear, who donated countless hours of their time and creative talent to promote my work; my daughter Samantha and my son, Benjamin—two of my most loyal readers—for their patience, understanding, and sense of humor while I was writing many of the stories, and for overlooking the missed moments and opportunities (I hope there weren't too many of them). I also want to thank Jessie and my dear friends Judy Lyon and Stephen Allison for providing me invaluable feedback on the title story, "The Year They Gave Women the Priesthood."

I am deeply indebted to my wife's great-great grandmother Ann Jewell Rowley and her family for their heroic sacrifices crossing the American Plains with the Willie and Martin handcart companies in the summer/fall of 1856. Excerpts from their family journals and personal histories appear in the story "Pioneers."

Finally, I thank my wife, Rebecca, for her unrelenting love, support, encouragement, inspiration, and ruthless editing—never pulling punches, my perfect muse at all times and through all seasons.

THE YEAR THEY GAVE WOMEN THE PRIESTHOOD

Change was in the air, a sea change, and we could all feel it although we never talked about it openly, especially not at church and definitely not in front of our wives. But the writing had been on the wall ever since the notorious *Hastings v. Illinois* decision. It was only a matter of time now, and we all knew it.

In case you've been living in a monastery for the past fifteen months, here's the skinny. In what the media called a shameless publicity stunt, celebrity entrepreneur Teresa Hastings sued the state of Illinois for the right to be legally married to her Kentucky-Derby-winning thoroughbred. The case made it all the way to the US Supreme Court where the plaintiff lost, but a Pandora's box was opened when the justices unanimously agreed that the primary consideration in any marriage relationship is consenting adult *humans* of sound mind. By extension, the court also ruled that neither the states nor the federal government could restrict marriage on the basis of race, creed, religion, culture, socioeconomic status, sexual orientation, or—and this was the backbreaker—the number of consenting adults—male, female, or other—who desired to be legally married to one another.

The decision was hailed as a watershed victory for the LGBTQIA+ community—no surprise there—but it also sparked celebrations among Mormon fundamentalists who'd been practicing polygamy on the sly for well over a century. Closer to home, the ruling opened the door for some postmodern revelation within the mainstream church. Faster than you could say "Twitter," church members flooded social media with speculative posts about the possible reinstatement of the law of plural marriage. Overnight, websites proliferated across the internet to get ahead of the game.

The Re-restoration of All Things provided an in-depth history of Mormon polygamy, including testimonials from early and current practitioners. By contrast, *Seven Brides for Every Brother* offered an online matchmaking service for men looking for additional wives and for unattached women interested in an audacious reinvention of matrimony.

Historically, in instances like this, the First Presidency would have nipped things in the bud by issuing an official statement for bishops and branch presidents to read to their congregations throughout the world, in this case assuring us that: (1) the recent Supreme Court ruling would in no way alter the church's current position on marriage; and (2) the 1890 Wilford Woodruff Manifesto that had banned the practice of plural marriage remained in force. In other words, one man, one woman. End of story.

Most disturbing (especially for women) was the lack of a response from church headquarters. No letters from the pulpit, no official proclamation on the churchofjesuschrist.org website, no emergency broadcasts. Nothing. And that deafening silence could only mean one thing: a major announcement at the next general conference in Salt Lake City. It was going to be a historic moment, an eternal gamechanger, and I for one wanted to be there.

Maddy was much less enthusiastic. She'd read the buzz online, and the prospect of sharing her home and her husband with another woman—or two or three—didn't exactly put a youthful bounce in her step. I tried to downplay the possibility, making offhanded but tone-deaf comments like, "Why would I ever want two wives—I've got my hands full with one!" But the truth is, many of my priesthood brethren were already window shopping for potential sister wives. They didn't say anything out loud, but you could tell by the way they snatched furtive glances at the young single women in our ward. I knew that look, and I knew their intentions because I was one of them. Specifically, I'd had my eye on Suzanne Horton, the bishop's daughter, who had just returned from an eighteen-month mission to Hong Kong.

Now I realize that, based upon what I've written thus far, you've probably branded me a first-class, low-life, skirt-chasing scumbag, especially if you are a woman. Fair enough. All I ask is that you read my entire story before crucifying me on the internet. You see, I know the politically and socially correct things to say here. But I'm trying to tell the truth without whitewashing or sugarcoating. Otherwise, what's the point?

So here are the facts. I loved Maddy with all my heart, but after fifteen years of marriage, I think she would have been the first to agree that, as a couple, we were stuck in neutral. If variety is the spice of life, I'd reasoned, then adding another partner to the mix might be just the spark to rekindle our withering love life. But let me be clear: I was the one who wanted to add to the spice rack, not Maddy. And all of the lofty talk about the holy celestial order and augmenting God's kingdom on Earth notwithstanding, reinstating polygamy would be a bonus for me, and a total bust for her, and I knew it. And so did every other priesthood holder who wasn't growing a nose like Pinocchio.

A month later—the first Saturday in October—Maddy and I were sitting in the great Conference Center in downtown Salt Lake City for the first time, marveling at the terraced rows of red theater chairs and the golden backdrop of fluted organ pipes that soared towards the vaulted ceiling like great Grecian columns. The world-famous Tabernacle Choir at Temple Square visually split the stand in two, with the women in aqua-blue dresses on one side and the men in white shirts and blue ties on the other. The seats below them were occupied by the twelve apostles and the First Presidency—the closest thing we have to church royalty—all wearing the de facto uniform of the holy priesthood: white shirts, black, gray, or dark blue suits, and conservative ties.

Following the opening hymn and prayer, our white-haired prophet rose from his chair and slowly approached the podium, gripping the sides as if it were going to fly away and take him with it. A munchkin-sized man, he'd always seemed ten feet tall standing behind that microphone, addressing us in a reedy voice that had calmed our nerves through a soul-crushing recession, two ill-conceived wars, and a slew of senseless school shootings that had claimed many of our own.

He exhaled slowly into the mic, as if in that one breath he were releasing the sum total troubles of the world. Then he spoke: "My dear brothers and sisters, one of the primary tenets of the Church of Jesus Christ of Latter-day Saints is our belief in the principle of continuous revelation. We are a dynamic church, an ever-changing church, ever moving forward to do whatever is necessary to build the Kingdom of God on Earth."

I reached for Maddy's hand, but she deftly pulled it away. The Conference Center was quiet as a tomb. Some women stared in stony silence while others shook their heads in pained anticipation. To my left, a middle-aged woman was leaning forward, elbows on her thighs and forehead propped against fisted hands, as if waiting for her executioner to pull the trigger. By contrast, Maddy looked like a statue of a pissed off Greek goddess.

The prophet released his stranglehold on the podium and leaned back, raising his voice: "The Lord in his infinite wisdom has determined that the time is right for all worthy females in the church, ages twelve and above, to be ordained to the holy priesthood."

There were gasps, followed by a long hush—shocked silence was more like it. Then, in an unprecedented breach of church protocol, a young woman leaped to her feet, thrust both of her lanky arms towards the ceiling, and shouted, "Wooo-hooo!" The entire Conference Center—well, the women certainly and many of the men—erupted in thunderous applause—another big no-no. There were high-fiving and a little seated salsa action, and even some kisses exchanged between couples. But the good cheer was short-lived as the prophet lifted a withered hand, gently summoning us to order. Our typically upbeat leader seemed filled with sadness as he leaned into the mic to deliver the second greatest proclamation of our generation.

"Brethren," he said, singling us out, "my dear fellow brethren in the royal army of God. Centuries ago, the Lord gave us a marvelous work and a wonder to perform here upon the earth. We have had seven thousand years to get the job done, but we have failed. Wars, poverty, hunger, pollution, crime, violence, racism, discrimination, contention, corruption—this is our legacy, brethren."

The prophet shook his head, choking down those last five words: *this is our legacy, brethren.* After a long silence, he continued: "The Lord has been patient with us; he has been long-suffering. He has given us every opportunity to prove our worthiness and good faith. But we have been remiss in our priesthood duties. We have taken our responsibilities lightly, too often regarding them as an imposition rather than as an honor and a privilege. His Spirit can no longer strive with man. For this reason, the Lord has seen fit to entrust that sacred duty to the women of the church."

The prophet asked the priesthood holders to stand—"any and all within the sound of my voice"—which included the millions who were following on TV, the internet, or the radio, from New York to New Delhi. I rose to my feet as did the hundreds of men and teenaged boys in the Conference Center.

"Brethren, the Lord giveth and he taketh away. From this day forward, all males will be released from their priesthood responsibilities, including all rights, privileges, and authority. We would like to thank those of you who have faithfully served in your callings and who have honored your priesthood over the years. Those who would like to give a vote of thanks to these individuals may do so by raising the right hand."

Several hands crept up, slowly, reluctantly. All male. Then a silver-haired woman raised her veiny hand, followed by another dozen. All female. Soon, hands were sprouting up everywhere, male and female, like a forest of human limbs spontaneously blooming throughout the Conference Center.

"Thank you," the prophet said. "The brethren may be seated."

I sat down and quipped to Maddy. "Well, no more 7:00 a.m. bishopric meetings for me." I was clearly in denial. Maddy was still in shock.

"To be perfectly clear," the prophet said, "brethren, you have all just been un-ordained."

The prophet then asked Sister Marjorie Palmer to come to the podium. A short, wiry woman with white helmet hair popped up from the anonymous rows of the congregation. She bounded up to the pulpit where she stood shoulder-to-shoulder beside our stooped prophet. A former general Relief Society president the sisters had nicknamed "The Energizer Bunny," Sister Palmer was no stranger to us. Now she was the new president of the church—the prophetess, seer, and revelator.

"All who can sustain President Palmer in her new calling," the prophet said, "please manifest by raising the right hand."

About three fourths of the hands rose, including mine because it always does. Maddy's hand went up like it was shot out of a cannon.

"Those opposed, if any, by the same sign."

Interestingly, there were no opposing hands.

Next, the prophet sustained two new counselors—Sister Makena Nalutuesha, a statuesque, middle-aged woman from Nairobi, Kenya, and Sister Hiromi Takenaka, a surprisingly young woman from a remote village in Japan. Finally, he sustained twelve new apostles, all women.

Then our former prophet addressed us for the last time. It was brief: "I admonish the membership of the church, male and female, young and old, to heed the counsel of your new priesthood leadership."

And with that, the men were out and the women were in. The former apostles and First Presidency rose in unison and humbly filed off the stand, taking one of the many empty seats that had been reserved for them in the front rows. Meanwhile, the newly sustained presidency and apostles took their seats up front. It was a seismic shift: the dark suits, white shirts.and red power ties giving way to fuchsia and lavender dress suits and the colorful, flowing gown of Sister Nalutuesha.

One disgruntled brother hollered from the gallery: "Brigham Young would have called down thunder and lightning!"

President Palmer didn't miss a beat. With a smile warm enough to melt the polar ice caps, she replied, "Yes, I agree wholeheartedly. Brother Brigham would indeed have called down thunder and lightning—to celebrate this historic event!"

The cavernous Conference Center rocked with joy. The women—from the willowy young Beehives to the osteoporotic great-grandmothers—were universally beaming. Maddy was certainly soaking it all in.

Then President Palmer squared herself at the podium and addressed us in a high-pitched voice that projected vitality and unwavering confidence: "It's the dawning of a brighter day, isn't it?"

More applause and a few "wooo-hooos!" that she instantly silenced with her uplifted hands.

She reassured us that every member plays a vital role in the church. Paraphrasing Paul, she reminded us that the hand is not without the foot or the arm without the leg.

"Do the eyes say to the ears, be gone! We have no need of thee? Heaven forbid! Likewise, we priesthood sisters throughout the world need the love and support of you brethren as we assume the leadership of this great church."

The men were no less important, she assured us. We'd just been assigned a different role.

President Palmer paused. On the jumbo TV screen, I thought I could see tears coming, but she managed to stanch the flow as she stared into the camera—and at us—with steely resolve.

"I need your prayers, sisters and brothers—*we* need your prayers." Then she punctuated her remarks with a clenched fist: "We will not falter; we will not fail. We will move this marvelous work and a wonder forward at a pace never before witnessed by humankind in any previous dispensation. The stone has been cut out of the mountain without hands, but it's been filling the earth at a glacial pace. We are going to change that; with God's help and guidance, the stone will now roll forth at light speed!"

Subtext: now that the women were in charge, the genie was finally out of the bottle. So, buckle up everybody!

Next, President Palmer read the names of a long list of seventies and other general authorities, who we promptly sustained. The prophetess then asked for patience as church units throughout the world were reorganized with new leadership. This, she assured us, would be completed by the following Sunday.

I leaned into Maddy and whispered, "Good luck with that!" I would eat my words.

⚷

And how did we men take "The Great Transposition" as it came to be called? There were some old-timers with patriarchal starch in their garments who couldn't embrace the idea of continuing revelation unless it worked in their favor (i.e., landed them a new wife or two). And there were a number of male-chauvinist types who simply couldn't handle the role reversal, having regarded the priesthood as God's official endorsement of innate male superiority. Many of these would apostatize and leave the church. Others conceded that their wives had always been better suited to manage the affairs of the church as well as the home and begrudgingly accepted the change. But for those of us who truly understood the purpose of the priesthood—that is, to answer the call to serve at all hours to all people in all places, even if they pee on your lawn after you've spent the night sandbagging their home in a Category 4 hurricane—we recognized this for what it truly was: a blessing in disguise.

Of course, we'd still have plenty of opportunities to provide service—President Palmer had made that abundantly clear—especially if manual labor was needed such as setting up chairs or unloading a moving van; we'd still be used as beasts of burden. But we wouldn't have the primary responsibility of running the show anymore. We weren't the movers and the shakers. We would be assigned things to do. We would be supervised. We would be presided over. Hence, no more early-morning or late-night meetings. No more Minute Man phone calls. No more panic attacks when the sacrament bread was missing. No more guilt trips. At that point, I was seeing a lot of pros and not too many cons.

That said, it didn't take long to acknowledge there was a new sheriff in town, at least in my house. At our first family meal following general conference, I instinctively asked our thirteen-year-old son, Tim, to say a blessing on the food. Maddy slid her hand gently over mine and gave her eyebrow a little lift that in a private context might have seemed flirtatious. In this case, it was a soft reprimand, and I quickly backtracked: "Or maybe save that for another time, Tim."

Maddy turned to Julia, her new priesthood-holder-in-waiting, and smiled: "Would you say the blessing, please?"

As if she and her mother were co-conspirators in a cleverly designed coup d'état, Julia smiled and replied, "Yes, Mother." She hadn't called Maddy "Mother" since their last knock-down-drag-out over the appropriate age for girls to get their ears pierced.

The next day, we held a family council to discuss how the new

policy would impact our home. I took my usual place at the head of
the table, with Maddy sitting to my right and seven-year-old Marshall beside her. Tim sat to my left with Julia next to him. When
I asked Maddy to say the opening prayer, her hand once again slid
over mine and gave it a gentle squeeze.

"That's right," I said. "Sorry about that."

Maddy smiled. "It'll take some getting used to. Tim, would you
do the honors?"

After that, I was reluctant to say anything unless called upon.
My instincts served me well. Maddy asked the kids if anything
special had happened during general conference.

Tim's hand shot up. "They took away the priesthood!"

Maddy smiled. "No, they didn't take it away. Heavenly Father
just decided that it's time for women to hold the priesthood."

"Yes, but they took it away from the guys! I don't get to pass the
sacrament anymore."

"That's true, Tim, but there are still lots of opportunities for you
to serve the Lord and your fellow humans." Maddy turned to me,
looking for a little backup. When I remained mute, she said, "Isn't
that right, Dad?"

"Yes," I said, smiling as big and wide as my face would allow.

"Julia'll get to pass the sacrament!" Tim said.

"Yes, she will," Maddy agreed. "When she's a little older. Won't
that be a nice opportunity for her?"

"It sucks!" Tim said.

"I know that's a bit of a disappointment for you," Maddy
soothed, "but you can still serve a mission and get married in the
temple and hold church callings."

"Not bishop!" Tim said. "Billy Horton says his dad's not bishop
anymore."

"No, he's not, but there are still lots of things he can be—Primary
president, Young Men's advisor, president of the Men's Society—"

"The Men's Society?" I said. "You mean like a Relief Society for
men?"

"Not exactly," Maddy explained. She'd been called as a counselor in the new bishopric. Along with the other recently anointed
female leaders in our stake, she'd been the recipient of a two-day

crash course during which a general authority had explained all of the church's new programs and policies. How the prophetess and her counselors had masterminded this blitzkrieg training effort worldwide in less than a week absolutely baffled me. It used to take our elders quorum two months to plan a father-and-son outing where everyone brought their own dinner and the elders quorum ponied up Dutch-oven cobbler for dessert. My point is, Maddy was now privy to all kinds of insider information. I was not.

"Not exactly," she explained. "The mission of the Relief Society was to nurture the sisters in the ward and to provide compassionate service generally. That's now a priesthood responsibility. In other words, the priesthood will be ministering to the needs of all members of the ward, male and female, young and adult."

"What if they're gay?" Julia said.

"Or trans?" Tim added.

"It doesn't matter," Maddy said. "All of God's children who live in our ward boundaries. The Men's Society will focus on issues related to adult male members."

"Like erectile dysfunction?" Tim asked. Apparently, he'd been watching late-night infomercials on the sly.

"Serious problems," Maddy said. "Of both a spiritual and temporal nature."

"E.D.'s serious, isn't it, Dad?" Tim said.

"Oh, it's serious," I chuckled. "No doubt about that." I have to admit I was enjoying this part of the discussion.

"What's E.D.?" seven-year-old Marshall asked.

Maddy rolled her eyes. "Never mind. Enough locker-room talk. I know you have a lot of questions—we all do, and I'm sure they'll be answered in good time. But for now, let's talk about what this means for our family—for us. So, did you notice anything different about our family council tonight?"

"We're not having FHE," Julia said.

"No, stupid! Mom's conducting," Tim said. "She's the one who says who has to pray now."

"*Gets* to pray," Maddy corrected.

"Mom's wearing the pants now!" Julia said.

"That's not true," Maddy said.

"That's what Jenny Draper says. Her mom's wearing the pants now."

"I think Kerry Draper's always worn the pants in that family," I said. Maddy gave me a you're-not-helping look.

"That's not true," Maddy repeated. "I still have my job as assistant principal at the high school and your father has his job with Canyon Realty. He'll still drop you off at school and pick you up. So, it really doesn't change things all that much around the house. Now, you know I've been called to serve as first counselor to the new bishop."

"Sister Perkins!" Julia clapped her hands. Tim shot her knife eyes.

"*Bishop* Perkins now," Maddy said. "That means Mommy will have some extra responsibilities at church. I'll have to go early Sunday morning for bishopric meeting and ward council. Tuesday nights, the bishopric will be making home visits. Wednesday nights, I'll be at the church for Young Men's and Young Women's since I'm assigned to those organizations."

"That sounds like a lot of time," Tim said.

"Well, it is! But the good news is, your father will be here. So, think of it as more quality time with Dad. Isn't that nice?"

"Not if he's cooking," Tim said.

Julia framed her face with her hands like that poor soul in Edvard Munch's *The Scream*. "Dad's cooking? Aaaaaah!"

"Sometimes, yes, when I have meetings."

Tim put a finger to his head like a pistol, closed his eyes, and pulled the trigger: "Pow!"

"Well, we'll work on Daddy's culinary skills," Maddy said. "I'm sure he'll be able to rise to the occasion."

"Thanks for that resounding vote of confidence," I said.

⊶

The long and short of it was, due to Maddy's new church responsibilities, I had to pick up the slack at home, especially on Sundays and evenings during the week. And how did this sit with me? Not too bad, really.

Take, for instance, our first Sabbath following The Great Transposition. At 5:30 a.m., in pitch-black darkness, Maddy slipped

11

quietly out of bed and into the bathroom where she showered and dressed. Then, still in darkness, she tiptoed into the kitchen for a quick bite before driving off to a bishopric meeting that would start promptly at 7:00 a.m. followed by ward council at 8:30. Meanwhile, I slept for another two hours. So far, I was loving this new arrangement! Yes, I had to have the kids ready for church at 10:00, but they could dress themselves—Julia and Tim for sure and Marshall with a little coaching. Besides, Maddy had already laid out everyone's Sunday clothes (including mine) along with a checklist of "to-dos" as detailed as the battle plans for the Normandy invasion. In addition, she'd stayed up past midnight preparing a fine Crockpot feast for lunch, pre-slicing the rump roast into neat little cubes, dicing the potatoes, zucchini, carrots, and onions, and storing each ingredient separately in a Zip-loc bag. She'd also made me a "Cooking for Dummies" cue card:

STEP 1: Drop all contents into Crockpot.
STEP 2: Add 1 cup water.
STEP 3: Plug in cord.
STEP 4: Turn on LOW.

And just to be sure I didn't foul things up, she'd placed two additional signs, one on the fridge (TURN IT ON LOW) and another on the door leading to the garage: BEFORE YOU LEAVE!!!!

Maddy's breakfast menu called for pancakes and scrambled eggs, but I decided to give the kids an opportunity to exercise their agency instead. So, I placed three bowls and four varieties of cold cereal on the kitchen counter along with an assortment of breakfast bars and called it good.

By 8:30, the kids were fed and dressed, so I gathered them together and read a few paragraphs from the *Come, Follow Me* manual. We still had a little discretionary time and Maddy had admonished us to use it wisely. So, I urged Tim and Julia to engage in personal scripture study or some other spiritually uplifting endeavor. For Julia, this meant updating her Facebook page in the name of missionary work ("building relationships of trust" we used to call this in the mission field). Tim informed me that he was retiring to his room to work on family history. Specifically, he was going to log on to *Norse Feud II* and lead a Viking raid on the

Irish coast, thus acquainting himself with his ancestors on both sides of the battlefield, the pillaged and the pillagers (a novel way, I thought, of turning the hearts of the fathers to the children and vice versa). As for Marshall, I plopped him in front of the TV and inserted a child-friendly church video.

With the kids anxiously engaged in good causes, I rinsed the breakfast dishes, loaded them in the dishwasher, and then descended into my man cave—a semi-finished basement with a 64-inch flat-screen TV. I settled into my recliner and watched the NFL pre-game show, a luxury that was strictly forbidden on the Sabbath, at least, on Maddy's watch. It had been a long time, and I had no idea that co-host Terry Bradshaw had aged so miserably.

I was able to watch the first quarter of the Cowboys–Eagles game and still make it to church in time for the opening hymn. Sitting on the stand to the right of Sister Perkins—now Bishop Perkins—Maddy was wearing the mauve dress suit she'd worn two years earlier when she was awarded district Teacher of the Year. My heart swelled with pride seeing her up there. I was also thinking: better her than me.

Sacrament meeting was pretty much the same except the girls handled the sacrament—two high school seniors blessing it and eight middle-school girls passing the plastic trays up and down the pews in almost flawless fashion. Brother Van Winkle spoke first, followed by Sister Van Winkle, so that was different too, but a breath of fresh air because Dorothy kept us all in stitches while her husband droned on in a monotone that could have put a charging lion to sleep. So, score another point for women and the priesthood!

For me, the only noticeable downside was Tim, sitting to my left, head bowed, looking as if his basketball team had just lost the city championship on a silly technicality. When petite Savannah White brought around the water tray, Tim took the little plastic cup, threw his head back, and downed it like a shot of whiskey.

The big split occurred after sacrament meeting when the women scurried off to the high council room for priesthood while the men ambled into the old Relief Society room. Our meeting seemed eerily reminiscent of our old priesthood gatherings minus the quorum reports. There were no table decorations. No one knew who was giving the lesson until Brother Lewis finally confessed that it was his turn and then proceeded to read a general conference talk on spiritual preparedness. We dismissed ten minutes early and loitered in the foyer debating whether or not BYU should have gone for it on fourth and two or punted with thirty seconds on the clock. (They went for broke, lost three yards, and Boise State kicked the winning field goal as time expired.)

During the post-service hubbub, as fathers and mothers gathered their children and herded them out to the parking lot, Maddy informed me that she had to stay and "handle the tithing" and then help set apart a bunch of people for their new ward callings.

"Don't wait on lunch," she said.

"Thanks," I replied enthusiastically. "We won't!"

⚷

Now I could amuse you with Mr. Mom type anecdotes about the transition to my new role—how I burned the waffles and washed the whites with the darks and committed the unpardonable sin of spreading peanut butter on the bread *after* the jam instead of before (Mom's way, which of course was the only true and correct way), but that would undermine the more serious intent of my tale. Suffice it to say that I was guilty of the usual blunders men seem to make when suddenly saddled with more domestic tasks. By the same token—like most of my fellow brethren—I managed to survive, and, eventually, to adjust (although "flourish" would be a bit of a stretch). I may not have run the ship as smoothly and efficiently as Maddy, but I did manage to sail it safely from port A to port B without running aground or losing any passengers. Or, as little Marshall was fond of saying, especially on Sundays, "Dad's way is okay, too."

All things considered, life was moving along remarkably well. If you were one of those power-tripping men who liked being the boss, giving orders, and throwing his priesthood weight around, the transition was painful, even humiliating. But for many of us, the recent change simply meant fewer church meetings and more time to pursue our own interests.

In fact, I didn't feel any real anguish until one day in late February when my little family gathered in the bishop's office following our Sunday meetings. A diminutive, freckled redhead who weighed maybe ninety pounds, Bishop Perkins shook each of our hands, starting with Marshall , then a sulking Tim, me, and Maddy the matriarch. Last but not least, she took my daughter's palm in a warm, two-handed clasp and smiled: "Today's the big day, Julia!"

She motioned to the chair in the middle of the room and Julia sat down. Then she turned to Maddy: "Sister Fletcher, would you like to do the honors?"

Maddy's smile had never shined so big and bright. She placed her palms on our daughter's head, gently crushing the brunette curls. Bishop Perkins's hands settled over Maddy's. I stood on the sidelines with my hands in my pockets as we all bowed our heads and closed our eyes, listening to Maddy's voice: "Julia Ann Fletcher, in the name of Jesus Christ and by the authority of the Melchize-dek Priesthood which I hold …"

Then I cheated, meaning I opened my eyes to see who else was cheating: not Julia, not the bishop, and certainly not Maddy, but Tim's eyes were wide open and full of anger and confusion. I'd promised Maddy that I would be supportive, so when Tim glanced my way, I gave him a little nod and shut my eyes, hoping he would do the same. He didn't.

The first part of Maddy's blessing followed the standard script. Like a seasoned veteran, she conferred on our daughter the Aaronic Priesthood, ordaining her to the office of deacon with all of the associated powers, rights, and privileges. But from there, her words flowed like honey, interweaving snippets from Isaiah, the Book of Psalms, and the Book of Mormon so seamlessly it was like a recita-tion from a single text, yet the words were hers.

When Maddy finally said, "Amen," I kept my eyes closed for a bit, wondering if this bizarre dream would end when I opened them. It didn't. Julia was already standing, shaking hands with Bishop Perkins who followed up with a maternal embrace. Then Maddy did the same, adding a kiss on the cheek and a whisper in Julia's ear: "I'm so proud of you!" Tim offered her a begrudging hand, but Julia grabbed it and drew him in like a dancer executing a well-choreographed move. "Come here, Big Brother!" she said and gave him a double-armed hug that even he couldn't resist. That broke the hard shell of his face and a big ivory smile popped out. All you need is love, I thought. Just maybe.

Then Julia turned to me. No handshake, no smile, but she threw her arms around me like she'd never let go. "I love you, Daddy!"

"I love you too, kid."

It was supposed to be a touching moment, our eternal family united in Christ celebrating the new order of things, but never in my life had I felt such a mishmash of emotions—joy for my wife and daughter but sadness for me and my son. It was the first time the loss of priesthood had reared up and bit me in the heart.

But this was only the beginning. Two months later I would stand like a wallflower at a junior high dance while Maddy and Sister Dickerson placed their hands on Marshall's head and called upon the powers of heaven to speed his recovery from a virulent staph infection in his foot. And six weeks after that, I would stand among the other Toms, Dicks, and Harrys in our ward and watch as my white-robed son stepped down into the waters of the baptismal font where Maddy waited in her spotless baptismal gown with open arms to receive him. Although I was allowed to act as one of the witnesses, it seemed like a consolation prize. I observed with gritted teeth, reminding myself that it is what it is. Suck it up and count your blessings. But I had no idea of the magnitude of the earthquake that was about to rock my smug little world.

⸻

At the April general conference, six months after The Great Transposition had been introduced, President Palmer stepped up to the podium wearing what had become the unofficial uniform of the priesthood: a white blouse and a red or lavender jacket with a matching skirt, scarf, and other accessory. She welcomed those in attendance and the millions who were following the broadcast on TV (which included me, Maddy, and our kids). She then gave a brief report on the state of the church. Since the last general conference, seven new temples were under construction, the number of full-time missionaries had doubled, and church membership had grown by almost a million members. Worldwide, the percentage of quarterly ministering interviews had ballooned from 42 percent to a jaw-dropping 93 percent.

Here President Palmer paused for a good-hearted grimace. "What happened, sisters?" she asked. Laughter rippled through the ranks.

Next, the prophetess debuted an official proclamation, titled "The World: Our Sacred Home-Away-from-Home." In a nutshell, the two-page, single-spaced document was a scathing reminder that God created this beautiful planet for us, and it is our responsibility to take care of it. Pollution, greed, and exploitation for profit were harshly condemned. We were counseled to read and discuss the new proclamation in our families, and each ward or branch was instructed to develop a plan to help its members be better stewards and protectors of the natural world both locally and abroad.

Overall, the new proclamation was well received, although there was some mumbling and murmuring among climate-change deniers. However, the politics of safeguarding Mother Earth was instantly upstaged by President Palmer's next pronouncement.

First, she reminded us of two principles that separate our church from all others: continuous revelation and the restoration of all things. "With that in mind," she said, "and given the favorable circumstances throughout God's kingdom on earth, the Lord has determined that the time is right to reinstate the sacred doctrine of plural marriage."

For the next thirty seconds, absolute silence reigned in the Conference Center. Then: gasps, grunts, groans, scattered applause, and a fair share of "wooo-hooos" and high-fives (initiated by women).

"To be perfectly clear," the prophetess explained, "under the new order, and pending approval from your local church authorities, worthy priesthood holders can now be sealed in the temple to additional husbands."

Nestled beside Maddy in the comfort of our living room, I stared mutely at the TV screen, trying to process what I'd just heard. Grinning good-naturedly in the pews while my wife conducted meetings from the pulpit; standing idly by while she ordained my daughter and healed my ailing son; smiling like a stooge every time she called on one of us to pray; playing second fiddle in all things spiritual in our home—all of these suspensions of privilege had been tolerable, even justified—righteous payback, especially within the context of centuries of masculine, might-makes-right abuse at the expense of women. Yes, yes, and more yes! I got all of that. But this was too much. Like Cain of old, I felt like crying out: "My punishment is more than I can bear!" Instead, I muttered, "Damn."

Maddy slipped her arm behind my back and began scratching it in slow, gentle swirls, an intimate gesture she used to share after lovemaking. In this case, I think she was trying to reassure me, but all I could feel was the slow wrenching out of my heart.

"Plural marriage?" Marshall said. "What's that?"

Julia the Aaronic Priesthood holder answered, cool and confident: "It means Mom can have more than one husband—although I don't know why anyone in their right mind would want that. Yuck!'

Maddy leaned over and kissed my cheek, but that was all. No defiant statement about one husband for her—"I've already got the best, so why do I need more?" "No one's telling me I have to take another husband!" "We're a team, just you and me!"

Nope.

Plural marriage spread through the church like wildfire. Leading by example, Bishop Perkins took two new husbands—Brother Bird, a sixty-something who had recently lost his wife to cancer, and Brother O'Connor, a good-looking young attorney who for reasons unknown to us had never tied the knot. Because there were relatively few unattached men with children still living at home, family size was rarely impacted by the new order. On the contrary, adding an additional husband or two to a household significantly reduced the child-to-parent ratio, which meant more quality time for everyone.

However, in instances where the new husband had children from a prior marriage, the size of the blended family could double or even triple overnight. This was the case when Brother Buchanan and his six children joined Sister and Brother Duncan's brood of two. It was commonly understood that these new mega-families had first dibs on the longer, center pews, while those who were single or had smaller families occupied the side sections of the chapel. Typically, the mother would sit in the middle with the two husbands bookending the children on either side. On the other hand, Sister Ridley liked to sit on one end of the pew with her three husbands evenly spaced among their nine kids. (Just a quick note that I think those three men looked about as miserable as three dogs sharing a bone.) Although the First Presidency had discouraged having more than four husbands, it wasn't prohibited, and, of course, the Law of Sarah was still in force, which meant that the first husband had to agree before any additional husbands were added to the family. The Catch 22—so eloquently described in section 132 of the Doctrine and Covenants but roughly paraphrased here—was that if a spouse refused to live the higher law, he was pretty much punching his ticket to hell.

I think Maddy was more sensitive to my feelings than most wives because, for the first few weeks, she never mentioned a word about the new policy. In fact, she'd been extra amorous lately, surprising me with the frequency, the ingenuity, and the geography of our lovemaking. For a while, I actually thought she might be one of those brave exceptions who simply refused to abide by the new order.

I lived that pipe dream for almost a month.

Then one night as we lay curled up together in post-coital bliss, she began coiling my chest hairs playfully around her index finger as she cooed: "What would you think about expanding our little family?"

"Don't tell me you're pregnant?"

She laughed. "No, silly. Would you like to add a husband to the family?"

I clasped her caressing hand and said, flatly, "I wouldn't like it."

Maddy was silent. She removed her hand from my chest, and I could feel her sweet warmth withdraw from me.

"Will you pray about it?" she asked.

"No."

I knew what was next: a friendly chat with Bishop Perkins that would go something like this:

"Brother Fletcher, do you have a testimony of the restored gospel of Jesus Christ?"

"Do you believe in the doctrine as outlined in the holy scriptures?"

"Do you believe we have a living prophetess, seer, and revelator who receives divine revelation?"

"Do you sustain the prophetess?"

"Do you follow her teachings and counsel?"

Yes yes yes yes maybe?

By this point, if you want to remain a member in good standing in God's church, you've been pretty much checkmated.

"Do you believe in the new and everlasting covenant of eternal marriage?"

"Do you believe that the principle of plural marriage has been re-restored in these latter-days?"

Follow it or fry.

I rolled onto my side, facing Maddy, head propped up by my hand. "I wouldn't like that," I repeated. "What's his name?"

"Brother Bayless."

I remembered him speaking in sacrament meeting shortly after returning from his mission to El Salvador. He had the tall, stream-lined look of an Olympic swimmer—broad shoulders tapering to a Superman waist. He also sported a head of thick, bristly red hair that wouldn't recede a millimeter until he was ninety.

"Quinn Bayless?" I said. "You're joking?"

Maddy pulled the sheet up so it covered her breasts, smiling coquettishly.

"Talk about robbing the cradle!"

He'd just enrolled in a pre-law program at the university. He spoke fluent Spanish and some obscure indigenous dialect, and he had a schoolboy smile that could charm a witch doctor. I hated him.

"He's a damn kid!" I said.

"I think he's very mature."

"Why doesn't he pick someone his own age! There must be plenty of young women running around … online … somewhere for crying out loud!"

Maddy looked down with an impish grin that said everything without saying anything. I'd seen that look fifteen years ago as she'd knelt across the altar from me in the sealing room of the Salt Lake Temple. It was the undeniable look of young love.

"You barely know this guy!"

According to Maddy, she actually knew him pretty well. He was an advisor in the Young Men's program, so Maddy had been seeing him every Wednesday at youth activity night.

"You know how it is. You're stuck there all night with the other leaders. You talk, you joke around. And remember that big youth conference in March? Brother Bayless and I planned that."

"And delivered the goods too, if I recall."

"Yes, that too."

"Great! Three days in the White Mountains together!" I was furious. "Have you two—ever—ever—" I was stuttering, hyperventilating. "Did you two have sex?"

Maddy sat up stiffly. "How dare you!" She didn't slap me, but she should have.

"How long has this been going on?" I demanded.

"What?"

"*This!* This whole I-want-to-marry-a-teenager routine?"

"He's almost twenty-five. He served a mission and he also did a four-year stint in the Marines."

"Wonderful! You want to marry Captain America! The kid can't even shave."

"Maybe not, but he can deadlift 400 pounds."

Maddy climbed out of bed, snatched her garments off the floor, and vanished into the bathroom.

I called after her: "How the hell would you even know that?"

The bathroom door opened and Maddy's head popped out. "He gave a bodybuilding workshop for the Young Women."

I flashed back several weeks to the Wednesday night Maddy had dashed off to Young Women's dressed in the black, skin-tight workout suit that made her look like Cat Woman.

"We're doing a lesson on personal fitness," she'd said.

"Well, have fun!" I'd said.

Idiot! Dolt! Imbecile! Bonehead! I should have seen it coming!

Maddy emerged from the bathroom wearing a dowdy plaid bathrobe.

"You're thirty-eight for pity's sake!" I said.

Maddy's face softened—surrendered was more like it—as a

gooey grin oozed from her lips. What had happened to my beautiful, accomplished, regimented-in-all-things, mistress of self-control, eternal companion? She held out empty, hopeless hands, as if she were a slave to her emotions. Cupid had shot an arrow through her heart and that was the end of it—and the beginning.

I reluctantly agreed that we should have a family council to prepare the kids.

⌛—

The next night we gathered in the living room where inspirational paintings (the Savior beckoning us to "Come, follow me"; the Salt Lake Temple at sunset) and framed axioms ("Families Can Be Together Forever"; "Come What May and Love It!") projected a cruel irony, at least, for me. The deepest cut was the large family photo above the fireplace. Taken a year ago on the north rim of the Grand Canyon, it featured Maddy and me in the center with Tim and Marshall to our right and Julia on the left, all of us wearing white shirts or blouses. It was a photo that would soon have to be amended. What was happening to my—*our*—little family? I lowered my head and could feel the tears coming, but Maddy gave me a gentle elbow.

"Come on. United front, remember?"

I looked up, sniffling.

"What's wrong with Dad?" Julia asked.

"N-n-n-n-nothing," I slobbered.

"Just allergies," Maddy said. "You know how he gets when the weather warms up."

"Not like *that!*" Tim said.

"It's the ragweed," Maddy said. "He'll be all right, won't you, dear?"

I nodded, still unable to suppress my sniffling.

"So, what's up?" Julia said. "I've got homework." Ever since her priesthood ordination she'd been acting more assertive.

"Well," Maddy said, "your father and I have a very important announcement."

Julia beat her to the punch. "Mom, are you getting married?"

"Gross!" Tim shouted.

"To Brother Bayless!" Julia said. "He's hot!"

Maddy blushed. "Well, now that the cat's out of the bag ..."

"That's so gross!" Tim said. Then he hurled the most damning insult possible at his mother: "You're *old*!" He bolted for the hall, but I grabbed him by the arm.

"Whoa, buddy. Where do you think you're going?"

Tim wrenched his arm free. "Mom's getting married and you're okay with that? Unbelievable! It's disgusting! *You're* disgusting!"

I took my son into my arms, stared into his teary blue eyes, and saw nothing but outrage. It was directed not at his mother or his sister but at me: How could you let this happen? How could you possibly have screwed everything up so totally?

In another generation, this would all be old news, no big deal, just as polygamy had been "just the way it is" generations ago. But he was a first-generation victim, suffering the loss of what had been his birthright as a male since the beginning of time.

I glanced at Maddy who looked as if she were standing on a forty-foot diving platform holding her breath. I briefly debated whether I should give her a vindictive shove or a helping hand.

"Tim," I said, "did you know your great-grandfather had two wives? Zenobia Carlson and Teresa Stockwell?"

Tim looked confused. "No."

"Well, he did!" I said. "Many years ago, God instituted the law of plural marriage and your great-grandfather obeyed it. And now your mother's going to have two husbands, me and Brother Bayless. And I guess I'm okay with that because the Lord's commanded it, so I kind of have to be okay with it, don't I? And it's not going to be easy, but we're going to make it work because that's what we do in our family. Okay? Can you help me with this?"

"Okay," Tim sniffled, wiping a hand under his nose. Then he opened his arms, I thought to receive my reassuring embrace, but instead he ran to his mother who looked over his fallen shoulders, mouthing me a giant *Thank You*! I couldn't remember the last time she'd messaged me such a genuine look of love. For a moment, I thought maybe this could work after all.

Then Julia had to rain on the parade. "Does that mean I'll get to have two husbands someday?"

"Maybe," Maddy said.

Julia smacked her fist into her palm. "Awesome!" I was surprised by how quickly she had changed her tune about multiple husbands.

"Don't go around crowing about it," Maddy said. "Besides, marriage is the last thing that should be on your mind, young lady. You should be preparing for a mission and college in that order."

Tim came up for air. "Will I have to share my wife with another guy?"

"Or two or three or four," Julia chided.

Tim's head dropped with an edge-of-death groan. "Do I still get to call Dad *Dad*?"

"Of course, you do, sweetheart," Maddy said. "He's your father and he'll always be your father."

"What do I call Brother Bayless?"

"We'll just have to see about that. I think Uncle Quinn might be a good start."

The rest of the family council dealt with logistics. We had four bedrooms, all located on the upper floor of our home with the master bed and bath on the south end, the guest bed and bath on the north end, and two smaller bedrooms sandwiched in between them and separated by a Jack and Jill bathroom. Obviously, Maddy would occupy the master suite. Julie would move into the guest room, and Quinn would share one bedroom with Tim while I would share the other with Marshall. Maddy and I agreed that it would be best if Quinn and I weren't roommates.

Of course, Maddy and I would discipline our children. If she and Quinn were blessed with offspring, they would keep their kids in line. Quinn and I had more flexibility in our schedules than Maddy who had to be at the high school before the first bus arrived in the morning and long after the last one left in the afternoon. So, Quinn and I would alternate days ensuring that the kids were awakened, dressed, fed, and safely transported to school. On the days Quinn was responsible for school drop-off and pick-up, I would prepare dinner, and vice versa. At church we would sit together as a family, with Quinn on one end, me on the other, and Maddy on the stand with the rest of the bishopric. In all things we would be a family with the exception of occasional husband–wife getaways. Above all, we would all work cooperatively and harmoniously together. We were going to make this work!

With that, Maddy directed us all to kneel down, after which she said a long, heartfelt prayer, speaking with the tongue of an angel.

⚬⊤

When Quinn and Maddy returned home from their week-long honeymoon in Cancun, I tried my best to look happy for them. To her credit, the moment she entered the house, Maddy bee-lined to me with a hug and a long kiss on the lips. "Thank you," she whispered, "for … everything!"

"I hope you two had a good time," I said without choking on the words. I was quite proud of myself up to this point.

"It was great!" Quinn said. "We did some snorkeling, sunbathing, visited the ruins."

And lots of copulating, I thought. Lots and lots of hot and heavy copulating.

"Well, great! It sounds like you had a great time." I wanted to put it in the rearview mirror, but Quinn wouldn't let it go.

"We went deep sea fishing, did some shopping, took a nice sunset dinner cruise on a sailboat …"

And copulating. Lots of rigorous, creative copulating. I get it, buddy. Pump the brakes.

"And then we took a tour into the jungle and rode the zip line …"

I grabbed Maddy's suitcase. "I've got this."

Quinn was still giving the kids a play-by-play as I trudged up the stairs.

A week later, on a school holiday, Maddy asked to meet with me privately in what had once been *our* bedroom. She smiled and motioned towards the king bed, adorned with a heavy floral spread and decorative pillows arranged neatly along the oak headboard. I recalled our old morning routine when the two of us would make the bed together. Each and every time she would walk me through her laborious step-by-step instructions: sinking her fist deep into the corner of the fitted sheet and then pulling it down over and snugly under the corner of the mattress—"Like this! Like this!"; spreading and smoothing out the top sheet; folding each corner at a perfect forty-five degree angle before lifting the mattress just high enough to tuck the sheet underneath it without disturbing the bed skirt; and, finally, measuring one palm's-width of bedspread below the mattress on either side—"No more, no less!"—before plumping and aligning the decorative pillows.

On a good day, when I was cooperating, the complete process took ten minutes, although it often felt like an hour as I rolled my eyes, sighing, grumbling, playing the long-suffering but compliant, henpecked husband, as if this were a demoralizing task way beneath my manly pay grade. In short, women's work.

Now it was all coming back to bite me. What I would have given now for one of those intimate, domestic moments, just the two of us, without the ubiquitous specter of Quinn hovering in the room!

Maddy was wearing her camo exercise suit. Post workout, her face was still flushed and pinpoints of sweat pimpled her forehead. Her brassy blond hair was tied in a pragmatic ponytail. She sat on the edge of the bed and smiled at me, patting the empty space next to her. I sat down, leaving a two-foot gap between us. She leaned over, slipped her arm around my waist, and gave me a gentle tug.

"Come on," she said. "I won't bite."

I edged over until I was almost touching her. I was so confused at the moment. It had been a difficult and awkward week of adjustments, especially at bedtime when Maddy and Quinn seemed to surreptitiously disappear into her bedroom. On the one hand, I felt like a little kid bracing himself for a soft-love scourging from his mother. At the same time, I was feeling those deep stirrings that a husband feels for his wife, especially in the privacy of their bedroom.

"Chad," she said, taking my hand in hers. The simple press of her flesh to mine was like a shot of desire straight to my heart. I turned towards her, my arm snaking around her waist, but she gently pushed it down. "Chad, that's not why we're here. We need to talk."

I withdrew my arm and lowered my head. She was still holding my hand, but now it felt wooden.

"Chad, I know how hard this is for you. Believe me, I know."

Desire dashed, hope gone, I was in no mood for a maternal pep talk. How the hissing, pissing, kissing hell could she know what I felt?

"But it's God's plan, not mine. Otherwise, do you think I'd be doing this?"

I stared at the carpet.

Maddy sighed. "Do you remember when Timmy was born? Remember how we held him in our arms and thought we could never love anyone as much as we loved him? Remember?"

I nodded.

"Do you?"

She wanted verbal affirmation. No ambiguity. "Yes," I said. "He was beautiful. Perfect from head to toe."

"And then two years later we were blessed with little Julia. Remember how much we loved her?"

I nodded

"Do you?"

I could see where this ship was sailing. "Yes."

"And did we love Timmy any less?"

"No."

"Or when Marshall was born? Did we love Timmy or Julia any less?"

I shook my head.

"You see? Love multiplies! There's plenty for everyone. The more you give, the more you *have* to give. Love doesn't diminish. It's not a cup you drain drop by drop. Love's infinite! It multiplies!"

"Maybe," I conceded, "but time and attention diminish. They're finite. Twenty-four hours in a day. More kids, less time and attention. Same with husbands." My language was deteriorating into Tarzan talk.

"That's true, sweetheart, and that's what we need to talk about. You know how we budget our time between work, church, and the three children? I need to do the same with you and Quinn. So, this is my proposal and I'd like to run it by you before sharing it with Quinn. Is that all right?"

Maddy was speaking in the calm voice of reason; it was the voice of a mother trying to reassure her little boy that the bogeyman wasn't hiding in the closet waiting to devour him for a midnight snack. It was not the voice of friend talking to friend or wife to husband and certainly not lover to lover.

"Sure," I said.

She explained that during the daytime the family would live in common quarters—shared meals, shared Family Home Evening and scripture study, shared family prayer, and so forth. One big happy eternal family. Household tasks would be divided evenly on a rotating basis between the three adults and, to the extent of their maturity and abilities, the three children. She had even designed an elaborate wheel-within-a-wheel-within-a-wheel chart designating days of the week, tasks, and who was responsible for what.

Then came the clincher. Tuesday, Thursday, and Saturday, I would sleep in Maddy's bed. Monday, Wednesday, and Friday would be Quinn's nights. Sunday she got a bye—"My Sabbath," she chuckled.

"That doesn't mean we're going to have sex every night," she clarified. "It just means that, when it's your turn, you'll share my bed and spend the night. If any of us are out of town or otherwise indisposed on our designated night, that's life. No make-ups, no swapping nights. Keep it nice and simple."

She squeezed my hand. "What do you think? Can we make that work?" Her voice had a pleading edge. For a moment she was the lovely bride of my youth again, not my reprimanding mother.

"Sure," I said.

"Thank you!" she exclaimed and kissed me on the cheek.

"You know, Quinn's a really neat guy and I think you two could become really great friends if you work at it."

I removed my hand from hers. "One step at a time, okay?"

She looked anguished, and I felt a surge of happiness.

"Will you try?" she said. "For me?"

"Of course," I said.

8—

Quinn must have agreed as well because that night, after the kids had gone to bed, the three of us watched an episode of *The Big Bang Theory* together, with Maddy wedged in between me and Quinn on the faux leather sofa. She clasped Quinn's left hand but, when she reached for my right hand, I tucked it under my armpit. I wanted her to feel at least an iota of the pain I was suffering. However, I quickly realized that Maddy was very content holding

Quinn's hand and might be equally satisfied if I skipped my turn in her bedroom too! I'd better take what I could get whenever and wherever I could get it. Breadcrumbs.

So, I reached over and slipped my palm into hers. Maddy looked at me and smiled. She was probably thinking this was actually going to work.

At 10:30 p.m. Maddy switched off the remote, turned to Quinn, and kissed him good night. "I love you," she whispered, and it was like a dagger in my gut.

"I love you too, *Angel Eyes*," he said, forcing a smile.

Every couple has their own private love language—pet names and little sayings spoken only between the two of them during those most intimate moments. And I realized that my Maddy—not *my* anymore but *our*—had become bilingual in the worst possible way, at least from my vantage point.

She turned to me and pressed her index finger lightly against my chest, smiling her impish smile. "I'll see *you* in a few minutes."

With that, she sashayed up the stairs, putting a little extra motion in her hips as she glanced back over her shoulder and smiled like a femme fatale in a film noir. To an outsider, it might have looked tacky, orchestrated, cliché, but nuts to that! It had the desired effect.

Quinn had strolled into the kitchen. I heard the fridge open and the faucet briefly running. Apparently, he was going to stall until I had ventured up to Maddy's love nest.

As I started up the stairs, my anticipation was ambushed by apprehension. Suddenly my pulse was racing like a spooked horse. This would be the first time Maddy and I had made love since Quinn had joined our family. And her youthful glow following her honeymoon in Cancun hadn't gone unnoticed. I wasn't a total couch potato, but I'd put on a few pounds over the last fifteen years—thirty-four to be exact. I wasn't Jabba the Hutt, but I'd grown a little thick around the middle. And ever since Maddy had broken the news about Quinn, I'd been drowning my sorrows in midnight milkshakes and Dairy Queen Blizzards. Quinn, on the other hand, was one of these fitness commandos who got up at 4:30 a.m. to subject his body to two hours of torture at the gym before breakfast. I liked to think that Maddy and I had always enjoyed a very satisfying sex life, but she'd never had any basis for comparison. Now she did.

Plodding upstairs, I told myself to relax, take a deep breath, this is just like riding a bicycle, but the what-ifs began assaulting me like little harpies. I didn't have a foot in the grave yet, but I wasn't in my twenties either, not like Quinn who could probably do it standing on his head if Maddy was willing. I'd been anticipating this moment for the past three weeks, really, and now sweat was sogging my armpits and my legs were turning to jelly. As I placed my hand on the doorknob, I could feel the last embers of desire quenched by a bucket of stone-cold fear.

I opened the door, slipped inside, and there she was, sitting up in bed in the semi see-through negligee that she reserved for special occasions—anniversaries, birthdays, special weekend get-aways, and (perhaps?) second honeymoons with a second husband. The little midnight ruffles were strategically placed to tease the mind and fire up the flesh. I was devastated. To further doom me, two candles were burning on either nightstand, releasing a sweet plumeria fragrance that was supposed to stoke passion but instead ignited panic and paranoia.

Maddy smiled, closed her book, and turned off her reading light. "Come," she whispered, and I could hear the silken fabric of her gown slither on the fresh clean sheets.

I wilted. I wilted in her arms. She tried all kinds of tricks to revive me, but it was hopeless—*I* was hopeless. I finally turned over on my side, facing away from her, and curled up like an infant in the womb. I felt her hand on my back, rubbing it gently and then stroking my head as she whispered, "It's okay, Baby. It's okay." Our love language had forever changed. I may as well have stuck my thumb in my mouth and sucked it like a popsicle

&—

Dr. Silverman says there's a vicious cycle to this—I can't even write the word, let alone say it; the most humiliating and self-loathing thing that can happen to a man in the presence of the woman he loves. And the cruelest paradox: the more you fret about it, the worse it gets. And I would think about it constantly—at work, at home, in the car, watching TV. I ached for another opportunity but dreaded it too. What if what if what if what if. Those damn harpies! That opportunity, of course, would come Friday night, but not until Quinn got his turn at bat.

He and Maddy returned from chaperoning a stake youth activity at about 11:00 p.m. First thing through the door, Maddy glided over to me, watching TV in the living room, and planted an affectionate kiss on my cheek.

"How'd it go tonight?" she asked.

"Fine. The kids are in bed."

"Wonderful! You're so good!"

"How's it going?" Quinn said, sauntering in like a hired gun who'd just cleaned up Dodge.

"I'm beat," Maddy said, "and I've got a big day tomorrow." She kissed me again and trudged upstairs as if she were wearing ankle weights—a good sign from my perspective. Following close behind, Quinn had a little more spring in his step. I watched as Maddy and then Quinn disappeared into the bedroom.

I puttered around in the kitchen a bit before going up to my bedroom where Marshall was curled up like a seahorse, out for the count. We shared the room adjacent to the master bedroom, and my bed was located next to the adjoining wall. Always looking after my best interests, Maddy had suggested that I move the large bed to the other side of the room and Marshall's smaller bed against the wall, but I'd nixed the idea. "This works better for me," I'd said, and Maddy could see that I was adamant. She held all the cards except for the Joker, which meant she had to capitulate on the little things in order to win the big ones.

"Okay, if that's what you really want," she'd said.

"Yes, definitely," I'd said.

Now I was going to pay for my stubbornness.

As I lay in bed, I tried not to listen to the sounds next door, at least at first. But the faintest noises seemed amplified, as if Maddy had mic'd her room just to torment me, and my ears picked up everything: the closing of her book, a rustling on the bed, soft sounds, whispers that slowly morphed into much more. I knew I should respect their privacy, but I couldn't resist. I pressed my ear to the wall and for the next fifty-eight minutes (yes, I timed it on my alarm clock) I listened to the impassioned sounds of love and, more specifically, their new love language. It culminated in mutual gasps of ecstasy—perfectly timed, a feat Maddy and I had never achieved in fifteen years of matrimony. As for the fifty-eight-minute stretch, I was a novice, a child.

It haunted me through the night as I reimagined my Maddy doing things to Quinn she had only done to me, and Quinn caressing her in places I alone had caressed. I felt a wailing anguish I had never before experienced or imagined. I clenched my teeth, pounding my head with my fists in anger and shame and rage. When I stopped, I could hear them exchanging joyful little giggles in the dark.

The next night, Saturday, I failed again in spite of Dr. Silverman's little blue pill.

"It's all right," Maddy cooed and quickly fell asleep.

Sunday morning, she left early for her bishopric meeting, so I awoke to an empty bed which I made to the best of my abilities. Then I meandered into the bathroom where Maddy's negligee was hanging by a hook, silently mocking me. Her bra was sitting on the sink, doing the same. I looked around, confirming my privacy, then placed my fingertips on one of the cups, smoothing them over the lace fabric, imagining her breast inside it responding to my touch as it used to. Then my other hand went to the other cup, my eyes closing as I drew a pair of slow, delicate circles—

"Dad!"

I jumped away from the sink as the door popped open and Marshall appeared in the frame.

"Haven't you ever heard of knocking!" I said guiltily.

He looked around the bathroom, confused. "What's for breakfast?"

"I'll be right down."

"I know, but what's for—"

"I said I'd be right down!" I snapped. Marshall's face drooped as he slouched away.

Over time we settled into a palatable routine. On Monday night we all had Family Home Evening together and on Wednesday night Quinn, Maddy, Tim, and Julia went to the youth activity. Tuesday night Maddy made home visits with the bishopric and Thursday night she had her yoga class unless there was some type of school function. I slept with Maddy on my designated nights—literally, breadcrumbs—and on Quinn's nights, I tried my best not to torture myself—that is, I tried to keep my ear away from the wall.

Gradually—and thankfully—the honeymoon period cooled. Maddy was putting in such long hours at the high school and church that her greatest desire now seemed to be a good night's sleep. By 10:00 p.m. she was exhausted. "I'm soooo tired," she would announce to all, stretching out the "o" extra long. Subtext: if you're sleeping in my bed, no hanky panky. In truth, I was relieved because it meant there were no expectations and, hence, no further humiliations. And I have to admit that I got more than a twinge of pleasure when Maddy played the fatigue card on Quinn's night. I loved watching his iron jaw hit the floor.

So, things were getting better—tolerable, at least—until one night after we'd put the kids to bed and the three of us had settled on the sofa to watch a silly rom-com. Maddy clasped my hand with her right and Quinn's with her left and exclaimed, "I've got great news! We're having a baby!"

Quinn smothered Maddy with hugs and kisses until she had to gently push him away. Then she turned to me, smiling awkwardly. "We're having a baby," she repeated, hoping I would play along, but it was pointless. Quinn knew, and he knew that I knew.

"That's wonderful," I said. "Great news."

Over the next few months, I tried my best to impersonate the happy father of a child that was all Quinn's, zero mine, no paternity test needed. Maddy updated her wardrobe with cute, form-fitting outfits that advertised her imminent motherhood and served as a constant reminder that she was bringing a new life into the world without me. In my mind, she was also shining a big, bright spotlight on my shortcomings as a man and a husband and whatever else.

In the meantime, I had to put up with Quinn's obsessive attention to Maddy's every little need: helping her up from the sofa;

elevating her legs; massaging her back, shoulders, and feet; preparing her protein shakes and vitamin-enriched fruit smoothies; sharing daily progress reports on Facebook and YouTube. All of which was bearable until Maddy started showing.

After that, a dozen times a day, Quinn would place his hand on Maddy's bulging stomach and smile his sappy, cheerful, all's-well-in-Zion smile. Maddy would smile back at him with equal quantities of gush and glow. Even the kids got into the act, pressing their palms on Maddy's belly and getting all goo-goo-eyed if they felt the slightest bit of movement. When Maddy asked if I wanted to touch, I politely declined.

"Are you sure?" Quinn asked, utterly baffled that I didn't want a piece of the action.

"Absolutely," I said.

The worst part was Quinn's cocksure grin, which I interpreted as a Hagar-like disdain that he disguised with dripping do-good-edness. Could he help me with the dishes? Did I want another serving of meat loaf? Could he cover my shift with the kids so Maddy and I could have a night out alone? Acting oh-so-nice—I couldn't stand it. Because nice is easy when you're on top. Nice is easy when your nose isn't being rubbed in it. Nice is so damn easy until you're suddenly told that the person you thought you were going to walk hand-in-hand with through the eternities isn't. Sorry, gotta share now.

My anger was burning so hot that I began to fear that one day the volcano would erupt, and I'd do something that could never be undone. I considered scheduling a meeting with Bishop Perkins, but then I'd have to lay all my cards on the table, including my bedroom fiascos. Call it false pride, male ego, toxic masculinity, whatever—I simply couldn't confess this to a woman. It would be degrading enough baring my soul to a man, but at least he might be able to understand this uniquely male brand of jealousy, humiliation, and rage. Besides, what could Bishop Perkins—or any bishop—do about it other than offer the standard spiritual Rx: fast and pray; read the scriptures; be patient and long-suffering in your afflictions, for they are but the twinkling of an eye in the eternal scheme of things; sex is only a small fraction of the marriage relationship, so put aside the natural man and love your wife as a sister and her other husband as a brother; the Savior through his Atonement has suffered all things including this: you do not walk alone.

Thanks, but no thanks.

So, I talked myself out of it and bit my tongue instead. Meanwhile, the list of irritating little Quinn-isms kept growing. One afternoon, I returned home early from work and found Tim and Quinn shooting hoops in the driveway. They quickly shuffled aside so I could park in the two-car garage, in keeping with our family agreement: one side was reserved for Maddy's Honda Accord and the other side for my Plymouth minivan. Quinn parked his old Nissan clunker on the street. As I rolled by, I waved to Tim who looked away guiltily, as if he'd just sold his soul for a Steph Curry jump shot.

"Want to join us?" Quinn asked.

"Come on, Dad!" Tim said.

"No, thanks," I said. "You guys look like you're doing just fine. Three's a crowd, you know."

I'd hoped this would hurt my son, which wasn't the most fatherly thing to hope for, but I wanted him to feel a bit of the rejection I was suffering. However, once again, my plan backfired. Tim interpreted my non-participation as a green light, and from that day forward he and Quinn were basketball buddies. Half a generation my junior, Quinn was also more savvy than me with social media technology and the latest video games. Even music provided common ground as they jabbered about rock bands and recording artists that were alien to my antiquated ears.

Julia saw in Quinn a more relatable ally as she navigated the treacherous waters of adolescence. One day she waltzed into the kitchen wearing a skirt that barely covered her bottom. I pointed to the hallway: "No way, Josefina! Upstairs. You know the rules."

I was direct, forceful, the father in charge, and quite proud of myself. But later, as I drove the kids to school, Julia pouted in the back seat, sandwiched between Tim and Marshall. Riding shotgun up front, Quinn told them a story about his big sister and her daily fights with their mother over wardrobe decisions. Instead of playing the heavy, he put a humorous spin on it, and by the time we arrived at the middle school, Tim and Julia were guffawing like punch drunk sailors. As Julia climbed out the backseat, Quinn said, 'Your mom and dad love you. You know that. They're just trying to keep you safe. It's a tough world out there, and you don't want to send the wrong message. Okay?"

Julia nodded obediently.

"Have a great day, Jewels!" he said.

"You, too," she said, and then whipping around as if she'd forgotten her head: "I love you, Uncle Quinn!"

"Same here!" he yelled.

"Nicely done," I said.

"Yeah, she's a great kid," Quinn said.

"Jewels?"

He smiled. "She seems to like it."

I gripped the steering wheel as if it were his neck.

As for Marshall, he already preferred Quinn's bedtime stories. "He's makes them up," he had confessed to his mom. "Dad reads from a book. Quinn makes funny faces and a different voice for everybody."

In retrospect, Quinn's transgressions were pretty trivial, but I'd become a giant pressure cooker and anything he did—big or small, right or wrong, intentional or accidental, real or imagined—turned up the heat a little bit more and a little bit more until one day—ka-boom!

It was a Saturday morning and Maddy had gone to the church for a 6:00 a.m. priesthood service project and a little grocery shopping afterwards. I was in the kitchen fixing hot chocolate as the kids sat at the kitchen counter wolfing down French toast—my day, my treat, extra syrup for all! We were off to a great start! I was asking the kids about school and their plans for the day, and they were actually answering me in complete sentences. Then Quinn ambled through the back door in his biker pants, fresh off a twenty-five-mile ride to the lookout station.

"Hey, how's everybody!" he said as he took a stool next to Tim.

The kids greeted him in joyous unison: "Hi, Uncle Quinn!"

Last night had been his turn in Maddy's bed and he was wearing his morning-after alpha-male smirk. As I handed Tim a steaming cup of hot chocolate, Quinn said, "Hey, I'll have some of that!"

It wasn't exactly a demand but an implication, and it was the way he'd said it—shoving an empty mug in my face, expecting me to hop to and fill it. Or maybe I'd just grown so insecure and paranoid that if he'd said, "Happy Saturday!" or "Holy guacamole!" I'd still have gone ballistic.

"The hell you will!" I said and reared back to deliver what I thought would be a head-spinning, jaw-cracking, right hook that would smear astonishment and humility across his glossy, smooth-shaven, poster-boy face and put him, once and for all, in his place—on the tile floor, on his butt, begging for mercy.

Apparently, in his spare time, while mastering two languages and perfecting the step-back jump shot, Quinn had also taken some martial arts training. In the split-second before my fist should have met his face, he whirled around, blocked my blow, and countered with a sledgehammer to my solar plexus and a side kick to my leg that sent me crumbling to the floor, clutching my knee in agony.

"What the hell, man!" I yelled.

"Dad! What are you doing!" Julia screamed.

"What am *I* doing? What the hell is Jackie Chan over there doing!"

"Daddy swore," Marshall said.

"You started it, Dad," Tim said.

Quinn was standing over me like some tribal war lord who'd just defended his goat herd. I couldn't let my kids see me go down without a fight, so I lunged at him, but he side-stepped me and slammed his foot down on my other knee.

"Son of a *bitch!*" I yelled.

"Daddy swore again," Marshall said. "Mom's gunna be ma-ad."

Quinn maintained his conqueror's stance as I dragged my crippled body to a chair and pulled myself up high enough to plant my sorry ass on it.

"You son of a bitch!" I snarled.

Quinn stared down at me with those baby-blue bedroom eyes. "Had enough?" he said, and then had the audacity to extend me a helping hand. I slapped it away.

Of course, just then Maddy walked in lugging two bags of groceries that she immediately dropped on the counter.

"What's going on here?" she demanded.

"Daddy swore," Marshall said.

"Chad had a little accident," Quinn said.

"What happened?" Maddy seethed.

"Accident? That a-hole took out my knees!" I was almost bawling, not from the physical pain but because I looked so pathetic, like a little kid in a playground squabble appealing for intervention. A kissy-boo on the wound.

Quinn held up his hands apologetically. "He threw the first punch," he said.

Maddy glared at me as if I were Satan at age five: "Is that true? Did you?"

She was mommy and referee. At that moment I realized I'd lost her, probably forever. I would never again hold her in my arms as a true husband, as man and wife; I would never again be her guardian and protector, if I ever had been.

"You!" she said, pointing to Quinn. "You should know better than to pick on someone twice your age!" (Now *that* hurt, much more than his cheap shot to my solar plexus.) "And you!"—pointing to me—"You need to get over it! Do you understand? Just get-ov-er-*it*! Now go to your rooms, both of you!"

Quinn glared at me as if I'd just goosed his mother. It's the first time I'd ever seen him angry or upset, and it gave me immense pleasure.

"NOW!" Maddy commanded.

I pounded up the stairs and into my room, slamming the door, fuming. How could I ever face Maddy or my kids again? I was a whipped dog, a shuddering little child in what had once been my home. I wanted to dissolve into nothingness. Instead, I punched my fist into the drywall.

"Stop that!" Maddy shouted from below.

She was fed up and fired up. That night, after the kids were in bed, she ordered us to the dining table, Quinn at one end, me at the other, with Maddy midway between us.

"You two need to grow up," she said. "This is the new celestial order, and you need to learn how to deal with it. I've been patient, I've been long suffering, I've tried my very best to accommodate both of you and your manly needs." She paused, waiting. "Well? Cat got your tongue? You both seemed to have plenty of tongue to spare this morning!"

I spoke first. "If this is supposed to be heaven, then I don't think I want to be anywhere near it."

I was expecting shock and dismay; instead, she called my bluff and raised me every chip on the table.

"Fine! Then let's go talk to the bishop about a temple annulment. I'll make the appointment."

I looked down.

"Well? Is that what you want?"

I mumbled a profanity.

"Can you raise the volume on that? I can't hear you."

"I said I don't want …"

"Don't want what? Come on, just say it!" She was in no mood for games.

I lowered my head and whispered, "I don't want you to do that."

She leaned back, crossing her arms like an impatient queen. She said she needed to teach us a lesson. As punishment, there would be no visits to her bedroom for a week.

Quinn shot me killer eyes. I countered with a syrupy smile.

"We're going to have to learn to live together as a family," Maddy said. "Do you understand?"

She turned to Quinn first, holding her glare like double sword-points until he nodded sheepishly. Then her angry gaze swiveled to me.

"Got it," I said.

"Now you two shake hands," she ordered.

Quinn lifted his suntanned arm as if it were an anvil and reached across the table. I gripped his hand intending to send a message, but he squeezed mine like a juicer.

"Okay, okay," I said. "I get it."

"Good," Maddy said. She motioned for us to stand so she could show the scripturally mandated increase of love, wrapping an arm around each of our shoulders as if we were The Three Musketeers—all for one, one for all. "We can do this!" she enthused. "We're a family, right? An eternal family?"

Quinn and I nodded.

"Then let's do it!" she said.

I looked at the Nike logo on her cross trainers and almost laughed.

❈

I divide sins into two categories: lowercase and uppercase. Lowercase sins are things like swearing when your football team blows a twenty-point lead in the fourth quarter or telling a white lie when your wife asks you how she looks in her new dress (this is also called a "survival sin"). By contrast, uppercase Sins don't just rock the boat; they capsize it, causing harm to you, your loved ones, and even innocent bystanders. Most uppercase Sinners describe their descent into darkness as a gradual process in which they were lured down a forbidden path step by step until they were too deep and lost in the woods to turn back. My fall from grace was more like an impulsive leap followed by a crash landing

This next part of the story is hands down the lowest point in my life. I'll share more of the juicy details later. For now, suffice it to say that I had a fling with a woman I'd met at the pool during one of Marshall's afternoon swim sessions. It was brief and awkward at times but torrid too. And, I have to admit, it felt quite good in the moment. Whenever guilt reared its ugly head, I punched back with a litany of justifications: Maddy had been neglecting me; I'd become a second-class citizen in her eyes, in her bedroom, and in our home; my manhood had been hijacked; I'd been usurped by a younger, sexier model; etc. etc. etc.

This strategy had actually worked until the day I returned home following my third liaison. As I slipped through the back door into the kitchen, I was startled to see Maddy all alone taking brownies out of the oven. She'd actually come home early—surprise number one. Then surprise number two: she twirled around with her million-dollar smile and kissed me on the lips: "Hi, handsome!"

Suddenly I could feel the guilt in my gut as if it were an evil alien that had been slowly sucking the last drops of virtue out of me.

40

"What's the matter?" she said. "You look like you saw a ghost? Was the staff meeting that awful?"

"I think I'm coming down with something."

"Poor guy. We'd better get you to bed."

The following week I tried to act as normal as possible, but Maddy sensed that something was amiss. Instead of grilling me with questions, she was killing me with excessive kindness: a playful pinch while I was bending over to load the dishwasher; an affectionate arm over my shoulder as I tried to tell Marshall an original bedtime story. Then Sunday night—her off night—I heard my bedroom door creak open and a few moments later Maddy was slipping under the sheets, whispering, "I thought you might like a little company tonight."

"What about Marshall?"

She laughed lustily. "Just try to hit the mute button at the moment of truth."

And—miracle of miracles—everything worked! Just like old times. The fact that she was five months pregnant was an unexpected turn-on in its novelty. Afterwards, as we cuddled on the narrow bed like two newlyweds, she purred, "That was nice."

"Yes," I said, exhilarated on the one hand but burning with guilt on the other. "It was."

If Maddy had just acted like her usual anxiously-engaged-in-a-million-causes, shoulder-to-the wheel, Wonder-Woman self, I could have kept my dirty little secret indefinitely. But her over-weaning kindness for no good reason was like death by a thousand cuts! Every little mannerism was another slice out of my heart—her habit of licking her fingertips and wiping them across Marshall's fallen bangs; the way she'd stand on one leg like a Masai warrior, bending just enough to work a stiletto heel onto her right foot, then reversing the process for her left. Even her obsessive to-do lists seemed endearing to me. When I realized that I'd jeopardized all of this—Maddy, marriage, family, reputation, my covenant standing before the Almighty God—for a roll in the hay (three rolls, actually), life became unbearable. I couldn't eat, couldn't sleep, couldn't think straight.

So I fed steroids to my rationalizations: this had been a blessing in disguise! It had fixed our (*my!*) broken sex life which had in turn saved our ailing marriage. This benevolent stranger by the pool had done us a great service!

Excrement! Male bovine excrement! That's what the greedy little alien feasting inside me said.

"What's the matter?" Maddy asked. "You look so sad."

Her sympathy was like feeding red meat to the alien. He'd built a bonfire in my bowels to rival the flames of hell and it was barbequing to oblivion whatever remained of my sick and sorry soul.

Enough! I finally bit the bullet and made an appointment to see the bishop.

⸻

The night we met in her office at the church, Bishop Perkins was wearing a red dress suit with gold buttons up the front. She smiled, shook my hand, and invited me to take a seat. In previous administrations, padded folding chairs would have been arranged in a square around the perimeter of the room with two or three in a short row facing the bishop's large cherrywood desk. Visitors would sit in the short row for tithing settlement, interviews, or other business, while the bishop occupied the judgment seat—a cushioned swivel chair—behind the desk.

By contrast, Bishop Perkins's desk was tucked away in the corner, almost as an afterthought. Papers and pamphlets were neatly stacked in "in" and "out" baskets. The folding chairs were arranged in a circle in the middle of the room, with no specified head, suggesting we were all children of God, all dependent on the Savior for our salvation. And it was no coincidence that the first thing I'd noticed on entering the room was not the customary portrait of the Savior wearing the red robes of judgment but a Minvera Teichert print of the two Marys—Magdalene and Jesus' mother—standing outside the tomb of the resurrected Christ.

I took a seat in the circle of folding chairs and Bishop Perkins sat down next to me, as if we were there for a friendly chat. After the preliminary small talk (How's the family? How's work? How are the kids? How are you adjusting to the new order?), she cupped her hands in her lap, smiled, and said, "What can I do for you, Chad?"

My fears and apprehensions vanished. Maybe this won't be so bad after all, I thought. Maybe we can handle this all in-house, just between the two of us—and God, of course—but leave Maddy out of it. Maybe the bishop will give me a firm slap on the wrist—informal probation. Don't take the sacrament for a few weeks, don't pray in church meetings, we'll temporarily suspend your church calling.

So, I told her how things had been very different at home since Quinn had joined the family and how he was the preferred partner now—you know—for intimacy. As expected, it was awkward and humiliating talking to a woman about my sex life. But Bishop Perkins had a genuine gift for listening without judging, her freckled forehead revealing nothing negative—shock, disgust, contempt, surprise, horror—none of that, only occasional winces that expressed sympathy and compassion. When I disclosed my repeated sexual failures, how the harder I'd tried the worse it had gotten, she touched my hand and whispered, "That must have been devastating to you as a man."

"Yes, yes—devastating! Absolutely!"

'That's completely understandable. So much pressure to perform, along with everything else on your plate."

At that point I was thinking: she gets it! This lady totally gets it!

So, I spewed out the rest of my story in an urgent, unedited torrent, describing how I'd sit in the bleachers watching as Marshall took his weekly swimming lesson at the Aquaplex.

"He made friends with a little girl whose mother just happened to be sitting next to me. After trading a few war stories about the travails of parenthood, we got to talking about our families. Her husband had been in the Marines serving in Afghanistan which, in her words, he seemed to love a lot more than his family because he kept signing up. He used to say it would take a silver bullet to kill him, but as it turned out (on tour number three) an IED did the trick.

"'I'm so sorry,' I said.

"But she seemed more angry than grieved. 'He knew the risks,' she said. 'He kept playing the odds and they finally caught up to him.'

"I wanted to change the subject. She was wearing a Texas Longhorns jersey, so I asked if she was a fan and she promptly fashioned both hands into the shape of twin hook-'em horns. After debating

the virtues and vices of the spread offense, I bet her a burger—
vegan for her; double cheese bacon for me—that my UCLA Bruins
would mop the floor with her Texas Long-johns on Saturday.

"I lost the bet. So, on a sunny autumn afternoon when Quinn
had the kids, Diane (fake name) called and told me it was time to
pay up. We met at a vegan burger place close to the Aquaplex where
I force fed myself a very poor imitation of real food. Afterwards she
invited me to her place to watch a replay of the 44–12 shellacking
on her jumbo TV screen. We didn't make it through the first quarter before we were rolling on the floor. By halftime we'd migrated to
her bedroom. Tammy, her daughter, was taking a nap.

"We repeated this two more times with the same basic script:
Texas versus Baylor and Texas versus Oklahoma State. And that's
how it all happened," I said.

Bishop Perkins's expression remained impartial. "How did you
feel afterwards?" she asked.

"Truthfully?"

"Of course."

"Fabulous!"

For the first time, the bishop's face shifted out of neutral. It was
subtle: a slight wince, as if she'd just been pinched. I backpedaled,
quickly. Apparently, this was not the time or place to be 100% honest.

"Well, not exactly *fabulous*—that's the wrong word. Maybe vindicated in some weird way."

"How so?"

"I guess I thought I wasn't really hurting Maddy. It wasn't like
I was taking something away from her and giving it to someone
else."

Bishop Perkins crossed her legs, angling a bit more towards me.
"No? What about the bond of trust and intimacy between the two
of you?"

"Not anymore!" I said. "She let someone else in the cookie jar!
She had her super boy toy Quinn."

"Boy toy?"

"That's what it felt like."

"So, was this about payback?"

"Payback? I didn't even know if I could function! Payback? I don't know. Maybe. Part of it."

"How so?"

"Isn't it obvious? She neglected me! She picked him over me!"

I was getting lathered up; the bishop remained calm.

"Do you think it's possible to love two people?" she asked.

"Not equally. Not like *that*. Not if you're a—" I'd almost stepped in it. Women in the church had suffered this indignity for half a century. Watch it, buddy.

"Not if you're human," I said.

Silence. I kept waiting for her to fill the void, but she didn't. A full minute passed—I actually watched the second hand sweep around wall clock.

"So why are you here?" she asked.

"I want to fix things."

"So, you feel something's broken?"

"Yes. Of course."

"And who broke it?"

I looked down at the carpet. The custodian had forgotten to vacuum. "Me," I said. "I broke my temple covenants. I broke sacred vows. I broke the trust between me and Maddy."

"But you said you felt fabulous—or at least vindicated."

"I did at first. But not now. I feel awful. Guilty. Horrible. Like a big black cloud's pushing down, smothering me day and night. I've hurt … I've hurt all the people … that I love the most!" I'm not a crier, but suddenly tears were streaming down my cheeks as I tried to spit out the last good pieces of my heart. How had this innocuous-looking little woman done this to me?

"And who are those people, Chad?"

I was sniffling. "M-m-Maddy. M-m-my kids."

"Quinn?"

This was a tough turd to swallow. "Yes, him too."

"So, you want to repent?"

"Yes, of course! That's why I'm here."

She smiled. "Okay, I just wanted to make sure because that's not what you said earlier."

"Yes. I want to repent. Definitely. Please."

"Do you believe you can be forgiven?"

"That's the whole point of the Atonement, isn't it? Though thy sins be as scarlet, through the cleansing blood of Jesus Christ they can be as white as the driven snow."

"Yes. Your sins *can* be washed away. But true repentance takes time and effort. You've taken the first critical step by coming here tonight: recognition. Acknowledging you've done something wrong."

I could already feel that black cloud lifting. She was in my corner.

"Have you told Maddy about this?"

Or maybe not. My head dropped and my heart sank. Telling Maddy was a deal-breaker, especially after her herculean efforts to build me back up again. She'd welcomed me back into her bed, but I'd already pooped in it.

"No," I said. "I haven't."

"Do you plan to?"

I looked up at her, silently pleading for a free pass.

"You know, Chad, what you've done has damaged the spiritual well-being of not just one but two families. What does this woman—Diane?—what's her impression of the church? Does she know you're a member?"

"I don't know. I doubt it."

Bishop Perkins grimaced. "You obviously weren't having gospel discussions on the pool deck."

I sensed a sarcastic edge, a fraying of her patience.

"Honestly, Brother Fletcher, I just don't see how you can go forward in your marriage—fix it, in your words—without sharing this with your wife."

I stared at the carpet, muttering as softly as possible: "Shit."

"Excuse me?"

My head popped up, blushing. "Sure—sure, of course."

"And do you think you should apologize to the woman? Diane?"

"Sure."

"Is that a yes?"

"Yes."

"And then discontinue any further relations with her—public or private?"

"Yes."

Another long minute passed; another slice out of my heart. Then I asked, hopefully, "Anything else?"

The galaxy of freckles seemed to leap off her face in utter astonishment. There was no neutrality in her expression now. It said in no uncertain terms: *are you freaking kidding me?* She rose from her chair and moved behind the desk in the corner, settling into the soft swivel chair. The judgment seat.

I added quickly—desperately: "Are you going to put me on probation?"

The crescents above each of her eyes arched like perfectly synchronized cats: "Probation? Brother Fletcher, you don't seem to grasp the gravity of your transgression. This is a matter for the high council."

"A church court?"

"It's called a disciplinary council."

"That sounds like a court to me. Why can't we just handle this in-house." I was begging now.

"I'm sorry, Brother Fletcher, I really am. But in cases where disfellowshipment or excommunication are possible outcomes—you'll have to go before the high council."

"Disfellowship?" So much for women with the priesthood being soft on crime.

"Or even excommunication—although that would be very rare. If it had been a one-time thing, we might have been able to handle it in-house—two adults caught up in a moment of passion—but repeat offenses? That's premeditation—much more serious. And believe me, this is for your benefit more than anyone's. The Lord and I and the high council want nothing more than to bring you fully back into the fold so you can know within your heart that that scarlet robe has been washed clean. This is the way we do it; this is the way the Lord does it."

All I remember after that is my full body numbness as I dragged myself out of her office and out of that building and into that cool November night. I could smell woodsmoke in the air. Thanksgiving was four days away.

I've screwed up everything, I thought. Everything.

When I got home, the kids were in bed and Maddy was watching TV alone in the living room.

"Where's Quinn?"

"He went to bed early. He's got a fifteen-mile run tomorrow morning."

Quinn was training for the Phoenix Marathon.

Maddy got up and strolled into the kitchen. I heard the microwave hum for twenty seconds. She emerged with a steaming mug of apple cider and handed it to me.

"Thanks."

"How did it go with the bishop?" she asked. I'd told her I'd made the appointment to discuss some personal issues, mostly pertaining to the new order.

"Not so good."

She winced. "I'm sorry."

I blew across the surface of the cider and took a long sip. "Me too. Have you got a minute?"

"Sure."

"How about an hour?"

She smiled and rubbed her bare foot along the length of my calf. "For you, I've got eternity."

"Don't bet on it."

⌐—┬

When I entered the room, President Butterfield stood up, followed by her two counselors and then everyone else in the room. I counted sixteen women total, all but one standing around a long, rectangular table with the twelve high councilors occupying three sides and the stake presidency at the head: President Butterfield in the middle; her first counselor, President Trujillo, on her right; and her second counselor, President Nansen, on her left. Adjacent to President Trujillo were two vacant chairs. In the front corner, removed from the table, stood Sister O'Connor, the executive secretary, armed with a yellow legal-sized tablet to take notes.

A large, attractive woman with the affable charm of a morning show host, President Butterfield shook my hand and motioned towards the two empty chairs. I sat down, and everyone else followed suit.

"Thank you for coming," President Butterfield said. "Is Madeline with you?"

I shook my head. Maddy had been willing, but I saw no reason to subject her to another blow-by-blow replay of my pathetic story, especially in front of her peers: a third of them were in her Thursday night yoga class.

A diminutive woman with jet-black hair that defied her age, President Trujillo cast me a reassuring smile that seemed to say, "You'll be all right! You're doing the right thing!"

President Nansen was harder to read. She had the soft, pillowy look of a doting grandmother, but her mouth was a stern little slit, trending downward.

Following a prayer, President Butterfield commended me for taking this very important and courageous step towards repentance. She talked about the Atonement of Jesus Christ and how it was a special gift to each of us but only if we accept it with a broken heart and contrite spirit.

"So, the angels in heaven are singing tonight," she said.

She then reviewed the charges, although she didn't call them that. "This is a disciplinary council," she reminded me. "A council of love. Brother Fletcher, look around at all of these good sisters. They're here tonight because they love you and want to help you."

I glanced around at a gallery of faces, all smiling and nodding with the exception of a sixtyish woman at the far end of the table who looked like an angry basketball coach. I noticed that about half of the coifs were silver, white, or somewhere in between, and the other half a mix of blonde and brunette with one redhead who also appeared to be the youngest of the group. Her perky smile brightened by a thousand lumens when she and I made eye contact. I tried my best to smile back.

Next, President Butterfield asked me to tell my story, so I did, but it wasn't easy. My behavior sounded so much worse when I described it to a larger group—that was part of it. But the other part was—and I'm just going to lay it out there—I was presenting my case to a tribunal of women, and I was suffering the consequences. Their smiles quickly vanished. I saw a few heads shaking and some faces grimacing. One woman mouthed to herself, "Poor Maddy!"

Another bowed her head, praying for my aggrieved wife and family, no doubt. Even Sister Trujillo seemed to grow stone cold. The angry basketball coach glared at me as if she couldn't wait to make me run punitive wind sprints.

I tried to explain how I'd gone from point A to point B—from heaven to hell—so quickly. For a few moments, I actually fashioned myself a martyr for my fellow brethren as I described the double whammy we were enduring, first by playing second fiddle to the women and now the whole new order thing.

"Imagine if you had to share your eternal companion with another woman," I said. "That's what men throughout the church are suffering every day." Then I felt like a damn fool. This time I really *had* stepped in it. In desperation, I laid myself bare before the council, bedroom failures and all. They stared at me as if I was speaking a foreign tongue, and maybe I was: men are from Mars, women are from Venus. Call me sexist, call me narrow-minded, but I can't help wondering how different that whole experience might have felt if there had been just one male face in that room.

When I finished, President Butterfield asked: "Do any of you have questions for Brother Fletcher?"

Several high councilors posed some standard questions: Can you commit to being completely faithful to your wife and supporting her as the priesthood leader in your home? Yes. Do you believe you can be forgiven of your sins? Yes. Do you have a testimony of the restored Gospel of Jesus Christ? Yes. Do you believe in the healing power of the Atonement of Jesus Christ? Absolutely.

After about thirty minutes of this, President Butterfield seemed ready to move on, but not before deferring to the angry basketball coach. She'd been listening with both forearms lying flat on the table, her hands balled up in fists.

"Sister Caputo? Any questions?"

Mentally I braced myself for a battering ram, but Sister Caputo looked down, shaking her head solemnly. "No, President."

I audibly exhaled, thinking it would be all downhill from here. I could feel the tension beginning to flow out of my body when a contralto voice summoned it all back again: "President Butterfield?"

It was the perky redhead, her right forearm rising up slowly, like a drawbridge denying me entry to anything ever again. "If I may?"

"Certainly, Sister Hawthorne."

Sister Hawthorne's cheerleader smile shined for a blinding millisecond before disappearing for good.

"Brother Fletcher, while you were engaging in sexual relations with this woman, did you ever consider the depth of pain and suffering you might be inflicting on your wife and children?"

I nodded.

"Is that a yes?"

"Yes."

"Then why did you do it?"

I turned to President Butterfield. "I thought I'd explained that already."

"Did you?" Sister Hawthorne said. "You made some vague references to your male ego, frustrated libido, your sexual limitations, and jealousy towards your wife's other husband."

"Yes, all of that and a whole lot more."

"If there's more, then, please, tell us. Tell the high council."

"It was a lot of things," I said. "Embarrassing things. Humiliating."

"Humiliating? Have you considered how humiliating your behavior has been to your sweet wife?"

"Yes."

"Then why did you keep doing it?"

I had no acceptable answer.

"And you did all of this while a young child was sleeping in the other room?"

"Yes."

"You did this to the wife of a Marine veteran who gave his life for his country?"

"Yes, but—"

"My question to you, Brother Fletcher, is why? Why did you show so much blatant disrespect to your wife, your children, your church, and your country?"

She was dropping all her bombs now, the whole damn cargo, blowing me to rubble. Even some of the high councilors were lowering their heads or looking away, embarrassed on my behalf.

"I don't understand, Brother Fletcher. If you love your wife and you're feeling neglected, why can't you just sit down and have a nice discussion about it? That's what I'd do with my husband. If we had a disagreement, we'd sit down and we'd discuss it. We'd find common ground and then we'd move on. But he wouldn't run off and have an affair."

Her strident blows had created a numbing effect. I felt nothing now except my anger warming up.

Her tone softened a bit. "Brother Fletcher, have you been to Gethsemane?"

"No, I've never been out of the U.S. except for a mission to British Columbia."

" I mean spiritually. Have you been to Gethsemane? Like Alma the Younger, have you felt that eternal anguish that penetrates to your bones? That stirs you to sincere repentance? It doesn't look like it to me."

I didn't know how many axes she was grinding, but more than enough to chop me down and feed me to the fiery furnace. I felt like scooping up whatever splinters of manhood remained and shouting back:

"All right, all right! Enough! I did something terribly wrong and I'd like to fix it. But none of you really know me. You don't know what's going on inside my head or my heart. And none of you are perfect either. You may have the priesthood, but I know things. Sister Johnson, you really love that year's supply of green tea that helps you keep that runway figure. And Sister Greenfield, I've seen you flip off a double-amputee fake Vietnam War vet panhandling outside Safeway. Sister Carlson, you've got the most active vibrator in the stake and you think anyone who votes for a Democrat has dick for brains. Hey, I read Facebook. If you haven't confessed it yourself, your family, friends, or enemies have confessed for you. There are no secrets anymore."

But I held my tongue because I didn't have a leg to stand on. I'd sat on their side of the table way back when. They were judging me because they'd been appointed by God to do so. They were just doing their job.

Sister Hawthorne tossed me a few more grenades before President Butterfield finally intervened.

"All right, any other questions?" She didn't wait for a response. "Then Brother Fletcher, we'll invite you to step outside for a moment while we discuss your situation."

I slipped out into the hall and sat in one of the half dozen folding chairs along the wall. I knew what happened next. The council would deliberate until they reached consensus. Then the stake presidency would retire to the president's adjacent office to talk and pray and render their final decision which would be presented to the council for a sustaining vote.

It was strangely quiet in the dim-lit hallway. I could hear a basketball pounding in the cultural hall and some slurred voices, but otherwise I was very much alone. My mind could have meandered any number of directions, but my imminent fate was not one of them. Whatever the council decided, I certainly deserved. At least they couldn't take the priesthood from me—that was a *fait accompli*, as they say. I thought with some misgiving about the many times I'd groused because I'd had to sacrifice a perfectly good Saturday afternoon to attend a stake priesthood leadership meeting or set up chairs in the cultural hall for a ward social.

Then I recalled a snowy February night four years ago. I'd been smitten by a nasty infection that had clogged my chest and sinuses, leaving me a coughing, sneezing, wheezing, aching mess. I was also running a fever of 103. For six nights, sleep had eluded me because of a non-stop, rib-splitting cough that laughed at over-the-counter meds. To spare Maddy my misery, I'd temporarily moved into the guest bedroom. On the seventh night—thanks to two humidifiers, a double dose of antibiotics and codeine, and sheer fatigue—I'd finally drifted off into a deep, sweet sleep that was painfully short-lived when the Bee Gees started screaming in my ears: "Unh! Unh! Unh! Stayin' alive! Stayin' alive!"

I fumbled around the nightstand for my cell phone and answered in a groggy, dying voice that belonged in a field hospital: "Hello?"

"Is this Brother Fletcher?"

"Yes." I'd hoped my raspy voice would scare him off. It didn't. I could hear the wind howling outside, flinging snow against the window.

He started speaking as fast as an auctioneer, obviously distressed.

"Oh, thank goodness! I'm so sorry to bother you at this hour, Brother Fletcher, but my wife and I were passing through town and we hit black ice. Our car slid off the highway just north of Skyline Park. *I'm* fine but Carol's in ICU and I need someone to help me give her a priesthood blessing. I tried to find the church directory, but there's no receptionist at this hour. So, I asked a nurse if she knew any Mormons in town and she gave me your name and number. I hope that's okay?"

Several things passed through my mind: why out of all the LDS people in town did that nurse have to know my name and number? And: why didn't this guy just give the blessing solo—he could do that in a pinch. And: was this *really* life or death? It was 2 a.m. Couldn't it wait until tomorrow? And finally: there were dozens of worthy priesthood holders in town who weren't hacking their guts out right now. Why not call one of them to crawl out of bed and risk a rollover driving to the hospital to give a random stranger a blessing?

"I'll be there in fifteen minutes," I said.

Brother Halliday, a burly little man with a blacksmith's arms, greeted me in the emergency entrance as if I were the Messiah.

"Thank you, Brother Fletcher," he said, "thank you so much for coming." He reached out with both hands to clasp mine, but I pulled them up like double stop signs.

"No no no! Nothing personal, but I've been sicker than a dog and—believe me, what I've got, you don't want to get." Dr. Lewis had said I was no longer contagious, but I wasn't taking any chances. Fortunately, my coughing had ceased when I got out of my car, a good sign.

Brother Halliday ushered me into the ICU unit where his wife was lying unconscious with elastic bandages wrapped like a turban around her head. Tubes and wires snaked from her arms, head, and chest to the various machines and pendant pouches of medications that were being pumped into her body.

"I've got oil," he said, holding up a small metal vial attached to a BYU Cougars keychain. He began unscrewing the cap.

"I'll do the anointing," he said. "if that's all right?"

I nodded but I was surprised. He was doing the more scripted

54

part and leaving the blessing portion—the heavy lifting, so to speak—to me.

I don't recall much of what I said, but when I had finished, Brother Halliday wrapped his mighty arms around me as if we were long-lost friends. When he finally broke away, he gripped my hand and pumped it vigorously.

"I don't care if you've got the bubonic plague!" he said. "I'm shaking your hand, brother! Coming out here on a cold, miserable night like this! Sick and everything!"

I tiptoed out to my car, careful not to slip on the ice. The wind and snow had let up a bit, so instead of blasting horizontally like bullets, the snow had become lighter and more playful, swirling about like little angels turning somersaults in the sky.

I suppose I've always been more of a lunch-bucket Mormon: tell me what to do and I'll do it—grudgingly maybe, but I'll get it done. One of my great shortcomings is that I seldom feel the Spirit in a powerful way—you know, a lightning bolt to the heart or a sudden flash of genius in the brain. But something peculiar happened as I drove home that night. On the one hand, the hacking and coughing that had been miraculously suspended during my visit suddenly returned with a vengeance. On the other hand, I had a strong impression that someone was riding alongside me. There was no still, small voice; no pat on the back. But I felt a heavenly presence in that passenger seat like never before, and I imagined him—or perhaps her—smiling, nodding, saying without words: *Well done, my good and faithful servant.*

When I slipped into the front door at 3:30 a.m., Maddy was standing at the top of the stairs in her bathrobe.

"Where have you been?" she said in a mom-like whisper—soft enough to not wake the kids but loud enough to stop a wayward husband in his tracks.

"I had to give a priesthood blessing," I whispered back.

"But you're sick!"

I looked up at her and smiled. "Yes, it was pretty awesome."

As I sat in the empty hallway awaiting my verdict, I thought: I'll never have to do something like that again. And then I thought: I'll never *get* to do something quite like that again. And: neither will my sons. It took me a moment to make the next leap: but Maddy will. And Julia. And that took some of the sting out of it. Then I wondered if the new order transcended planet Earth, sweeping across the eternities and the innumerable worlds in it, tipping on its head all of our traditional notions of the true order of heaven? So, the last shall be first and the first shall be last?

Maybe there was still time to mend our ways and be recommissioned into God's royal army. Or maybe that ship had sailed. Maybe my generation would have to die off like the Children of Israel staggering through the desert for forty years with an Egyptian hangover. We just didn't get it—I know *I* didn't. But maybe there's hope for my son or my sons' sons.

A few minutes turned out to be an hour and a half. President Butterfield invited me back in and I retook my seat. She forced a smile, but her eyes were red and growing moist, a precursor to delivering bad news. She thanked me again for coming and applauded my courage for taking the first big step on the long road to repentance. I didn't like the adjective "long."

"Brother Fletcher," she said, her voice assuming a formal, legal tone: "The council has determined that you will be disfellowshipped as a member of the Church of Jesus Christ of Latter-day Saints." She then enumerated a list of things I could no longer do: take the sacrament; pray or teach in any church meetings; hold a church calling; attend the temple. A year ago, she would have added to her list: exercise your priesthood authority in any way. Next, she reviewed the coulds: attend church; pay tithing; assist at service projects; provide support in a volunteer capacity; attend church functions. My progress would be reviewed in a year and, upon the recommendation of my bishop, the council could re-evaluate my spiritual progress for possible reinstatement to full fellowship. Did I have any questions?

President Butterfield was dabbing her eyes with a Kleenex as were several other sisters. In fact, two boxes of Kleenex were circulating around the table. Only Sister Hawthorne didn't partake. She sat with fisted forearms on the table, like a pair of clubs that had been lowered in the name of justice.

President Butterfield's frown slowly curved into a crescent smile.

"Brother Fletcher, this may seem like a sad affair, but the angels in heaven are celebrating right now. Our brother who was lost has been found!"

This is a court of love, she kept saying, and I must confess there was nothing but goodwill expressed by those women, Sister Hawthorne notwithstanding.

When I stepped back outside, I was surprised to see Brother Cooper slouching in one of the folding chairs looking as solitary and abandoned as I had three hours ago.

He glanced up at me with a peculiar mix of humiliation and hope. "You too?" he asked.

I nodded. "Yep. Me too."

He sighed, resigned. "Maybe we should make a T-shirt."

IN A BETTER COUNTRY

But now they desire a better country, that is, an heavenly ... (Heb. 11:16)

"You don't have to go," she whispered, the morning grogginess in her voice betraying an urgency that was futile but necessary.

"I know that," he mumbled.

"Bishop Carson said—"

"I know. I know what Bishop Carson said."

She twisted onto her side, freeing an arm from the sheets. "You're going alone then."

He shoved another T-shirt into the duffel bag and zipped it shut.

"Okay, fine," she muttered. She would crawl out of bed now, throw on her terrycloth bathrobe and slippers, and hope that no one recognized her driving down the freeway at first light.

He had faithfully dispatched his morning duties: lugging the trash can out to the curb for Friday pickup, unloading the dishwasher, walking Cleo to the end of the cul-de-sac and back. But instead of his perfunctory routine of feed and flee, he had lowered himself to one knee, running a hand gently along the spine of their black lab.

"We'll see you later, girl," he whispered, and she had stopped chomping on the dry nuggets to gaze up at him with doleful eyes, as if divining his future. Framing her face with his hands, he leaned in close, inhaling her doggy breath. "Man, you stink!" he said and rubbed her head briskly before turning away.

8—¬

During the fifteen-minute drive to the airport, Margie stared straight ahead, her profile a flashback to the other times he had failed her—blue eyes iced over, chin tilted high, Geena-Davis lips puckered, not for a farewell kiss but to blow him off. As the Camry idled outside the entry, Mark maneuvered out of the front seat and grabbed the duffel bag and day pack from the trunk. When he leaned in to kiss her, she turned her head and gave him the back side of her unadorned hair. He inhaled the smell of a restless sleep, of dried sweat, fear, and anger.

Okay, he thought. *You're just making it easier.*

"Thanks for the ride," he said and, in one quick motion, shut the door and waved goodbye—more like a sarcastic salute. He didn't look back but heard her drive away long before the sliding glass doors rolled open to welcome him.

⚬—

There were four legs to his journey, the first three by plane: to Phoenix, to El Paso, to a polysyllabic south-of-the-border city he could barely pronounce. A bus or train or burro would take him the final leg.

Or so he hoped. He had no directions, no itinerary, no game plan—nothing except the duffel bag, the day pack, a billfold with $200 cash, and a map torn from a *State Farm Road Atlas of North America*. His destination was a tiny drop of blood on the loins of northern Mexico.

Rinsed clean by last night's thunderstorm, the small mountain town he called home positively glistened: the pine trees and the little homes positioned neatly around them, the rolling greens of the golf course, the brick buildings downtown. As the plane gained altitude and curved south, he caught a final glimpse of the mountains, the sun washing across their snow-packed peaks, turning them gold.

Flying had never bothered him, not even in these puddle jumpers where you sat shoulder to shoulder and rode the wind like a cowboy on a bronco that couldn't decide if it was going to buck or break. But the roar of the engines was certain to amplify the siren in his head that had started after the phone call and hadn't left since. He pressed his palms to his cheeks and let his middle fingers slide down over his ears, trying to head it off, but it was too late.

He gazed down at the forests of ponderosa pine, chagrined at their resemblance to his own thinning scalp—spikes of hair surrounded by patches of sunburned skin. But the pines shortly gave way to sagebrush and chaparral as the desert rolled out like a rumpled old carpet crowded with legions of saguaro cacti.

Within the hour they were descending into Phoenix—to his eye, an intestinal mosaic of asphalt, concrete, and terra cotta inlaid with turquoise swimming pools. As he looked down on the rush-hour traffic stuttering along the gray arteries of the city, he wondered: How many other icy farewells this morning? How many happy returns tonight? How many broken hearts and good or bad surprises? Did God really keep an inventory of each and every one, meticulously monitoring the comings and goings of the human race? Not just in this world but worlds without number? Every fallen follicle accounted for? Or was the monitoring more like wearing spiritual ankle bracelets? Then was He a glorified hall monitor or the Grand Chess Wizard maneuvering the pieces one bewildering step ahead of the devil? And did the devil ever catch up? Did he ever checkmate God? Was it a never-ending winner-take-all, or a best-of-seven series? A best-of-dispensations? Was it possible for Satan to outfox the Fox? Win some battles but not the war? Was Sean maybe a casualty of battle or a victim of friendly fire? Or did some guardian angel fall asleep at the switch—take a donut break when he was supposed to be watching Sean's backside?

Stop it. Just freaking the hell stop it. He snapped the rubber band on his wrist three times, hard.

He had a one-hour layover, which would have given him time to check his duffel bag if he had wanted to, but it was small and he had packed light: a change of garments, two clean T-shirts, a pair of jeans, a shaving kit, and a light jacket. In his day pack, he carried a pen and notepad, a John Grisham paperback, several granola bars, a pocket-sized Spanish/English dictionary, and a driver's license for ID. No debit or credit cards. He had heard enough horror stories about *gringos* getting thrown in jail and being forced to max out their plastic.

He took a seat in the waiting area where the weatherman on the TV monitor was bracing the Phoenicians for their tenth consecutive day of 100-plus heat. Mark tried not to think about home, but his thoughts fled north to earlier that morning when he had soft-stepped upstairs to say goodbye to Stacie, sleeping soundly under the open window on the last day of school. Nothing out of the ordinary except that he had lingered in the doorway a few moments longer than usual, taking in the details of her life: a poster directly above her bed of a leggy, pony-tailed Mia Hamm executing a goal kick; the wind chimes in the shape of leaping dolphins tinkling in the breeze; a collage of every certificate, note, Valentine, letter, or postcard she had ever received covering the wall behind her bed. Her chubby little arm was wrapped around a soccer ball as if it were her best friend.

This morning he had noticed a particular sweetness in the malformations of her face: the thick, pouty lips, the bulbous forehead, the eyes from another planet. He had knelt down by the bed, put a hand on her brow, and smoothed back her bangs. "I fixed your flat," he had whispered.

She had mumbled something—slurred, semi-intelligible.

"There might be a slow leak, but it should be okay until I …" *Come home?* The last two words had stumbled out like an accident. Part plea, part question, a two-headed hitchhiker who can't decide which direction to go.

Eyes shut, still dreaming, she had lifted a hanging hand. "Thanks, Daddy."

8—

A full-sized jet carried him east across the southern desert and into a yellow haze from a massive forest fire that was trying to devour the upper half of Mexico. Squeezed into a coach seat, reading the details, Mark snapped the front page of the *Arizona Republic*, smiling meanly. Retribution, he thought.

He had figured that El Paso would be a sneak preview of the Third World to come, and the airport didn't disappoint. The effect was partly due to the paint-stained concrete floors and the plastic sheets draping the corridors, half-snagging the industrial dust, but mostly it was the echo of Spanish everywhere, from the garbled announcements over the intercom to the mounted TV monitors where men in suits and ties reported the latest breaking news.

Mark followed the bilingual signs (*Puerta/Gate; Salidas/Departures*) past the concessions—Burger King, souvenir shops, sports bars—down a long corridor opening into an enormous hall that was empty save for a small chair beside an open doorway in the far corner. He passed through it, followed a carpeted corridor around two corners, and dead-ended at a deserted counter with a large number 22 posted above it. Mark double-checked his boarding pass—22, 1:22—then checked his watch: 11:10. Two hours to kill.

He sat down on a vinyl chair and opened the Grisham paperback—a random grab off his bookshelf. He tried to read, but after four pages he realized that absolutely nothing had registered. He started over; but failing again to focus, he put the book aside. It was 11:15. Stacie would be lining up for lunch now. Hopefully her reading circle hadn't been quite as catastrophic as the day before. Margie would have returned from her morning walk, finished tidying up around the house, and was probably out making home visits. Her calling as Relief Society president had been a godsend. All of that free time she'd had to think and mope and heap blame and second-guess had been replaced by good works: lifting up the feeble hands, changing bedpans, delivering hope on a cookie sheet. Mark wondered if her anger had simmered down. Was she thinking about him, or had she mentally dispatched him for the weekend? Or longer? His return ticket was open, although he had estimated three or four nights. You'd have thought he was leaving for a year. Or checking out for good. What she didn't know she would always deduce. Crazy, idiotic, foolhardy, stupid, head-up-the-ass idea, she had called it—throwing propriety and position to the wind (mother of the ward, the shining example). She rarely cursed, but when she did, you knew she meant business. She was pissed.

At 12:50 a man in a gray suit and a woman in a scarlet dress and black hose entered the waiting area and quick-stepped to the counter. Mark sprang to his feet a little too quickly, startling the woman, who arched a brow. Mark fell into line behind them and tried to eavesdrop on their three-way, but the matronly Latina behind the counter was speaking in a very rapid dialect that bore no resemblance to anything he had retained from two very distant and inattentive years of high school Spanish. They may as well have been speaking Cantonese.

His three brothers and his sister had all served Spanish-speaking missions for the church—this trip would have been duck soup to them—but inspiration had called him to work stateside, in scenic Minnesota. Best mission in the church, they used to say as part of the conditioning. Best stateside mission in the church, he and his companion would mutter on the sly.

He wondered now if his negative-Nellie attitude back then had greased the wheels of fate against him and his house ... wait: we don't believe in fate. Justice, yes; punishment; natural and unnatural consequences; guilt; payback ... all of that we've got in abundance, a six-thousand-year supply—but fate?

Best mission in Minnesota.

The plane looked more like a rocket—small, sleek, silver. Squeezing through the doorway, he found himself sharing the eighteen-seater with a group of Mexican professionals, all middle-aged men except for the woman in the red dress and a tall, leathery *gringo* who was wearing a disappointed but deadly look, as if he had just failed a James Bond screen test. They sat in single seats divided by a two-foot-wide aisle.

The Aeromexico pilot and copilot looked official enough in their white shirts and ties and bronze badges, but they kept fiddling with the control panel like teenagers playing video games. The plane labored off the runway, fighting the oppressive pull of gravity. When it finally broke free, it seemed to climb the stairway to the clouds like an obese dog, lunging and grasping at each step. Mark looked through the tiny portal and noticed the wing straining up and down in the turbulence. The *abroche su cinturon* sign began blinking in panic-stricken red; and a moment later, the plane lurched and dipped dangerously downward. Pilot and co-pilot were frantically working the switches as the plane bucked and rattled through the swirling white air. Mark focused on the rivets along the wing, wondering if at any moment they might pop off like buttons on a too-tight dress. James Bond was reaching for his barf bag. The pilot and co-pilot were no longer laughing.

Mark felt unusually calm, as if imminent death would be a form of honorable release. He started to say a silent prayer, but a blast of wind—something—smacked his side of the plane, summoning up Margie's words and Bishop Carson's warning: *If you go, you go solo.* He had done his praying a priori.

As the turbulence simmered and the plane leveled out, the *abroche su cinturon* light died. The pilot said something over the intercom in Spanish that made everyone else chuckle. Peering grimly through the portal, Mark could see nothing but a gray infinity beyond the wing. Recalling old axioms: *Sometimes you have to leave to come home again.* Or the motto framed on his son's wall: *Return with honor.* How about just plain *Return?* Return in one piece? Return, period?

An hour later the plane began its descent. As the clouds thinned, he saw a vast, flat land of beige-on-brown parchment stained with scattered clumps of trees and a river winding across its length like a long, lazy signature. The yellow haze, compliments of the southern inferno, cast a surreal, coastal fog over the city, although they were 200 miles from the sea. Little wind-up planes cluttered the sides of the narrow runway.

The plane set down gently. The co-pilot said something to Mark that he didn't understand, but he nodded back: "*Gracias.*" As he stepped onto the portable stairwell, his hand shot to his forehead, blocking the sudden glare. He fumbled for his sunglasses. They slipped through his fingers, and as he lunged for them, he lost his footing. Behind him the woman in red gasped as he grabbed the metal railing, sparing himself a long rough-and-tumble ride to the blacktop, but not before his side slammed hard against the railing, his left leg scraping along the steps. He swore softly as pilot, copilot, the woman in red, and all of the other passengers swarmed around him—or so it seemed. There wasn't possibly enough room for all of them to converge on the stairwell, yet it seemed as if they were collectively helping him up, speaking to him in urgent Spanish, dusting him off, genuinely concerned about his welfare. Too embarrassed to feel any pain in the moment, he politely waved them off: "*Está bien, gracias, está bien.*"

He continued down the stairs, ignoring the ache in his ankle yet knowing that, by tomorrow morning, it would swell up like a grapefruit. One of the young professionals handed him the remains of his sunglasses, and Mark thanked him curtly: "*Gracias.*" His word for the day. He really just wanted to get on his way and forget about the incident. Talk about a greenhorn! He may as well have worn a sign on his back: *Kick me, I'm stupid. Rob me, I'm a tourist.*

He hobbled across the blacktop as the sun clawed at his face. The runway looked like boiling water. By the time he reached the sliding glass doors of the single-story building, his shirt was soaked and sticking to his back. He had dressed for warm weather—short-sleeved, button-up shirt, beige cotton pants, Nike sneakers—but this heat was downright savage.

The airport was small but clean and carpeted, with large glass doors and windows creating an aquarium effect that far outclassed the concrete tomb in El Paso. Mark retrieved his duffel bag from the carousel, passed through customs, and—with gestures and very broken Spanish—bought a ticket on a shuttle bus. The shuttle belched and bellowed three or four miles down a desert highway before pulling into a large parking area full of old cars and their rusted ancestors. He shuffled across the yard into what looked like a gigantic warehouse with little glass-enclosed shops along one end offering snacks, novelties, bottled water, soda pop, ice cream. There was a game room for the children with pinball machines, plastic cars and mini rockets to mount, and video games with annoyingly loud sirens and flashing lights. A long series of countertops stretched across the opposite end of the building below large marquees advertising the various bus lines: *Estrella Blanca, Caballero de Azteca, Paloma Blanca.* In the center of the building, Mexican families sat in rows of vinyl chairs bolted to the cracked linoleum floor.

He had no idea which line to take. He gravitated toward the counter with the biggest, brightest, cleanest-looking sign, *Paloma Blanca*, although the second "A" was hanging like a key on a hook. *Don't judge a book by its cover*, he reminded himself; but in this case, it was all he had to go by.

Mark changed $150 to pesos and kept the other $50 in American dollars for the trip home. At the counter, a young woman greeted him with a big smile tainted by a distracting gold rim around each of her two front teeth. Mark handed her two 100-peso bills. She gave him back a ticket and two twenties, spewed out a blur of words, and pointed to the schedule on the marquee. He was disheartened to see that the bus didn't depart until 17:40—5:40 p.m. his time—and would not arrive at his destination until almost midnight.

"*Sí*," he said, fumbling with his wallet, the ticket, his change—adding as an awkward afterthought: "*Gracias.*"

The big clock on the south wall read 3:05, and his watch showed 3:02. That he was traveling in the same time zone gave him a strange sense of comfort. Whether by his watch or theirs, he had two and a half hours to burn.

He browsed around the glass-enclosed shops and bought a liter of water which he promptly guzzled down, then strolled over to the restroom, a little annoyed that he had to feed the turnstile five pesos. The interior was surprisingly cool, although that creature comfort was mitigated by a septic stench and a steady, trickling sound as if someone were at the urinal trying to break a world record. In fact, there was only one other patron, a middle-aged man rinsing his hands in a stand-up porcelain washbasin minus one corner. The man shook the excess water from his fingers and sauntered outside, leaving Mark alone.

It was a little spooky—the dim lighting, the perspiring concrete walls, the stale smell of neglect. But he savored the moment of solitude. From the moment he had landed in El Paso, he had felt like a stranger in a strange land, surrounded by people who did not understand his language or his intentions or his grief. He could only imagine what the locals were thinking of this blue-eyed giant moving through their midst.

He turned sideways and checked his profile in the water-spotted mirror. Unlike Margie, who had maintained her maidenly figure over time, he had taken on the fat and freckled look of Auric Goldfinger. He wondered if it was the cumulative baggage of fifty-two years on the planet or the stress of the past year that had doomed him to droop prematurely. He was an easy target, like Stacie—heavy for her age, slower on the draw, and clumsy, too. (The school kids teased her mercilessly: "Spacey Stacie has no brain, won't come in out of the rain.") He may as well have been parading around in a clown outfit. The locals weren't ogling him—they were too polite for that—but he could feel their eyes trying to read him as if he were a story in an unknown tongue. He lifted his chin, squared his shoulders, put a bit of iron in his eyes and lips. Better, he thought, giving the hem of his shirt a tug and tightening it over his bulging belly. No, there was no subtlety here, no blending with the crowd, but he had not come to blend.

He couldn't make much urine—a bad sign in this heat—so he quickly finished his business, bought two more bottles of water, and took a seat in the waiting area. Several big ceiling fans were waging a relentless but futile war against the suffocating heat. The locals seemed to take it in stride, a few older women casually fanning themselves, indifferent to the inertness of the clock, but Mark was genuinely suffering. Reminding himself to stay hydrated, he broke the seal on another water bottle. He leaned back and tried to relax amid the mustachioed young men in T-shirts and blue jeans, their wives dutifully holding babies and diaper bags. Across the way, a Tarahumara woman half Mark's height was selling tamales from a metal bucket with a towel over the top.

He gave the Grisham novel another try, but his mind kept detouring to a passage in the Book of Mormon in which the prophet Nephi is commanded by the Spirit to cut off Laban's head so he can secure the brass plates—the sacred record and genealogy of his people: "It is better that one man should perish than a nation dwindle in unbelief."

Nations wouldn't perish in this instance, but *he* might—if not from the heat of the sun, then in the fires of hell. "Vengeance is mine, saith the Lord. ... I will forgive whom I will forgive ... but for you it is required to forgive seventy times seven." Bishop Carson had quoted those scriptures ad nauseam during their many private meetings.

Carson was a mild-looking man whose Ben Franklin bifocals and innocuous comb-over screamed white-collar accountant, although actually he earned his bread repairing diesel engines. But he spoke candidly, a tack Mark had found refreshing after the barrage of clichés, casseroles, and sympathy cards. And he could speak with some authority about loss, his wife Sherry having survived several

rounds of hair-and-energy-thieving treatments before finally suc-
cumbing to cervical cancer. She had been thirty-five.

"Your son's in paradise. You don't need to worry about him—you
need to worry about you. He passed his test, but you're still taking
the exam. And how you react is a large part of that. The real question
is: will you be worthy to stand in Sean's presence on the other side?"

Mark knew the party line on trials, tribulation, adversity. He
used to dish it out himself when he was a bishop: There must be
opposition in all things—no good without evil, no pleasure without
pain, no spiritual growth without suffering, endure it well, for all of
this will give you experience, and I the Lord God have descended
below all things … Job crawling on all fours through the refiner's
fire … God gives his toughest trials to his toughest Saints.

"You still have your son," Bishop Carson had said. "And you
always will."

At some point during the conversation, Mark's head would
drop as his voice wrestled with itself, his fingers dragging down
the length of his face as if it were putty. Margie's arm would slide
across his shoulder, drawing him in close as he wept a bitter mix
into his hands. They would kneel together as the bishop offered
a prayer—for faith, hope, courage, perseverance, enlightenment,
understanding. Mark would pray for forgiveness and the ability to
forgive, the sweet miracle of letting go. Margie would continue to
rub his back, comforting him as a mother comforts a young child,
assuming that this was the turning point, that they were really,
finally, at last, heading home again. She would be right about the
first part but not the second.

A week later, they would be back in the bishop's office, Margie
squeezing Mark's hand as he stared glumly at the crystal candy jar
beside the box of Kleenex already plucked clean. Sitting behind
his desk, Bishop Carson would listen patiently once again, offering
similar counsel and a similar prayer, and the next week the same,
and the next week and the next until one evening he cut Mark off
in midsentence: "Mark, Mark, Mark … Listen to me. Listen carefully to what I'm going to say." The bishop sighed deeply, slowly,
exhausted. "Mark, it's not easy for me to tell you this, but you are
guilty of the greater sin here."

Mark tilted his head to one side, as if trying to clear water out of his ear. "Excuse me?"

"Pride," Bishop Carson clarified. "You're stewing in it. I understand your hurt. I understand your anger. But this is destroying you and your family. You need to humble yourself and ask God for forgiveness and just let this thing go. You've got to move on."

Mark's eyes closed slowly, as if he were dozing off. This *thing*? Move on? Like it was a football game and the home team just got whipped? This *thing*?

And then his eyes opened, glaring. "Ask God to forgive *me*? And what about this—this—this—" He couldn't even finish the sentence, couldn't finish the curse. Could only spit and stutter: "That is so like you—so like you people to sit on your h-h-h-igh horse and j-j-j-judge! Ask God to forgive me? And who's going to f-f-f-forgive God … for not protecting his s-s-s-servant? Isn't that what you tell these kids? Called to serve and all? They're just kids, you know. Kids!"

Mark was standing, throwing his hands haphazardly around the office, waving accusingly at the framed picture of the Savior who was observing quietly on the wall: "Ask *him* maybe!"

The bishop listened calmly, his fingers laced together, elbows forming an isosceles triangle on his desk. "I think he knows a little something about suffering," he said. "And I think his Father knows a little something about losing a son."

"That was with purpose! That was by design! Don't you think I know that? Everybody knows that! He gave up his, but he got him back—almost immediately back. He's God. He's big picture. I'm little picture!"

The bishop didn't flinch. "How do you know Sean's death wasn't by design? Or didn't have purpose? Isn't that the truest trial of faith? To believe even when we don't see or understand?"

Mark was jabbing his finger at the little bald man behind the desk. "Don't patronize me! You don't—you haven't—all of your—your boys …"

Margie pressed her palms to her ears, screaming above his scream: "Stop it! Stop it right now!" And then, in the silence that followed, "Please?" Then it was her turn to sob. That was the end of the conversation and of their visits with Bishop Carson.

That was a year ago. In the months that followed, Mark had crawled deeper and deeper backwards. Each night, after a mostly silent dinner, while Margie self-medicated on Turner Classic Movies, he retreated to the dark privacy of his study where he explored the vagaries of the internet. Sometimes he filled out nonsense questionnaires or entered bogus sweepstakes; other times he read the *New York Times* or the *Washington Post* or obscure publications from small farm towns hiding in the breadbasket of America. He checked the bizarre junk being auctioned on eBay and sometimes bid a few dollars, no more. He avoided porn sites but became a cynical reader of gossip and entertainment columns and the ASU Sun Devils sports webpage.

He went to bed late, got up late, and dragged himself to work late. He was curt with his staff and even worse to his customers. No one dared say anything—not even his typically blunt-as-a-hammer secretary or Ray, his co-owner and best friend since high school. He tried to pick fights, but no one took the bait. He was grieving, and they gave him wide berth. Ray told him to take some time off, take Margie on a vacation—to Europe, New Zealand, somewhere fun and far the hell away from all of this.

His daughter became a veritable stranger and genuinely suffered from the void.

"Dad, come on up!" she would call into the hall at bedtime.

Every night he used to read her a story. Now her mother came instead.

"He's busy tonight."

"Again?"

"Yes. Again."

He used to leave her little notes every morning: *Dear Stacie, Have a dolphin day!*

Now, when she announced brightly, "Dad! I had a dolphin day!" he would mumble in his milk. Her disappointment was palpable.

He missed her first two soccer games of the season; and when she burst into his gloomy office, proclaiming, "Daddy! I scored a goal!" he muttered perfunctorily, "Good for you," and continued fondling the mouse, scrolling down and entering another mindless bid. After that she quit reporting.

One night after Stacie had gone to bed, Margie slipped into his study and softly shut the door. The lights were off, his face half lit only by the glow from the computer monitor, a ghost-like facade. His right hand was cupped over the mouse, and she put hers over it. He continued staring at the eBay offering on the screen, an old football allegedly used by Joe Montana in high school.

"I want you to know," she whispered, "that I've loved you since the first time we met. Our first date. That night when I got into bed, I thought to myself: That's all I want in life—Mark and a couple of children, and I'll be happy forever. And that's never changed. I want you to know that. But this has got to stop. All of that love: you're killing it. It's killing us—our family."

He continued staring blankly at the monitor.

She lifted her hand. "You need to do something," she whispered. "I want my husband back. I don't want this morbid stranger living in my house anymore."

She leaned over and kissed the back of his neck. Then she slipped out into the hall and quietly shut the door.

⟊⟶

4:35. Margie and Stacie were at the Harkins Theatres now for the rush-hour show—a family tradition for the last day of school. They would throw the usual prohibitions to the wind and junk out on buttered popcorn and Pepsi. Super-size? Bring it on! This one day of the year. School's out! Let's party! Afterward they would grill hamburgers and loiter on the deck, watching TV outside as the sun dipped below the pines.

Mark gazed around at the sea of alien faces, reminding himself that he was the alien here, a dollop of winter in this land of smoke and sunlight. A little Tarahumara girl was dozing off beside her mother, who was already asleep in the next chair. The girl's head tilted slowly to the right until it suddenly struck the mother's shoulder, startling them both awake. They traded looks, briefly confused, then erupted in laughter. Mark started to smile, then sat up stiffly, wrenching his head away from mother and daughter. Focus! Focus! Reverie, nostalgia, sentimentality—they were the enemy today.

At 5:20 he stepped out into the boarding area where a small crowd had gathered near a sleek silver bus that looked newly minted. Idling beside it was a big brown monstrosity that looked like an old school bus made over by a street thief's hasty paint job. Mark's heart sank when he noticed the words *Paloma Blanca* hand-lettered in white paint across the dented, dust-crusted flank. Noxious black fumes poured out of the rust-eaten exhaust pipe. Through the chalky haze, the late afternoon sun burned a blood-orange.

Weaving his way past the luxury liner, Mark scolded himself: *Next time shop around, stupid! Grow a brain, numbskull!* Then he quickly repented. It was better this way. This is why he had come: to travel as Sean had traveled, second class, with the goats and chickens, not to fat-cat around like an American tourist. He wanted to eat what Sean had eaten, sleep where he had slept, smell what he had smelled. He wanted to suffer as Sean had suffered. That same culture shock and initial ineptitude with the language. Sean's first companion was a native from Mexico City, Elder Ortega. A nice enough young man, but Sean couldn't understand a word those first few months. When Ortega met up with the other Mexican missionaries, they would jabber away while Sean stood there grinning stupidly, pretending to get the punchline when he may have been the joke.

Mark showed his ticket to the uniformed little man who motioned for him to leave his duffel bag by the collection of bandaged suitcases and cardboard boxes that had accumulated outside the open belly of the bus. Mark boarded and headed to the back, averting his eyes from the other passengers. His body had always seemed a burden that moved at odds with his spirit, but never before had he felt so big and clumsy and out of place, like Gulliver among the Lilliputians. Still, he recognized his size as an intimidating asset; and settling into the bench seat in the very back, he stretched his oak trunk legs and assumed a look of cool detachment: arms folded across his soft but bulging chest, shoulders square, jaw clamped tight. *Don't mess with me*, his body language said, although if someone did, he would be pretty helpless. He had no training in the art of self-defense. All of his life he had been a gentle giant, playing the fun-loving peacemaker. Playground bullies had kicked sand in his face and pantsed him outside the girls' locker room; they had pissed and pooped in his mess kit—and all of that, okay. Turn the other cheek, walk away, take the high road. For him, okay. He could take all of that. But this other … No. No Mr. Nice Guy. No gentle bear. No water off a duck. No forgive and forget. No turn the other cheek. No kiss and make up. There would be no pissing in his son's mess kit.

As the last few passengers boarded, Mark silently noted the incursions on the world he had left behind. There were no goats or chickens on board, but the outside was soft-sale camouflage compared to the ravaged interior. Peanut shells, candy wrappers, and clots of dried mud spotted the floor; the vinyl seats were split and frayed; the cracks in the windows were angry asterisks. These he had almost expected. Harder to process was the little shrine near the driver's seat where a large picture of a brown-skinned Virgin Mary cloaked in a green gown gazed gently back at the passengers. Red and gold tassels dangled from the rearview mirror, and the face of a young girl smiled inside a frame of pink macramé. Etched above it, in bold, medieval letters: *DIOS ES AMOR*.

At 5:40 the bus bellowed as it backed out of the shady overhang, allowing the sun to resume its grueling work. Within minutes the interior felt like an oven that someone had switched from low to broil. The locals remained statues, stoic and indifferent even as sweat rolled down their earth-colored faces. Mark unscrewed the cap on his last water bottle and began sipping methodically. He stood up and wrestled with the nearest window until it finally gave, but the air gusted in like dragon's breath, so he sat back down and resigned himself to a long, hot ride. He could feel the globs of sweat colonizing in the soft folds of his belly.

He observed quietly as the bus lumbered through a maze of convoluted streets, intermittently stopping to pick up more passengers: a young Tarahumara family, the father carrying an infant in one arm and a toddler in the other, the skinny mother on crutches, her left ankle swaddled in an Ace bandage. They took a seat near Mark in the back, the woman staring straight ahead, her almond eyes big and glossy, beautifully so, but expressionless, as if her head were mounted on a wall, telling silent tales. Or maybe she was simply contemplating the whereabouts of their next meal?

Mark turned his attention outside where colonial domes and arches rose majestically above onerous billboards and row upon row of simple shops and hodge-podge homes of mud, plywood, cardboard, concrete, and corrugated metal. Every city had its unsightly neighborhoods, he knew that, but the bus had been rumbling along for over an hour now, and the scenery was growing progressively worse. Where were the elegant stone plazas and fountains? Why were they traveling the eyesore route? Welcome to second class ...

He was beginning to feel sick now, a little nauseated. Was it the fumes from the bus, the smoke from the south, the city smog, or the early summer heat? Or maybe the to-and-fro tottering of the bus as it rounded each corner like a boat about to capsize? The other passengers were opening their carry-on sodas and bags of chips or removing warm tortillas from plastic bags. He should have brought more water. Food, too. Chips, crackers, something besides his stash of granola bars. Dramamine, *por favor*?

He pictured Sean riding the bus here for the first time, his first solo trip away from home. *Bienvenido, Elder!* Was it a grand adventure in his eyes? Or did he too look at the small, broken homes and the hand-me-down laundry drying on the line and long for a safer, cleaner, more familiar place? Pine trees and snowboards. Their little big boy all grown up. In his letters he had tried to sound upbeat and positive, but the subtext was painful; he was hurting badly. In their return letters, they had quoted platitudes: "Forget about yourself and go to work ... put your shoulder to the wheel ... lose yourself to find yourself ... return with honor."

His son had never voiced a direct plea to let that cup pass. Mark had pretty much put the kibosh on that at the airport. So he had written about dogs falling off rooftops and his linguistic miscues—telling people he was *embarazado* (pregnant) when he meant *embarazoso* (embarrassed). Stand-up comedy mingled with scriptures. In this way, he had survived his first six months in this city that looked as if half of it needed to be power-washed and the other half delicately feather-dusted. Humor had been his savior, at least in the beginning. And then they had transferred him to the village in the mountains where it was pure and clean and safe.

Within a month, the tone of his letters had changed. The humor was still there, but now he spoke of his "great love for the people." He must have repeated that a hundred times: "wonderful … humble … salt of the earth … spiritual … a believing people. You tell them about Joseph Smith's vision in the Sacred Grove, and they have no problem with that, not like the ever-skeptical white people. 'Yes,' they'll say. 'My uncle, he had a vision too!'" Always ending his letters with the obligatory guilt trip: "We Americans have been blessed with so much—not just material wealth, not just cars and toys and stuff, but power too, the power to do good or evil in the world, or to sit on our hands and do nothing. The ultimate spectators. Those of us who hold the priesthood especially have a solemn obligation to …" Fill in the blank. Yes, yes, we're all under condemnation. Mark shook his head, half smiling, half cringing at the heavy-handed general authority jargon so typical of young missionaries who had finally lost themselves in the work. Which was exactly what he and Margie had been fasting and praying for …

No. Don't say it. Be careful what you wish for … pray for. See the grand design. Leave it in God's hands … Get over it … Move on …

Shut the hell up.

They were rolling deeper into the innards of the city: store windows fogged over with dust, newsprint patching up corroded walls, more signs: *Carta Blanca Cerveza … Tecate … Dios Te Lleve … Floreria Claudia … Fruteria Olivas … Vidriomex*. A man with no legs was sitting a few feet from the corner holding out a Styrofoam cup. More like that—an entire street of them, men and women without legs, arms, eyes, mouths. A street of missing parts and pieces. As the bus roared into a busy intersection, the city became a giant pinball game of mad taxis, swerving cars, screaming sirens.

This was not Puerto Peñasco or some other little tourist town where you could lounge on the beach and barter for cheap souvenirs and sip your virgin margaritas on a veranda overlooking a tranquil blue bay. This was real Mexico, raw Mexico, and it had lost its luster. He found himself arguing internally but angrily with God: *Why so many born in these circumstances, with their future sealed in a time bomb? Why are these dealt a pair of deuces while others get four aces?* He winced at the banality of his argument. He sounded like Sean in his combative high school days, raging against God's ways to man. His voice would erupt, his rosy cheeks burning, especially when Mark dismissed his harangue with a patronizing smirk, with rolling eyes: "Don't worry, Marge! Old Sean's just trying to save the world again!" Sean would shove his plate aside, shake an accusing finger at his father: "All you people care about is your stupid house, your stupid cars, your stupid Botox!"

In those explosions of passion, Mark—a child of the down-with-everything-but-me, do-your-own-thing sixties—always felt his own past rearing up and biting him in the butt: *touché*. Sean disdained the fact that his father had devoted his entire life to selling top-of-the-line bed mattresses. Smiling condescendingly: "Relax, son. Your mother and I have been around the block."

Sean had sworn that he would never, ever, under any circumstances, serve a full-time mission for the church.

It was dusk before they reached the outskirts of the city; and as the bus turned southward, Mark took one last look at its ragged silhouette on the horizon. A gigantic Mexican flag was undulating defiantly and ironically above the ruins—something odd and strangely triumphant about it, like a besieged city stubbornly refusing to surrender.

As the bus steamed through the countryside he saw automobile graveyards, gardens of old tires, sway-backed horses roaming barren fields, rock walls three feet high sectioning off rolling hillsides where a lifetime of litter was masquerading as snow. More billboards: *Di No a Drogas Para Que Tu Vivas Mejor ... Gabrinando por Gobernador ... Carta Blanca.* And a parting image just before nightfall—two men lying side by side in an empty boxcar, the heartbreak that was Mexico.

But at almost the same moment, Mark zeroed in on a mud-domed house with a big orange fire dancing licentiously in the front yard. Barefoot children in T-shirts were kicking a soccer ball as a matronly woman tended the fire and a young mother sat on a stump of concrete nursing her baby. Hands on hips, the father was peering at the bus through dust-fogged eyes. Mark's heart spasmed momentarily. He couldn't pinpoint the feeling until it was replaced by another: envy.

He leaned back and tried to sleep, but his thoughts kept escaping north to the mountains. They would be returning from the movies now, Stacie chattering nonstop about the last day of school, the tearful goodbye to her teacher. In his absence, Margie would man the barbecue tonight, and Stacie would ask if they could make microwave popcorn—too bad Dad isn't here to make his world-famous homemade shakes and fries, they're the very best, right, Mom? Margie would smile and say—hopefully—yes, too bad.

Something was intruding—a thumb pressing on his head, right at the tender temple, trying to divert him home. He reminded himself that he was an emissary carrying God's mail. Everything else was the devil's diversion—Lucifer in a top hat and coattails, mixing excrement with sunshine to play the upper hand.

Leave it in God's hands, Bishop Carson had said. And so, in a manner of speaking, he had. There were asterisks to every commandment.

Margie's parting words forced their way back into his head: "Don't call me. Don't call and tell me you're in some Mexican jail."

He wondered if that missed kiss outside the airport would be their last. He started mentally writing her a letter, but two lines into it he shredded the thing angrily in his head. He was aching inside and out, but that was okay. It was good to feel it deep and hard and stinging, like acid in his veins. That's how Sean had felt it. It was good that he was traveling second class. Hell, maybe it was third class. Not quite without purse or scrip but with a few pesos in his pocket. Good that he was thirsty, dry, itchy, sweaty, hungry, homesick—that word! Sean had never painted it that way. Kids. Nineteen-year-olds. To them it was an adventure. A two-year camping trip. Living off tortillas and beans.

The bus stopped briefly at each little outpost to let more people on or off, and for every burro crossing the road, but never long enough for him to get out and take a leak or buy a candy bar. It lumbered relentlessly through the barren flats until it was consumed in desert darkness, the only break an occasional pair of headlights speeding toward them like twin comets that thank goodness always managed to stay on their own side of the road. He had heard stories. There was no bathroom or reading light on board, just the smell of sweat and exhaust and the fried desert air, and wondering where they were, where they were going, and when they were going to get there. He may as well have been sloshing around in the belly of a whale.

At some point, the air outside grew cool enough to warrant moving closer to an open window. Shortly after, he could sense the extra pull of gravity as the bus began laboring uphill; and within the hour he could see campfires burning at the edge of the world. The bus began slowing down but never quite stopping as the other passengers stood up and shuffled to the front. Pine tree silhouettes were keeping watch over a small village of log cabins. Tarahumaras in headbands and shawls were moving slowly in and out of lantern shadows. A longhaired mutt was lying on a porch beside a man with a face like driftwood. His hawk eyes seemed to be staring directly at Mark, condemning him personally for a long, sad history of dead ends, or perhaps reminding him that he was on foreign soil now.

At last, the bus came to a complete stop, and the other passengers began shuffling out into the night. Mark wondered if this was his stop, but when he stood up, the driver glanced up in his rearview mirror and shook his head.

It was another hour of torturously slow climbing and winding, but eventually Mark saw a nest of lights glowing up ahead. This time the driver switched on his little dome light, nodding, but Mark was already in front of the door, thanking him profusely. Before his Nike sneakers had even touched the broken pavement, a pack of local boys swarmed around him as if he were a star-crossed celebrity. When the driver opened the side panel to remove Mark's duffel bag, a flurry of arms reached out for it, like a fish feeding frenzy.

It took all of two seconds to identify the leader—a tall, slender boy with black bangs drooping into furry eyebrows that made a straight, unbroken line across his lower forehead. The exact countenance of the boy he had seen in his dreams. The giveaway? The gold Rolex watch on his left wrist—Sean's high school graduation gift from Margie's parents.

"Carlos?" he whispered aloud, but his voice was swallowed up in the commotion.

On second glance he looked even younger than Mark had imagined—thirteen, maybe fourteen—a street-smart smirk as he oozed to the front of the pack, deftly released a younger boy's hand from the duffel bag strap, and made it his own. Slinging the bag over his shoulder as naturally and expertly as a sailor heading off to sea, he smiled at Mark and asked: "Where you go?"

In plain pants, huarache sandals, and a baggy blue-on-green print shirt, he was not dressed much differently than the others. It was the way he wore the shirt, with the tails loose and reckless and the top buttons undone, showing off his glabrous chest.

"A place to sleep—*dormir*?" Mark clasped his hands together against the side of his face and tilted his head.

The boy nodded vigorously. "*Sí, sí.*"

His lanky legs seemed to flutter in the darkness as Mark hobbled along trying to keep pace, his ankle throbbing anew as blood flooded back into it. He followed the boy down a narrow street lit by a solitary lamp, the cone of light marking the point where the cracked pavement gave way to cobblestone. They turned left down another narrow street and right down another, and just when Mark thought they were going to disappear into the darkness of a third, the boy stopped abruptly outside an eight-foot adobe wall. A wrought-iron lantern cast as much shadow as light on a small wooden sign with letters in cursive and a painted picture of a turquoise butterfly: *La Mariposa.*

"*Aquí está!*" the boy announced.

As Mark pressed two twenty-peso notes into his hand, the boy's eyes widened in such a way that Mark couldn't tell if he had tipped way too much or way too little. "I need you tomorrow. *Mañana.*"

"*Mañana?*"

"Yes, *mañana.* Twelve o'clock. *A las doce. Aquí.*" Mark pointed to the ground.

"*A las doce?*"

"Yes—I mean, *sí. A las doce.*" He felt as if he were back in high school Spanish, performing Mrs. Velasco's tedious pattern practice drills.

"*Sí, sí, sí.*"

He interpreted the rapid succession of *sí*'s to mean he had paid the boy generously. Mark thanked him again; and if it hadn't seemed so contrary, if not outright sacrilegious, he would have thanked God as well.

"Carlos, right?"

For the first time since their encounter, the bravura drained from the boy's mahogany face. "How you know ..." and he took a gulp of air—for inspiration or composure—"name?"

Mark shrugged: "Lucky guess. *Suerte.* Tomorrow, *a las doce,* okay?" He held up a handful of bills. "*Mañana.* Don't be late."

As Mark watched the boy's elusive frame blend into the shadows, one thought kept going through his head: *The Lord hath delivered him into thy hands ...*

⸻

The hotel was nothing fancy but decent enough for $20 a night. There were two levels arranged around a small courtyard of dirt and gravel where you could sit in plastic lawn chairs and contemplate the red flowers spilling out of big ceramic pots. The sound of Mexican trumpets and accordions was blasting through the open doors of a small bar.

The night attendant was so short his chin barely cleared the counter where Mark carefully placed 200 pesos. His stubby fingers curled up, swallowing the bills, as he handed Mark a room key fastened to a strap of leather imprinted with a turquoise butterfly. In broken English he said that breakfast was served until nine.

Mark said *gracias* and trudged up the wooden stairwell, passing lacquered doors of knotty pine until he located the ceramic tile with the number 12. He entered, hoping for cooler air and was marginally rewarded: no refrigeration but a ceiling fan created an artificial breeze that took some of the sting out of the heat. He dropped his backpack and duffel bag on the bed, drew the blinds, and popped the window, allowing in some fresh air along with distant strands of Mexican music.

The room was small but clean and comfortable—maybe too comfortable for his purposes: tile floors wonderfully cool to the touch, wooden beams ribbing the ceiling, the bedcovers, turned down for the night, sporting an exotic native design. Hanging on the wall directly behind the wooden headstand was a framed oil painting of a white woman in her early twenties—long, straight hair covering one shoulder and half-hiding behind the other. Mark wondered what mixed message was lurking behind this posed portrait of a strawberry blonde in a Mexican peasant dress. There was an innocence about her—the rosebud lips that had not kissed many lips, the optimistic eyes that had yet to see the dark side of the moon. On second look, and even more so on the third, she seemed hauntingly similar to Margie as a young college student. He hadn't known her back then, had only seen photos, but she would have been quite a catch. How she had evaded the hordes of horny suitors until her late twenties bewildered him almost as much as why she had fallen for the likes of him. "Desperation," she had cooed into his ear in their early years, back when life was simple, plausible, sexual.

She would be in bed now, reading a Dorothy Sayers mystery. Stacie would be in bed as well—or maybe not: the last day of school, curfews were typically lengthened. Maybe she had been invited to a friend's house for a sleepover, and they were up late watching TV or something. He hoped so; she needed more of that.

He smiled, recalling her very first soccer game. She had been nine, a newcomer who had stumbled and bumbled through the initial practices. To appease the league rules, the coach had sent her in to patrol midfield during the waning minutes of the game. Instead, she had bolted after the ball as if her little heart were trapped inside it and she was trying to get it back. He would never forget the image of her sprinting downfield, legs and arms churning, chest thrust forward, head angling back, like a cartoon character in super-acceleration—mouth and eyes wide open, tongue hanging out, expressing nothing but sheer joy.

She had angled across to the goal, braking, spinning, chasing the ball back to midfield, and so on, up and down and back and forth, completely oblivious to her coach screaming frantically from the sidelines. He had finally run onto the field and grabbed her by the arm: "Stacie, Stacie, sweetheart, play your position! You'll kill yourself running all over like that!" And she had nodded, nodded,

tongue wagging, but he may as well have told a thoroughbred to
walk or a malamute not to pull. She had spun around and streaked
across the field, while the poor coach had appealed to the crowd
with a histrionic shrug.

She was not big or fast or particularly skilled, but—jeez!—she
loved the game. Loved the ritual of putting on her shin guards, her
matching headband, her purple jersey with the number 10; loved
to stuff her Adidas bag with her little sports drink, her cleats, her
purple-and-gold sweats and sling it over her shoulder. Tough as
nails, too. On defense she confronted every opponent as if it were
a personal vendetta. No one got by her without a slide tackle or a
foot in the shins. Not dirty, just tough. Scrappy. All of her inner
hurt and anger were converted to energy on the field.

It seemed strange—even unjust—that he was down here in this
cheap but clean hotel, while they were up there, a thousand miles
away, under the same moon, the same stars, the same sky, yet he felt
galaxies removed from them.

He meandered into the bathroom, trying to remember what he
had come here to forget, and almost bumped into a small wooden
table with a water bottle beside a ceramic bowl. The thirst that had
dogged him throughout the long bus ride suddenly returned. He
grabbed the bottle, broke the plastic seal, threw back his head, and
swallowed. The water was as warm as pee, but he didn't care. He
emptied the bottle in seconds. He turned on the tap, started to refill
it, then dropped it in the sink, scolding himself: *This was Mexico,
dipstick!* The last thing he needed now was an attack of the Revenge.

But his throat felt like a desert, and his efforts to lick the dry-
ness from his lips resulted in tiny threads of flesh sticking to his
tongue. He tried to urinate, but only a few pathetic drops squeezed
out, the yellow-green color of antifreeze. The telltale sign of dehy-
dration. What now? Walk down to the bar and buy some water?
They'd probably charge him triple. He was too tired. Tomorrow. He
could wait until tomorrow. They probably only had liquor anyway.

He stripped down and spread his body across the bed, which
was firm and solid but about six inches too short. He closed his
eyes and listened to the soft, steady revolutions of the ceiling fan
as more Mexican music intruded through the open window. The

female lead was crawling to the high notes, the men yip-yip-yip-ping in the background. In the relative silence of the room, the ringing in his ears suddenly became loud, shrill, obnoxious. Mark turned onto his side and tried his very best to not dwell on anything even remotely related to home.

◦—

At first he thought it was the morning call of desert birds, but then he remembered that he was in the mountains now. Rolling onto his back, he peered up at the ribbed ceiling through blurry underwater eyes and realized it was the monotonous chit-chit-chitting of the fan. He tried to sit up, but everything ached, as if he had been clubbed from head to toe with a baseball bat. Sunlight was slanting full-force through the window, catching the corner of the bed. The sweat had dried on his garments, leaving them stiff and salty. He had brought only one other pair and was saving those for the trip home, so he would just have to make do for now. Crawling out of bed, grumbling—*stupid, moronic bus ride; I'm too stinking old for this*—he caught himself again: good. Let it hurt. Deeper. Harder.

He showered under a stingy trickle of water, the showerhead so low he didn't even attempt to wash his hair, and besides he wasn't going to risk a truant drop sneaking between his lips, raising havoc with his bowels, and sabotaging his mission. Okay, so maybe he was being overly cautious, maybe even paranoid, but he felt like a marked man here, a six-foot-six blob of *gringo*, and he sensed the subtle elements of the country conspiring against him because it was their turf and he had come to take one of their own.

Two wooden tables had been squeezed into the hotel entryway, converting it into a cramped dining area. One table was empty and the other was occupied by two young women and a gangly young man in a tank top. Although Mark felt relieved to see other white faces and to hear his native tongue, he noted the abrupt, if brief, break in their conversation as he took a seat at the adjacent table. He suddenly felt terribly and incredibly old.

They were roughly Sean's age, college kids doing what college kids do best. Mark only half-heard their casual chatter but couldn't block out the morning-after bravura of the young man. Mark tried

84

to bite back the urge to ask God, once again, why he had carelessly looked the other way when Sean, his anointed servant, was standing naked in the crosshairs, yet he allowed these kids—wanderers, adventurers, good-timers—to roll merrily along through life, unfazed and unscathed. Okay, so they hadn't made the same covenants as Sean, weren't born under the yoke of Ephraim, but still ...

A slim-hipped girl in a flounced skirt floated up to his table and, before he could decline, poured coffee into his mug, then set a bowl of cereal in front of him. Moments later she returned with a plate of steaming refried beans, scrambled eggs and chorizos, salsa, and warm tortillas. He tore a tortilla in half, munching on it slowly, as if it were medicine, then picked haphazardly at the beans, reminding himself that he needed fuel in his tank, although he really wasn't all that hungry. Thirsty, yes, and when the server placed a shot glass of orange juice on the table he gulped it down instantly, hoping she would return with a refill. She didn't.

He tried to ignore the college kids, but now they were talking about a canyon with waterfalls.

"Oh, it was soooo awesome!" the brunette kept saying. "Soooo awesome!"

Mark turned slightly, his wooden chair scraping the tile floor. "Excuse me."

The brunette did a double take, as if a statue had suddenly come to life. An unsightly silver ring pierced her left nostril, and bits of blue glitter sparkled on her eyelids, yet Mark marveled at the simple beauty of her face: no lines, no wrinkles, just rosy, sun-blushed cheeks. The legacy of the young.

"I'm sorry. I couldn't help overhearing—you said something about a canyon?"

The brunette's eyes darted guiltily between her two friends, as if she had just revealed a sorority secret, but her expression quickly relaxed. "There's a really cool canyon a few miles out of town," she said.

The blonde was wearing a turquoise halter top that made a token effort to rein in her copious breasts; the brunette looked athletic in a sleeveless T-shirt and sports bra. The brunette wore her hair long and straight; the blonde's was in a ponytail.

Mark asked if it was within walking distance.

The young man's goateed face scrunched up. "It depends. How long is long?"

"It's maybe four or five miles, I guess," the brunette said. "But there's lots of locals who can take you. Just go to the plaza. They're all over the place."

Mark nodded. The brunette thrust her hand into her macramé purse, searching briefly before pulling it back out like a magician who had reached for the rabbit but came up empty-handed. "Damn!" She continued ferreting for something. "You didn't come here to see the canyon?" she asked a little suspiciously. Why else would anyone come to this middle-of-nowhere town?

Mark shrugged. "Nope. Just passing through."

The blonde crossed her nut-brown legs. They were lean and sinewy, like a marathoner's. "Wherever the wind blows?"

"Yep. Blowing in the wind."

"Must be nice," she said.

"Sometimes," he said, cringing at the irony. In a teenage fit, Sean had once told him that he lived his life with the passion and daring of a Benedictine monk.

His meal barely touched, Mark left a few coins on the table for the serving girl, slipped out the wooden entry gate, and followed the dirt road leading to the heart of town.

In daylight it was much easier to get his bearings. Two high ridges studded with scrub pine and giant boulders flanked the village like protective walls to the east and west, with railroad tracks and a narrow highway running north and south, dividing the town in half. A whitewashed shrine bulged conspicuously out of the top of the western ridge, and although the sun had long since muscled its way above the eastern edge, its brightness was dampened by the sulfuric haze from the south: Mexico was still burning. Mark reminded himself to check out train departures for the return trip. Anything beat the *Paloma Blanca*.

His ankle felt painfully stiff, as if it had been nailed to his lower leg, but he tried not to limp as he passed a school where young children in uniforms—burgundy pullovers and black slacks for the boys, white blouses and burgundy skirts for the girls—were jumping rope, kicking soccer balls, and playing tag on a large slab of cracked concrete inside a chain-link fence.

The town itself was about the length of two football fields; and within a few minutes, Mark found himself standing in the plaza, empty save for a small gazebo in the center, a few iron benches around the perimeter, and a handful of small trees shrouded in the morning shadows of a Catholic church. By far the most commanding presence in sight, it was a towering structure of immense stone blocks stacked six or seven stories high with turrets at the four corners and a huge wooden door, bolted and girded with wrought iron, protecting the entry. A large stone cross protruded from the Alamo hump at the top center; and a large bell half-hiding in the upper recesses clanged at regular intervals, summoning the faithful to mass. Everything else in the village looked tiny and insignificant by contrast.

A few Tarahumara women in flamboyant skirts and puffy pastel blouses meandered in and out of the nearby shops. Otherwise, there was not much human traffic.

Still thirsty, he ducked inside a shop with a sign that read *Farmacia* and took four bottles of water from the glass-encased refrigerator. The shop was poorly lit by two bare bulbs, and the windows appeared foggy although there was no moisture in the air. The lack of light made everything—the bottles of medicine, the candy bars under the glass countertop, the cans of soda pop on the shelves, the racks of postcards and cheap souvenirs—appear old and obsolete.

A little humpbacked woman drifted up beside him so stealthily that he didn't notice her until he almost knocked her over when he turned to go.

"I'm sorry," he said over and over. "*Lo siento*. I didn't see you— I'm so sorry. *Lo siento. Muy … muy lo siento.*"

The woman was wearing a tri-colored shawl in spite of the early morning heat. She asked him in a tiny voice, as if reciting from a Berlitz script, "May-I-halp-you?"

"*No, gracias,*" he said. "Just looking. *Solamente ….*" and he aimed a finger at his eye.

She smiled, her teeth like a pair of split bowling pins. She was so incredibly short that Mark felt as if she were staring directly at his navel. He noticed a postcard of a waterfall, so he picked it from the rack and paid for it along with the four water bottles.

His appetite recharged, he strolled across the street to the bakery, bought two cinnamon rolls, and then sat in the shade drinking until two of the water bottles were empty. It was only 10:30, but his shoulders were collapsing and his eyelids closing, and he didn't fight it. The sun had found a break in the shade and was gently working the back of his neck like a slow hypnosis.

He and Margie were standing in the bleachers under the field lights, the aroma of popcorn, hot dogs, and cigarettes overpowered by the smell of the rain-soaked grass. Spectators in plastic ponchos or hiding under umbrellas were screaming as the muddied, bloodied players lined up on the three-yard line, water to their ankles, the lights on the scoreboard showing HOME 14 VISITORS 10. There was a weird instant of silence as the quarterback pitched back to a big farm boy who lowered his head and barreled through a split-second chasm in the line like a human dump truck. The collective hometown groan turned to ecstasy at the nasty clash of helmets—the human truck stopped cold for a moment before dropping back flat in the mud, inches shy of the milky stripe. Number 55 was already on his feet again, staring down like a victorious gladiator. The defeated opponents dragged themselves to the locker room while the home team swarmed around number 55, confetti flying, horns blowing, the soaked cheerleaders shaking their pom-poms in a rainy, foggy, surreal moment. The boy hero, amid the commotion, stopped and aimed his index finger across the swampy field directly at Mark. His smile alone could have stanched the November deluge. At that moment, Mark thought that he could never feel happier. And two years later, he thought he would never feel sadder, lonelier, angrier, or more vulnerable.

He had held up fine at first, fielding the call from the mission president, his hands and voice finding Margie and easing her into a chair, onto the bed, and back into the fold, even while she stumbled around, drugged on denial and sleeping pills. He held her steady at the graveside as the wind tugged at the hem of her sky-blue dress, adding insult to injury by throwing it up around her thighs a full three seconds for observers to catch an embarrassing eyeful. Then he guided her back to the hearse and steered her through the Relief Society luncheon, the smorgasbord of Crockpot delights and Jell-O desserts, helping her, eventually, to find a fragment of her smile as the well-intentioned guests offered hackneyed condolences: "He's in the celestial kingdom with Heavenly Father ... He must have an even greater mission to perform on the other side ..."

But one day ... a week, a month, six weeks later ... a single word passed between them: "Mark?" and then a nod. He folded up the morning paper, and together they climbed the staircase, pushing open the door of Sean's room for the first time since the phone call. It was like diving into the rabbit hole, the role reversal so instant and obvious. Her pioneer stock took charge as she became her old pragmatic self again, stripping the bed sheets as coolly and indifferently as a maid tidying up a motel room. She cleaned out the drawers, the closet; and then she started boxing up the assorted verifications of his life: trophies, certificates, baseball cards, CDs, the spiked dog collar he had worn one Halloween, the puka shell necklace an admiring classmate had sent him for graduation. All of it. There would be no morbid shrines here.

Mark had watched, dumbfounded. Each item tossed into the box was like a mini burial. Finally, she had snapped at him: "Hey, are you going to help, or are you going to just stand there with your hands in your pockets?"

He knelt down, reached randomly under the bed, and pulled out a sheet of plywood with miniature tanks, artillery, and plastic soldiers glued to the surface—Sean's recreation of the D-Day invasion. He and Sean had stayed up all night with matches and red nail polish authenticating the display by meticulously burning and bloodying the limbs and faces of selected soldiers. The project had won first prize for Hobbies and Collections at the county fair. Mark fingered one of the soldiers, snapped it free, held its match-blackened face up to the light, and broke down weeping.

11:15. He stood up, tossed the empty bottles into a trash receptacle, and headed back to the hotel to meet the boy named Carlos, still uncertain what he was going to do and how he was going to do it.

When the boy arrived, he looked a bit surprised, probably

because there was no luggage for him to carry. Mark smiled, summoning up some dictionary Spanish. "*Quiero ver la cascada,*" he said, showing the boy the color postcard of the waterfall. When the boy hesitated, he flashed a 200-peso bill, which elicited an enthusiastic response. The boy himself looked like a picture postcard with his lazy black bangs, baggy beige tunic and matching pants, and tire-tread sandals. Mark did not overlook the gold Rolex that appeared even brighter and brasher at midday.

He followed a few steps behind as the boy led him down a dirt road that wound through the south side of town. Within a quarter of a mile, it was just the two of them, traversing scrub pine that soon gave way to sketchy forests of ponderosa pine. The boy moved like an antelope, stretching his lean legs so swiftly and effortlessly that he probably could have sprinted up the mountain. Mark had read somewhere that the Tarahumara Indians had a ritual where they ran for over a hundred miles. A marathon was child's play, a morning warm-up. Mark had no idea if Carlos were Tarahumara or if he were even Indian, but he obviously had been nursed on endurance from the cradle. The kid had the lungs of a lion.

Feeling every ounce of the eighty surplus pounds in his gut and butt, Mark was sucking air as the incline steepened. He tried to minimize his pathetic wheezing; but it was hopeless, so instead he lagged several yards behind, out of Carlos's hearing. He did not want to appear weak or handicapped or anything but large, powerful, formidable, scary. A colossus who could crush and destroy at will. Instead he felt like a giant stick of butter melting in the Mexican sun. The boy was probably sneering to himself: another fat American who any second is going to whip out his cell phone and call the rescue squad. He'll phone in for a golf cart or helicopter to drag him up the hill.

Mark wouldn't give him the satisfaction. The intermittent flashes of gold on the boy's wrist were sufficient motivation. Panting, gasping, the smoky haze adding rust to his lungs, he kept his trunk-like legs moving, slowly but deliberately, ignoring the pain in his bum ankle, grimly determined not to stop unless the boy did, which was not until he had gained the top of a false summit that flattened into a grassy meadow stretching a hundred yards—the calm before the storm—before melding into a gruesome staircase of broken rock and stone that zig-zagged up the bare and rugged flank of the mountain.

The boy paused, hands on hips, barely winded as he waited for Mark to catch up. He said something in Spanish, and Mark (sucking air, trying not to) nodded. "*Está bien, está bien,*" he said, assuming the boy had inquired about his condition. Maybe he had called him a dumb gringo. Maybe he had told him to get the lead out of his fat ass so this silly hike wouldn't take all day. Maybe he had said, "Give me every peso in your pocket!" Or maybe he had said, "Are you tired? Do you want to rest for a while? Am I going too quickly?"

Mark removed the two water bottles from his day pack and offered one to the boy who said *gracias*, took a long swig, and wiped his forearm across his mouth.

"Is it far?" Mark asked. "*Es lejos?*"

The boy shook his head. "*No, no. Está cerquita.*"

He wanted to ask the boy a thousand questions. Why aren't you in school today? Do you do this every day? Your parents—what do they do for a living? What do you want to do when you grow up? Have you thought about leaving the village—moving to the city maybe and going to school? Are you Catholic? What does that mean to you? Do you believe in God? The Ten Commandments? Punishment? Justice? Do you know what justice means? Where did you get that nice-looking watch? Was it given to you? Why are you wearing it if it wasn't given to you and it is not yours? Do you know the owner of that watch? Do you know where he is now? Do you know what happened to him? Do you know he has a mother and father, like you do? How do you think your parents would feel if you didn't come home tonight—if you suddenly disappeared and no one ever saw you again? Are you prepared for what comes next? What were you thinking when you did whatever you did to the owner of that watch? Do you ever think about him now? Does he visit you in your sleep like he visits me? Is there anything whatsoever in that pea brain adolescent head of yours? Do you know what God is going to do now? Do you understand that I'm just the messenger here? Don't worry. It will be quick and completely unexpected.

91

Just like Sean. You caught him off guard, bending over to tie his shoes or maybe tying yours for you? Caught him red-handed in an act of stupid kindness when you thought no one else was looking. But someone's always looking. God is always looking through his all-seeing eyes. Vengeance is mine, saith the Lord. For it is better that one man die than a nation dwindle in unbelief. For it is better that one boy die ...

So many questions but none that he could articulate in a foreign tongue that to his ear was a blur of vowels and congested consonants.

The boy pointed toward the cliff and marched on with Mark following a few steps behind: not so passive now, not so locked into survival mode, his eyes scouring the ragged wall of yellow rock for opportunities.

They labored up the switchbacks for an hour before reaching another summit, then followed the trail through a section of forest spotted with blue and gold flowers. They squeezed between two giant boulders constricted so tightly that, for Mark at least, coming out the other end felt like a birthing. Next the boy led him through a tunnel of leafy trees and overgrowth. Heads lowered, they moved rapidly toward the circle of light at the other end until they found themselves standing on the lip of a sheer cliff that presented a sudden and spectacular view of the canyon. On their side, the barren walls plunged a thousand feet straight down to a slow-flowing highway of dark green water. The other side, equally steep, was lusciously layered with pines, shrubs, vines, flowers. Mark did not understand the magic or climatology (or the theism) that decreed one side of the canyon Desolation and the other Eden, but the distance between the two was only a few hundred yards.

The boy pointed across the divide: "*Las cascadas!*" he announced, and Mark followed his finger to a point midway up the cliff where water blasted out of the woolly pelt of flora and plunged 500 feet in a twisting ribbon of silver magnificence. The daredevil fall looked like one of those preternaturally gifted superheroes that can stretch itself from heaven to earth, crashing on the boisterous bottom only to instantaneously reconstitute itself into a satin-smooth flow except where the protruding rocks made rippling white tears in the fabric.

The majesty of the scene demanded a moment of silence, even

from this boy who had witnessed it countless times before. Mark, too, watched in awe.

"*Nos vamos!*" he shouted and waved Mark forward.

Moving with the alacrity of a ballet dancer, the boy pranced along the edge where one false step would have sent him hurtling to oblivion, and Mark could see firsthand the easy accident. He was quickstepping now, against his better judgment and abilities, yet he somehow managed to dog the boy's heels, knowing he had to act soon, that if he waited too long the trail would widen and reduce the margin for error. He tried not to look down. There was a dizzying sense of vertigo, and he had to keep the advantage of surprise. *I have delivered him into your hands* ... There would be no debate, no second guessing. It would be swift, instantaneous, clean.

And it was: the boy pausing for a moment to gaze down into the canyon as if for the first time—hypnotized, it seemed, by the steady, silver shimmer of the falls; Mark sneaking up from behind, clamping one arm around the boy's throat, the other wrenching his arm down and around, pinning it roughly behind his back; the boy screaming in Spanish as he tried to break free but, his arm being trapped, only able to arch his back, pleading in pathetic grunts and squeals.

Mark tightened his stranglehold, surprised by the surge of power in his arms. "You little shit!" he growled. "That was my boy! That was my son! What did you think—that you could just kill my boy and just walk away, did you?"

He was cheek-to-cheek, spitting into the boy's ear: "Did you think you could just do that? Do that and wipe your hands and just walk away?"

The boy tried to twist his neck free, but Mark reined him in roughly and shoved a knee into the boy's spine, hard, seething like a jilted lover. "Now you'll see. Now you'll feel like he felt ... see what he saw going down."

And then he was dragging him to the edge, the boy kicking and thrashing, but the adrenal rush had turned Mark into Superman. He could have plucked the boy up with one hand and hurled him into the river. He released his stranglehold and grabbed the boy by his hair, jerking his head back, stretching the fragile neck until the Adam's apple seemed to be straining like a rat trapped under the skin. Mark thought he could easily snap it—yes, snap his head right off and throw it into the river. Good riddance! One quick, hard yank—but better, less obvious, a little push, a little nudge over the edge. Just another dumb hiking accident.

The boy was crying now, whimpering, resisting a little but not much. Did Mark maybe feel a little sorry for him? Maybe just a little? Hell, no. Hells bells, no. Whimpering little shit. Then finish it. Finish! No, let him stew and suffer a little longer, pre-play in his head that skydive without a parachute until the fear and panic killed him. Till the mini macho peed his pants.

But in that instant of hesitation on the edge, even as he reminded himself to not lose courage—not a voice exactly but a thought, sentiment—yes, all of that, surely, but this boy too has parents, a mother and father who will wonder about his whereabouts, suffer and weep and grieve, wondering over and over what pathetic piece of human sewage has done this terrible, horrible thing.

Only what he had done to others. Maybe many others. Well deserved. Well earned. Only what he was willing to do and more. They would go to the church and pray over the lanky, broken body; burn incense and wave palm fronds and flowers; do whatever it is they do. A kid. A stupid, thoughtless, reckless little kid trashing his life for a silly gold watch. He felt like Abraham of old, the knife raised, teeth clenched, poised to finish the job … Then do it! Do it! Do it now! But Sean's voice, a soft hand on the shoulder, rushed to the rescue: maybe the details of the dream had been confused, maybe the watch had not been stolen but given willingly, a gift maybe in one of Sean's big-hearted, save-the-world missionary moments, maybe …

In that instant of hesitation, something—a fist, a hammer, a spike—slammed into his upper thigh, high and tight, near the groin. He bellowed, he howled, but it was the shock more than the pain that made him relax his hold just enough for the boy to duck, twist, and wrench himself free.

He tightroped briefly along the edge, and then he was gone, his black mop flip-flopping as he bounded down the trail—left, right, left—as if he were paralleling to the bottom. In the mix of sun and shade, his angular body flickered like an old silent movie.

Mark hollered after him: "Come back, you little sonuvabitch!" But it was a half-hearted cry that chased the boy only part way down the mountain and then quit because by then he was not sure of anything anymore.

Except the knife in his upper thigh which had suddenly become very real. He used both hands to remove the blade, which the boy had buried to the hilt. He didn't know if that part of the knife was even called the hilt, maybe that was just for swords, but it was buried up to that part. He withdrew the blade slowly and in a weird moment imagined young Arthur removing Excalibur from the stone. He felt nothing at first because the adrenaline was speeding so maniacally through his body. But the blood was real, and there was plenty of it spreading quickly across the upper half of his pants. Removing the knife was like unplugging the dike, and he was tempted to stick the blade back in to stop the bleeding. He didn't know much about these things—he sold beds and mattresses, for crying out loud, and had barely passed his first aid merit badge, and that was forty freaking years ago. But there was an artery down there, he knew that—a great big one—and if the boy had gotten lucky and nicked it, he was a dead man—he knew that too. The femoral artery. That was it. Blood gushing out like water from a broken faucet. Just the thought of it chased the blood from his head to his groin and he thought, *That's it. I'm done.*

But not yet. He managed to half-sit, half-fall on a rock shelf where he reminded himself to keep cool, stay calm, keep cool, stay calm. The boy had buried it deep, maybe hit the bone. Mark didn't want to look but knew he had to. So he peeled off his T-shirt and tried to tear it into strips, but it was much harder than it appeared to be in the movies, so he finally bit into it, chewing a small hole and ripping the thing in two, more or less, then tore one of the halves into ragged quarters and the other half into long strips.

He unzipped his pants and pulled them down for a better look at the mess that was his leg—and now his life—and pressed a piece of his shirt against the oozing blood until it was thoroughly soaked, then applied another piece and held it firm until the bleeding stopped. He took one of the strips and wrapped it around the semi-soaked bandage knotting it tight but not tourniquet-tight. But the blood soaked through again, and when he removed the bandage, he inserted his thumbs into the wound, gently pulling the lips apart until they opened like a dumb, dark mouth—hell itself bubbling inside. His eyes clamped shut against his will; he fought and fought but couldn't force them open.

When he finally did, he was lying on the ground with his pants halfway down, his garment top exposed, and his face in the dirt. But he was still alive, which meant he had been luckier than the boy who had missed the fatal artery. His pants were an awful, ugly mess, but the bleeding had stopped, thank God. And then he remembered to really thank God because he was going to really need him to get out of this mess alive. The bleeding had stopped but the boy was probably back at the village by now saying who knows what to who knows whom? He had sprinted down the trail as if he were on fire, but these rat-pack kids always had an escape hatch, a way back home. He'd probably told his parents, the police. The whole village probably knew by now, and before long they'd be coming after him with machetes and bullwhips. Besides, he didn't have a leg to stand on, literally or figuratively. Well, there was the boy's knife, which happened to be inserted into Mark's leg. Try explaining that to a judge. *No hablo español.* Or his sudden change of heart that kept him from hurling the urchin to a speedy and accidentally-on-purpose death. Quid pro quo. That was a change of heart, wasn't it? Father? There, at the last instant, second guessing? Playing Hamlet? Or was that strike three and I'm out? Judging our actions and the workings of the heart. To even look upon a woman to lust after her ... Intent is everything. But didn't I balk on the intent—my second and third stuttering that allowed him to houdini out of this?

His thoughts were scatter-gunning everywhere. Stop. Think. Focus. Deal with the moment, save the metaphysical crime and punishment, sin and suffering, eternal judgment stuff for later. He had to get back to town, get this thing cleaned up, sewn up, before the Mexican microbes infiltrated and took his leg, if not his life.

He picked up the knife—small, about a four-inch blade, although at the moment it looked as big as a Bowie knife and for sure it was infested with germs having been employed to gut chickens or goats or who knows what. The serrated edge had made his ugly wound even uglier. He thought he recalled hearing a clink on impact, something even nastier than the raw puncturing of his skin. Striking the bone, maybe, and if so, was that bad? Of course it was bad, but how bad was it? Doesn't matter—doesn't doesn't doesn't. It is what it is and now keep your head screwed on straight and deal with it.

He tossed the blade aside and, reconsidering, picked it up and heaved it deep into the canyon, then wondered if some goatherder or federal agent might see it glistening in the sun. Idiot! You could have buried the dumb thing. Could have done a million other things besides throw it out there for anyone to find. And with your prints all over it.

He needed to act quickly. There was no one in sight and that was good. He couldn't go back to town, not like this, all covered with blood. The boy probably had an uncle or a brother or father who was probably the police chief or the sheriff or whoever doled out justice here, and wouldn't they just love to throw his sorry American ass in jail? Wait. Calm. Stay calm now. Stop. Breathe …

Okay. Okay. Okay, so now he would hike back toward the village, find a place to hide, wait there until dark. A shady spot out of the sun, close to some water, hopefully, to clean out the wound. He would sneak back to the hotel at dark—if he could just get back to the hotel room and clean himself up …

He thought it wasn't right to wear his garment top like a T-shirt, in the open with nothing over it, but was it any better to carry it in his pocket like a giant handkerchief? *What would Jesus do?* If he removed the top, the sun would fry him like an egg, so he left it on and started the long walk back, limping on the left leg now instead of the injured right ankle which he didn't even notice anymore.

Halfway down the mountain, he saw through the pines a fortress of rocks about fifty yards off the trail, so he veered toward it thinking, *This will do.* It was a ten-foot wall of boulders that formed a kind of horseshoe with an oval hole at the bottom, wide enough for him to crawl through. On the other side he found a shady grotto in a stand of trees with thin strips of bark peeling off like badly sunburned flesh—the way his skin would look tomorrow.

He lowered himself to the bed of dirt and leaves and tried to relax beneath the cribwork canopy of branches and pine needles. He thought he was protected, but fragments of sunlight still sneaked through the overgrowth, burning slowly but deeply into his arms and face and neck. His lips and mouth were parched, and he wanted water in the worst way. *Should've brought more; should've shared less; shouldn't have guzzled it all at once.* But he tried to ignore all of that and the little army howling for food in his belly. What surprised and amazed him the most was the wound. Even though he knew it was there and it bothered him some, there was relatively little pain, and he didn't know if that was good or bad.

He tried to rest—not sleep, because if he dozed off, he might not wake up again. He started counting down from 100, and then he tried reciting the Articles of Faith, and then began singing old Beatle songs, church hymns—anything to keep his brain working. But jeez, he was thirsty and the sound of falling water made it even worse, although it was probably just the wind in the trees or the ringing in his ears, and besides, water would draw a crowd on a day like this and he couldn't afford any witnesses.

And so he began praying—a nonstop monologue directed partly at himself, partly at God, partly at Margie—not so much prayer as a blitz of uncensored emotion mixed with bits of contrition, despair, and personal pep talk: *We can get through this thing, can't we? Of course. All things possible in thy book. All things, right?*

Thus, he waited, trying to rest without falling asleep as the sun dragged its gassy, liquored body across the Mexican sky. When it finally touched down on the rocky horizon, he pulled himself to his feet and began a crippled but hasty descent toward the preliminary lights of the village.

The mixture of dusk and the ubiquitous haze made for convenient camouflage; and by the time he reached the outskirts, night had fallen, and he could hear music playing in the plaza. He followed the darker streets, ducking behind a tree here, an old barrel there, detouring to avoid a small but persnickety dog guarding the entrance to a house of mud and sticks. Eventually he found the walled exterior of the hotel, slipped through its wooden gate, staggered across the patio, and climbed upstairs to his room, hoping no one had seen him.

Water. He needed water fast. He bolted into the bathroom and lowered his head into the sink, determined to guzzle straight from the tap and suffer the consequences, but he pulled out at the last moment. *This close*, he scolded himself, licking his brutally chapped lips. *This close on so many levels.*

He showered, scrubbed the wound the best he could, tore a bathroom towel into strips, and made a temporary bandage. He put on his other garments, clean jeans and shirt, and stepped out into the warm evening, heading toward the pillar of light hovering over the village, silently praying that the pharmacy would still be open and the crowd too busy to notice an oversized American in a maroon ASU Sun Devils T-shirt and blue jeans gimping along their cobbled streets.

He was in luck because it was Friday night, and every man, woman, and child from every two bit town in northern Mexico seemed to have descended on the plaza where a five-piece band was playing in the gazebo—brassy, sassy trumpets punctuated by the intermittent booming of a bass drum. The crowd was circling around it like a slow-motion whirlpool—one that kept changing its mind and reversing direction: an old couple dancing a slow-but-smooth two-step, the mustachioed husband in shiny black shoes, his wife with her silver hair in a bun; younger couples swiveling their Latin hips centerstage or cuddled on the cast-iron benches. Mature women and their teenage daughters sauntered into the arena with shawls over their shoulders like graceful butterflies, the ends trailing behind them. A young man in a white dress shirt and tie was sitting imperiously on a stainless-steel throne while an old-timer spit-shined his shoes. Sidewalk vendors sold their wares, and Tarahumara women with bulging bundles on their heads wove adroitly through the crowd as the human traffic flowed in and out of the shops, the bakery, the open-air food stands. For Mark, the smells of fresh-baked delights and meats sizzling over flaming grills were tantalizing reminders that he hadn't eaten since midmorning. Through all of this, the little band played on with astounding volume and energy.

Watching from the shadows, Mark was startled by this other slice of Mexico. He wondered how this abundance of simple joy had escaped him earlier. In almost every face, he observed laughter; and even in the silent countenances of the Tarahumaras, he sensed a quiet contentment. A pack of children seemed deliriously happy kicking a plastic bottle back and forth across the bricks. He couldn't remember the last time he and Margie had danced like the silver-haired couple circling in front of him … couldn't remember the last time they had danced. The energy was so addictive that for a moment even he was tempted to step out and join the swirling, whirling mass. Then he saw, through a momentary gash in the crowd, two images that reined him back. The first was a young mother in rags huddled up with three small, barefoot children on the street corner, her open hand, dark and withered, extended to passersby. She could not have been a day over eighteen. The second was the sloping shoulders and mop-haired head of Carlos.

He was coming in Mark's direction, maybe not intentionally but this was no time for even a chance reunion. Mark dipped his head and hobbled down a side street until he found, to his relief, the pharmacy still open. An old Tarahumara man and his wife were at the counter buying tubes of something. They smelled like a campfire.

Through the glass counter he could see tiny boxes and plastic bottles with warped wrappers and faded lettering that betrayed their natural shelf life. One bulb was burning behind the cash register and the other on the wall near the entry. Otherwise, the store was cast in evening shadow.

Mark consulted the list he had made in the hotel room, carefully trying to pronounce each item: *alcohol*; *aguja*, needle; *hilo*, thread; *vendaje*, bandage. The hunchbacked woman behind the counter scrunched her face on his first try but smiled on the second, nodding, pronouncing the word correctly: *a-goo-haa*.

As she bagged the items, he grabbed as many bottles of water as he could carry, a can of soda, and two candy bars. Turning to go, he felt his eyes shutting down again, and he grabbed for the counter, trying to steady himself. The woman looked at him curiously—no, gently; it was a gentle look of concern—and asked him something he couldn't decipher. He smiled, nodding, trying without words to reassure her he was fine, just fine, *está bien*, he said—later thinking it should have been *estoy bien*—but for now he just wanted to get out of there (*gracias, muchas gracias, está bien, estoy bien*) before the wound started bleeding through his pants and he caused a panic in the house.

He gathered up his things, stepped outside, and felt marginally better, well enough to stop and buy half a dozen tamales from a streetside vendor because Sean had said that anything hot was safe to eat.

In the hotel room, he ate and drank ravenously, tearing the husks off the tamales and wolfing them down, guzzling bottle after bottle of water. It was lukewarm, but he didn't really care right now. He ate and drank way too much way too fast and stopped way too late, but he didn't care. When he was so stuffed that he thought his belly would burst, he rolled over sideways on the bed and lay there for several moments, trying to psyche himself up for the nasty task of dressing his wound.

For this, he placed the remains of his bathroom towel on the bed and removed his pants, wincing as he pried apart the gash, an ugly, jagged ravine. He poured the rubbing alcohol directly into it, then flung himself back onto the bed, snorting and swearing and chewing his upper lip so he wouldn't howl the roof off because the pain was so deep and sharp and savage, like the knife going in and out all over again. He could have gotten something milder, hydrogen peroxide for instance, which he wouldn't have felt at all, but he couldn't pronounce the words in Spanish, although that was only part of it. More to the point, he wanted the bite, the sting, the torture of hot lava pouring into his groin. He wanted the punishment. So he administered a second round, biting on a washcloth, chewing it almost joyfully as the clear liquid burned hot and deep, whispering his son's name: "Sean … Sean … Seany boy …" And then he flopped back on the bed again, staring at the ceiling fan monotonously chopping up the air, reminding himself that this was the easy part.

It took him six tries to finally thread the needle; and when he did, he almost messed it up on purpose, but finally he forced the tip into the tough, fat flesh of his upper thigh, and yes, the first one was awful—the worst by far—and jeez, it hurt, it hurt, it hurt so damn much, and you had to really muscle it through the stubborn skin and across the great divide, but you had to sew it up, didn't you? Of course, you did. But the second was a little easier than the first, a little less bite. And the third pass was a little easier still, not that any of it was easy. But by the time he had looped the thread through from one end of the gash to the other he had come to almost enjoy it. It was his punishment for stupidity, clumsiness, carelessness, shortsightedness. It was his final tribute to his son who had died nobly in service to his God. Each poke and plunge felt like a hot, angry stripe. Like penance. At the end of the gash he pulled the thread around tight, tying it three times for good measure. Tears streaming down his face, he raised the remains of the last tamale to his lips, took a triumphant bite, and then collapsed face down on the mattress.

When he woke up it was still dark outside and the blood-red digits on the alarm clock read 12:17 which seemed impossible because he wasn't tired or even drowsy and it had been well past 10:00 when he had returned from the plaza. Was he so strung out and depleted that he'd slept through the night and the day and into the next night? Or maybe three nights and two days? He had no idea, none. Outside it was perfectly still, perfectly quiet, the only sound the inexorable ringing in his ears. He thought that maybe he was still sleeping except the room was too familiar, too tactile, and had none of the eccentric distortions of a dream. And the pain in his upper thigh was all too real. It felt as if someone were bludgeoning it with a hammer. He unwrapped the wound and cursed at the sight of a red-hot ring around his artless ladder of sutures. He poured more alcohol over the wound, savoring the sting, knowing better but still hoping that the harsher the bite, the more potent the potion. But there was no stopping the throbbing or the sweat lacquering his body or the fire in his flesh. He thought maybe the room was just really hot, or maybe he had a fever, but either way there wasn't much he could do about it until morning, so he opened his Grisham paperback and tried his best to focus as night crawled leglessly toward dawn. He tried not to watch the laggard progress of the clock or clutter his mind with calculations but did anyway: the train left at 4:00. Eleven and a half hours plus four hours makes fifteen and a half hours. Seven hours to the city, arrive at 11:00. Twenty-two and a half, round it off to twenty-three. Figure an hour to get from the bus station to the airport, get a ticket, et cetera, et cetera. The plane left around 9:00 a.m. Add eleven to midnight, one hour, plus another nine makes ten, which equals thirty-four. An hour flight to El Paso, kill two more at the airport makes three and an hour to Phoenix makes four. Thirty-eight total. Puts you in Phoenix about 1:00 make it 2:00 to be safe. Wait another hour for the next puddle jumper, 3:00 plus an hour in the air and you're landing about 4:00. Add an hour for glitches, screw-ups, Mexican time. 5:00. Flying in over the peaks at 5:00 p.m. ...

He worked the numbers over and over again, mixed with flights of guilt, regret, anger (*stupid, stupid, stupid* ...), prayer, and escalating pain; and at some point during the mental mishmash, he managed to doze off again.

The sun had been up for a few hours, but he stuffed his bloodied pants next to the wall on the other side of the bed so the maid wouldn't see them if she started to clean up. Then he made the final call for breakfast. He didn't want to risk going into town and seeing the boy or the police, so he returned to his room until checkout time at noon. He was not too surprised to see two extra nights tacked on to the bill, which he promptly paid, smiling at the young woman with the long braid. Then he limped toward town on the less-traveled south side, marveling at the orgy of colors: shawls of bougainvillea coating adobe walls, flowered vines dripping out of clay pots, young mothers in multi-toned fabric sweeping the walkways of simple homes painted outlandishly loud colors: scarlet, orange, turquoise, pink, chartreuse. They were so bright and bold and in your face that Mark found himself limping along with a little more bounce in his step and a little less gravity in his countenance.

The midday sun had cleared the streets except for a few mangy dogs stretched out on slabs of shade and a young woman slipping into the open doorway of the church. Mark considered following suit, but first he had to attend to his leg. He entered the pharmacy and bought *una cosa para matar el dolor*. Something to kill the pain. Butchered, but the best he could do on the fly. The old woman smiled at him as if he were a regular customer now and handed him a small bottle with faded lettering.

"*Es fuerte?*" It is strong?

The old woman nodded vigorously: "*Sí! Es muy fuerte.*"

"Good," he mumbled, "because I need *muy, muy fuerte*."

The old woman held up three fingers. "*Tres pastillas*."

Mark repeated the gesture. "*Tres?*"

More nods; more vigor. "*Sí! Tres*."

Mark bought four water bottles and found a patch of shade where he swallowed three pills and hoped for the best. Even in the shadows it was scorching; but he toughed it out, watching from afar as a few brave hearts ventured out into the sun—old women lugging plastic bags swollen with the day's groceries; a middle-aged man and his young sidekick pushing and pulling a giant desk across the cobbled streets on a comically undersized hand truck. No sign of Carlos.

The pills made him drowsy but did nothing to reduce the pain. It was tolerable when he was at rest; but if he put any weight on his leg it was like smashing it with a hammer. But he was melting in the heat. Gritting his teeth, he limped across the plaza and disappeared inside the church where he was jolted first by the sudden plunge in temperature—the place felt refrigerated—and then by other sensations: the exquisite silence, the vastness of the space, the darkness pricked by a few strategically placed lights and little rows of votive candles burning up front and along the sides, the flames wriggling like goldfish in tiny bowls—all of that—but most unsettling to his Mormon mind was the giant statue of the Virgin Mary in a flowing robe of royal blue, posing dead center in the front on a pedestal in a three-dimensional frame of tendrilled gold. She was staring down at the almost vacant rows of dark wood pews, not with eyes of long-suffering but with a cool detachment, arms extended, hands open, awaiting an embrace. The wall behind her was a giant mural of long-faced martyrs and suffering saints divided by four golden columns that urged the eye upward to a domed ceiling populated by chubby cherubim. At the foot of the statue in a small glass box the Virgin's immaculate Son gazed down from his cross with bowed head and despondent eyes, a golden crown on his head, the prints in his hands and feet barely visible, like little afterthoughts.

At first the ubiquitous look and smell of gold was appalling to him, especially in a town so small and poverty-stricken, lacking in things of the world, but Mark reminded himself of the Kirtland Temple and how the Saints had willingly and joyfully crushed their heirloom china to a fine powder that would sparkle from top to bottom whenever the sun touched the temple walls. Duty. Sacrifice. Love was smeared somewhere in the mix. And what force had moved these massive blocks of stone, bent double under the cracking whips of friars and conquistadors? Wasn't that how it had come down here? Every nation had its dark underbelly.

To the right near the front, a young woman with a thick braid of black hair was kneeling between the pews, head bent, eyes closed, lips moving softly and swiftly. A balding old man entered clutching a straw hat in both hands. He dipped his hand into a stone container bulging out of the wall, crossed himself, limped up to the altar in front, genuflected, then crossed himself again before kneeling behind the front pew.

Mark watched for several minutes, but neither the man nor the woman moved. He closed his eyes and tried to feel the Spirit, but the pain in his groin outshouted his prayer. There was certainly reverence here, he couldn't deny that, and respect—a willing submission to God. More than *he* could claim. His antsy prayers were even shorter than his lovemaking. In and out, man.

To call them simple hearts was condescending. Believing hearts. Yearning hearts. Trusting and devoted hearts. He, on the other hand, had come all this way, for what? His eyes slowly climbed the giant stone blocks that had been hoisted five centuries ago without power-driven motors or machines. The sweat, blood, and tears of a nation. And what nation? Whose people? Father Lehi's truant offspring? Or God's chosen children, biding their time until he hands back the deed to the Americas for good—all of it, north and south?

Mark looked up at the porcelain face of the Virgin Mary—smooth, shiny, aloof, indifferent, and so very white. Yet the longer he looked, the more it seemed to warm and soften. Here was a woman who could understand the agony of loss without divine scaffolding and eternal vision. So maybe the frigid pallor and unblinking eyes were more self-defense than apathy and indifference. She had been there, steeled and softened not by vicarious hypothetical loss but daily, finite, mortal, belabored pain and suffering. She knew the score in simple human terms.

He tried to imagine Sean among these people, walking down this aisle with his companion on a preparation day, checking out the local sights. His bristly blond hair and all-American smile could have lit up the night, couldn't it? Or more likely the pure spirit vibrating between the two, a *gringo* and a native carrying their leather-bound scriptures, the twin sticks of Joseph and Judah. Sean would have been respectful here, wouldn't he? Not a snotty, ugly American cowboying around as if he owned the place.

The smell of incense was strong, and flowers too, although he couldn't see them in the darkness. The smell of stone, cool and damp, the smell of history. Mark closed his eyes, listening: The silence was deep and prolonged, patiently waiting for an answer. It was the sound of deafness, the sound of a god who is not angry or amused but simply indifferent. And yet ... and yet ... and yet ... It was comforting here; not exactly the same God he worshipped but close enough for the moment. He felt safe—alien but safe. Here he could hide from the boy and the sun and the heat of the day and the tentacles of his own history. Like Jonah. Like Job.

He took a seat in the very back pew and began whispering to the God that he had grown up with and had loved and trusted and, to the best of his abilities, had obeyed. Except this time it was not a prayer of demands and entitlements or of anger and accusations. Nor was it a prayer of defeat, but of resignation.

He leaned forward, head bowed, eyes closed, elbows braced on his knees, waiting for an answer. The silence was immaculate, the only noticeable sound the sirens ringing perniciously in his ears. He thought he heard voices—the angels overhead murmuring among themselves? And then he sensed another presence take the cavernous chill out of the air. He was certain it was Sean who had settled down beside him, but he was afraid to look, afraid that he would break whatever cosmic spell had allowed his son to momentarily sneak back across the veil. He had waited over a year for this, had fasted and prayed and pleaded for this. He kept his head down, eyes closed. He felt many words, heard none, but he would remember four: *Poppa, I forgive you.*

He looked up: no Sean; no anyone. The old man with the straw hat and the young woman were gone. He was alone.

He limped down the center aisle toward the rows of votive candles, knelt down in spite of the pain, and confessed before the cool-eyed Virgin and her ever-suffering Son the real reason he had journeyed to this faraway place.

The day they had said goodbye to Sean at Salt Lake International it was snowing miserably—a frenetic explosion of white innards soiling the sky. Sean looked twenty pounds thinner than when he had entered the Missionary Training Center eight weeks before. He wasn't a pencil-neck, but he had dropped the lethal linebacker's mass in his chest and shoulders. His summer tan was gone as well, and his pasty cheeks made his blue eyes look radiant but spooky. He had seemed disoriented; he was smiling but his smile seemed forced. The other missionaries in his group—all in the unmistakable white shirts and plain ties, clipped bangs and sheared side-hair—seemed to be reveling in the gala of the send-off: back-slapping fathers and grandfathers, doting mothers and sisters, girlfriends momentarily breaking the "arm's distance" rule to indulge their missionaries with a departing hug. Laughing, joking, teasing, well-wishing. Some tears too, but no histrionics, no flood-gates opening, just moms dabbing their eyes as they bravely sent their boys off to serve the one and true God.

When Mark reached out to offer a farewell embrace, Sean had startled him, wrapping both arms around his father as if he had just returned from the dead, then pulling him in close and tight—tight as he hadn't since he was a frightened little boy in Dr. Lewis's office holding a homemade bandage to his bleeding forearm.

Except that in the airport he didn't cry, although in retrospect (always the damned retrospect!) the force of his embrace had been a louder, more desperate plea. And Mark had felt sick inside, a crisscrossing nausea as he reassured himself, *No, no, no, this is normal, this feeling of loss at departure. He's on the Lord's errand. This is right. This is good. He can't back out now. He'll regret it for the rest of his life and forever after. This is what Mormon men do; it is their work, their glory, their Father's business.* And then his boy had whimpered, called him something he hadn't since grade school: "Poppa ... oh,

Poppa, please …" Looking beyond his shoulder and into the goggle eyes of Elder Simmons from Pocatello, Idaho, Sean's gawky, geeky, computer-nerd of a companion waiting calmly and patiently (and bravely!) in the wings—in that instant he had been ashamed of his son. And in the next instant, the ugliest thought: *What would we tell people? What would people say?*

Mark gently extricated himself from his son's bear hug, looked into his watery eyes which seemed to be pleading for an honorable out. In his mind he answered flatly: *No.* To the boy, he replied with a smile and a manly pat on the back: "You'll be fine. You be good now." His boy nodded, sniffling as he turned and, head bowed, trudged toward his companion who greeted him with a comforting hand on the shoulder. But later Mark would second-guess that decision, that double-pumping, double-crossing nausea, the ambivalent voice of the Spirit waving him on and off, and it was he—not the boy—who had played the coward, too damn chicken to listen. Later he would be ashamed of being ashamed.

⚷

At 3:30 he stepped back out into the sunlight and limped over to the train depot to buy the ticket that would start his journey home. The window was closed, and the small crowd appeared unconcerned by the fact, so he played along. A stocky middle-aged woman was standing guard over a cardboard box the size of a coffin lashed together with twine and duct tape. Behind her stood a young mother with a baby sucking vigorously on her breast, while a little boy with a blue headband clutched the hand of a wiry old man.

Mark checked his watch and tried to tap it faster. No train in sight. A Mexican train running on Mexican time. He eased through the crowd to the shady side of the depot, but it didn't help. The flesh was dripping from his face. He closed his eyes, reminding himself to hang on, hang tough, he would be home soon, but each minute crawled by as if it too were wounded.

When he looked again, the boy was standing twenty feet away—a defiant little angel in his pale slacks and tunic, one hand on a jutting hip, the other dangling at his side, the gold watchband pimping in the afternoon sun. Mark returned the glare in kind, refusing to let go. For what seemed like minutes but were probably only seconds, the two remained like that—a pair of gunslingers, each waiting for the other to make the first move. Finally, Mark tapped his wrist where his boy's watch should have been, then crossed both hands over his chest, striking it twice. With a shrug and a smirk, the boy pivoted on the heels of his tire-tread sandals and sauntered into the growing commotion of the crowd.

Another minute passed, and then a surge of families descended on the depot dragging more bandaged boxes and suitcases. Mark couldn't afford to lose his seat, so he joined the human flow edging toward the tracks.

Moments later the silver train rounded the bend—not the newest or shiniest model but a beauty in his eyes. Even the deafening bellow of the horn and the shrill protest of the brakes sounded melodious. He noticed that the sulfurous haze had disappeared. For the first time since he had crossed the border—how many days ago?—the sky was clear, blue, chaste, clean. Had it changed from foggy-smoggy yellow to pure blue during his brief retreat inside the church? Or had he simply been too preoccupied—too self-involved, as Margie would say—to notice the change earlier?

A uniformed officer had entered the area, and Mark hoped it was a routine patrol, not some Mexican dragnet to seek out and strip-search the fugitive *gringo*. Mark stepped forward, grabbing the handrail with one hand, his duffel bag with the other. He tried hard not to grimace but failed miserably as he pulled himself up the first step, dragging his bum leg behind. One down, three to go—do they have to make these steps so damn high? When the porter with the toothbrush mustache reached down to help, Mark looked up, smiled, shook his head: "*No, gracias*." Sweat was oozing from every pore, it seemed, gluing his garments and shirt to his chest and back, his legs so damp he had to check for blood leaks. His life had become a permanent hot flash. He tried to pay for his ticket, but the porter shook his head and motioned him on.

Easy now. To the back. He scanned the coach—a few families packed into the bench seats, a man in a white business shirt and tie reading the Mexican daily, a young Tarahumara woman in a dress as colorful as a fruit salad sitting all alone staring out the window.

Mark sidled down the aisle and eased himself onto the cushioned bench seat. A fist of foam protruded from a gash in the seat cover next to a sticky soda stain, but otherwise it looked clean, adequate. No, not adequate—beautiful. It looked absolutely beautiful!

He leaned back and propped his leg sideways on the seat, hoping to take the sting out, but it felt as if some wild beast were gnawing on it. Watch check: 4:35. The coach was almost full and no one else was boarding, but the train continued to idle. "Come on," he muttered. "Get this crate moving! One down, three to go. We can do this!"

Peering out the window, Mark noticed the young man in uniform huddled with a half dozen of his sidekicks, talking animatedly. Lots of arms slicing and dicing the air, fingers pointing here, there, the train. One of them motioned toward Mark's window, and he looked abruptly down and away, instantly regretting it—Stupid! Stupid! Stupid!—like some cheesy spy movie. He closed his eyes and began whispering a desperate and disjointed prayer: *Father, please, I know what I have done rather tried to do attempted but didn't didn't I stopped my heart was on the verge yes absolutely yes but I stopped or you prevented in your grace wisdom love cutting me slack again I didn't deserve but still stopped and did not please now I'm so sorry of for everything that but the rest too my way I've been acting those thoughts contrary lack of faith and not trusting your grander bigger better vision didn't couldn't see for that blinded by you know who how that is you know all things of course you do please if you could of course you omnipotent omniscient ombudsman can once again look with fondness where did that come from have I ever said anything cast a fond eye on your servant Mark doesn't have quite the same ring as David or Solomon or Joseph the one-syllable ordinariness but please if you could see feel it in your heart to carry me lead me guide me walk beside me safely please one last look touch taste they're coming aren't they coming and there's no escape now no way out now nowhere to go now but …*

And then he felt a slight tug in his lower back, and for the first time since his little journey had begun—for the first time in over a year, really—he smiled. Honestly, sincerely. They were moving. He sat back and let the adrenaline drain from his body. His shirt was soaked, his heart was thumping, but he closed his eyes and braced his fists against his forehead, whispering aloud: "Thank you, Father, thank you thank you, thank you. I don't know what else to say right now except thank you."

When he opened his eyes, it was pitch black and he realized they were passing through a long tunnel. He felt strangely at peace in the darkness. Safe. He could feel the train laboring—this was the brief uphill part; once they reached the summit, they would fly all the way to the city.

The pain in his groin tightened and burned. Should have gotten something stronger. None of this *tres pastillas* stuff. Something to knock it out for the count, at least until he got home. Got to catch it early, though. The ugly red around the sutures was normal, wasn't it? A little redness? But jeez, it felt hot. His whole body was on fire. He could check again, but what's the point? He just wanted to get home in one piece. Two pieces, Father. A dozen pieces is okay. Just get me home.

He imagined the puddle jumper angling into the final descent, the magnificent view of the peaks still striped with snow, Margie waiting for him, the look of relief and hopefully joy on her face as he passed through the sliding glass door into the terminal. The long embrace, kissing her as if he really meant it, and her kissing him likewise. They would go to the Red Lobster for dinner. Grilled salmon. A big baked potato smothered in butter and sour cream. Screw cholesterol, screw calories for the night. He would tell her all about it—the trip, yes, but all of the stuff going on internally, too. In his head, his heart. Not too much, though. Omit the dark and gory details. Keep it upbeat. Keep it positive. She had been through enough already, and he'd put her through even more. Apologizing. He would apologize. Tell her how sorry he was and—yes, how much he loved her. He loved her. He didn't realize how much. Not like this. Hurting your heart to even think about it. He would say that to her. What? What was he going to say? He had fourteen hours to figure that out. Give or take. Grilled salmon crusted with macadamia nuts. That was her favorite. They could rent a movie afterwards. One of those romantic comedies she liked. Meg Ryan. Something light. Something fun. Sit on the sofa with a blanket and just sit. Watch. Enjoy. Enjoy the moment. He prayed for that moment.

They were passing a small village of log homes where late afternoon fires were burning. Mark gazed out the window, sleepy but ecstatic—or was it really ecstasy? He was overwhelmed by a simple but immutable sense of joy. The pain in his groin was growing colder; he'd have to get it checked out when he got home. Doc Flanders would fix him up. The crotchety graybeard would scold him for being a stupid idiot—*Who do you think you are, some kind of superhero? You could have lost your leg, or a whole lot more!* Margie would chastise him, too. A little bit; not too badly. He hoped to see her nice face—the one with the smile she tried to hide but couldn't suppress. Cleo would be all over him—tail wagging, high-stepping, turning circles. And the little one—no holding back. She would drop everything—dolls, chocolate milk, book, telephone. She would drop it all and come running, and this time he would fall to his knees and thrust open his arms, big and wide, and he would receive her—close, tight, permanent. Have a dolphin day, kiddo! Have a freakin' double-dolphin day!

The train rolled past craggy cliffs with pine trees leaning out across the tracks like acrobats—a tough land of harsh valleys and odd alliances where cacti grew alongside evergreens. Through the forest mesh he saw a small homestead—a simple box of logs caulked with mud, a column of smoke, laundry hanging on the line like a row of colorful pennants. An old woman with a blue scarf over her head was sitting out front, her hands working industriously on something. She looked up and watched a moment as the train passed. Mark lifted his hand and waved to her. Of course, she couldn't see him; he was a dark blot on the window, if that, but he lifted his hand and waved anyway. He wanted to reach out, hand her something, touch, speak. This is where his boy Sean had served, his little corner of God's vineyard. Had he spoken to this old woman? If not her, then surely dozens like her. Mark smiled. He pictured his son and his companion, two young giants in white shirts and black pants, backpacks slung over their shoulders, plodding across this rocky field to speak to this old woman. Do they realize we are sending our hearts? Our souls? Our best? Our very, very best?

Mark was smiling but shaking too. Had they turned on the air conditioning? He didn't know they even had A/C. Suddenly he felt cold. He crossed his arms and clasped his triceps, rubbing them briskly. Maybe he was coming down with something, a sneaky Mexican bug. Or was it simply the excitement, the anticipation: four legs on this journey, one down, three to go.

He looked out at the forest—pine trees spaced randomly, with lots of daylight in between. A man in a white tunic was leading his oxen toward the homestead. Farther off, a young Tarahumara boy with a red headband and baggy white pants was chasing a soccer ball across a barren dirt field surrounded by pines, like a private little stadium. He was all alone but may as well have been playing before a crowd of thousands the way he charged up and down the field, his shirt tails trailing behind like banners, booting the ball, chasing it down, zigging and zagging with such speed and energy and glee. Like Stacie—sweet little Stacie. Chasing the future into a corner, slide-tackling it on its ass. Feet barely touching the ground.

He was flying, wasn't he? Inside the amphitheater of pines. Ponderosa pines? Yes. Yes, he was almost certain of it. Those tall, asymmetrical, goofy-looking maverick evergreens. Yes, he was sure of it. Just like back home. His little mountain town. He leaned back, sleepily ecstatic. A lovely chill had crept into his feet and was climbing up the inside of his leg, into his groin. Cool. Nice.

And now he noticed something else: he listened for it very carefully, but the ringing in his head was gone. Gone. For the first time since the phone call he listened to the beautiful symphony of silence. He was feeling warm again. Warm and cold together, the pain passing through him now like Novocain. He closed his eyes, smiling. Home. He was going home.

Then he says something about apples. Big red ripe ones, perfect on the tree; how we each start out like that, but every sin thereafter is a big or little bite out of us, depending. This girl, this Rachel, she'd been gnawed right down to the core. "But the seeds!" he exclaims, his suntanned cheeks peppered with hope, jubilation. "The seeds can be planted and a whole new tree with perfect fruit can grow—right, Brother Conklin? That's the Atonement, isn't it? If you really, really believe?"

But his older sister, the one the mean boys call *La Gordita*, has been playing the what-if game, planting seeds of her own: "What if when you get back, she needs to repent—*again?* I know someone just like that, a good friend, in fact. Abused as a kid. Her uncles, her stepfather, they all used her like Kleenex. Everybody's easy before she started junior high. It's a pissed-on world, a pissed-on life. My friend, she finally got married, sure, but she's so screwed up now they still haven't had sex yet and it's going on four years. I'm just trying to warn you, Jake. Believe me, I've been there. Still am. Always probably forever will be. Two kids, two men, no husband. I'll be waiting tables till the Millennium. Once you're in the garbage heap it's damn near impossible to climb back out."

"Sour grapes," he says. "Maybe my sister's just jealous because she doesn't have someone like ... well, not to sound conceited or anything, but someone like me. And Rachel does. Or will. Maybe. I mean, I'm still—what do you think, Brother Conklin?"

I've met her only once, at church: a shy, spindly, self-conscious girl with dishwater blond hair half-hiding her face, John Lennon glasses on an Afghan hound nose. A gun-in-the-back smile. He says she knew he loved her because it was three weeks before they kissed and even then, they never went all the way. Some kind of personal record. He knows she loves him because the last time on her sofa she withdrew her hands abruptly and stared at her sandals on the ragged carpet, counting crumbs as she delivered her verdict: "If you don't go on a mission, Jake, I don't want anything to do with you."

A week later he removed the ring from her engagement finger and slid it on the fourth finger of her other hand: "Just friends, okay? I need to stay focused now. If I can do that, if I can keep my head in the game, God will bless us both—do you know what I mean? I'm doing this for the Lord. Not for you. Not even for us."

Big sister talked him into that: "Don't you think it would be better if … Don't you think it's only fair that … Don't you?"

Afterwards he went to Hunan West for moo goo gai pan, but everything tasted fecal. He called her that night and repented: "Will you marry me?"

She wept two years in one night.

He dreamed of threshing Laban's fields for seven years while Rachel waited naked in her tent.

The night before departing for the field he stopped by looking very missionary in his white shirt and navy-blue suit, his curly brown hair clipped off at his ears. "We all have this perfect Mormon girl in mind," he says. "You know what I mean, Brother Conklin?"

I smile, nod. Sure.

"But … well …" Then he proceeds to tell me a little something about fresh red apples, seeds. We stand in the cramped entry of my claustrophobic apartment where boxes remain stacked five high, a stubborn refusal, or hope. Six months ago he and his fellow priests moved all my earthly belongings out of the fine white house with the vaulted ceilings and into this red brick building where the train moans plaintively at midnight and the laughter of my children resounds every fourth weekend. Sometimes. Back then he still wanted to play pro baseball, a catcher for the Texas Rangers—chest and shoulders swelling his sleeveless T-shirts.

I wish him well, tell him how proud I am, how he's made the right decision. In Sunday quorum meetings I have told him countless times about the proverbial best two years of my life in Ecuador.

"Seattle, Washington? *¡Qué bueno, amigo!*" I remind him he will have the rest of his life to be married. "An eternity, Jake!" Maybe.

There is nothing else to say now. Hands hidden in his pants pockets, he awkwardly scans the room—dirty dishes stacked like leaning towers in the sink, newspapers scattered on the shag carpeting. The stink of old kitty litter, of solitude. Eventually he smiles, but it is like a crack in a brand-new windshield.

A honk outside rescues us. The handshake, the hug, a little joke at the door ("Well, I got rid of another one ..."). Another smile and a half-salute as a curly brown head appears around the corner: "Jake! Hurry! Dad's waiting!" It is a perfect miniature of the Boy Scout I prodded up the Bright Angel Trail six years ago. These eternal *déja vus*. He wraps his thick arms affectionately around his little brother's neck and rubs his knuckles into his scalp. As they skip along the cement walkway like a couple of school kids, I want to call out like Friar Laurence: "They stumble who run too fast!" Or bearded Prospero: "Tis new to thee!" Instead, I holler: "*¡Vaya con Dios!*" He stops, turns, wrinkles an eye. "God be with you," I whisper and softly close the door.

GHOSTS

The Janitrol furnace that had kept them warm for nineteen winters gave up the ghost late Friday afternoon, minutes after the last repair and parts shop had closed for the three-day weekend. Trapped in a veritable icebox, during a long, sleepless night, Dale was forced to re-examine the wisdom of installing an attractive, eye-pleasing fireplace of malpaís rock (his preference) instead of a utilitarian woodstove (hers). Thanks to his bullheadedness, aesthetics had overruled pragmatics, and he now found himself alone and without heat on Christmas Eve.

Last night the cold had grown so intense he was tempted to call the bishop for help, but his pride had overpowered his suffering. Besides, that would have been a bridge back.

What pride? he muttered to himself.

But he knew.

So had she.

Dale hooked a finger between two horizontal slats, drawing the lower one down a fraction, peered outside, and grimaced: stars, zillions of them, shining like frozen tears. Clear skies meant another cold one. He could barely hear the mixed-and-matched voices of carolers rolling down the street like a slow ocean swell: Shirley Stedman's annual Christmas Eve block party. Dale had already closed the blinds and doused the outside lights to discourage any holiday do-gooders from paying him a charity visit. But for good measure he quickly hit the family room light, leaving the house in inhospitable darkness. He waited by the front door until the chorus of "We Wish You a Merry Christmas" crescendoed and faded, then flicked the light back on, pulled the thermal blanket around his neck and shoulders, and settled back on the leather sofa, close to the

119

tiny space heater he had disinterred from his basement. Ten seconds hadn't passed before he heard a loud rapping at the front door.

Dale knew he couldn't ignore the visitor because he'd just turned on the light. He tried waiting him out, but the knocker persisted until Dale reluctantly opened the door.

"Brother Watson! Mele Kalikimaka!"

A tall, gangly, Quixote-looking figure was ensconced on his doorstep.

"Excuse me?"

"Merry Christmas!"

Dale flipped on the outside light for a better look. It was Wayne Hampton, wearing faded blue jeans with frayed cuffs and a flaming red-and-orange aloha shirt. He was holding a coconut in one hand and a pineapple in the other. A white puff exploded from his lips with each breath. Just beyond the Sahara of snow in his rolling front yard, Dale noticed several cars—Toyota Camrys, Honda Accords— parked in front of the Desmond's home. Bundled up against the weather, couples bearing wrapped and ribboned gifts were marching up the long, sloping driveway lit by luminarias.

Dale had never liked Hampton. He didn't dislike him exactly, but he had never warmed up to the man. His looks were as odd as his mannerisms, with that stringy blond mustache and goatee dripping from his chin like Spanish moss, and a nose long enough to hang your hat on. He had an annoying habit of wheezing between words, as if breathing through a box like Darth Vader. Even more irritating was the way he would size you up with those bulbous blue eyes and an overconfident grin that, in Dale's opinion, was totally unwarranted; the giant Adam's apple that jerked around as if a bird were trapped in his throat; the junky Rambler station wagon with the spare tire lashed on the roof rack; the antique washers, dryers, and refrigerators rusting in his front yard that also happened to be the lone eyesore in the neighborhood. What right did he have to parade around with such beaming optimism? A new move-in to the ward, Wayne wasn't privy to Dale's recent history, which may have partly explained his unwitting obtrusiveness. Several times he had tried to make a home teaching visit, but Dale had averted each attempt.

"Thanks," Dale murmured, reluctantly accepting the two exotic edibles. "Well, Merry Christmas!" Smiling falsely, he started to close the door, but Wayne had edged into the entry like a cunning salesman. He noticed that the interior icebox effect was turning each breath, his and Wayne's, into a little cloud of cumulus. He reminded himself to breathe sparingly and discreetly lest he arouse Wayne's suspicion.

"Like I said, Mele Kalikimaka!" Wayne blew on his reddened knuckles. "Mind if I come in for a minute?"

You already have, Dale thought. But it would be rude to say no, especially tonight. Dale wondered, sourly, if this might be the answer to his earlier plea for help. If so, he wanted to repent and for God to renege. *Lord,* he mused sarcastically, *I'll take my chances with the elements. Make this guy evaporate, pronto!*

"Sure," Dale conceded.

Wayne stepped into the entryway, rubbing his bare hands briskly. "Boy, it's cold in here, too! Colder than out there, almost!"

"I left a window open earlier," Dale lied. "To get some fresh air."

Wayne's bushy eyebrows contorted as he took silent inventory: no tree, no twinkling lights, no colored bulbs, no advent calendar, no smiling papier-mâché reindeer pulling a fat little papier-mâché Santa across the window seat; and no miniature salt-dough wise men peering down at the baby Jesus in a Popsicle-stick manger. All of that disappeared when she did. Wayne motioned towards the bed sheet Dale had thumbtacked to the walls, creating a sagging curtain between the kitchen and the family room, a desperate (but surprisingly effective) attempt to contain the modest warmth generated by the space heater.

"New curtains?" he quipped.

Dale's smile came slowly, as if a razor blade were being drawn carefully across his face.

Wayne dropped to one denimed knee and placed his hand over the metal floor vent. "It's like ice! You sure your furnace is working?"

"Yeah, I think so. It was, anyway."

"Well, let's have us a look!"

"That's okay, really. You don't—"

But Wayne was already striding down the hallway in his big

clumsy snow boots, through the laundry room, and into the adjoining garage, with the intuitive foreknowledge of a cat burglar.

Wayne removed the louvered metal cover and genuflected before the silver furnace. He twisted a brass clasp, shutting off the fuel line, then switched it back. "Got a match?"

Reluctantly, Dale trudged inside and returned with a small box of wooden matches. Irritated at first, now Dale was flat-out angry. He'd spent all day in this sub-zero Antarctica he called his garage trying to breathe some fire into this damn machine he laughingly called a furnace. His nearest brush with luck had occurred shortly after dark when, inexplicably, the furnace had issued three short, hard gasps before sputtering out for good. Dale had dropped to his knees on the concrete floor. He'd felt like bawling but instead offered a short, heartfelt plea for help. Seconds later his hands had begun shaking like a diviner's, not from the fires of the Spirit but the cumulative wrath of the drop-dead cold. The arctic tremors had spread quickly throughout his body until he was convulsing like an epileptic. He'd staggered through the back door, down the hall, and into the bathroom where he'd twisted on the faucet and plunged his phantom fingers under the hot water, tossing handfuls onto his face and throat, heedless of the volumes streaming down the front of his winter coat.

When he'd finally paused to look, he'd flinched from the stranger staring back at him in the bathroom mirror: bulging brown Pekinese eyes; thin, stiff bangs, flattened by his ski cap; zinc oxide lips; bushy, twisted brows. Most alarming was the mouth, a deeply grooved frown that arched down to the tip of his chin. After thawing out in a hot bath, he'd layered himself in coat, sweater, thermal underwear, and ski cap, and then had curled up on the sofa chair with a thermal blanket. And now, when he finally had a chance to get somewhat warm for the night, this church busybody was dragging him back out into the cold again for who knows how many more hours of freezing futility. Who did this knothead think he was, Merlin the Magician?

Dale handed him the box of matches, noting the red warning label on the panel: EXTREME DANGER! DO NOT ATTEMPT TO IGNITE THE PILOT WITH A MATCH OR OTHER OPEN FLAME!

"Well," Wayne said, "we've got gas. Now let's see—"

He struck a match and stretched it towards the two parallel rows of metal tubes, near the igniter.

"Hey, you're not supposed to—"

There was a loud bolt, followed by a spooky whoosh as small blue flames bloomed along the metal tubes.

"Yep, we've got flame! Now let's see if we've got ignition."

Dale had to confess that the sudden appearance of fire, the promise of heat, momentarily filled him with a rush of warmth that had been absent in his home this holiday season, even with the furnace working. But his hopes were crushed when, inexplicably, Wayne switched off the gas, instantly killing the flame. Dale lunged for the offending hand. "What are you doing!"

"Let's have a look at that igniter."

He really didn't have a clue, did he? The rumors were true. Hampton wasn't playing with a full deck.

"Got a screwdriver?" Wayne asked, oblivious. "A flathead?"

Mumbling crossly, Dale ferreted through an old toolbox until he produced three flatheads of different sizes. Wayne rubbed his chin pensively before selecting the middle one. Dale looked over Wayne's bony shoulder as, arms and elbows jerking and quirking, he performed minor surgery on the machine.

"Aren't you freezing in that shirt?" Dale asked.

"Nah!"

"I've got a coat if you'd—"

"Got it!" he said, withdrawing his head from the exposed belly of the machine. He held the part up to the lightbulb overhead, examining it like a scientist: a small square of metal with two short porcelain tubes set parallel to each other, and a stiff wire curving inward from each tube, like calipers. "Yep, this is the old model, all right. A real dinosaur. Let me see what I can drum up."

In a surprising feat of athleticism, Wayne snapped from his kneeling position to his feet, like those Cossack dancers in the Nutcracker. "Be right back! Don't go away!"

Wayne pressed the remote bar, and the garage door rattled open slowly and noisily. "You got some WD-40? You ought to grease those runners! Well, stay warm!"

The streetlights had cast a golden glaze on the snowy expanse, rendering the look of a desolate outer space city. In the frigid semi-darkness of the garage, Dale watched the rangy figure trot off into the magical night, a little miffed, a little annoyed, a little amused, but mostly overwhelmed by an old sadness, and a nagging guilt.

⚷—

His father had once said they were oddly, even tragically matched, like a pair of star-crossed lovers in a Greek myth: inextricably bound yet doomed to imminent disaster. In some ways Dale had spent most of his life trying to prove his father wrong. In other ways he seemed determined to fulfill the prophecy.

He first saw her late one afternoon as he was rushing out of the library en route to his 5:00 p.m. class. As the daily recording of the national anthem began blaring across the bucolic Brigham Young University campus, twenty-thousand-plus clean-cut, bright-eyed students stood at robot-like attention: she alone had refused to stop. From the library steps, Dale watched curiously as the young iconoclast in paisley skirt, sandals, and macrame shawl slalomed around the obedient bystanders crowding the walkway. One of them, a towering, blue-eyed Aryan, hollered at her in righteous indignation, "Hey! Stop for the anthem!"

She never broke stride, never looked back. "I will when Nixon does!" she hollered over her shoulder.

⚷—

It was 1972. Watergate was nothing more than a swank hotel in downtown Washington.

To further ruffle the feathers of the self-anointed Patriot Police, she committed another unpardonable by veering off of the concrete path and marching defiantly across the middle of the lawn, a collective gasp trailing behind her.

The instant the music stopped, Dale lit out after her: up a flight of stairs, across an expansive parking lot crammed with economy cars and station wagons, and up a residential street lined with elm trees whose naked branches pierced the twilight sky like giant pitchforks. She turned left on one street and right on another, gradually ascending into a little universe of box homes that

124

cluttered the foothills of the mighty Wasatch. A slight winter chill still lingered in the April air, but bits of spring green and gold had begun to bleed through the massive white wall that sheltered the little university town from the rest of the planet.

Dale believed in spiritual promptings, to a point. Since returning from his mission to Argentina almost two years ago, he had dated dozens of marriage-minded mannequins, and in every case the Spirit had ordered him to bail out—sometimes in a front-seat whisper, other times with a clarion call. He didn't know if the Spirit or lame curiosity had directed him to follow this unusual young woman to her residence, nor, at the moment, did he really care.

She turned into a short, narrow driveway leading to a small brick home where two tricycles and a host of Fisher-Price toys were scattered across a dormant lawn. He cleared his throat: "So what's wrong with Nixon?"

She turned. He was expecting something, or someone, quite different: cast-iron jaw, sledgehammer chin, maybe a little hair bristling her upper lip, tougher eyes, a scar on the cheek perhaps, or a tattoo—a knife, a flower, a hammer and sickle. A peace sign. Something.

Lightly freckled, her face looked soft, gentle, Madonna-like. An angel's.

But her tongue cut like a razor: "He's a crook! They'll put him behind bars! Mark my words!"

"Is—is this—is this your house?" Dale found himself stuttering and he never stuttered.

"I rent a room in the dungeon."

"The dungeon?"

"The basement. It's cheap. Twenty a month for a bed, a bathroom, a hotplate, and a refrigerator. What more do you need?"

Dale nodded. Sure. Right. What more?

Dale knew he didn't believe in love at first sight, but she must have. How else could someone like her have fallen so wholly and instantly for someone like him? They were the Owl and the Pussycat.

"I'm Dale," he said.

She smiled. "Hello, Dale. I'm Verna. How long have you been back?"

In the summer of 1974 Richard M. Nixon resigned from the presidency in disgrace. Six months later Dale and Verna were sealed for time and all eternity in the Salt Lake Temple.

Verna liked to think it was a storybook romance, but in fact Dale's parents, multi-generational members of the Mormon aristocracy in Mesa, Arizona, had opposed the union. Yes, she was intelligent, ambitious, hard-working, all the more admirable for having pulled herself up by her bootstraps, defying genetics and genealogy to put herself through school, but ... *This is life*, his father, the silver-haired surgeon had argued, *not the movies*. She had no lineage, or at best a broken one, and a dubious past. She was still wet from her baptism, for pity's sake. There was more, much more, to consider in a marriage. She's not just going to be your wife but the mother of your children and our grandchildren

All his life Dale, the firstborn of seven, had obediently jumped through the requisite hoops: Eagle Scout, seminary, mission, and now temple marriage.

"So, what's wrong with that?" he said.

"You're making your bed; you're going to have to sleep in it."

"As long as she's in it, I'm okay with that."

His father was shocked. So was Dale.

"Don't, Dale. I know what you're thinking, but the novelty will wear off and you'll regret it. She's like nailing jelly to the wall."

"I like jelly," Dale said, emboldened. "Jam, too."

"What's that girl done to you? You've never talked like this before."

Dale smiled and shrugged. "I guess I've never been in love before."

"You think this is funny? Don't expect me to bail you out when this all goes off the rails! We've got six more kids to put through college. Do you hear what I'm saying?"

"Loud and clear, Dad."

Hordes of Dale's aunts, uncles, cousins, and shirt-tail relatives attended the sealing ceremony. On Verna's side, a half-brother hobbled into the reception wearing mangy brown hair to his shoulders and a thrift store suit.

After graduating that spring, they drove across the country in his old Ford Pinto, resurrecting it once with baling wire and again with the laying on of hands, to attend law school in Baltimore, conveniently distant from relatives of either tribe.

Their first Christmas was celebrated in a tiny apartment with a bedroom so small they had to shuffle sideways to get around the queen mattress on the floor. Too broke to buy a Christmas tree, she constructed a hearth out of cardboard boxes, painting the bricks red, the mortar gray, and golden flames wavering in the grate. At a yard sale she bought a string of twenty Chinese lights for a dollar and strung them around the perimeter. Christmas Eve they shared a simple dinner, half of it from cans. Alternating verses, they read the scriptural account of the nativity and sang a few carols. Dale was accustomed to a vast Christmas Eve gathering of family and friends, complete with baked ham, candied yams, and eggnog flowing like a river—an all-night festival of conversation and song. But their evening was still young, barely 8:00 p.m., and they had already exhausted their itinerary. All that remained was their modest gift exchange.

She opened hers first, a pocketbook of Shakespeare's sonnets, thanking him profusely. Her gift to him was a soft bundle about the size of a small pillow, swaddled in butcher paper she had decorated with Crayola markers: a solitary star shining above the domed silhouette of Bethlehem. Unwrapping it, he looked at her oddly and forced a smile. It was a heavy wool scarf, the ugliest plaid affair he had ever seen. He looked at her oddly and forced a smile. "Thanks," he said. "This is—it's really cool."

They sat at the little kitchen table with the warped Formica veneer trying so hard to appear happy. But the bright-eyed baby face that had greeted her that first day in the foothills of Provo sagged with sadness.

"What's the matter?" she asked, leaning across the table and stroking his forearm. "It's Christmas!"

"I'm fine," he said, but his smile was an anchor waiting to be dropped.

"You look so sad."

"I'm fine."

"You miss your family, don't you?"

"No."

"Yes, you do. I would if I …"

"If you what?" he asked a little more sharply than he'd intended.

"If I had a nice family like yours."

"Look, I don't miss them, okay?" He waited a moment for his anger or frustration or whatever was eating him to subside. "And I'm sorry for barking at you like that."

"You don't bark. Dogs bark."

"Oh, I don't? Then what do I do?"

"You kind of scowl—maybe like an alley cat when you take his food away."

"An alley cat, huh?"

"Yeah. An alley cat."

Then he turned the tables on her. "I'm sorry, Verna."

"Sorry about what?"

"This. I didn't mean for it to be like this."

"Like what?"

"This!" he shouted, and she winced—feeling guilty, the cause—as his arm swung out and around, encircling the entire apartment—the cramped kitchen, the paint-peeling walls, the cheap plastic dishes, the tiny ground-level windows buried under snow.

He would remember her expression at that moment and carry it with him to the grave. Although he didn't fully appreciate it at the time—wouldn't until it was too late, really— at that moment he realized that she absolutely adored him. It wasn't the puppy-dog admiration that had trailed him through his letterman days in high school, but something altogether different. He had wondered, at that moment, if he could ever possibly love her as deeply as she appeared to love him.

He waited for her to say the obvious: "Hey, cheer up! We have a home, food, a nice soft bed. The snow's falling but it's warm. I have you." But she had other plans.

"Aren't you going to try it on?" she asked.

"Sure," he said, slowly unfolding the pathetic piece of cloth. Hidden inside he found a collection of objects: toothbrush, toothpaste, a bar of soap, a hand towel, three packages of trail mix.

"Are we going camping?" he asked sourly. "This looks like a survival kit."

"It is a survival kit!" she said. Popping up, she reached across the table and grabbed his arm. "Let's go!"

He gazed around the tiny apartment incredulously. "Go where?"

"Come on!" she said, tossing him his down jacket. "And don't forget your survival kit!"

As she led him up the dark stairwell to the ground floor, he pressed her for details: Where are we headed? What's going on?

She remained elusive. "It's important," she replied, "for families to establish Christmas traditions."

"I agree. Now would you mind telling me about ours?"

She smiled. "Trust me," she said, and they stepped out into the frigid night.

The snow had stopped falling, but the wind had stiffened, tugging curtly at their winter coats. As they plodded through the ankle-deep snow, she instructed him to read the note taped to the tube of toothpaste. Reluctantly, he did: *Please deliver to someone less fortunate before the clock strikes twelve on Christmas Eve. If you fail, you'll turn into a mistletoe and spend the rest of forever hanging from a rafter watching happy young couples kissing passionately in broad daylight. Good luck and God bless.*

He stared at her, uncertain whether to laugh or cry. What on earth had he gotten himself into? They were so totally, absolutely different. Maybe his father had been right. Nailing jelly to the wall.

She blew him a kiss. "Smile," she said. "It's painless."

They hadn't gone half a block before they found an old man in a threadbare windbreaker curled up asleep on a metal grate, trying to salvage some subterranean heat. Dale quickly surveyed the igneous moonscape that was the man's face, his prickly pear chin and gaping mouth. A green ski cap covered his head, and his stubby fingers poked through his mittens like bloated worms. Dale knelt down, gently lifted the man's head, and placed the bundle underneath it. Rising, he gazed down the street where a handful of colored lights were blinking on the grim storefronts, barred and locked up for the night. For a moment he thought he could hear carolers belting out a hearty Christmas tune, but the distant screaming of a siren chased away those holiday illusions. Dale removed his down jacket and placed it tenderly over the old man.

As they hustled back to their apartment, Verna hooked her arm around his waist and leaned her head against his shoulder. "I love you," she whispered.

He hastened his pace, humbled, embarrassed, something.

"Next year," she panted, trying to keep pace with him, "you get to make the kit and I get to do the honors."

Such was the birth of their Christmas Eve ritual. Each year they alternated roles, one person creating the kit, the other delivering it. During their law school days, when they lived downtown, it was quite easy to find a needy soul. But as Dale's practice flourished and they moved higher and higher up the hill, their search for worthy recipients became more like an annual odyssey. Their survival kits grew bigger and more elaborate as well, until they found them-selves purchasing Alpine backpacks from R.E.I. and stuffing them with dome tents, mess kits, sub-zero sleeping bags, and a week's supply of food. But they were always faithful to their tradition, even when they returned late from a Christmas Eve party or the year he contracted a nasty virus that chained him to his bed for a week. Even the year he broke her heart.

❦

Last year was the first time in thirty they had missed their Christmas Eve ritual. He'd sat up all night in the sofa chair waiting for her, hoping and praying that God in his infinite mercy would part the veil and allow her to pass through for a few moments to offer a bit of comfort to a lonely man staggering through middle age. In retrospect, he'd longed to see her not so much to perform their annual ritual but to talk, to apologize, to tell her the many things he couldn't because it had happened instantly, so fast. An hour would have been heaven, but all he really needed was four seconds. Four words. "Thank you. I'm sorry." Make it seven. "I love you." Eight. "Always."

In retrospect, it had been a silly, naive, childish hope—a Christmas wish far beyond the permissible pale. Death would have been the next best alternative, death and reunion. But taking his own life now would have jeopardized theirs together in the hereafter: there was that much religion left in him, or fear. So, while he didn't actively seek out death, he'd taken no precautions to avoid it. Late one night as he was meandering down the cul-de-sac, a black pickup truck had swept around the corner of a merging side street, tires screaming, engine roaring, headlights coming at him like a pair of Nolan Ryan fast balls. Instead of diving for safety, Dale had sauntered towards the speeding fireballs, unflinching, wearing a smile that had unnerved the driver even more than the impromptu game of chicken. The driver had managed to swerve around him, hollering a string of obscenities in his wake, but at that point Dale had realized deliverance was a distant country, and many miles remained in his journey. Lonely miles.

He was awakened by a loud, yet intimate, rapping at the front door. Groggily, he cast aside the thermal blanket, rising from the sofa like a drunk in a rowboat, and trudged across the family room. Pushing open the French doors, Dale confronted an invisible wall of ice. The oak bannisters, the Tewa pottery occupying the antique nightstand, the walnut coat rack, the chandelier, the framed portrait of the prophet—everything in the entryway looked cold, sterile, cryogenically bound. A thin layer of ice framed the vertical window beside the door. He placed his finger tentatively in the lower right-hand corner and scratched, confirming his fears: the plague had crept inside. It began squeezing his bare scalp and mercilessly pinching his ears and the tip of his nose. Each breath blossomed ash-white before his eyes. There was a cold, creepy presence, as if the Ghost of Christmas Future had moved in for the night.

Dale yanked open the heavy oak door.

"Come in! Come in! You must be freezing!"

Wayne's mouth arched into a clown-like smile. "Not too bad." He was still wearing his aloha shirt, his bare arms pebbled with goose bumps, the blond hairs levitating from the chill. He was holding a cigar box overflowing with assorted metal parts, wires, tubes—a mini junkyard.

Wayne stepped eagerly into the frigid entry, his free hand buried deeply in the pocket of his faded blue jeans.

"What time is it?" Dale glanced at his wristwatch. "Eleven-thirty—hey, you didn't walk all that way, did you?"

Wayne shrugged. "It wasn't that far."

Dale silently chastised himself for being so self-absorbed and inhospitable. Verna would have been disappointed in him—not angry or ashamed, but disappointed. She would never have turned someone out the night before Christmas, or any other night. She was always bringing strangers home, rescuing them from the camps and shelters and freeway on-ramps, the *will work for food* folks. One night she brought a mangy couple she'd seen hobbling across the railroad tracks. Their clothes were ragged, and they reeked of urine. Dale greeted them guardedly in their majestic entry, then pulled Verna aside. "What are you doing? Are you nuts?"

"They need a bath."

"I can smell that!"

"And a place to sleep."

"Sleep? We can't—they can't—"

"How can we say no?"

"We don't know anything about these people!"

"So, let's get to know them."

She smiled at him, fluttered her eyelashes, not mockingly but flirtatiously, and whispered, "Inasmuch as ye have done it unto the least of these—"

"Come—come in here," Dale said, directing Wayne into the family room and seating him next to the space heater. He placed the thermal blanket over his shoulders. "You want some hot cocoa?" Dale was already moving towards the kitchen counter.

"Yes. Yes, that would be nice." Wayne's lips looked pale, dangerously blue.

Dale pulled open a cupboard and rummaged around until he located the box of Carnation hot chocolate. He tore open two small packages, emptied each into a mug, filled the mugs with water, and placed them in the microwave. He punched several buttons on the control panel. The machine purred softly as he scanned the refrigerator for snacks: cheese, carrot sticks, lettuce, cranberry juice, a half loaf of twelve-grain bread. Verna's vegetarian tendencies had gradually prevailed over the years.

"Are you hungry?" he asked. "Will you eat a grilled cheese sandwich?"

"Wonderful! That would be great!"

Wayne seemed genuinely pleased, which eased some of Dale's guilt. He was not ready to admit that perhaps it even made him feel good as well.

Dale cut several strips of Wisconsin cheddar, slathered Shedd's Spread on four slices of twelve-grain, and placed the sandwiches in a frying pan, checking them periodically. The microwave bleeped. He quickly removed the two mugs, stirring the chocolate froth bubbling darkly on top until it formed a rich, smooth blend. He offered the bigger mug to Wayne, whose face was beginning to appear less paralyzed and more its saggy old self.

"Thanks," he said, sipping loudly. "This is great! Wonderful!"

Dale retrieved the two grilled cheese sandwiches, and the two men sat side by side on the sofa and ate.

"You should have asked me for a ride," Dale said.

Wayne took a slow sip and smiled. "You should have offered."

"True."

Wayne wolfed down his sandwich and began licking his greasy fingertips.

"Let me get you a napkin," Dale said, rising. "Want another? There's plenty?"

"No, no! I'm fine."

When Dale returned, Wayne was sitting on the carpet, leaning back against the sofa, his legs crossed yoga-style, crowding the penurious warmth of the space heater. Dale sat beside him on the floor.

"So, what made you come here tonight?" Dale asked. "And don't say you were prompted by the Spirit. I used to be a bishop. I know the script."

"And all the tricks too, I'll bet."

"All of them. So, tell me, the bishop put you up to it, didn't he? Or old Brother Wyman. He's always trying to light a fire under the high priests."

Dale was bantering, trying to thaw the ice that he himself had hardened. Wayne peered thoughtfully into his mug, as if he were reading tea leaves. "I guess I just didn't want to be alone tonight." He looked up, but this time his face cracked like plaster from his effort to smile. "I wanted some company. I thought you might want some too."

Dale nodded cautiously. It was one thing to share food and shelter; it was something else to assume associations.

"Yeah," he said, "I lost my Cheryl five years ago."

My Cheryl? It sounded so intimate, so endearing, so—human? Odd, or perhaps indicative, that he had never regarded Wayne in a married state, or any other state. He tried to picture Wayne and his wife. A watery image from *American Gothic* formed in his mind.

"It's hard," Wayne said. "Isn't it?"

Hard? Which part? Before or after? Giving or receiving or taking away? Dale recalled fights that seemed so picayune now, sandbox quarrels over infertility, adoption, vacations, his second marriage to racquetball, hers to whatever cause was en vogue at the time: save the rainforest, save the spotted owl, walk for hunger. Things that should have been mere asterisks to an otherwise beautifully told tale had been blown grotesquely out of proportion in his memory. His grief, he realized, was grounded less in loss than in regret, little things he had and hadn't said or done; wishing he'd graciously taped over this or that part of their life story.

In retrospect, he had secretly hoped that over the years she would grow out of her idiosyncrasies. But while he had climbed the ladder socially and professionally, she had moved laterally, if at all. At forty-five she still wore funky broad-brimmed hats to church, and long paisley skirts to her ankles. "The Hippy Lady" the church kids called her behind her back. When they moved into their dream house—a gabled Victorian manor that, more accurately, was *his* dream house—it annoyed him that she didn't seem to fully appreciate his hard-earned bounty. When she joked about "great and spacious buildings" and too many rooms to clean, he took it personally.

The day after he was called to serve as bishop he took her out to lunch for a heart-to-heart. He was looking so handsome and professional in his three-piece suit, like a junior general authority. While she had the Thai salad, he ordered ahi Hawaiian-style, and they sat in an intimate little booth overlooking the canyon, talking casually. Towards the end of the meal, he mentioned his new calling.

"Oh, you'll be wonderful!" she said. "I just know it! You always are!!"

Twenty-seven years and she still adored him. Somehow she

had managed to overlook his moodiness and after-cracker fits, his exacting insistence that the dishes be stacked just so.

Not just for him, he explained. But for her, the mother of the ward now. Setting an example was so important, especially to the youth. Avoiding even the appearance of evil.

"So, who's evil?" she asked, batting her eyes seductively. She still wore no makeup except for a touch of blue under her eyes. It was beginning to show now, her cosmetic indifference, and all those years loitering in the sun without protection. Little webs were engraved on her cheeks and grooves spread from the corners of her eyes like spokes from a wheel. Still, she hooked her foot around his, tugging it gently, teasingly.

"No one's evil," he said. "That's not what I meant. I think you need to be—look, will you knock it off for a minute? Can't you be serious for once? I think you need to be, oh, a little more fash-ion-conscious, that's all."

She was silent for what had seemed like a short lifetime.

"Verna?"

"You really want me to do this, don't you? I mean, it means a lot to you, doesn't it?"

"Yes. Yes, it does." And then he had said the one thing that she could never forgive. "My church career ..."

"Okay," she said, dabbing the corners of her lips with her nap-kin. "Okay, I can do that."

She asked for the check, although he paid the bill. They kissed and parted company: he drove back to the office in his Lexus, while she zoomed off to the mall in her little Subaru where, in her words, recorded in her journal: *I strolled into Dillard's like a rich bitch and bought out the store: dress suits, heels, three-piece drop-dead showcase stuff.*

He was forty-nine that summer; she was forty-eight. They would share three more years together, more or less.

He was trying to recall how it had gone that October morning, who had cast the first stone? Was it him, mumbling something about her half-brother's devil-may-care, ship-without-a-rudder existence, how he was brave and adventurous with the macho stuff of the world, but in the spiritual wilderness of commitment and sacrifice, he was a total washout? Or had she started it, sensing his annoyance, beating him to the draw: "Of course you don't want to! It's spur-of-the-moment, unplanned, unscheduled, unapproved by sixteen committees and four show-of-hands!"

It went back and forth like that, childishly, thoughtlessly, and then cruelly: "And most of all, it just might be fun, heaven forbid! Just because you're afraid of your own shadow doesn't mean you have to lock the rest of the world in a box!"

Contrary to her accusations, Dale's fear of flying wasn't entirely irrational. Shortly after his eighth birthday, his Uncle Lenny and favorite cousin, Chris, were flying down to attend Dale's baptism when the Cessna suddenly dipped and spun, and what had at first appeared to be a simple sky trick ended up a tragic pillar of smoke and fire on a sahuaro-studded desert in central Arizona. Dale and his father had watched from the runway where they had arrived right on schedule for the landing.

"You're not going up in that Tinkertoy plane with your half-cocked half-brother. End of discussion!"

But she had mentally drawn a line in the sand. No more knuckling under—she'd even used that phrase: "And I suppose you expect me to knuckle under again?" Afterwards came a dark period of second guessing: if he hadn't been so insistent, dictatorial, pig-headed, maybe she would have relented. Or if he'd agreed to join her. Maybe she was just testing him to see. If he'd gone with her, things would have run smoothly. No gasping engine, no twirling free fall, no smoke and fire. At worst, they would have died together. But why did she have to ride the damn plane to begin with? Why didn't he just grab her by the arm and say NO! NO, YOU WILL NOT GO! Why didn't he back off for once? If he'd just let her see the worry in his eyes. If he'd told her about his cousin Chris and Uncle Lenny. No, he had to have it his way, always his. He was the priesthood holder; he was the boss. But it wasn't even that: no one could have lorded it over her by virtue of the priesthood or any other hood. No one could have unless she allowed them to. And why had she allowed him all those years?

As a bishop he used to wonder how some of his most staunch Latter-day Saints could lose their faith so quickly. Now he knew. The words of comfort and logic he used to shower on others

(Adversity is part of life … the refiner's fire … if God answered all of our prayers all of the time … Mortality is the twinkling of an eye, and then we'll be united eternally …) suddenly rang hollow. At best, God seemed coolly indifferent; at worst, sadistically ironic.

"Well, you know what they say?" Wayne was hunkered by the sofa now, cradling the cigar box of junk.

"What's that?" Dale asked. He was still sitting on the floor cross-legged, close to the space heater.

"It's always hardest on the one who stays behind." Wayne hopped to his feet and began marching down the hall.

"Hey, where are you going?"

"Work to do!"

Three hours later, the two men were kneeling side by side in the freezing garage, not in joint prayer but in a desperate effort to work a miracle in the cold belly of the furnace. The cigar box was almost empty, the misfired parts forming an altar to futility on the cold concrete floor. Dale's hands were tucked under his armpits, and he was rocking slowly back and forth, trying to generate some warmth, as Wayne jerry-rigged yet another old igniter with a pair of needle-nose pliers. Both men were wearing down jackets and ski caps that Dale had salvaged from the basement. Although they were in no grave danger yet, the bitter cold had lowered their defenses, and like doomed men in a Himalayan blizzard, they began sharing confidences. At one point, Dale asked Wayne about his wife. "Do you ever get over it?"

Wayne withdrew his head from inside the furnace and smiled sadly. "Nope."

"That's encouraging."

"It does get better, though. The first year was awful. At first, I'd look around and see her everywhere: as a twenty-year-old in faded blue jeans strolling to the post office, at thirty-five checking out the vegetables at Safeway. One day at the mall I saw her from behind. Twenty-four or twenty-five, streaked blond hair past her waist and cheerleader curves. I picked up the pace, began weaving through the Saturday crowd. When I finally caught up to her, she was standing in line at the Sears charge card place. I reached out and put my hand on her shoulder and gave it a little squeeze, in a certain way, like I used to do. She looked back with a split-second smile, as if she were expecting me, but in that moment my Cheryl disappeared, and I was looking at a total stranger, although all I remember now is her mouth, this big giant pit with red around it and the awful sound coming out, like a broken siren, and then a thousand rent-a-cops, pot-bellied old guys in uniforms, reaching for their guns like it was their first time ever, and the woman's still screaming like a siren and I'm standing smack there in the middle while the rest of the store's crowding around to watch. And there's a dozen folks from church or work or the neighborhood, folks you really know, you know. And next thing they're putting cuffs on me, and I'm standing there with my eyes closed, wishing, praying that everyone else has theirs closed too, hoping they can't see me because I can't see them. But it was never the same after that. The bishop, when I explained it, he said he understood, things like that happen, no harm done, really, but I really ought to be more careful from now on—you know how people are about things like that nowadays. I said yes, yes of course, I'll do that, Bishop, I will. But it wasn't another week before I was released as Blazer Scout leader and made secretary to the high priests. You just get so lonely some-times, you know what I mean?"

Dale nodded. "So, have you got any plans tonight?"

Wayne reburied his head in the machine. "Fixing your furnace, I guess. Give me that flathead, will you?"

Dale handed him the tool. "Why don't you spend the night here?"

Wayne's elbows jerked and pulled as he inserted the jerry-rigged igniter. "Okay, give me some gas."

Dale twisted the brass clasp.

"Power?"

Dale inserted the plug into the outlet and turned the pilot knob to ON. Dale's heart soared as he heard three quick clicks, like tick-ing teeth. A thread of laser-blue began writhing as if it were being tortured. Then nothing.

Dale's shoulders collapsed. "Damn!"

Wayne calmly removed the igniter and, with the pliers, twisted one of the wires inward a fraction of an inch. "Amazing what a teeny tiny little adjustment can do."

As he reinstalled the igniter, Dale watched from behind.

"You never give up, do you?"

"Nope."

"Do you think you'll ever remarry?"

"Nope. Do you?"

"I don't know. Maybe. Do you think that's wrong?"

"Nope."

"You just don't want to remarry? You said you were lonely."

"I try to keep busy."

"You know something? I think my wife would have really liked you."

Wincing, Wayne tightened the last screw. "Why do you think that?"

"I don't know. She just would. And believe me, that's a compliment."

"I believe you. Gimme some gas, please."

Dale turned the fuel valve and twisted the pilot knob: he heard the ticking teeth; the blue thread wriggled like a worm on fire.

"Come on," Wayne muttered, tapping the screwdriver against the metal frame. "Come on."

The furnace issued a deep, consumptive breath. There was a moment's silence, and the cold belly belched blue flames. It was a modest show of pyrotechnics, but to Dale it seemed like sheer wizardry, as if Prometheus had just pulled off a cross-cultural whammy, stealing fire from the Norse gods. He gazed fondly at the gawky Christmas Eve intruder who had become a miracle worker.

"You did it," he whispered.

As blue flames bloomed along the metal tubes, Dale listened for the first warm breath to puff through the interior vents. And for a moment he thought he heard a jubilant shout from within, as if a dear old friend had been magically raised from the dead.

KUWAIT CITY

Slouching in the belly of the C-141, through the oval glass we could see the black cloud endlessly billowing above the desert city, a parting gift before the enemy had cut and run. Thank God we didn't have to jump.

As we stepped off the plane, oil clung to our faces and fatigues like leaden sweat. We were driven by jeep to a city of tents the color of autumn back home. A woman veiled in black watched us from her balcony as if peering through a mail slot.

Inside we met our commander, a wizened little man with a walrus mustache. He showed us a plastic device the size and shape of Linda's diaphragm case.

"Landmines," he said. "They dropped about ten million of them. They don't kill, just maim. It ties up more personnel to care for a maimed body than a dead one. Dead's easy." He looked us over, obviously unimpressed. "It's usually pretty quiet during the day. No one goes outside in this godawful heat. But right about now it starts cooling off a bit—that's when they start coming."

It was 6:15 Kuwaiti time. They called this "orientation."

We followed him into the operating quarters. "Filthy richest country in the world," he grumbled. "If you're a Kuwaiti citizen, the government builds you a palace when you marry. They fly you to Switzerland or the States for gall bladder surgery. Make a vacation of it. They all cleared out before the first bullet. They were sipping daiquiris in Miami Beach while the non-citizens were left behind to fight. I'm talking about the Filipinos, the Palestinians, the servants who are nothing but de facto slaves. Suffering, you know. Sacrificing. Just like we're suffering and sacrificing. Doing their dirty work. They remember the length of their nose."

The tent flap opened, and two men wheeled in a gurney occupied by a spindly boy who looked a bit younger than my nine-year-old. I saw Brent's hound-dog eyes as he asked me once again:

"Dad, why are you going over there?"

"Dad, do you have to go?"

"Dad, when are you coming home?"

"Dad, are you going to die?"

And Linda, still fluctuating between anger, grief, and incredulity: "You didn't have to do this. You volunteered. Why are you doing this? Why are you—"

I had pointed to the massive SUV in the driveway and the Audi shining like a silver bullet beside it. "That," I'd said. "Those. Much given, much expected. Right?"

I did not tell her the other half: a plainness in the work at home. A descent into the ordinary.

Half of one leg was gone and the other was badly mangled, as if a shark had bitten off the left after sampling the right.

The head surgeon held up two saws: "Choose your weapon."

"Wait a second," I said. "I think we can save this one."

But he had been too long in this business. His eyes were ice cubes squeezed between his cap and mask. "Suit yourself."

Three other surgeons entered, masks on, scalpels flashing, like an organized mugging, each cutting in his area of expertise: one for the intestines, one for the head, another for the heart. I took the legs, the remains of the day.

We began digging for shrapnel as if it were gold, the dwarf air-conditioning unit gasping as it labored to defray the heat seeping through the canvas. Eight hours and infinite sutures later, I raised my bloody, latexed hand to high-five each member of our crew, as if we had just hit the buzzer beater to win the NBA title: "We did it! We saved the leg!"

I hoped the head surgeon was smiling behind his mask.

⚮

My first day off I pay one of the locals to drive me out to the Highway to Hell, a six-mile-wide strip of burned and abandoned tanks and artillery stretching halfway to Baghdad: long barrels twisted like pretzels, melted treads, barbequed bodies shriveling in the sun.

My guide speaks very little English, but I think he has acquiesced, so I climb up on a tank to see for myself. The sun through the open hatch drops a small circle of light inside, enough to see the essentials. Enough to see enough: blackened control panels, wires, and monitors. I climb down inside where I find my next surprise: a small photograph taped to the panel. I peel it off, hold it up to the light, and marvel at the image of a young woman, unveiled, as stunning in her facial nakedness as most pinups in the States. Two little dark-haired boys, one standing on either side of her. Somber, serious. Twins? Future bearers of the sword? Kids. Like mine. Like the boy whose leg was chewed off by a landmine. They want to run and jump and play ball. The universals of war.

Dad, where are you going?

Dad, when are you coming home?

Dad, are you going to die?

Linda?

I wonder if the father of these twins managed to escape, or is he one of the char-broiled bodies disintegrating in the sand?

I notice something on the floor amidst the blackened miscellany. It looks like Aladdin's magic lamp: brass with a fired-on greenish-black patina. Spoils? The last loot before fleeing town? I wonder if this tank might have outrun the desert demons had its operator— the father?—not paused to snatch this souvenir. I am tempted to rub it, just for fun, to summon up the mighty genie inside and make a wish, but at that blasphemous moment the upper lid slams shut, sealing off the light. Groping, I try all possible knobs and buttons, but the hatch remains locked. I locate a vent, open it, and air blows in like a blast furnace. In vain I holler to my guide. Through the horizontal slits I watch his vehicle vanish like a mirage.

I remind myself to remain calm, and the first hour I am successful. I work slowly and methodically to finagle an escape, but the metal monster is a stranger to me, and every orifice is sealed save the one vent. The second hour I grow more frantic. I pray and plead to God for deliverance, some sweet miracle that will unlatch the frozen lid. I push, I shove, I pound. I expend all of my remaining energy trying to thrust my fist through steel.

By noon I have stripped down to my priesthood garments, and my body is slathered with sweat. The vent provides me fresh oxygen, but each swallow scalds my lungs. Through the louvered opening I cry for help, but my language is a stranger here, indifferently devoured by the Arabian wind.

By late afternoon the last drops of moisture have oozed from my skin, and the baking is almost complete. My coffin is a kiln. I search my pockets for something to write on and find the dollar bill Brent gave me at the airport: "For good luck, Dad!" I try to print legibly, but my hands are schizoid seismographs. I hope she can read the word DEAR. I hope she can read the word LINDA. The word LOVE. And BRENT. And SORRY.

Thoughts flit in and out of my head like birds in search of an easy meal, leaving disappointed. Occasionally one lingers a bit longer: a conversation with my grandfather when I was a rebellious teenager. The subject was cremation. He had called it an abomination unto the Lord. "How can your spirit rejoin your resurrected body if it's all ashes blown hither and thither?"

I had countered in kind: "What if you're blown to bits in a war? What if a lion eats you? Will you be resurrected in its digestive tract?"

I had not reckoned on melting to death in a steel box in the middle of Earth's biggest, junkiest, wealthiest sandbox.

More conversations with my grandfather. The day he cautioned me against driving through Central America alone. I was halfway through college on scholarship and had a free summer to burn.

"No worries," I shrugged. "I figure when my number's up, it's up. That's what the scriptures say."

"Not if you foolishly compromise it," my grandfather contested. "Paul was protected from serpents because he was on God's errand. He wasn't recklessly playing with fire. He wasn't out trying to show off."

Had I come to this desolate land to show off? To play with fire?

"You could at least look a little sad," Linda had said.

"Do you want me to cry? Would that help?"

"Yes."

I try not to lament the span of life I have short-changed my-self. I try not to think about the many things I will miss, but they pour ruthlessly into my head, punishing me: ball games, recitals, Christmases, vacations, graduations, weddings. Out of the swirl a single image emerges: Linda and Brent standing in a field of yellow flowers with mountains in the background. He is beach-tan, wearing shorts and a T-shirt, and she is in a loose summer dress, hand on hip, a light breeze twisting a few strands of hair across her face. They are standing side by side waving to some stranger. "Come!" they seem to be saying. "Come on!" They are smiling, and it is killing me to watch.

Nightfall brings a cool respite, but I can feel my body shriveling like a marshmallow in a fire. I peel off my final covering, first the top, then the bottom, and place them in a neatly folded bundle by my side. And now I am utterly naked in my pitch-black tomb of steel. I could look outside for stars, but I have resigned myself to a noiseless, nameless exit. I feel weak and inert, yet my fingers continue exploring in the dark. When they locate the lamp, I feel an illicit surge of hope as I am tempted, once again, to rub its bony surface, just in case a miracle is lurking somewhere within; just in case the laws of my God bend a little differently in this strange desert place where magicians turned serpents into straw and sand into black gold.

I peer out the side vent and see the full moon rising out of the desert like a great domed edifice commissioned by the ancient kings. My fingers tighten around the lamp, my last resort now. Will mystery rescue me? Will magic? If I try this, do I forfeit the other? Or is my God the lord and master of pragmatics: whatever works? Or will this constitute betrayal in the final crosshairs?

I give my God one more chance, although he is not a god of chances. Once again, I ask him—beg him—to please, somehow, someway rescue me from this anonymous end. I assure him that I will not be so reckless and cavalier in the future. I promise that I will do better and be better. Husband. Father. Doctor. Everything. I acknowledge that he alone can save me, not this silly piece of fash-ioned brass, although I do not quite discard it. I do not toss it across the floor, into the deep dark, as a final demonstration of my faith.

Instead, I barter a little, like Father Abraham. Am I not going about thy business here? Did we not save that young boy's leg? And many lives, many more legs? Do I too not help the lame to walk? Inasmuch as I have done it unto one of the least of these … Would it not have been much safer and easier for me to stay home watching March Madness? Then where is thy shield? Where is thy comfort? Where are thy angels riding to my rescue? Oh, God, Father, all things are possible unto thee: deliverest thou me?

I have tried the latch a hundred times, but I close my eyes and try once more. This time, inexplicably, I hear the telltale click, my ram in the thicket. My heart stops, then almost punches through my chest. I barely have the strength to push the lid open, but I manage. As my head emerges through the hole, it feels as if I have surfaced from the bottom of the sea, gasping for air. The desert breeze embraces me with cool, gentle hands.

I monkey down the steel siding, my bare feet plopping on the sand. The cemetery of scattered wreckage appears ghoulish in the silver light, like an eerie dream. I begin walking towards the east where the full moon fills the sky like the faceless countenance of an omnipotent God. He is neither frowning nor smiling.

Go, he says, and sin no more.

A PSALM FOR THE MAN WHO HAS EVERYTHING

From the get-go we told you she was out of your league: pom-pom waving prom queen bee of everything, whose twinkling blues and Instamatic smile sank hearts like doomed galleons and made lap dogs of half the football team (the other half settling for the post-party leftovers).

You were half-drunk on a six pack and your buddy's double dare when you hopped her backyard fence at midnight and tossed pop-corn kernels (oh so corny!) at her bedroom window while howling an off-key serenade, like a coyote in heat: "Mi-chelle, my belle ..." Forcing her outside to slap duct tape on your mouth. The first kiss was three months away, but her hands like warm lotion on your cheeks were ample bait. "Stop it," she whispered. "Stop it, please." And you did.

But the poems you taped to her bedroom window greeted her each morning with a mix of Dr. Seuss silliness and devil-may-care bravado that was, like, totally against her rules. Totally. Next came lunchtime diatribes that rattled her perfectly calendared conveyor belt world: marriage–mommy–grandmommy–grave, with a lot of potlucks, service projects, and church stuff in between. You spoke of islands where life was as simple as a straw mat, a hammock, and fresh fruit you could pluck from the trees; where every morning some new mystery washed ashore and your daily business was to solve it, rewrite it, or ignore it. Totally.

After a hundred days of this she started to see through the glass a little more uncertainly. Her adorable little twin nieces seemed much less adorable feasting greedily on her sister's milk-bloated breasts. Suddenly she saw her future in a bottle and wanted to cast

147

it out to sea or smash it on the tinted windshield of her mother's Lexus minivan: *bon voyage*! She was sixteen.

For two years her parents wrung their hands and beat their chests and fasted and prayed for divine deliverance from this walking, talking, neo-hippy freak. And just when it appeared that all was lost, the boy who juggled Pink Floyd, Greenpeace, Karl Marx, and J. R. R. Tolkien suddenly got religion.

Or maybe it was her drawing a line in the sand: me forever or never. That eternal ballbreaker.

Or maybe because your parents (paisley throwbacks to the dead-ended sixties) so adamantly said no that you said yes, and they said no way and you said yes way.

You cut your hair like an accountant and got a job bussing tables at the steak-and-lobster place. By summer's end you'd bought two used suits and a dozen white shirts and joined the army of God, bearing your new name and title like a medal over your left breast: *Elder Collins*.

For one year, eleven months, and two days, the fires of the Spirit and the unspoken promise of her farewell kiss fueled you through the concrete maze of Mexico City as you tried to keep your eye on the ball and your head in the game, even as hope faded with the growing interim between each aerogram: *You are an ordained emissary of Jesus Christ taking his gospel to this forgotten people; thrust in thy sickle, for thy time here is but the twinkling of an eye ...* The slam dunk came on a Thursday night after you and your missionary companion baptized the Fernandez family, all eight of them.

The letter was short. *I'm sorry. I'm really, really sorry.* You had twenty-eight days before your honorable release.

Everyone in the world including your mission companion, your mission president, and even your usually goofier-than-goofy parents told you, in so many words, to dump the chick and move on, but there was something unjust unfair unacceptable about it. You had become another dumb statistic: *Dear John-ed* in the home stretch.

And so, you returned with honor and an asterisk to our little town where we thought you would eventually grow old and die alone in a one-bedroom condo on the east side with a flower garden you didn't have to tend and an artificial lawn you didn't have to mow and a future you didn't have to live.

We told you and told you and told you to get the hell out, but you stayed anyway. You found good, steady work at the cabinet shop, insisting that that was what you really liked to do, work with your hands. And you reminded us that your parents had had you late in life and they were getting older and you were it for them. You said nothing about the girl who was a young woman now or the man she had chosen, but we all assumed the obvious.

He was tall, of course, with mannequin good looks and the square jaw of an action hero, an ex-quarterback/returned missionary born of parents who were not only goodly but wealthy. Pioneer and corporate pedigrees that made him lord over half the valley. He was mayor too, and someday would run for governor and who knows what else? All of which meant she lived in the triple-decker on the hill and drove the biggest, shiniest sports utility vehicle in the county.

At church we offered you small and cautious callings while he was fast-tracked to the top: Young Men's president, counselor in the elders quorum, elders quorum president, counselor in the bishopric, and, finally, bishop. Meanwhile, she gave birth to twins—a little girl who would grow up to be heartbreakingly beautiful and a boy who would morph into the handsome captain of the football team. All of which left us (and surely you) wondering why the rich, handsome corporate/ bishop types who already have everything else always get the pretty girl as well, although we knew better: that was precisely why.

So, you watched their lives grow from afar, at church socials and ball games and the annual county fair, always keeping a safe and private distance, trying not to be obsessed with it, although we knew you were. And you did so well for so long, until that seem-ingly innocuous night when fate would finally hunt you down: the church Valentine's Day dance, adults only.

You have come solo, of course, but have chosen to sit alone even though the other solos have all gathered at one table. Normally you would have entertained them with subversive asides about the clodhopper feet of Brother Miles and Sister Cunningham's Bride-of-Frankenstein hair. You can be quite the stand-up comic when you get on a roll, especially with Sister Hanley always sitting a little too closely and laughing a little too generously, trying a little too hard to coax a dance from you.

You're forty-seven years old, the proud owner of the only cabinet shop in town. You've done well for yourself, all things considered. But you buried your father five years ago and your mother shortly after Christmas. You have no brothers or sisters, no nieces or nephews, and for the first time in your life you've been hearing footsteps. You don't want to feel sorry for yourself, but tonight you just don't feel like putting on a show. Tonight, you really just want to be left alone. Then why did you come at all? Why not stay home and watch reruns of *Battlestar Galactica*? Good questions, but tonight you've got no answers.

So, you sit by yourself and, once again, trying very hard not to, you watch The Woman You Cannot Have. She's wearing her Russian spy outfit: black trench coat belted at the waist, curves showing despite the heavy fabric. The heels of her black velvet boots click confidently as she crosses the wooden floor, arm-in-arm with her handsome husband. Delicately but lethally tipped, her boots seem like bewitching weapons on her slender feet. Her auburn hair cascades grandly from her crown to her shoulders, half-hiding one eye, bouncing ever so slightly, like the rest of her, as she sashays by your table. For a moment you think she's maybe doing this intentionally, to rub your nose in it, but you know better: you're invisible, at best an embarrassing footnote buried in the pages of a previous life.

She and the bishop/mayor/tycoon/husband saunter past long tables laden with punch bowls, vegetable trays, chocolate fountains, and platters of artery-clogging desserts. They finally stop at one of the many small, circular tables arranged around the perimeter and dimly lit by festoons of leftover Christmas lights.

She removes her coat with assistance from the bishop/mayor/tycoon/husband, and there she is, in your face again: a form-fitting cross-my-heart-and-hope-to-break-yours dress, bright red, that hugs her hips tantalizingly tight, with a white kerchief around her throat for a dash of contrast. Only a small stripe of leg is visible, from the top of each boot to the bottom of each knee, but the black, semi-see-through hose teases your imagination beyond the dress, the boots, and whatever else remains between this and all of that.

It hurts, it absolutely hurts you to look at her for more than a moment.

For some reason, tonight, you want to smack the man standing next to her with a stick. Or a baseball bat.

But you have to admit he looks dapper in a three-piece suit, with the slightest gray peppering his pompadour. And the way he leads her around the dance floor, like the enchanted prince courting a Disney princess, you have to admit. You try to convince yourself that beneath the Valentine's Day smile she is secretly miserable in her by-the-book life. You try. Even as he guides her back to their table and helps her settle into her chair. Even as he saunters over to the table of solos you have eschewed for the night and, one by one, offers each of the ladies his arm and gives each (oldest to youngest) a little joy ride around the gym.

And then, surprisingly, he veers off towards one of the married women. It's a bit of a shock to Sister Allen who glances at her grizzled husband whose metal walker is resting against the table. It's highly irregular—never been done before in this church in this town; at least not to our recollection. Caught off guard, Brother Allen shrugs and smiles and nods all at once. There's silence at first, troubled brows and hushed mouths that gradually grow into smiles as the brittle senior skates around the floor for the first time in a decade. It's a green light for the rest of us as the bishop/mayor/tycoon/husband works his way from the old timers to the young mothers and even to the newlyweds, the husbands smiling and playing the good sports because he is, after all, the Lord's chosen vessel, the anointed father of the ward. And we all appear to be okay with it—a slight breach of tradition, true, but nothing illegal or untoward; no sacred covenants broken. Everyone seems to be having a good time, with the exception of you—a parable suddenly festering in your head, the prophet Nathan calling out King David: *a poor man had a lamb that he loved; the king who had many herds took the lamb and butchered it to feed his guests. What should be done to the king?*

You don't know why this bothers you so much, but it just really damn does. When you look down at your hands, you notice that you've twisted your paper napkin into a tightly constricted rod, like a missile. Right now, you'd like to dip it in poison and throw it at the Man Who Has Everything, but he's too far away and there's no lethal liquid within reach except for the fountain of flowing dark chocolate, so the missile hangs limp in your hand.

The others are still smiling and chit-chatting, but you've had enough. You rise, cross the floor, and stand before the woman you have loved from a distance for far too many years. Summoning up every ounce of gall and courage, you extend your hand, tilt your head slightly, and stammer: "M-m-m-ay I have this d-d-d-ance?"

Her mouth opens slowly. You will remember forever after that astonished scarlet oval and the matching and sudden blush on her cheeks. Her mouth tightens as it closes. The music seems to have stopped, and the dancing too. We are all watching—those of us who know the history leaning into those who do not, whispering quick updates as we savor your strained smile and her perturbed politeness. You alone hear her response: *I'm sorry, but I think that that would be inappropriate.*

And there it is—that word! Inappropriate. Not a slap in the face but a slow, long-suffering incision.

You stand there, a little stunned, a little dazed, and then a little pissed off. Inappropriate. That mealy-mouthed, chicken-hearted, gutless, cop-out nothing word. And was it any more appropriate, her husband the bishop/mayor/tycoon making the rounds with everyone else's wife? One dance. One simple, three-minute, for-old-time's-sake, inappropriate dance. Throw a dog a bone for pity's sake! Break a sweat for something besides your power aerobics! Get your nose out of the clouds and mingle with the underlings!

You're ready to spew it all out, twenty-six-years-worth, but out of the corner of your eye here he comes, John Wayne in pinstripes fox-trotting to the rescue. The baritone radio voice, the voice of trophies, diplomas, certificates, success, privilege; the voice of the blessed, the chosen, the endowed: "Is everything all right here?"

"Yes," she says. "Brother Collins here was just saying hello."

Brother Collins? Not Robert, not Bob, not Bobby. A cold, formal kiss-off.

You nod, smile stupidly, run your fingers through your fallen and receding bangs. Of course. Brother Collins Here was just saying hello. Now he'll say goodbye, won't you, Brother Collins Here?

Yes, of course.

And so you do. Goodbye, it was nice talking to you, nice seeing you again. Nice imagining you.

You say none of this but think it, all the way back across the dance floor to your folding chair where you sit down alone at your table and stare straight ahead until the music starts up again. He gallantly extends his hand, and she rises like a duchess, hooks her arm around his, and together they glide out to the middle of the floor where all of us, you hope, are watching. And then you slide off your chair and leave the room, quickly.

You don't hear, but can imagine, our collective sigh of relief. Even the folks at the singles table are glad you're gone. Even Sister Hanley, who briefly contemplates rushing outside and catching you in a vulnerable moment, quickly snuffs out the last spark of hope she has quietly and faithfully guarded all these years. You've crossed an uncrossable line—finally, inevitably, and it's just so obviously obvious now to everyone: you're just too damn weird. Mentally washing her hands of you and our silly little dead-end town, the next morning she will buy a bus ticket to Bakersfield, California where (we think) she will spend the rest of her life working the cash register in her sister Lucille's flower shop.

You too will disappear, but not for good, showing up two hours later in the exclusive hilltop neighborhood. You know better than this, but it's Saturday again, and you're all alone and inappropriate, and will be again and again and again. If you're caught, there will be repercussions. All the rumors and behind-the-back whispering and finger-pointing will rise to a thundering crescendo. There will be humiliation and restraining orders, maybe even a church court; you may have to lay yourself at the mercy of the Man Who Has Everything.

Idling beside the little metal box mounted on the metal post, you press the numbered buttons and the wrought-iron gate swings open, allowing you to enter. You know the code because you've built custom cabinets for over half of the mansions in this guarded, gated community. The uniformed young man in the booth knows you by sight and waves as you pass. Yes, it's late but you've been known to burn the midnight oil meeting the demands of this finicky but well-compensating clientele.

You notice a light on in the draped living room. You drive around the block twice before rolling to a long, slow stop fifty yards down the street where you cut the engine and the lights. A pregnant moon is shining through the gnarled branches of oak and elm, casting you and your Ford Cherokee in striped, twisted shadows. Gently you pull the handle, ease the door open, and slip out into the frosty night. You've dressed darkly: black overcoat, black sweats, black gloves, black ski cap. So pathetically cliché.

You begin crawling on all fours across the dormant front lawn, your hands and knees receiving the cool moisture of the grass. In your haste, you trigger the motion sensor; instantly you and the yard are showered in midday brightness, like a giant flashbulb trying to catch you in the act. You scramble for the bushes along the perimeter and hunker there until the blast of midnight sun has dimmed and darkness has returned. Then you resume your approach, this time on your belly, slowly, inch-by-inch, until you reach the brick wainscoting. On your knees now, you press your eye to the glass right where the two halves of the drapes meet, even as you scold yourself: *no no this certainly isn't behavior nowhere becoming a temple recommend holding priesthood bearing Latter-day Saint get out of there get out of there get out right now!*

Are you violating covenants? Doing that which is impure? Unholy? Unchaste? Totally classless? Yes. Yes. Yes. Yes. Yes.

But you look, noting the zebra-striped shields from Africa, the framed photograph of the Salt Lake Temple bedizened with Christmas lights, the Navajo rug that covers one wall, and the colossal family portrait that consumes half the other. And then you see his crown jewel.

Still in her red spy outfit, minus the trench coat, she is tidying up, plumping pillows and rearranging them on the leather sofa, while he watches by the counter. The necktie gone, the shirt collar open, the white sleeves rolled up to mid-forearm, he looks downright dashing. As she bends over to gather up some plates and glasses from the coffee table, he approaches from behind and laces his arms around her waist. She straightens up abruptly, a trace of exasperation or fatigue in the sudden collapse of her shoulders. His hands move quickly, as if to catch them, and he begins gently kneading the back of her neck. She appears annoyed: not here, not now, please. Seeing this, you enjoy a twinge of satisfaction, even if she doesn't. Her head turns, eyes rolling in your direction, as if she knows you're watching and the two of you are somehow in cahoots. In that moment you read this little secret, that the past twenty-six years have been against her better judgment. In that moment you forgive her—for the rude kiss-off tonight, for the cold aerogram when you were counting the days in the slums of Mexico City, for the years of invisibility afterward. You forgive her for what you both have become.

She closes her eyes wearily—yes, she is weary, tired of this prefab life, and he'd better not press the issue, had better not press anything

But wait: her neck is softening a bit, relenting now. His cunning hands are prevailing as her neck arches forward and her eyes and mouth slowly open as if she's enjoying it, absolutely enjoying it although you are hating it but loving it but hating it, too.

You want to watch, but you also want to throw something. Pull a brick out of the wall and hurl it through the window, through the bishop/mayor/tycoon/husband's head. Why not? Why the hell not? What do you have to lose? Your life? Wife? Eternal salvation? You lost all of that twenty-six years ago: *I'm so sorry. I'm really really sorry.*

Get out now. Get thee hence. The devil in your head. The devil in your heart. Stop it now now now stop.

You absolutely, positively cannot believe you are doing this, but you absolutely, positively are.

You need to withdraw. You must. You should go home and make yourself a nice turkey on rye with avocado slices and a strawberry–banana smoothie. Nonalcoholic comfort food. Watch Colbert or *The Tonight Show.*

But you can't. You watch as his hand deftly unclasps the microscopic hook, pinches the zipper, and lowers it down the length of her back, the scarlet dress splitting at the nape of her neck and peeling neatly and evenly apart, one triangle falling open to the left, the other, perfectly symmetrical and synchronized, falling to the right. The dress is coming off. It gathers a moment at her hips before sliding down her legs. And now she is perfectly packaged in her white undergarments, enticingly shaded from the waist down by her sheer-black pantyhose. Your breath is pulsing on the glass. *Stop. Stop it now. Don't you know don't you know what you're doing here?*

His hands are reaching around her, touching and caressing, the ever-patient lover gliding through his progressions. She is turning to meet him, to receive him—the two of them working on each other, their tangled hands groping, squeezing, searching.

They are standing and embracing with pools of clothing around their feet. Her hands are touching him where you have fantasized and prayed and, in your very best dreams, imagined they would touch you. There is urgency now in his hands. And in yours.

You should look away, in deference to her. And if not for her, then for yourself.

You can't. You must see this to its inevitable conclusion—must see that last look on her face, that final passage of pleasure.

Or maybe not. Maybe things will go awry tonight: a censuring hand; an abrupt withdrawal; a humiliating malfunction. Some juicy stain on their picture-perfect world.

But this will not happen tonight. You watch as she melts in his arms and he lowers her gently onto the plush white carpet and commences his exalted work. There's no stumbling or bumbling; it appears perfectly choreographed yet perfectly natural. And he's magnificent! A god! Together *they* are magnificent, god and goddess. And you are condemned all over again:

Thou shalt not covet.

Thou shalt not envy.

Thou shalt not commit adultery in thy mind or in thy heart.

Thou shalt not drool on thy neighbor's doorstep.

Thou shalt not creep and peep.

You watch as he spreads his exquisitely sculpted body over hers and the gentle rhythm of mating begins. You watch her oval-mouthed ecstasy, and it all looks so damn perfect that you want to scream or swear or stand up and cheer or something, or you don't know what the hell what anymore.

In that instant, you forfeit all hope.

You know you shouldn't, but you watch right up through the

final and mutual rapture and you even stay to watch some of the cooing and caressing aftermath.

But now you've seen enough—too much! You spring to your feet and turn full-circle, the security lights dousing you in midday brightness, but this time you don't care. The neighbors may see you, the naked lovers, the security patrol, a coyote ferreting through the neighbor's trash—everyone may see. So what? So what so what so reeking freaking what?

Arriving at your three-bedroom home on the west side, you slam your car door and then your front door, and then you scream: not a yell or a bellow or a howl, but a good, old-fashioned, from-the-deepest-reaches-of-your-soul primal scream. You put your fist through a framed photo of yourself at age thirty commissioned by your parents in a private studio because they wanted to preserve you in your prime. You ignore the cuts on your knuckles and the shards of broken glass on the floor. You say good and good and good. You are out of control and you know it, but you don't give a rat's nipple right now. You hurl a ceramic mug against the wall and scream again. You acknowledge the presence of Silas, your golden retriever, cowering under the coffee table with a bark of your own: "What are you staring at?" He slinks into the kitchen and you say, "Good! Now you're talking!" You rip off your silly black ski mask and pathetic gloves. Good! Good! You look up at the yellow water stains on the ceiling and then down at the dog stains on the carpet and then survey the cramped living room for other targets: a mac-ramé wall hanging hand-made by your ex-hippy mother; a poster of Pink Floyd's *Dark Side of the Moon;* a portrait of Christ gazing at you with a peculiar blend of pity, disappointment, and rebuke. You bark again: "What are you staring at!" It's not a question.

Then you have a little shouting match with God, except God doesn't shout back. You have some questions, and you want some answers. Straight talk for a change. None of this "search the scrip-tures" prattle. No "faith precedes the miracle" stuff. You want raw, unfiltered answers.

You begin simply, with one thundering word: Why? You repeat it three times, each with a little more grit before the final *Why the hell!*

You want to know why God plays favorites? Why does he pour

sunshine on some and dump shit on the rest of us? You don't apologize for your French. You remind God that this is not a prayer—it so totally isn't!

At first you speak for all mankind, but then it turns back to you. Didn't you do the right things? Didn't you serve a mission? Didn't you give up your old mopey-dopey ways and come fully into the fold? And now, don't you honor your covenants? Don't you pay tithing, read your scriptures, pray, visit the poor, the sick, the widows—do do do; don't don't don't?

You're foaming and fuming and you want to throw more things. You're swearing at the Almighty, mingling expletives with scriptures, and you don't give a damn. You don't want to hear about no respecter of persons! Don't bore you with sermons on equity and justice and fairness and the rest of that sweet slop!

But you sound so petty and you know it, so damn petty saying it out loud, and yet it sears you to the bone: Rejoice in the good fortune of others! Okay, hallelujah! Hosanna to the Lord! Cry me a Jordan River! The Man Who Has Everything could have had any any any girl, his pick of the princess litter; so why her? Why did it have to be her?

You remind God (again) that you served a mission, all right— played the faithful servant in the concrete jungles of the most polluted city on Earth. And in your absence your presence was erased. Trumped and dumped. Thank you thank you and more thank you! Wait! You hear a voice, the still small chuckle from the other side. Chuckle? Oh yes, because you're certain that God finds this all so very amusing, your petty private angst. Small petunias to him. You can hear his watertight rebuttal over the holy megaphone: Did I promise thee the woman? No. Did I promise thee any woman? No. Did I promise thee touchdowns and convertibles or a palace on the hill? Did I promise thee ease and comfort?

At first God lobs you softballs: Would you prefer that The Woman You Can't Have be miserable? Abused? Beaten? Depressed? Frustrated? Maligned? Raped? Killed? Paralyzed?

No no no no no no no of course not.

He mentions Job scraping off his boils and Joseph Smith shivering in Liberty Jail. And just in case you've forgotten, he reminds you of his Only Begotten boy sweating blood in Gethsemane. He tells you to stop by the elementary school next week and visit the east wing where they educate, to the extent possible, the little children with gyrating eyes and drool dripping from their mouths, permanently strapped to body boards.

You tell him you know you know you know. It could always be worse, but it could also be better, and that's your whole point. Why so much of this for some and so freakin' little of that for others? Why? Why the hell?

Hell? Freaking?

He says you still don't get it. Butcher, baker, candlestick maker isn't the point. CEO, brain surgeon, naval commander. It's not the point.

Then what *is* the point? Just what the hell is it?

His voice grows soft and he calls you by name. You think for a moment you can actually hear it. The night the mother of all blizzards closed town for a week you went out in the ugly, howling heart of it and helped Bishop Johnson dig out a poor wayfaring stranger whose truck had rolled off the highway and into a ditch.

So? So? Anyone can do that. Any poor or rich or middle-class anybody can do that.

True, but you did it. Brother McMillan stayed in his nice warm home and watched the Lakers make mincemeat of the Utah Jazz. So did Brother Avery and Brother Davenport. And it wasn't even a playoff game.

Funny, you say. So, God has a sense of humor.

Of course I do. I invented sex.

Now you're smiling a little, softening.

Is this supposed to make you feel better?'

No, but it certainly made that poor banged up stranger feel better. And it should have made Brothers McMillan, Avery, and Davenport feel like three able-bodied amoebas with four-wheel drive and studded snow tires.

In that moment you have a flash of insight, call it revelation. It comes not from a still small voice in your head or some platitude from seminary scripture mastery but the old vinyl records your parents used to play on Saturday mornings (surely, you were convinced, then and now, to annoy you) while you scrubbed the toilets and cleaned the two bathrooms, your fair portion of what they had called "Saturday Jobs." First, the sweet guitar strains of Crosby, Stills, Nash, & Young counseling you to love the one you're with if you can't be with the one you love. And then Mick Jagger's razor-blade voice telling you that you don't always get what you want but you can still get what you need.

As those two tunes filter through your head, God tells you he needs you here, not necessarily here in this town but here on planet Earth. There will be more midnight phone calls, stuff like that. He tells you you're doing okay. You don't turn on the tears at the pulpit, but you're gold in a crunch, and he likes that. He loves that. He tells you to keep doing what you're doing but don't be afraid to step outside the lines. Try a little harder; look a little harder. He tells you to trust him, really. And then he tells you to let her go. He calls you brother; he calls you son; he calls you friend. The room grows quiet and you notice that Silas has slinked back under the coffee table and he's looking up.

When you finally wake up it's almost 9:30 a.m. You call Sister Hanley, but there's no answer. You want to apologize for last night. Or ask her out. Or maybe both. You definitely want to do something. You call her again at 10:00 and again at 10:30. At 11:00 you call her friend Sister Mitchell who says she left early that morning. She doesn't know where exactly. Doesn't know why either.

You tell her to tell Sister Hanley that you called. Please. You say please again, and she says okay. You say thank you. Twice.

Then you go online to Cheap Tours and book a trip to India. It's where you had always dreamed of going before you met *her*; before church and the mission and all of the painful aftermath; before your mother contracted the disabling disease that gave you the perfect excuse to stay.

SELFIE

I couldn't believe what lay on the sidewalk although not so surprising really come to think of it after the rain and the thunder
that wasn't thunder but metal on metal mixed with fiberglass and
steel-belted radials traveling 60 70 80 mph maybe faster both
ways head-to-head mass-times-velocity-equals crash but what did
you expect you told him over and over and over and—wah! wah!
wah!—but he was a kid you said all right so maybe not a kid-
kid but twenty-one going on twenty-two going on forty-five Pfc
USMC semper fi Superman with a big red indestructible S on his
chest fair game legal tender but still in your eyes mind heart still
your blue-eyed baby boy who had dodged bombs and bullets in Afghanistan the Taliban couldn't kill him or Big Mac breakfasts but
now this and there it was lying on a slab of concrete his last testament in a tiny black box smaller than a wallet but like I said not a
heap big surprise after all come to think of it amidst the accordi-
on-ed hood and the upside-down helplessness of a desert tortoise
on its back and the jigsaw pieces of glass and mirror sparkling
like treasure in the early morning sun and his body still strapped
to the leather seat one hand frozen to the steering wheel and this
last pure piece of him flying free but you don't want to know that
all you want to know are colors you want three but here's four:
blue the color of his eyes and his jeans boot-cut pre-bleached and
shredded on the knees; pink the color of his tongue in a full-throt-
tled laugh like a kid on a roller coaster; red which was splattered
everywhere; and black the instant of impact and the color of my
days ever since that moment landing smack in the middle of the
very spot here now at my feet of equal ownership, this: a selfie of
his last blotch of bliss.

SENIOR GIRLS SOFTBALL

They don't spit and chew and scratch themselves like the guys. Instead, they tug daintily at the side-seams of their skintight pants and fiddle a bit with their bangs in between pitches. I suppose it's no accident their headbands match their purple jerseys. Socks, bracelets, earrings too. But they throw like the big boys, all easy wrist and elbow, and swing the bat with teeth clenched and menace in their eyes. I can remember when any ball hit was a guaranteed home run, the infielders stumbling and bumbling like the Keystone Kops while the outfielders counted butterflies or searched for four-leaf clovers. "I got it!" "No, I got it!" "No, me!" "Who's got it?" "I do—I think! No, you take it!" "Me?" "Don't you?" "Who's got it?" In the bleachers we smiled, shrugged, clapped a lot, groaned a little, and shouted, "Nice try!" Or nothing at all.

I watch you now on the mound going through your brow-mopping, sleeve-shaking, belt-tugging, between-pitch ritual like a seasoned pro, as if this were the World Series, every pitch the game-breaker. You scrape your cleats across the rubber, bending at the waist—your throwing arm dangling like a Neanderthal's as you finger the ball, a little white melon, the full moon in your palm. You check the catcher's sign. Shake. Shake. Nod. The burly redhead in the box takes a slow practice swing, freezing it a moment like a long-barreled weapon aimed right between your eyes. A threat? A promise? A prayer? Yours, perhaps? Or has your God abandoned you today? If so, I'm to blame for that. I'm half winner here, hoping to take all.

The count is three and two; two outs; the winning run on second and the tyer-upper a feisty little cyclone dancing around on third thanks to a cheap infield hit and shortstop error. "Not your fault!" hollered your bullish little coach with the powerlifter's shoulders. "Not your fault, Tracy! Shake it off!"

The late afternoon sun is half-hidden behind the pines, a golden bird trapped in a crooked cage. Shadows are spreading across the field like water on a paper towel. Chatter attacks from all sides— "Hey, badda badda badda badda! Hey badda badda badda!" "Come on, Lupe, wait for your pitch! Wait for your pitch now!"—but you're deaf to it. For almost seven innings you've managed to block out the raucous crowd, the passing traffic, the airplanes droning overhead, and the turmoil at home. Another broken dish. Another midnight rant. Another stone-cold goodbye. Your mother and I don't see eye-to-eye on this. Or much of anything lately. No secret there. It's only a matter of time before we all have to take sides. In the meantime, I argue with her own ammo, compliments of a dozen rounds with the full-time missionaries:

"God blessed her with a golden arm. Divine gifts shouldn't be buried under a bushel."

"It's the Sabbath."

"She's sixteen, old enough to choose for herself, don't you think? Free agency and all that good stuff."

"Maybe. But she's mine, not yours."

"And whose fault is that?"

"Yes, whose?"

I'm the only smoker in the stands, and this is one of the few places where my nicotine habit hasn't been outlawed, at least not yet. Nevertheless, I do my best to conceal my lethal white cartridge in between puffs. I'm sitting in the front row at ground level. A little girl with dust powdering her hands, knees, and face toddles over and stares at me with the sad countenance of a World Hunger Relief commercial. I smile, exhale, and lower my cigarette under my leg. Her newly minted eyes regard me suspiciously before she slowly backs away.

The opposing coach has called time-out to confer with the batter. When he finishes, he pats her on the shoulder and gestures to the antsy little dancer on third. Time-in.

You are a freckled ice princess with your blond ponytail hanging below your waist and your blue eyes lasering in on the catcher's mitt.

"Come on, Tracy!" I holler. "One more pitch! Blow it by her!"

Your hand and glove go to your belt. For a split second, you are a penitent priest awaiting an eternal verdict. Your right arm drops, then whips around like a propeller, the ball almost scraping the ground the instant before it turns into a streaking comet. You blink. The telltale thud in the catcher's cushioned leather echoes the stentorian voice of the man in executioner's garb as he jerks his thumb back as if pulling the lever on the gallows: "Steeee-rike!"

The sky briefly flares, then darkens. At that moment you are the sun with eight purple planets swarming jubilantly around you. I detect a crack in the ice: a smile.

And I have won on both accounts. And lost.

PIONEERS

My wife Frieda could have worked for Cecil B. DeMille or Steven Spielberg, given her cast-of-thousands knack for the spectacular. Take tonight for instance. In the name of fellowshipping, and to beef up our numbers, she has invited two other families to join us in our weekly Family Home Evening activity. She has also borrowed a life-size model handcart from the Millets, made ten trail signs (wooden, authentic, hand-carved), and staked them out at odd intervals along a bumpy dirt-bike trail behind Witherspoon Park: *Nauvoo, Mississippi River, Council Bluffs* ...

Sixteen of us, ages five to fifty, have gathered around the first trail sign, reluctant teenagers in Teva sandals and Oakley sunglasses, the younger children in costume: blue jeans, straw cowboy hats, paper bonnets, long loose cotton dresses to the ankles. Big, blue-eyed blondes, the seven Boyak girls look like a tribe of Swedish immigrants, while the Huntingtons bear the swarthy genes of the south. We (the Tolmans) are a fifty-fifty mix.

Following an opening song and prayer, Frieda introduces tonight's lesson, "Our Pioneer Heritage," and objective: on this balmy midsummer night, we will take turns, by family, pushing and pulling the Millet's handcart from Nauvoo to the Salt Lake Valley, stopping at each trail sign to read the note Frieda has diligently thumbtacked to it.

While Frieda fields questions from the children ("Is it a race?" "No." "Do we get a prize?" "Maybe."), my eyes and thoughts drift south to the grassy playing field where a middle-aged man in a tie-dye T-shirt is chasing two mop-haired boys around a fortress of wooden logs and rope nets, growling like the Cowardly Lion of Oz. Their happy shrieks are echoes from a time not long ago when

I too pursued my son around the jungle gym: "I'm the Hot Lava Monster! The Hot Lava Monster! Grrrrrr!"

"Hey, Dad!"

Andrew motions for me to join him at the front of the handcart, an unfinished plywood box with a wagon wheel on either side. "Come on! We'll be the pullers; Mom can be the pusher!"

Pusher? This unwitting allusion to my sixties youth elicits an unexpected grin as I step over the handle, resting on the dirt, and position myself beside my son. The cart and its load are laughingly light by pioneer standards, yet the handle, a two-inch-thick pine dowel, feels like lead in my hands. Gripping it, my son innocently taunts me with one of my own aphorisms: "Come on, Dad, be a help, not a hurt!"

Frieda hollers from the rear: "Hey, let's get this show on the road!"

Straight ahead, the sun is slowly being sucked under the hilly horizon. Framed in Rubenesque clouds, it's a gaudy image, idol-atrously surreal, like the golden calf caught in quicksand. From its fiery center, a steamy pink residue floats towards the blue-gray mounds amassing overhead. The swollen sky looks and smells like rain. I estimate thirty minutes before the first drops fall. Silently, I pray for a swift, hard downpour that will chase us under the ramada and rescue me from tonight's ordeal.

We drag the handcart along the narrow trail, the Boyaks and Huntingtons sauntering alongside us in the surrounding weeds and wildflowers, chatting innocuously. I wear a smile throughout, even when the Boyak girls break into song, like the Von Trapp family: "Put your shoulder to the wheel push a-lo-ong! Do your duty with a heart full of so-ong! We all have work! Let no one shirk!"

Pausing at the second trail sign, *Mississippi River*, Frieda gazes north where a jet plane is angling above the mountain—red, white, and blue lights winking on its wings like patriotic stars. Interlacing her fingers behind her neck, with a quick but disciplined motion she lifts her hair up, deftly withdrawing her hands so that the ebony coils settle gently, like soft little springs, on her shoulders. This motion, which in words sounds long and calculated, takes a fraction of a second and seems as natural and routine to her as taking a breath of air.

We relinquish the handcart to the Boyaks. Andrew snatches the envelope thumbtacked to the wooden sign and pretends to read: "Bad water. Half your party gets dysentery and croaks." He grips his throat, gagging, and flings himself backwards onto the dirt, his skinny bare legs issuing a few spasmodic kicks, like a cartoon death. His clownish antics have not escaped the obsidian eyes of Connie Huntington, a lithe little gymnast who inherited her father's poker face and her mother's bewitching black hair. Noticing her noticing him, Andrew claps his hand over his mouth in mock horror and adds a couple kicks for an encore. Frieda casts him the evil eye, momentarily throwing ice on his antics, and then proceeds to read the true contents of the envelope, the first of several excerpts she has copied from the pioneer journals of her ancestors:

> *Leaving New York, we went by train and boat to Iowa City and after a short delay, to one of the worst journeys that was ever recorded. We were lighthearted and worked with zeal preparing our hand carts. Because of the great demand for carts of the previous companies, the wheels were made of green material. We met morning and evenings for devotional exercises. On one of these occasions Brother Levi Savage, who was returning from a mission, spoke and portrayed the intense sufferings the saints would have to endure if we started so late in the season to cross the plains, the thoughts of which made him cry like a child. Captain Willie sternly rebuked him for such a speech. He was afraid it would dishearten the saints, and told us that if we would be faithful and do as he told us winter would be turned to summer. But subsequent events proved Elder Savage was correct ...*

As Frieda's voice summons up spirits from the dust, I begin rewriting in my mind procrastinated passages from my personal history:

I met Frieda at a spring singles dance. I'd just turned forty, but she was six years from crossing that middle-age milestone that seems to stand up and scream out with quiet desperation: LAST CHANCE! (for temple marriage, eternal family, exaltation, et cetera). Ironically, I'd resigned myself to celestial singlehood, which is to say, I was no longer looking for a mate, eternal or otherwise, only occasional companionship to share a movie, a concert, a meal, an evening of TV and microwave popcorn.

I'd been coaxed to that evening's function by a well-intentioned friend who introduced me to Frieda (who looked as unenthusiastic as I felt). Commiserating over the punch bowl, we soon discovered we'd both planned a backpacking trip into the Grand Canyon over Memorial Day weekend. "Small world!" I proclaimed, and when she smiled, her teeth sparkled as if half the Milky Way had taken up residence there. By the time a crew of resurrected Credence Clearwater wannabes had finished a tortuously long rendition of "Susie Q," we agreed to hike the Grand Canyon together.

Unchaperoned? Well, why not? We were both mature adults, temple-endowed, returned missionaries. We shared the same code of ethics and virtue. Who needed a chaperone?

Our only child was conceived in a moment of ecstatic sin in a dome tent on a sandy bank at the bottom of the Grand Canyon, as a chorus of frogs sang approvingly in the faint trickle known as Monument Creek. Afterwards, lying together on my sleeping bag, her head on my chest, I asked the inevitable:

"Was that your first time?"

"Could you tell?"

"I wouldn't know."

She gave my arm a gentle squeeze. "I love you," she whispered, and we dozed off like that.

We were married civilly that week, and eternally shortly after, following the requisite channels of sackcloth and ashes. A sympathetic stake president kindly abbreviated the standard year's probation prior to a temple sealing.

※

Colleen and her seven daughters maneuver the handcart towards Council Bluffs. Bradley Boyak nudges me in the ribs. "See? That's why you need more kids!" I laugh, nod. Is that right? No kidding? Like my son the thespian, I too am playacting, but in an altogether different manner. I seriously wonder if I'll be able to complete this ersatz journey to the Promised Land. Gazing down the dirt trail that gradually wraps around the northern rim of the park, I find it hard, near impossible, to believe that only two years ago I finished first in my age category in our local Mountain Man Triathlon: a mile swim across Emerald Lake, thirty-two miles on bicycle around the lake's paved perimeter, and a six-mile run up Anderson Mesa and back.

Up ahead, Billy Huntington, sporting a thick, dark mop spilling over shaved sidewalls, is flirting with the oldest Boyak girl, a double-braided Brunhilda wearing a too-tight T-shirt that proclaims: *Abstinence: I'm Worth It!* Frieda is strolling alongside Gary Huntington, a tall, stout accountant with a sailboat, a palatial home on the golf course, and a brand-new head of hair, partly subsidized by a life insurance windfall: a little over a year ago he lost Cheryl to a gruesome battle with ovarian cancer.

Frieda's arms are folded just below her chest, so that it appears as if they are hoisting up her breasts, supporting them like shelves. They look especially full tonight, milk or love-laden, thanks to the tight fit and the flimsy cotton fabric. Her suntanned hand lights on Gary's shoulder, gently as a bird, and slides down the length of his arm. It's an innocent gesture, as simple and spontaneous as a little girl's smile, and she has no idea how deeply it wounds me.

Wedging myself between them, I ask Gary if he's been to the lake lately? When he asks me if I've lost weight, I laugh, patting my belly. "I think I've gained a little, actually." Call this a pink lie: survival. Frieda nods reassuringly. "Oh, he has. He really has."

When I tell Gary it looks as if he's lost some, he beams proudly: "Ten pounds!"

"Watch that Sizzler salad bar or you'll start looking like me!" Bradley Boyak says, sneaking up behind us.

"Salad bar nothing!" Colleen cuts in. "Try Dairy Queen Blizzards!" Everyone laughs but Frieda.

At Council Bluffs we sing the first verse of "Come, Come, Ye Saints." Cynthia Boyak reads the note tacked to the trail marker:

We left Iowa City on the 15th of July 1856, in what is known as The Captain Willie Handcart Company. This Company consisted of 500 souls, 120 handcarts, 5 wagons, 24 oxen, and 45 beef cattle. We were happy in the thought that we were going to Zion, and the 100 miles all went well, the scenery being beautiful and game being plentiful, and the spirit of joy reigned in these Camps of Israel. However, on the 4th of September, our cattle were run off by a band of Indians. This proved to be a great calamity.

I'm not superstitious by nature, especially when it concerns religion. I prefer to picture God as a benevolent, loving father rather than the Old Testament vindicator of hellfire and fury. However, I'm no revisionist whitewasher either. God will temper justice with mercy, but justice will be wrought, sometimes down to the seventh generation.

Consequently, from the moment I learned Frieda was expecting, I begged Heavenly Father not to punish us as he had David and Bathsheba, delivering up a dead child. "Do anything you want to me," I pleaded, "but not Frieda, not the baby."

Nine months I waited on pins and needles, all the time hiding my anxiety from my wife, assuring her that everything would be fine, just fine, although in my dreams I was forewarned of a troglodyte-looking creature as my sole heir. In the delivery room, when the baby's head crowned, I rushed forward to count fingers, toes, eyes, ears. Ten, ten, two, two. Perfect! Our child was a perfectly beautiful brown-eyed baby boy.

I treasure that moment of delivery, as I do the moment of conception and all of the good things leading up to it. And if this is the price I have to pay ex post facto for Andrew's unblemished birth, then I've got no complaints. God may work in mysterious ways, but I don't believe that he operates in ledger book fashion—not if the Atonement is a bottomless pit that no amount of sin and misgiving can overflow. I don't believe that my present condition is the result of past transgressions, or payback for private covenants years ago. And that's exactly what makes this whole thing so damn difficult.

⚸—

Frieda continues talking to Gary Huntington, talking right through me. She doesn't do this to be rude or to inflict pain. That's just Frieda.

"Gary," I say, pointing to the handcart. "You're up!"

Gary calls to his two teenage boys, who reluctantly surround the handcart, mumbling and murmuring in the manner of the two original Lamanites. They quickly get into the spirit of the occasion, however, trotting side by side humming the "Bonanza Theme."

Bradley Boyak hitches his blue jeans a little higher on his

bullfrog belly and invites me to join him and Gary for a racquet-ball game. "You ever played racquetball?" No, but I'd sure like to. Tonight? Oh, no, not tonight. Tonight I have to …

I invent an excuse: grade papers, mend the garden hose, fix a leaky faucet, build a garage, pole vault over Mt. Rushmore. Anything.

Bradley nods. Maybe some other time then.

Sure. Yes. Please. By all means. I'd really like to.

Colleen floats up beside me like a big Hawaiian queen in her multicolored muumuu and wraps a motherly arm around my bony shoulders: "Brian, are you cold?" Caught off guard, I almost topple over. "A bit," I reply. This is a blue lie: the long-sleeved shirt and baggy pants are intended to conceal the hasty disappearance of my flesh. The extra T-shirt underneath adds false bulk. I smile extra big, extra wide, even as the invisible agent, my unholy ghost, gives the corkscrew in my gut another sadistic twist.

Everything hurts now. I bruise like a banana.

I remind myself to walk, laugh, smile. Whatever happens, I absolutely must smile. Last night, during what I'd thought was a private moment, Andrew sneaked into my bedroom and caught me hunched over in the rattan chair. "Dad?" When I looked up, his face grew small and sad, like a balloon losing air. He was wearing his new baseball glove on his left hand, holding a ball in the right. He must have heard me groan.

"Don't you want to play catch?"

"No no—it's not that. Of course, I want to play catch. I always want to play. It's just that—bad day, Andy. I got a little bad news is all."

"I'm sorry, Dad."

When I got in bed later that night, I found his old teddy bear, Snuggles, propped up against the headboard. A half-joke. Warm fuzzy comfort.

Another time it was Frieda. Late one night she crawled out of bed and shuffled down the hall and into the kitchen. An hour passed before she returned.

"You okay?" I whispered.

My iron-willed wife began sobbing in her pillow. I turned over, groping for her face in the dark, exploring it gently with my hands, kissing her tenderly. "Hey, what's wrong? What's the matter, sweetie?"

"I'm worried," she sniffled.

"Worried? What about?" I asked.

"You!" she barked.

I tried to laugh it off. "Me? You don't need to worry about—"

"I heard you mumbling—then you got up—all the weight you've been losing—the doctors—"

"I'm fine," I insisted. "I got up to pee, that's all. You didn't want me to pee in the bed, did you?"

She laughed—a small, cautious laugh. Over and over, I reassured her, kissing her cheeks, her chin, her eyelids, everything except her potent lips: I'm fine, fine, feeling better, stronger every day.

I curled up behind her, my front to her back, and kissed the nape of her neck. Several minutes passed before she reached back, grasped my hand, and placed it gently on her belly, her fingers silently counting mine in the dark.

The next morning, we joked about it, embarrassed, self-conscious, uncertain what to do or say.

"I mean, you wake up in the middle of the night and suddenly you say to yourself, 'Now what's *really* important?'"

"Don't kid yourself," I said. "You were just trying to seduce me."

"You wish!" she said, and her smile caught momentarily, like a bad lock, as she read my mind: *you're right*. And: she's right. Intimate little jokes that were no longer funny.

⚲

Dusk has buried the last bit of sun, and the pine tree silhouette fringing the horizon has turned to black lace. We plod on past a solitary home where fruit trees spill over a wooden fence and a wiry teenager, naked from the waist up, sits on a tree stump finger picking a steel-string guitar. Drawn by a primordial magnet he doesn't comprehend, my son has drifted to within three feet of Connie Huntington. Does he have any idea his gait is miming hers exactly, stride for stride?

Gaining the Missouri River, we take over again, Andrew jockeying his way to the rear. "Boys in back, girls in front!"

Billy Boyak reads excerpt number three:

Now the weather was getting cold, rations short and work hard and sister

Eliza became weaker with the cold and hunger each day. One of those cold bleak days her life of hardship ended and she passed away and was buried along the trail. With hope and courage, we joined the company and the little ones trudged along day after day, until their feet would bleed and yet I was unable to assist them, only with encouraging words. (Many times I wrapped a blanket around them while I dried their frozen clothing by the fire.) I remember well the last time we crossed the Platte River. It was almost sundown when I got to camp. My clothes were frozen so that I could scarcely move. I stood by the fire with a blanket around me while mother dried my clothes by the fire. She often said she would be the happiest woman alive if she could reach Zion with all her children.

Sometimes the pain is almost unbearable, like the weekend Frieda took Andrew to a soccer tournament in Albuquerque while I stayed home, ostensibly with a strained back. Saturday morning, Jim Reynolds, an old running buddy, stopped by to see how I was doing. He had no idea the spasm in my spine was nothing compared to the rodents chewing up my insides.

I looked like hell: baggy sweatpants, baggy sweater, ski cap, whiskers dripping from my chin. I could barely make it from the sofa to answer the front door. Jim tried to appear oblivious, but he couldn't miss the stains on the floor and the dirty dishes stacked in the sink.

We talked. When's Frieda coming home? Tuesday. You okay for food? She left a two-year's supply of frozen dinners. Still going to work? In body, not spirit.

Then I began shaking uncontrollably, hot and cold needles streaking and freaking up and down my body everywhere, and just as suddenly I was itching all over, clawing my arms, chest, legs, and stockinged feet.

Jim looked worried, but I told him I was okay, just a little chilled. He said, "Hey, I've got just the thing! Let's get you over to the Athletic Club and put you in the Jacuzzi. That'll warm you up real good!"

It sounded like a good idea, but it backfired. The instant I slipped into the hot, bubbling water, my eyes blackened, my body melted, and I went under. Jim pulled me out, helped me to the concession stand, and bought me a 7-Up, thinking that maybe I just needed a sugar fix. Instead I vomited over and over until there was nothing left inside me to spew out. He had to carry me in his arms, like I was a baby or his bride, into his Land Cruiser. Curled up in his front seat, dry heaving, I told Jim I wanted to die. It was the first time I'd admitted it to anyone.

Then he started bad-mouthing Frieda. "She should be here, nursing you, not gallivanting off to Albuquerque." But I told him no, stop, shut up. Just shut up, please. You don't know what you're talking about. You mean well but you don't understand. I made him promise not to repeat what I'd said to anyone. "You're my best friend, Jim. I have to count on you." That was a yellow lie: Frieda's my best friend. Was.

Jim said okay, have it your way, but I looked like a clock slowly winding down. He said I looked like Death eating a cracker.

⚷

Fortunately, it's a short walk to the next trail marker, and I let Andrew and Frieda do most of the work up front. Bradley Boyak walks alongside, enthusiastically informing me that there really wasn't all that much game on the Great Plains until the farmers came and started growing crops. "Well, buffalo maybe, sure, but as far as the other ..."

I finger the plastic vial in my pants pocket, debating whether or not to pop the lid and surreptitiously slip one of the sea-foam green capsules into my mouth. If I do, within thirty minutes, the dagger will be withdrawn from my gut, leaving only a residual ache and sting for the next four to five hours, but my body and brain will close up shop, and I'll be a walking zombie for the rest of the night. That's the tradeoff, as Dr. Clark likes to call it.

Each green capsule is a last temptation, a micro-dose of suicide, which is why I try to hold off until bedtime. Usually.

"Hey, loser!"

It's Andrew, reminding me that I'm falling behind again. I release the vial and mentally slap the offending hand as if it were a disobedient child's. Bradley reads the excerpt at Winter Quarters:

One night when we were to go to bed hungry, Sister Rowley got two very hard sea biscuits, that were left from the Sea Voyage. She put the biscuits in their frying pan and covered them with water, and placed them on the fire to heat. She then asked our Father in Heaven to bless them, that there may be sufficient amount to feed our hungry children. When she took the lid off, we were all happy to see the pan full of food. We all thanked our kind Father in Heaven for such a wonderful blessing.

The second hardest part will be trying to explain to my son something I don't understand myself. First there were the doctors, a whole slew of specialists. We held a family fast, then a ward fast. I've received three priesthood blessings. After the first one, administered by Jim Reynolds, Andrew glowed with innocent optimism.

"You're going to be all better now, right Dad?"

I glanced at Frieda, whose smile looked as if it were being held up by guy-wires.

"God willing," I said.

My son's instant grin confirmed what was a given in his mind, for what reason could God, who is perfectly good, possibly have for not healing his ailing father, a righteous priesthood holder, a high councilman, and, of course, his one-and-only dad?

Blessings two and three were administered in more exclusive company, minus Andrew.

I keep postponing that inevitable talk, not because I'm secretly expecting a miracle cure, but because once I state the obvious, things in our home will never again be the same. They are different enough now, but at least we maintain a charade of normalcy. And I want to preserve that for as long as possible. In the meantime, I mentally rehearse the script, hoping that when the moment arrives, Andrew will know his lines better than I know mine.

8—⸸

As we cross the Platte River, a little irrigation ditch that even the smallest in our pioneer party can leap with a single bound, Bradley hands out sticks of beef jerky. "Here, have a pioneer snack!" I thank him and take a giant bite, chewing voraciously, although it, like everything else I put in my mouth, tastes fecal and raises havoc within. When I think no one is looking, I spit it out like a wad of tobacco. But I'm too slow on the take, and one of the Boyak girls catches me. She kindly averts her eyes, embarrassed for me, and I avert mine.

Fort Laramie is a boulder at the top of a ridiculously gentle rise that sucks and squeezes the oxygen from my lungs. By the time

I reach the summit, I'm panting like an asthmatic. Breathing is futile, like trying to blow up a balloon with a hole in it. I smile at everyone: Frieda, Andrew, Gary, Bradley, Colleen ... "Nice scenery," I gasp, motioning to a weedy area where thistles with fat purple bulbs and yellow flowers bloom.

Colleen eyes me nervously as Gary reads the note:

We were delayed at times on account of our handcarts becoming rickety, having been made of green timber. We would have to wrap them with rawhide, saved from the animals that had died or been killed for beef. The hide was cut into strips, and these were used to wrap the rim of the wheels when the tires became loose. The end of a strip was fastened to the felly by means of a small nail to hold it in place. As the weather became cooler with more storms, the tires tightened up, and the hide strips wore through and the pieces were left hanging to the wheels. I remember pulling some of these pieces off and roasting the hair off and eating them.

I'm still trying to comprehend the lessons I'm supposed to learn from this. Empathy for the chronic sufferers of the world? Gratitude for the little pleasures in life, like enjoying a sunset meal with my family? Pride goeth before the fall? Or is this a final test of my spiritual mettle?

I search the scriptures daily for comfort and relief: If I walk into the very jaws of hell, fret not, for you have trod a thousand miles in my moccasins. Am I greater than thee? You will give me no trial or temptation greater than I can bear ... There must be opposition ... Those you love, you chasten ... (Then, sir, love me a little less, please.)

Or are you reducing me to a cross for someone else to carry? Is this Frieda's trial too? Unconditional love, patience, long-suffering? But why instruct her at my expense, or vice versa? Is this your way of pushing the envelope? Putting our feet to the refiner's fire? But why burden us both? And why create crosses? Hasn't the planet got enough to go around already? All the screaming orphans! You know I really think sometimes this would be a whole helluva lot easier if I were suffering frostbite and cholera to build the New Jerusalem. At least I could go down swinging and leave some kind of legacy behind. Something besides stained sheets and a bottle of painkillers. Because right now I'm not feeling one bit noble or courageous, in case you haven't noticed. Right now, I'm feeling weak, tired, humiliated, degraded, ashamed, abandoned, used up, worn out, cast off, and pretty pissed off at life, death, the universe, and just about everything in it!

Do you, Richard Tolman, comprehend the fabric of eternity?

I know that line! I KNOW ALL OF THAT! Doing a job on Job. Curse God and die. Thy ways aren't my ways. You see the big picture; I'm living in the lowly here and now. To you, it's the twinkling of an eye; for me, every day it's hell freezing over and thawing out again. I hate this! I hate it! Do you know what it's like—oh, of course you do! You know everything! Then tell me, how do you do this graciously? How do you do it without being a pain in everyone's butt including my own? How do you—oh, I know. I know I know I know I know I know. But, Father, I wanted to grow old *with* her, not without her.

⸺⚷⸺

It's our turn again, already, to drag the handcart. "Come on, Dad!" Andrew hollers, grabbing me by the hand. "Let's get in back! Let's be pushers again!"

Yes. Let's. And thank God that it's downhill. This quarter-mile trek has exhausted me. I feel, and probably look, a hundred years old. I'm counting the minutes until I can swallow that sweet green capsule that will mercifully deliver me to another time and place, where I inhabit a new and glorified body that can outrun, outjump, outbike, outswim, outlove anything remotely resembling what I've turned into. On the outer edge of the park healthy young couples are swatting tennis balls inside a chain link cage. The clouds are big black boxing gloves colliding in slow motion as lightning pulsates ominously on the mountain. Frieda begins singing in her soft, haunting alto: "Come, come, ye saints, no toil nor labor fear …"

By the time we reach Independence Rock, a slightly bigger boulder than Fort Laramie, my body is numb but nauseated, the double ache you feel when the Novocain wears off. I turn away from the group, trying to gather myself and clear my eyes, which are blurring around the edges, like windows frosting up in winter. I resist the pending blindness, nagged by an irrational fear that if my eyes shut now, they may never reopen. Emily Boyak reads:

On the 12th of October, Captain Willie was forced to cut our rations again, this time to 10 ounces for men, 9 for women, 6 for children and 3 for infants. Leaving the Platte River, we soon came to more hilly country. We dragged along, growing weaker every day with our provisions getting lower. We had to leave everything we had no immediate use for and toiled on in our weakened condition with very little to eat until we came to what was known at that time as the 3 Crossings of the Sweetwater. Here the last dust of flour was dealt out, and the next morning we found 18 inches of snow on the level. Captain Willie and a man by the name of Elder left our camp in search of help.

One night, I woke up drenched from the waist down, and not with sweat. I let out a grotesque groan: "Noooo!" Frieda rolled over to comfort me, stopping abruptly as her hand searched the sheets: "Brian? Oh, Brian!"

I crawled out of bed, peeled off my soaked garments, and ran a hot bath. In the meantime, she changed the bed sheets, covering the wet spot with a towel. But I hid in the bathroom until the alarm bleeped at six-thirty.

"Brian!" she said, knocking on the door. "Brian, I've got to get in there! I've got to get ready for work."

I didn't look at her when I passed by. I couldn't. She didn't say anything about it, which was good in some ways, worse in others. When I returned from the office that afternoon, there was a box of Depends on the bathroom sink. That night I stayed up until she went to bed, then curled up on the living room sofa. I'd barely dozed off when I felt the soft press of her body behind me, her voice whispering in my ear. "I want you in there, with me."

"I won't wear those damn things!" I said.

"That's okay," she said. "It was a bad idea."

There were moments like that, when she could be so gentle, handling my ego like a delicate little bird. But other times, the stress and strain wore her patience threadbare, like that awful afternoon in Dr. Clark's office, after shelling out another thousand dollars for

more X-rays, lab work, an alphabetical battery of acronymic proce-
dures signifying nothing.

"So, what you're telling me," Frieda said belligerently, "is there's
nothing wrong!" She crossed her arms threateningly, like a hitman
with a bone to pick—or several to break. She wanted a name for
the damn thing—a fancy, ugly, polysyllabic, Latin-sounding, vali-
dating name.

Dr. Clark cleared his throat and clarified. "Whatever the problem is, it's not showing up on the charts."

"So, it's psychosomatic!"

"No. The pain is real—very real. And his condition is obviously …
We just can't detect—"

"Psychosomatic!"

As they tilted with semantics, I sat on the edge of the exam-
ination table like a little child being metaphorically cut in two,
Solomon style. They sounded like a cranky husband and wife
bickering over the spoils of their imminent divorce. I had become a
third party in the debate, having given up hope months ago.

"I don't know how long, if that's what you're asking. It could be
years."

"That's not what I'm asking!"

"Look, we'd nuke the damn thing if we knew what it was!"

A week later, Frieda and I had it out, more or less. It was
Christmas Eve, and we were up late wrapping a few last-minute
gifts to slip under the tree. I wanted to talk about it, she didn't, but
I kept pressing her, like a pathetically desperate lover, until finally
she said what I knew she'd been thinking for some time: I was self-
ish, obsessed, a one-track boor; all I ever thought or talked about
was myself, my silly condition.

I exploded. I roared at her. "YOU THINK I ENJOY THIS! YOU
THINK I LIKE BEING THIS WAY! YOU THINK—"

She closed her eyes and took a deep, calming breath, choosing
her words carefully. "When we got married, I think we both had
certain expectations …"

"Expectations! What you're really saying is, if it were cancer or
leukemia, that would be different. But somehow this is all my fault!"

I waited several moments, then answered for her: "The bottom line is, you can't respect someone like that—someone who allows something like this to happen. And you can't love someone you don't respect."

No answer. A rough, angry tearing of paper. Creasing and folding. "Is silence assent?"

"Pass me the Scotch tape, please."

⸱⸱⸱

I imagine myself back in their lonely camp—tired, hungry, my flesh burning wherever the cold has chewed it to the bone, and no relief in sight. My eyelids close without resistance as the first faint drops of rain tickle my face. For a moment, I see myself sprinting down the sandy trail a few desperate feet ahead of the pack, the salty sweat dripping in my eyes, half-blinding me, the lactic acid hardening like cement in my legs and arms. With every stride, I can hear terrible snapping sounds. They may be twigs or they may be bones. If they're mine, I can't tell. I'm beyond pain or thanksgiving. My eyes are pinwheels, the world around me a psychedelic blur of blue, brown, and green. Yet I hear Frieda's voice above all the others cheering me as I stagger across the finish line, feel her hands on my shoulders easing me down onto the pavement, her lips softly touching mine. I hear words of love and praise and miracle whispered in my ear, words I thought had been lost at the bottom of the Grand Canyon.

When I look again, Frieda is watching me with the most peculiar expression, a mixture of fondness, love, compassion, and fear. Her eyes seem to ask, across the mass of friends: You okay?

I almost smile. I almost bow my head and say yes.

She grabs the handle on the handcart and orders everyone to heave-ho: "Let's go; we've got weather! Let's hightail it to Zion!"

As if on cue, a crooked scimitar splits the blackened sky. Seconds later, a bomb explodes and the mountain roars like a badly wounded beast. Suddenly, it looks and sounds like a scene from *Die Götterdämmerung*. Any moment, Wagner's Valkyries will swoop down to gather up the warrior dead.

The sixteen of us swarm the model handcart, speeding it past Fort Bridger without stopping as the summer rain pellets down.

Plucking the note from the trail sign, Frieda reads one-handed as she walks and pulls:

When we broke camp, we waded the Sweetwater Springs. Here the country began to level out again, for we could see the campfires for hours before we reached them. In traveling after night through the frost of that altitude, my brother, Thomas's right hand froze while pushing on the back of the hand-cart. My brother, John, overcome by exhaustion, was laid by the roadside to await the sick wagon. When he was picked up, he was frozen in 2 places on the side of his body nearest the ground. When Thomas got to the fire with his frozen hand, it soon presented a sad picture. It had swollen up like a large toad. That night we had to make camp without water. Twelve people died and in the morning 3 more died. All 15 were buried in one grave. Mother had to melt snow to thaw our hair from the ground where we slept. My brother, John, and I had pulled together on the same cart from Iowa City. We toiled on, doing the best we could, until he became disabled the evening we reached South Pass. My two younger brothers, Richard and Thomas, being too small to render much service.

Five minutes later we are all gathered around the barbeque pit near the ramada where Frieda staked the last trail sign: *Salt Lake Valley*. The sky is a big ugly bruise, but the rain has softened to intermittent spittle, more refreshing than annoying. Kneeling beside the lacquered wooden bucket, Bradley flicks a switch that sets his automatic ice cream maker in motion. Frieda offers some closing remarks about our debt to our pioneer ancestors, admonishing us to demonstrate similar faith and resolve in our equally trying times. "Our trials are different," she says. "Theirs were snow, hunger, thirst, disease. Physical villains. Ours are much more subtle and devious ..."

"Like MTV," suggests Colleen gravely.

"Or Democrats," quips Bradley Boyak.

Colleen reads the last excerpt:

When we arrived at the last crossing of the Sweet Water, Cyrus H. Wheel-lock of Don Jones's party met us with provisions. He could not restrain his tears, when he saw the conditions the saints were in. Some of the people were so hungry that now they had food they were unwise in eating and died from the effects of it. Louisa herself was very sick and while traveling next day lay down on the snow and begged Mother to go and leave her. We had been 3 days before relief came and many had died with hunger and cold. 14 being buried in one grave at Pacific Springs. My brother John and Thomas were both badly frozen. But on the 19th of November 1856 Mother was truly rewarded for her faithfulness in arriving in Salt Lake City with all her children. Although she had laid her frail, sweet stepdaughter Eliza on the plains, she was privileged to bring all her lambs to the fold. As soon as she arrived, she had a piece of sagebrush removed from her eye, which had been causing her a great deal of pain for some time.

Sometimes I hear him howling late at night, flinging hail like wedding rice against the glass, calling me out. The morning after, I can see his breath and fingerprints on the window, marking the spot where he's been watching, like a peeping Tom or a cat burglar casing the house. I imagine him in different guises. Maybe he's a used car salesman, Tex Earnhardt with a ten-gallon hat and a bolo tie, straddling a Brahman bull: "Come take advantage of our Mother's Day sale! A one-thousand-dollar rebate on all …" Maybe he's Monty Hall screaming, "Come on down, and Let's Make a Deal to End All Deals!"

More often, though, he comes not as a dark-hooded clansman but the kindly, frosty-haired grandfather with swollen arthritic knuckles who, from his sickbed, mesmerized my child's mind with bear-hunting tales. He puts his gnarled hand in mine and leads me towards the translucent veil where I can distinguish the sketchy silhouettes of my father and mother on the other side, waiting eagerly to greet me. I hear sweet, angelic music, and voices as tranquil as the sound of summer rain.

I step boldly forward, but each time, nearing the threshold, I'm stopped by reconsiderations. Am I being lured away prematurely? Seduced by a little travail? Once I cross the line to that kinder, gentler place, I'll never be able to cross back again; this border check is final and unforgiving. The smiling attendant in white asks if I have fruit, knives, or other mortal contraband? He doesn't tell me in advance what or how much I can take with me. Or is this the great leap of faith? Discarding all earthly pleasures and pains to move on to a bigger and better? Are we ants in a jar blinded by the security, or insecurity, of the known?

Come, follow me.

Try it; you'll like it.

But he doesn't tell me that I just may miss the smell of peppermint and jazz and woodsmoke on a cold winter morning. Doesn't remind me I'll never again stand on top of Engineer Peak gazing across the Colorado Rockies, or watch my boy execute a slide tackle or bear his testimony in Japanese at his missionary farewell; or make love to my wife, or cook her a Spanish omelet, or make her laugh. Not in this life. And he doesn't tell me that someone else will.

⚷

As we commence the closing song, the last verse of "Come, Come, Ye Saints," Gary Henderson leans towards my wife and whispers in her ear. She turns and smiles at him oddly. It is a gesture of friendship, but not altogether friendship. I'm surprised at what a striking couple they make, but not altogether surprised. And I wonder: What am I doing here, beside Bradley and Colleen, when I should be over there, between Andrew and Frieda?

We squeeze under the ramada for refreshments, Bradley's homemade root beer floats. The kids devour theirs in seconds and then sprint off to the playing fields, half of them tossing their Styrofoam cups into the trash can, the other half dropping them thoughtlessly on the ground.

"Pick that up, you litterbug!" Colleen scolds one of her errant seven.

As the Boyak girls play keep-away with a soccer ball, Andrew assumes a catcher's crouch behind a paper plate. He punches his fist into his baseball glove and hollers to me: "Come on, Dad! Throw some smoke!" Frieda flashes me her Milky Way smile, the one I can't refuse. I trot over to accommodate.

Andrew tosses me a fluorescent-green tennis ball and begins flashing fingers between his skinny, bare thighs. I paw the imaginary rubber, shake off his first sign, okay the second. Leaning back, I cock and lift my left leg while wrenching my right arm geekishly behind my back, delivering a cool sidearm fastball at the ankles in the manner of Don Drysdale. I tell my son *nice catch, wayta block that plate*! I add a little play-by-play from my sandlot days, dating myself: "Runners on first and third, two outs, bottom of the ninth, Mantle at the plate, Maris on deck ... Here's Drysdale with the windup, the pitch— curve ball, got him swinging! Mr. Clutch takes three and sits down!"

Grinning, Andrew glances over at Connie Henderson, watching from under the ramada. Her thread of a smile quickly widens to a half-moon. Noticing me noticing him noticing her, Andrew looks away, happily embarrassed.

The tennis ball feels like a shotput in my hand. Every pitch is a cigarette, shaving two hours off of my life. Or two years. Yet for a moment, surely the first this evening, perhaps the first in months, I enjoy a brief respite; call it peace. And to me it's as miraculous as those two sea biscuits were to Frieda's starving ancestors as they huddled around the campfire at Winter Quarters.

So, I wonder, second guess: Does God grant us these occasional Kodak moments as a celestial carrot to keep us going, enduring to our predestined end? If it's a trick, a holy ploy to persuade me against my will, it almost works.

I look at the ramada where Frieda is laughing, her voice floating effervescently above the crowd. If I exit early, she'll have as many suitors as Penelope, panting at her door. And unlike the crafty Queen of Ithaca, she won't have the luxury of unweaving by night what she has woven by day. She will remarry in time. Of course, the lucky fellow will have her on loan only. But I wonder: while she is sharing her life and body with someone who is at his best while remembering me at my worst, will these last two years obscure the previous eleven, and in her heart will she belong to this stranger, although by eternal covenant she'll be mine? Or will she? Is there reneging on the other side? If the heart plays more or less fondly?

But my selfishness is showing—or my humanness. If I truly love my wife, won't I have that other inevitable talk, the one I can't even begin to script in my mind? Or is this where I draw a line on the law of consecration?

Another silver flash above the peaks, followed by more mountain bellows, and a shot of cool summer spray. As Gary and Bradley begin packing up the ice chests, the women holler to the children who stampede across the field like a herd of wild ponies. We load up our vehicles and say our farewells. Gary magnanimously offers to return the handcart to the Millets—he insists—sparing me the burden of dragging it back the half mile I brought it. (Thank you, my priesthood brother, or did you know all along?)

By the time we arrive home, the rain has stopped, and the clouds are breaking up. Andrew, running on the infinite energy of youth, rounds up his friends for a short game of flashlight tag. Exhausted from her Cecil B. DeMille production, Frieda collapses on the living room sofa to catch the last ten minutes of *Star Trek: The Next Generation*. I tell her to go to bed; I'll take care of things. "After a performance like that! What a show! You really outdid yourself—"

She smiles and thanks me for all my help, extends her hand. "I never could have done it without—"

I load the dishwasher, sweep the kitchen floor, and call Andrew inside. It takes a while, but eventually he bursts through the back door, hot and winded. By the time I trudge upstairs he is sitting up in bed, poring over strategy manuals for his *Wing Commander* game. I plop down beside him and wrap an arm around his bony shoulders. Kisses are out: he's too old, too tough, too almost-junior-high.

"Good night," I say. "Don't forget to say your prayers!"

"Okay."

"I love you, Andrew."

"Love you, Dad."

I linger in the doorway admiring his perfect little face, and the way his chest lifts and settles like a gentle ocean swell. There's something I need to tell him, something about Connie Huntington and the secret smile that passed between them, but I'm not sure exactly what. Is now the time for our inevitable talk?

He lowers his *Wing Commander* book and looks up, annoyed. "Do you have a staring problem?"

I smile, blow him a mock kiss. "Don't forget—"

"I know, I know."

When I reenter the family room, Frieda is crashed out on the sofa, while Worf the Klingon warrior tries to negotiate peace with a bizarre-looking hermaphrodite from Planet Somewhere. Frieda's face appears to have aged in her brief sleep. Scrunched against the sofa pillow, her lips look swollen and pouty; her mouth sags sadly, and the skin around her eyes appears wattled. Threads of gray are tucked strategically behind her ear. And I realize that she too is growing older. I bend down, brush her ringlets back, and kiss her tenderly on the cheek, as if for the last time.

Then I slip out the sliding glass door, past Frieda's flower garden, and kneel in my private spot between two Gambel oaks. My eyes rise to the heavens where a half-moon is squeezing between two bulging black clouds, like a breech birth. When its full face appears, I see this image: Death eating a sea biscuit. Splitting it with me. That skull-faced smile. It's a fluorescent tombstone: the dimmer, lesser glory I may inherit if I'm judged solely by the intentions of my heart.

I bow my head, close my eyes, and begin my nightly talk with my Father. Tonight, I don't debate the justice of my plight or petition for an early release. I don't rant and rave about my powerless position. Tonight, I thank him for carrying me safely to the Promised Land. I assure him I'm not being facetious. I thank him for those priceless moments on the mound throwing sidearm strikes to Andrew, and for fifty-one years on this beautiful planet, eleven years with beautiful Frieda. I thank him for the pioneer men and women of steel plodding across the wind-swept plains, wearing rags on their feet, pulling strips of rawhide from the handcart wheels and chewing them for dinner.

Ten minutes into my prayer, I'm feeling better, stronger. I think maybe I can skip the green pill tonight. Just maybe. But first I have some questions about this wonderful promise called resurrection, our bodies gloriously restored to their youthful prime and vigor. I ask him, what if you never had a prime? Suppose you were born armless or legless or eyeless or clueless? Then what of body restoration? Or suppose you prefer blue eyes to brown, or the nose is a little too hooked in your opinion, the hips a bit too wide? Will there be plastic surgeons in heaven? Or will it be more like shopping for new clothes, a mix and match of body parts with racks and racks to choose from? Will we be uniformly bleached celestial white? Or will brown, black, red, yellow, and California tan be among the color options? Will there be mountains to climb, races to run, kisses to give and receive? Or have I run my last footrace—in the here and in the hereafter?

I tell him it's all academic, beside the point. I want Frieda. I want Andrew. Anything else is icing.

LOOSE CONNECTIONS

Toby Dalton didn't earn many merit badges—in fact, he barely earned the pedestrian rank of First Class—but his scouting deficiencies were easily redeemed by his father, a sportswriter for the *L.A. Times* who, once a year, spotted our entire troop tickets to an L.A. Dodgers game. Box seats, right behind home plate.

Toby's father wasn't a member of the church, but Sister Dalton was, though she didn't always dress like it. Tall and shapely with arctic blond hair trimmed shaggily at the shoulders, she liked to show a lot of leg, even at Sunday services. She favored miniskirts with fishnet stockings, a look popular among the blossoming young girls at our junior high school. We all thought she was the cool mom. We assumed she could dance to our kind of music simply by the way she moved, her heart-shaped hips swaying to a secret beat that wasn't the province of our homemade, whole-wheat mothers of Zion.

Other than the Daltons, who were half-and-half, there were only three LDS families in our neighborhood. Whenever my mother drove up to the junior high in her two-tone, twin-fin Saratoga clunker, the other kids would nudge and snicker. Their mothers drove Cadillacs and looked more like Sister Dalton. Although my mother always greeted me and my older sister with a smile and a cheerful "How was your day?" Kara was cruel in the back seat. She would cover her head with a gym towel, clap her hands, and shout loud enough for outsiders to hear: "Home, James!" The kids on the curb would point and laugh, while my mother silently ignored them: kids will be kids; dickheads will be dickheads.

Usually. If she was having a bad day, she would stop the car and scold us. "Snot-nosed little ingrates" was her favorite epithet. She also liked to remind us that she'd driven all the way from Tarzana to pick us up so we wouldn't have to take the school bus, and this was her thanks! We treated her like dirt—just like dirt! She would usually finish with some kind of token threat: "Who do you think I am, your slave? Your colored maid? Well, I'm not! And you'd better remember that, or you'll be *walking* home next time!" We would be penitent for a season, or at least for the remainder of the drive home.

One particularly bad day, she said nothing, not even her usual cheerful greeting as we climbed into the back seat. When I peeked at the rearview mirror, I noticed tears shellacking her cheeks. Even my flinty little heart softened for a moment.

"Mom?" I said. "What's wrong?"

"You have no idea," she sniffled. "No earthly idea."

She was quiet the rest of the drive and most of that evening.

My father came home late that night, which wasn't unusual. He often had church meetings or something going on at the high school. I was already in bed when he arrived home and should have been asleep, but I wasn't. I could hear my mother's voice in the kitchen. She was angry, speaking in the same sharp tones she sometimes aimed at me and my sister. She wasn't screaming, but she wasn't holding back either. I heard the word *hypocrite* two or three times and *tramp* half a dozen. By contrast, my father's assertive voice was reduced to a meek whisper. There were several long stretches of silence, and during one of them I dozed off.

When I woke up the next morning, my father was gone and my mother was quiet at breakfast.

"Where's Dad?" I asked.

"He left for work."

"Already?"

"He had to go in early. Eat your pancakes. You're going to miss the bus."

"I have to take the bus?"

"Yes. Now hurry up."

A few weeks later we struck it rich when Mr. Dalton gave our scoutmaster tickets to watch Sandy Koufax pitch against the Chicago Cubs. My father readily volunteered to help chaperone and provide transportation, which meant we could squeeze three other scouts into the back seat of his Plymouth Valiant, with me riding shotgun up front. That was the plan.

Even though Mr. Koufax threw his first pitch a good four feet above the catcher's grasping mitt, it turned out to be a pitcher's night. Outfielder Lou Johnson would get the only hit and score the lone run on a throwing error. I can still see him sprinting home, eyes bulging as if bloodhounds were snapping at his heels. Mr. Koufax would retire twenty-seven consecutive batters, striking out fourteen of them, including the last six. Zeros lined the scoreboard except for those three aberrations: one hit and one run for the Dodgers; one error for the Cubs. When he fanned Chicago's last hope, Harvey Kuen, a galaxy of flashbulbs lit up the stadium. Blue seat cushions sailed out of the stands like square Frisbees at the beach. In seconds they checkered the infield. Teammates in Dodger blue stormed the mound and hoisted Mr. Koufax to the stars.

I have a generic recollection of the obvious: the smell of hot dogs and cigarettes, roasted peanuts and chocolate malts. The giant orange ball with a white 76 in the center mounted on a flagpole. The scoreboard flashing PERFECT GAME!!!! The shared euphoria of the fans as we merged into a single mass and poured out the exits.

What I recall most vividly, however, occurred an hour before Mr. Koufax's first erratic pitch, as my father's car was following the trail of red taillights snaking up Chavez Ravine like a river of molten lava. We'd all met at the church prior to the game—twelve scouts, three cars, three adult drivers, and Sister Dalton in a zebra-striped miniskirt and a cream-colored blouse that fit so tight you could see every lovely curve and crease in her upper body. At the last minute she'd decided to attend the game, and who could protest? She held our admission tickets in her black suede purse. She'd also decided to ride with us. She sat up front, in my place— my mother's place, if she had been present—which I resented at first.

However, my resentment soon turned to curiosity and then to something else that seemed at once confusing and exhilarating. I'd never seen Sister Dalton so up close and personal, and I couldn't take my thirteen-year-old eyes off of her. From the back seat I watched her silver earrings dangling like fishing lures and her soft jawline moving in a slow, liquid rhythm as she worked on a stick of gum. I wondered if the Marilyn Monroe mole on her left cheek was real or cosmetic. One thing was certain: the prominent bulge of her breasts was authentic and magnificently magnified each time she turned sideways to talk to my father, who answered her tersely, his eyes fastened to the pavement.

While I tried to avoid the appearance of leering, I did look long enough and hard enough to discern the lacy outline of Sister Dalton's brassiere. This stoked within me a reaction that felt exhilarating, embarrassing, uncomfortable, and shameful. Every time she took a breath it seemed as if the seven seas were in motion, and I was riding one of its fatal waves straight to hell.

As my father's car followed the laggard traffic towards the parking lot—a vast desert of blacktop filling up quickly—an old VW bug packed with college kids pulled up alongside us. One young man with wild Einstein hair pressed his hands and face to the glass like a lizard in a cage. Another man with a sketchy mustache poked his head out the passenger window, shouting: "Sir! Hey, sir! The young lady can come with us!" He gave a wolf howl, and the car sputtered off, leaving in its wake a trail of noxious car farts.

Sister Dalton turned to my father, who in my eyes had always been little more than an innocuous high school math teacher, and asked, "What did they say?"

My father stared chastely at the road, pretending not to hear. Sister Dalton twisted her buoyant body to face him more directly, addressing him not as "Brother Harrison" but by the nickname he and my mother shared alone: "Hanky, what did they *say*?"

In the rearview mirror I saw my father's eyes close painfully, as if Sister Dalton had just inserted a knife into his liver. "I think they were trying to say you're cute," he grumbled.

Sister Dalton giggled like a teenager, waving the remark aside as if it were a pesky fly. Her body angled towards my father's, her red-tipped fingers circling the crisp, plaid arm of his sport coat, tightening briefly, then letting go. I stared at the negative space between them, their silhouettes like two pieces of a puzzle yearning to be pressed together, locked tight, whole.

LETTER WRITTEN TWO DAYS AFTER HIS EXCOMMUNICATION FOR CONDUCT UNBECOMING A LATTER-DAY SAINT

Dear President,

You don't know what you don't know. I once had a woman who swayed on the dance floor like a tall, slender tree in a summer breeze. Men circled her like sharks at first, then obedient planets. I knew I had it good but … that's an old song. I still write her on occasion to say it wasn't her fault.

Fault? Tell me, what is this gift, this peculiar birthright? I humbly, respectfully, return it. But the kindly old couple in white points to the neon sign behind the counter: *Sorry. No refunds or exchanges.* Then may I, please, share my gift with my brother? They appear anxious, even a little perturbed, when I ask. The woman resembles my maternal grandmother, eyes like the sky after a rainstorm, while the man bears an unfortunate resemblance to W. C. Fields. Both manage to smile. "Would you seriously want to do that?"

You don't understand your own hesitation, but I do. You think you are being so brave with your sledgehammer compassion, but I dare any one of you to descend into the pit with me for even ten minutes. I will light and lead the way, unraveling a ball of yarn like Theseus in the monster's maze. A guaranteed trip home. Just ten minutes with this Minotaur. He too bears your head, your arms, legs, loins. The resemblance, you will see, is uncanny. But remember: this is no TV show. You must meet yourself to understand yourself. Little boys become big boys; little girls, big girls. Boys kiss girls and girls kiss boys.

Or is it really so simple? Isn't it more like the Moon with its many changing faces? If the body is ninety-eight percent water, and the Moon its mistress, and Moon and water are woman ... You complete the syllogism. God inscribed his preference on our hearts and in our minds. So we inherit two hard drives. For some they match. Most, you say? If God's inscription is as sure and indelible as the hallowed engravings on your Golden Plates, then our faulty human software is to blame. Or maybe not. Maybe this was God's intent from the beginning.

Listen, please. She offered herself on a platter of midnight lace, like a magic potion, a cure. She was exemplary by all measures. The virtuous woman of Psalms. But listen: they have tried all manner of do-goodedness and therapy. I have slept with electric eels. I have knelt at the holy altar and cradled a weeping woman in my arms. I have clubbed myself for passive resistance and have watched her face crack a thousand times like a bad-luck mirror. I have suffered her fed-up taunts and attacks and have witnessed the resurrection of my manhood in forbidden company.

I went home alone, curled up in my stucco box, and tried to hibernate until God returned with his terrible, swift sword. I made love to myself a million times and hated myself a million more. I read many books. In my loneliness, I cried out to the skeletons in my closet. I cried to God, who appeared in a white sailboat on perfectly calm waters: Peace be unto you! I positioned myself between good and evil, instructing them each to prop an elbow on the table and clasp hands: Go! And they arm-wrestled for my soul.

What you don't understand is the bad guy isn't necessarily the one wearing the skirt or chasing it. The good guy, I think, is whoever will kiss the leper even though every kiss is a time bomb. I am three parts this, two that. It's not oil and water but cake and ice cream. Bread and butter. Or can be. I am what I am not. You are. I look in your eyes and see sadness. I look in their eyes and see storms. We frighten them to fury.

The pews are filled with noise. Lies. Promises. Courage in a plastic two-liter bottle. For best results, read the scriptures and gargle caffeine-free Coke twice daily. Only God knows my hands, my fingers, my heart.

Someday maybe you will understand a fraction of our despair.

I don't know when or how. Nor do I wish this hell upon you or any of them. You did what you had to do. You followed the book. You followed the rules. But I hope, I pray that I am permanently in your thoughts as you sit down to carve your Christmas bird tonight, to the delight of your congregated loved ones. I hope, I pray that I am ever-present in your thoughts as you lie down with your lovely wife. Maybe when she is gone and your children have moved out, you will begin to comprehend. Maybe, when you trudge home to a weekend of tin foil dinners in front of your flat-screen TV (the iciest of lovers), or yourself—maybe. As you crawl into an empty bed in an empty house, I hope you hear my voice amidst the terrible silence. But even then, remember: for you there is an end eventually, the promise of resurrection and reunion. We, on the other hand, are eternal.

HOW WE DO DEATH

The night he heard the news about Katie Morgan, Frank Williams couldn't sleep. Earlier in the week he'd said some things, not maliciously, half-teasingly, really, to get a little rise out of Stella. "I swear she never smiles. She stalks the halls at church scowling like the Terminator."

"Katie? She has a very good sense of humor. It's a little bizarre sometimes, but—"

"I've never seen her smile. Ever."

"Well, you wouldn't either, if you were married to Roger!"

Roger. Another point of guilt. Something about the office-supplies salesman had always grated Frank. That phony-baloney, deep-bellied laugh and the way he gripped your hand Sunday mornings, staring you in the eye as if reaffirming the NATO Alliance.

"How are you today, Brother Williams?" His aura of one-upsmanship.

"If Katie doesn't tell him where his head is," Stella said, "he'll forget he's even got one!"

She switched off the light and curled up on her side, in her "deep sleep" position. After playing possum several moments, she finally sighed. "Frank? I'm tired, do you mind? I'm really, really tired."

"Try Geritol," he grumbled, giving the covers a tug. "Try vitamin E. Try ginseng. Try anything."

"Oh brother! Grow up, will you?"

"Won't I?"

He hoped so. Fast. Because there was another point of guilt, peripherally related. Less than forty-eight hours before "the incident," Frank had seen Katie at Walker Park. White shorts, a M*A*S*H T-shirt, lace-up midcalf sandals, she was hoisting little

Linda by the hands and swinging her up and out and up and out. Later, Frank would recall the red Kool-Aid stains circling Linda's mouth and spotting her white T-shirt, and the way her baby belly bulged beneath it, and her felicitously piercing "Wheee!" each time she arched into the air, and the exultant cries of his daughter Cassie swinging on the rings—"Watch me, Daddy! Watch!" But mostly he would remember Katie. At that moment she had appeared so young, healthy, athletic—her stern jaw and acute edges softened by the autumn sunlight, red threads glittering in her crisp blond curls, her bare calves firm and glossy. He had felt—oh, not a sexual draw, really, but surely a sensual one. She had been the simple country subject of Homer Winslow or Cezanne. And that image would haunt him for two reasons: it was the last time he saw Katie Morgan whole, and she was smiling.

Or maybe not quite the last time. And maybe not just a sensual draw. That night Katie had appeared to Frank in a dream. They were driving home from church together, alone. They never made it: halfway there they checked into a Motel 6 where they undressed each other swiftly, hungrily, like two famished souls who had suddenly entered the land of milk and honey. Katie slathered him from head to toe with coconut butter, licking him in places he hardly knew he had. Frank was so hot that when she kissed his bald pate, it sizzled.

Although he knew better, Frank would always sense an original connection between their transgression and the ultimate results: the wages of fantasized sin. His only consolation was that it had been her suggestion, her wink, her hand on his thigh. "Come on," she had whispered, leaning into him. "Be daring!" She had smiled like a bride—an experienced one.

Frank's dream proved prophetic, more or less. Two days later, Katie and Roger left town for the weekend, alone. The first time in nine years. They checked into the Hilton in Scottsdale. Except they never made it to the king bed. At least that was how Frank imagined it, "the incident," the first of many to follow. Roger unzipping his pants while Katie prepared herself in the bathroom, the sudden lunge, followed by the sequential tearing of the shower curtain, like big buttons popping. Then a hollow thud and the godawful thrashing and flip-flopping, like a five-and-a-half-foot fish out of water. He ran. "Katie!"

Thank God the bathroom door wasn't locked.

⌗━

"It's … inoperable." The young doctor looked up from his clipboard for the first time since … whenever. Overnight his baby smooth cheeks had stubbled. Patches of sweat darkened his light green tunic. "It's … I think that maybe …" Her hand reached out from the bed and touched his. "It's okay," she whispered. "It's okay."

Later, Dr. Griner, the extra-special specialist, showed her the MRI: two walnuts perched atop her brain like little Siamese twins. "We can't cut," he said clinically. "Not without inflicting permanent damage."

Katie nodded. Okay.

When Ann and Brenda, her visiting teachers, came with flowers and balloons and M&Ms in a glass jar, Katie squeezed each by the hand and smiled. "But they don't know anything about the power of the priesthood. My patriarchal blessing says—it promises—I'll live to see my grandchildren. I've got a family to raise. Four … four children," she said, almost choking on the words.

Brenda's upper lip trembled; Ann smiled knowingly.

"After all," Katie said, gripping the bedrails and with gritted teeth pulling herself upright in bed. "We're all in the same boat, really. We don't any of us know when we're going to go. You, me, Roger. It could be today; it could be twenty years from now. They'll try to shrink it and buy some time, I guess."

How much? they asked without really asking.

"Whatever the good Lord gives me. Enough."

She was brave—everyone said so. Her third day in the hospital, she forced herself out of bed, legs quivering like tubes of Jell-O as she dragged herself to the toilet, shaking her head violently when the nurse rushed in to help: "No! No! No!" She refused pain shots, sleeping pills, medications, even Tylenol. Even when they stuck tubes in her neck and in the sides of her head. "I've got to keep my mind clear. I've got to keep my senses now. Especially now."

"She's a fighter," they said. "If anyone can …" But Dr. Griner cautioned against giving her false hope. She fought it; she fought him: with faith, hope, her Tennessee stubbornness, and, yes, her macabre sense of humor. Brain tumor jokes. "What do you do when someone has a seizure in a swimming pool?" "Throw in the laundry."

The day after her second biopsy, when Dr. Griner entered with his usual doom-and-gloom report, she sat up in bed, head bandaged, legs crossed yoga-style, and began chanting like a Hare Krishna. Griner's jaw dropped. Katie threw her head back and roared: "Get me a tambourine, Doc! Get me a tambourine!"

She came home two weeks early. Her two boys were playing football in the driveway. They dropped their ball and ran over, butch blond heads glistening with sweat, and pressed their hands and faces lizard-like against glass. Her head was turbaned with gauze, her eyes bloodshot, her face red and swollen, as if she had been in a brawl. She raised her hand, which seemed delicately small, and waved. Michael and Jamie stared a moment, then smiled impishly. "Mom?"

Nights were the worst. At home, in her sleep, the walnuts would fog up and transmogrify into crabapples, shriveled breasts, giant testicles. A condor would swoop down with talons clicking and pluck them up, always dragging her along for the ride. Sometimes it was almost comical, like the sausage stuck to the woodcutter's nose. But more often her voice was smothered by the whirlwind, a great sidewinding of sand and ice. Ultimately, she was awakened by a child's whimpering, which turned out to be her own: lullaby sighs downstairs. And then the invisible shredder would kick into gear, labor pangs in all the wrong places, and she would curse the lout for snoring through it all—knowing in her mind he hadn't abandoned her intentionally; his spirit was willing but his flesh had succumbed to exhaustion, joining the semi-dead. She would place her palm on his sandpapery cheek, stealing warmth like a pickpocket.

Nights were the worst. When the smell of woodsmoke seeped in through the cracks and the pines were inverted broomsticks dipped in pitch. Each phase of the moon became her brain, her little life through a telescope: a fake smile, a seahorse, an embryo, a skull.

But in the morning, there were eggs to fry, lunches to pack, hair to comb, teeth to brush, faces to wash. After waving to the yellow school bus as it spewed out a tail of blue exhaust, she would walk home via the greenbelt, past the sledding trail where Roger often took the children on snowy days. Knee-deep in the morning mist, the Indian summer breeze curling the hem of her gown, she became a love-lost heroine in a Gothic romance. Sometimes she almost felt herself walking across the firmament, angelically—or like that great Water-Walker of old. Other times, she trudged home like a wounded soldier in retreat. Always, inevitably, she would stop and kneel on the same grassy patch, head bowed, eyes open, feeling every follicle of sunlight on the back of her neck and each pine needle piercing her kneecaps. She would listen to the private silences—bird flight, the blue morning air, spirits rising from the frosted grass—listening, beyond sound now, only to feelings, the faint hairs growing on her freckled forearms, the dark little continents burgeoning in her brain. Always, inevitably, she would close her eyes and re-ask the obvious: What now? Why now? Why me? Why *us*? Mentally searching the scriptures and conference talks for answers: For the rain falleth upon the good and the evil alike. There must needs be an opposition. The faith of a mustard seed can move mountains. By little things I make great things happen. I give you weakness that you may be strong. And, surprisingly, she took comfort in these reminiscent fragments. A stubborn confidence hardened within her. No. No. No. She gripped the iron rod and refused to let go.

But then her other half countered: Was she being punished for poor parenthood? Lack of gratitude? Not being thankful for all she had? For always seeing the glass half empty? You think you've got it so rough—here, take this! Her doctrinal mind knew better: God doesn't work that way. He wouldn't. He couldn't.

But he has. He did.

And then she would think about Roger and the children and how they would get along without her. And felt guilty about every little thing—Linda throwing her arms around her as she hustled off to work: "Don't go, Mommy! Don't go, pleeeeez!" How she would cry and carry on until she finally had to shove her away, for both their sakes. Hollering at the boys for tracking snow in the house. Yelling at April. Bitching at Roger about the damn house, his job, late hours and rotten pay. Suddenly all the little

spilled-milk crises that had rocked her world seemed laughable.
Almost. She wished it were a year ago, she and Roger laying shin-
gles in the August sun, the smell of hot pine sap and the tangy red
earth. To swing a hammer again! To lug laundry down the stairs!
And then she would gaze up at the mountains, which now seemed
a thousand miles away yet close enough to reach out, touch, burn
her hand on the hot autumn colors, or prick herself on one of the
steepled tips, as the Sleeping Beauty had pricked her finger on the
cursed spinning wheel. She wished she were that beautiful princess
and could sleep for a decade or two, until her children were fully
grown, and then reawaken, whole, to embrace them in their adult
beauty. Wasn't that the promise of the resurrection? The great glory
to come? Ten years, twenty, fifty, a century—it was all the twinkling
of an eye, wasn't it? Until Christ the Handsome Prince would bend
down and awaken all his sleeping brothers and sisters with a magic
kiss. She looked towards the sun, glowing brilliantly above the
mountains like a renewal of the promise, and for a moment, all was
well, with the air so clear and blue and the little trail of clouds like
puffs of God's breath—soft, floating answers to her prayers. But
then a crackle, some floppy-eared dog prancing by, and the ugly
other would switch back on, the steel teeth gnashing and grinding
to the impossibly ancient smell of gunpowder and coonskin caps as
she clenched her eyes again: No! No! No! No! No!

<hr />

The Relief Society sisters brought dinner four or five times a
week, and Saturdays Ann and Brenda came to the house to clean
and help with the laundry. Stella said she could help too, but Ann
and Brenda said no, they could handle it. "Thanks anyway. We're
her visiting teachers. We're glad to do it."

Stella said so was she. "Glad, I mean. To do it."

At fast and testimony meeting Bishop Turner asked the congregation to please remember Katie Morgan in their prayers.
Thereafter, every public prayer included a reference to Sister Morgan. Frank and Stella concluded all their daily family prayers with
"and please bless the Morgans." Kent McMillan, the elders quorum
president, called a special fast on Katie's behalf and that night went

to the house and gave Katie a priesthood blessing: "You will be healed," he proclaimed authoritatively. "You will live to raise your four children. The Lord has revealed this to me. Be of good cheer."

Frank didn't see Katie again until she came to church five weeks after her first seizure. Her face was big and bloated in spots, shrunken in others. Like a Cabbage Patch Doll's. Chubby cheeks and pinpoint eyes. She sat in the side pews with her family, head covered with a paisley scarf, a brown shawl over her shoulders. Silent. Like a refugee who can't speak English and isn't certain if she's truly welcome. Timid. Afraid. Even though everyone shook her hand. Even though the Relief Society sisters all hugged her. They smiled and said how good to have you back! And she smiled and said in short, clipped syllables: Yes. Good. So good. To be. Back. Very good to be. Over the next few weeks her language would return with remarkable eloquence before vanishing for good.

Frank would make four visits to the house, each inspired by an ambivalent blend of curiosity, duty, brotherhood, and the common suffering that unites human beings in distress.

And guilt. There was his adulterous dream, yes, and things he'd said about Katie earlier. And Roger. Katie joined him in the elders quorum now, "just in case." In his confederate-gray suit, back arched pompously, he appeared to be bearing his cross a little too piously and self-righteously, Frank thought, although he knew he shouldn't be critical. Walk a mile in his moccasins … Judge not that ye be not … Acid rain may fall on you too if you're not careful … Still, every time he looked at Katie, sitting there like a damn mannequin, he felt himself getting angry at Roger, as if he were an unwitting accomplice.

Frank's first visit was the night before Halloween. A fat-faced moon was rising out of the pines. Katie was asleep upstairs.

"I'm fine," Roger said, flashing his salesman's smile. "We're fine."

Frank noted encouraging indicators. Taped to the slanting drywall of their cozy A-frame were three paper banners lettered in carnival colors: I'M GREAT!!! I'M HAPPY!!! I'M WONDERFUL!!! Even the freshly carved jack-o'-lantern on the kitchen table grinned with ghoulish optimism. Before it sat a slimy, stringy pile of pumpkin seeds and 3x5 cards: *Guess how many? Michael. Jamie. April. Linda.* Paper ghosts and skeletons were smiling on the walls.

But there was an odd odor in the house. A moldy-bread smell. Pants and jackets were draped over the sofa and soiled clothing piled in the laundry room. Peanut skins freckled the shag carpet. Cheerios spotted the kitchen floor. The TV room was an obstacle course of Fisher-Price toys. The children drifted quietly in and out, like solemn little spirits that any moment might fade away and disappear.

"We're fine," Roger sighed, but his face looked like a tire that had suddenly gone flat. "Yeah," he said, pulling a slimy thread from the pile of pumpkin seeds, "we're just trying to get back into a routine."

☙—

"A tumor is like a growth—a bad growth. There are two little walnuts that keep getting bigger and bigger …" He had tried to explain it to them a dozen times, but Linda was too young and Michael almost seemed too old and April appeared too guilty, as if it were all her fault. Jamie was the only one who finally came right out and asked: Is Mom going to die? "We don't know." What else could he tell them? Faith, hope, miracles. The power of the priesthood. They'd heard his broken record a thousand times now. "I don't know, Jamie. I don't know, April, Linda, Michael. Not if we can help it. Not if God can." But then he corrected himself. "Heavenly Father's will. Not ours. It's in his hands."

But he could read Michael's adolescent scowl perfectly, his mumbling, grumbling lips: Why does God want to take my mother? Why does he need her more than we do? He's supposed to know all and see all and have all. Why our mother? Why us? What did we do wrong?

Or waifish April with her greasy blond hair, her apologetic droop: What did *I* do wrong?

☙—

"*You* need the priesthood blessing," she said. "Not me. Where I'm going, they take good care of you. Not like here."

Roger glared at her. "You're not going anywhere!" he said—hollered. She looked down at her cupped hands, felt like crying but smiled instead. "What's the difference between an Osterizer and a person having a seizure?"

Roger's smile came slowly, belligerently. "I don't know—what?"

"An Osterizer's got an on/off switch."

"Very funny," he said. Smiled. Laughed.

But he bought a do-it-yourself estate planning kit—just in case. Always just in case. "Not just you—it could be me. Driving to work, coming home. Who knows?" They talked about life insurance, trust funds for the kids, CDs, Ginnie Maes. They talked money—*she* did. First thing, pay off the mortgage. Get that monkey off your back. Childcare. For Linda. A fulltime nanny would be best. They discussed everything but a new wife, a new mother. He wouldn't allow it. "Not negotiable," he said, closing his black binder.

⚷

She fought it: every microwave meal she made, every cake she baked ("I did it all by myself!"), every bowel movement absolutely on her own. Every letter she wrote, and she wrote reams. Dear Ann, Dear Brenda, Dear Bishop Turner, Dear Editor, Dear Roger…

Dear Stella,

Thank you for the apple pie. It was wonderful!!! You have always been such a wonderful friend. It's not easy babysitting Linda. Thanks.

I've been thinking of a lot of things lately. Right now, I'm thinking about a lousy, rotten day last winter. We were building the house, living in that cold, dark, dreary basement in the meantime. The kids were at school, Roger was making his rounds, and Linda had kept me up all night again crying her head off. And it was snowing again—like the whole sky was falling in little littered bits and pieces. I was sitting by the woodstove trying to get warm, feeling sorry for myself, thinking about the Jeppersons vacationing in Hawaii and Bishop Turner's big Victorian house with the hot tub, thinking how they have everything and I've got nothing but a half-built house we'll never be able to pay for. And then feeling ugly and guilty about my feelings. Cursing God in my heart for dealing me such a rotten hand. And just about the time I'm ready to do something I would have regretted, guess who comes trooping down the stairs with a plate of chocolate chip cookies, whistling a silly Primary song? "Happy winter!" you said. "Let's celebrate!" And while we were gorging ourselves, you opened the newspaper and checked the weather. "Ha! Honolulu: Cloudy. Rainy. Record lows. Ha! So much for Gladys Jepperson's suntan!" And then we laughed. It felt so good. It was the first time I'd laughed in so long. We talked about our bratty kids, our boring, horny husbands, church—all the forbidden topics. And for a day at least I was truly happy. I don't know what good spirit prompted you to stop by, but thanks.

Stella, I've always admired you, but I felt intimidated too. You're a classy Californian and I'm just a country hick. I could never figure out what you saw in me. This experience has helped. There's pride in everything if you look deep enough.

Love,

Katie

P.S. I just want to be a mom. I just want to sit at the kitchen table and make Valentines with my kids. I just want to cook a nice breakfast and put on their coats and then go and wave goodbye and watch them run to catch the bus just in the nick of time.

8—

"You build walls, you know. Fences. But at dark, that's when they all crumble. Driving around from client to client, you're okay all day until suddenly out of nowhere it hits you like a rabbit punch. Especially at night, driving the empty highways—all that time and space to think and second guess. What if what if what if? You're almost home where you can't hide in your briefcase. I keep telling her, 'I'm okay. I'm handling it, I'm handling it.' I don't know. Maybe she's right. I'm only human. Boy, am I ever only human."

Frank placed his palms gently on Roger's head and, in the name of Jesus Christ, blessed him with faith, hope, courage, endurance, health, strength, wisdom in dealing with his wife and children. "Your suffering is intense; it is great. But it's through our trials we truly come to know and understand our Savior. God's ways are not our ways. His thoughts aren't ours. He knows what is best, and we must have faith in his infinite wisdom. Call upon us for help, Roger, in this time of need. Let us help in that truest sense, brother-to-brother. God bless and strengthen you, Roger. God bless …"

Roger rose from the kitchen chair slowly and tentatively, like a cripple who has just been healed. He turned to face Frank whose hands hung limply at his sides. Roger started to say something, but Frank wrapped him in a bear hug and the two husky six-footers wept in one another's arms.

⊶

She had refused medication. She had also refused to make a farewell video for the children. It was Roger's idea. "No! I don't want them to remember me like this! Not like this!"

At first she had hated looking at herself. Every morning she would confront the bathroom mirror and monitor the rapid metamorphosis of her face: the chipmunk cheeks scrawled with radiation blush, the pencil-point chin, the shiny, lopsided skull that chemotherapy had stripped bald. She would stare and stare until it all became a miserably bad joke, and then she would curl her fingers and cackle, witchlike: "Mirror, mirror on the wall, who's the ugliest ... baldest ... most ravishing ... gorgeous ...?" More than ever she had envied the trim figure and high cheekbones of Stella Williams—Stella with the luscious chestnut brown hair that swung so playfully, tauntingly, below her hips.

But as the pain grew worse—the *real* pain; not of self-image or ego, but the blunt, raw hurt of a thousand rusty zippers on her skin that some invisible sadist kept tearing open and tugging shut all night, all day—the others no longer mattered. Flesh, hair, lipstick, pantyhose—it was vanity, all vanity. For dust thou art, and unto dust ... Her only redeeming virtue was her courage; she would be brave. As long as she could drag herself to church, to the toilet, in and out of bed, she was the hero, the victor. But it hurt, hurt like hell. It *was* hell. Merely moving her fingers shot icy needles up her arms, straight to the bullseye in her brain. Every cell in her body seemed to be frying and freezing simultaneously. Tying her shoes or rinsing a dish was scaling Mt. Everest. Massaging her back, Roger's fingers were like rodents chewing through her flesh. Who cared about mascara and eyeliner?

At night, she could feel the slow, cautious rhythm of the mattress, could hear his hastened breathing, the creaking of bedsprings and the sudden relaxation and simmering of his heart. She said nothing at first, sparing him the humiliation. God forgives little indiscretions—little indiscretions in lieu of bigger ones. It all seemed so silly to her now, although she tried to understand his need, this sticky, urgent male need of his; tried to re-feel the phantom passion, but there was nothing. It was gone. One night, she even said yes yes yes, but it was like being impaled by an oak tree; she thought any moment she was going to split in two. She said it was good, it was fine, right up to the final cry he maybe mistook for pleasure—maybe was just hoping was really a pre-death shriek: the fires of hell spearing her in the groin. Like triple-transitional labor. The end. He knew, really, but neither of them would say so. He thanked her and thanked her, but after that night, he left her alone.

Still, Sunday mornings she would struggle into a dress, trudge downstairs, and present herself to her family: "Behold, the Elephant Woman!" They would smile cautiously. She was winning.

Then one morning at church her scarf fell off revealing a gigantic potato head—lumpy, scarred, stapled. And she laughed. She didn't care anymore. She honest-to-God didn't care.

But after the Inquisition Chamber, when they stapled her skull back together again, lying in the recovery room, she held out her veiny little arm and whispered to him: "Was I brave?"

"Of course. You're always—"

"Honey?"

"Yes?"

"I'm tired of being brave."

He bought the Demerol. Within a week she was on morphine.

❧

Stella had always felt weird about hospitals, cemeteries, funerals, things like that. Maybe because she had watched death take her mother so slowly and gruesomely when she was only twelve. Since then, even the smell of rubbing alcohol made her nauseated. But with some prodding from Ann, she made what she thought would be her last visit to Katie at home in bed. Katie answered her with winks. At first, she tried to bolster her friend's sagging will. "Katie, you haven't given up yet, have you?"

Katie's eyes closed slowly, an excruciating yes.

"Whatever happens, Katie, you'll have left your children a greater legacy than I will if I live to be a hundred. Your courage, your faith, your fighting spirit … You're an example to us all." Wink.

"You make our biggest hurts seem microscopic."

Wink. Wink.

Stella sniffled, wiped her eyes. "Well, next time I'll write down all the boring, dull things I do so I'll have something real to talk about."

Katie shook her naked head. Her frail hand reached out, freckled and scaly, and found Stella's. "You're not dull," she whispered. "Or boring. I always like talking to you."

Stella looked away, hiding her tears. Ann took Katie's hand, stroking it gently as she chatted about mundane matters, as if Katie were a sick little child with a cold. After several moments, Stella turned on her angrily. "Stop it, Ann! Stop! I can't pretend like that. I can't—"

Driving home she apologized to Ann for her outburst.

⸙

"I keep seeing her strapped in that padded chair, in that damn hospital dungeon. There's a helmet on her head with tubes and wires spiraling out of it, like one of those medieval cures for the insane. Her neck's bent like it's broken, and her mouth's all crooked and hanging. They've got her arms strapped at shoulder-level, like she's on a cross. I'm thinking, Blood of the Lamb … Blood of the Lamb … Then they turned on the juice and I couldn't handle it. I ran outside like chickenshit Peter, until they were all through."

⸙

On Thursday the women from the hospice came. "We'll make it as painless as possible," they said. "We'll let nature run its course."

Roger considered this a moment, then panicked. "But what … what if she catches pneumonia or something?"

The women gazed at him curiously—such interesting old eyes, kindly yet stern. "What would you have us do?" they said.

Roger stared at the kitchen floor. For the first time in eight months he noticed that it was speckled with peanut skins.

⸙

At fast and testimony meeting Roger stood at the pulpit and read the testimony Katie had dictated to him two months before. There were thanks for favors and apologies for petty offenses. A passionate restatement of her faith in Christ and of the truthfulness of

209

the church. Thanks to Roger, her children, Bishop Turner, the Relief Society, her visiting teachers, Ann and Brenda. And Stella Williams; a special thanks to Stella. In closing: "If I had to go through the pain and misery ten times, even a thousand times all over again, and died afterwards, I would rather do that than live forty more years the way I was, gnashing my teeth in lukewarm nothing."

⊙—

It was almost time for her medication. He didn't want to give her injections, he said. That was a last resort. "Once I use the syringe, then she can't drink water, and once that happens, she can't eat. That means an I.V. And *that* means ..."

Frank nodded dumbly. He was trying not to, but his eyes kept drifting to the far corner of the living room where Katie lay inert in a bed with plywood sidings: boxed in. One fleshy white arm lay atop the sheet like a lump of pork fat. Frank noted the half-full catheter bag beside the bed and the bedpan underneath. Lilting melodies from *The Little Mermaid* video drifted in from the family room where the children were sprawled out on the floor staring at the TV monitor in the dark. Clothing was strewn about; the moldy-bread smell had settled in permanently. Wads of Kleenex overflowed the wastepaper basket and spotted the linoleum floor like paper turds.

Katie shifted in bed and groaned.

"Her spirit's trapped inside that body," Roger said, and an image flashed in Frank's mind: a giant beast caught in the tar pits, helplessly sinking. A dumb beast, roaring without sound.

Roger pressed his fists to his forehead. Slouched in the folding chair, he looked like a broken prizefighter, his blond cowlick hanging in his eyes, his belly swelling the lower third of his green sweatshirt. He had put on ten pounds since Frank's last visit. Stress, tragedy, had been sending him to the fridge.

"It's over," Roger said. "Right now, she's carrying eight thousand rads in her brain. Griner says a thousand rads, dispersed over the whole body, will kill you like *that*." His fingers snapped crisply. "She's a fighter. She's going down with her boots on. But unless Jesus Christ comes through that door and says, 'Take up thy bed and walk ...' We're just waiting now."

210

Pot-bellied Linda strutted into the room, swiveling her shoulders like a sumo wrestler. "I want to see Mommy!" she demanded playfully. She pulled herself up on the plywood sidings and rolled over onto the mattress, bouncing lightly up and down, big-eyed, grinning like a little demon. Katie's head bounced in unison, a lopsided volleyball.

Frank couldn't pry his eyes from her giant head. A ring of short, scruffy hair wound around the base while an even thinner trail ran down the back of her skull, like a scalp lock. A big bulge protruded from the near side, spidery veins glowing through the whiteness like blue filaments, or like a little light bulb growing inside a much bigger one. This, Roger explained, would keep swelling until the elasticity couldn't accommodate it anymore. And then ...

Frank caught himself counting the indentations where the head plates had been stapled back together. Gruesome little bites. He thought: Dear God, I will never ever ever feel sorry for myself for anything again.

Linda removed something from the plastic bucket on the bed and held it up. "What's this, Daddy?" She was barely three and didn't understand, but at the moment her antics were more annoying than endearing.

"Tissue paper."

She held up a Tampax. "What's this?"

Roger thought a moment. "A stick."

Linda giggled. "No, it not!"

Roger looked at Frank and sighed. Beat. Beaten. "I'm afraid to remarry. What if something like this happens again? I couldn't live through this. Not again." He called to the other children: time for bed. His tone was gentle, conciliatory. A token cry of protest rose from the family room, but the TV soon went off and the children shuffled upstairs to bed like little robots. Linda had cuddled up beside her mother and was feigning sleep.

"I've got the answer," Roger said. He was staring into the living room, half-hypnotized, speaking to the yellow flames swaying lazily behind the glass panel of the fireplace. "I'll buy myself a Porsche—I've always wanted one, you know. And then when I want to get warm at night, I'll go out and sit in it and turn on the heater. And when I've had a hard day and I need coddling, I'll turn on the control panel and a nice, sweet voice will say, 'There, there, Roger, now you just sit back and relax now ...' And then those automatic seat belts that drop down from the ceiling will reach around and hug me tight." He chuckled, but the deep belly gusto was gone. It rang hollow. Frank reminded himself that it was just talk, idle talk. It meant nothing. He was just trying to cope, that's all. A man's not accountable under those circumstances. What would he do in Roger's shoes? Suppose it was Stella—*her* potato head, *her* spirit trapped inside that lump of flesh. Changing *her* diaper, cleaning out *her* catheter, spoon-feeding *her* morphine ... Whatever gets him through the night.

Roger mentioned the insurance money. It was a good policy—a great policy. No one could tell him the Lord didn't have his hand in all this. Three days before her first seizure, for no good reason at all, he'd doubled his life insurance and taken out a policy on Katie. "The Holy Ghost must have grabbed me by the pants and dragged me down to MetLife."

More talk. Pragmatic prattle. He was tired, exhausted. Talking in his sleep. Can a man be held accountable for sleeptalking? For dreams? Nightmares? Roger checked his watch. "It's about that time," he sighed, and trudged into the kitchen, returning with a large spoonful of medication—brown goop. He knelt by Katie's bed so he was facing her backside, away from Frank. He carefully lifted the bed sheet. Frank saw a slice of Katie's white buttocks through the gap between Roger's arm and ribcage. He winced as he watched Roger insert the spoon into her anus. It took several moments. Then Roger lowered the sheet and returned to the kitchen. The spoon clinked in the sink.

"It's hard," Frank said when Roger returned. "I lost my mother when I was seven. She left six of us—the oldest was barely two." He wasn't sure why he had said this. Courage. Roger was going to need far more courage than even Katie now. He remembered: the over-sweet stink of flowers, the forlorn faces of his brothers and sisters watching the melted cheese grow cold on their plates. His father clutching the telephone receiver, his face knuckling up like a fat fist. Bishop Packard's words of assurance at graveside: "Life is like a voyage," he said, "and those of us standing in the port watching the ship disappear on the horizon are lamenting, 'She's gone! She's gone!' But those waiting on the other side—mothers, fathers, grandparents, ancestors—they're all shouting, 'Here she comes! Here she comes!' While one party grieves the departure, the other celebrates the arrival." Everyone nodded. Amen, they said. Then they all marched off to eat. Sixteen different casseroles. A dozen varieties of potato salad. That evening, Frank's father gathered the six children for family prayer: So we all pull together now. We press on. We adjust. We adapt. It's the human way; the Mormon way. Your mother's in Paradise. No more pain, no more suffering …

But that night something strange happened. Around midnight Frank was awakened, not by the sound of his older brother snoring in the lower bunk, but an unsettling sensation. As he opened his eyes, the lights from a passing car momentarily flooded the room, and in that split-second Frank thought he saw a man standing in the doorway. He looked sad, like a heavenly messenger bearing bad news. Frank's first impulse was to scream, but as his eyes readjusted to the darkness, he realized that it was his father. He looked like a black-and-white negative, his head, arms, and lower legs shaded by darkness, and the rest of his body, from his neck to his knees, blanched white by the priesthood garment he wore like a second skin. Frank was barely seven, confused and afraid, so he rolled onto his side, facing the wall, and pretended to be asleep. Moments later he felt a slight tug on the bed, then heard creaking sounds as his father climbed the wooden ladder, lifted the blanket, and crawled in behind him, pressing close, his front to the boy's back. Frank could feel his father's warm, rhythmic breaths on the back of his neck, intermittently broken by what sounded like suppressed weeping. He waited, trying not to move, not to breathe even. He felt his father's hand slide over his little belly, stroking it softly, slowly. That was all, but it felt so strange. He lay there for an hour staring at the darkened wall, until his father's hand dropped limply to the mattress.

There was a whimper upstairs, and a cry. "Daddy! Dad-dee-ee!"

Roger excused himself and plodded upstairs as if such distress cries were commonplace. Frank could hear him talking, comforting. Then a groan: Katie.

He crept over to her bedside. Linda had fallen asleep under her mother's fleshy arm. He briefly monitored the subtle rhythm of her body swelling and shrinking. Life. And then he saw the giant beast screaming silently in the tar pits.

Frank looked around guiltily to make certain no one was watching. His fingertips pressed gently against Katie's great potato head, exploring its lumpy surface curiously, startled to discover little patches of fuzz. Like an infant's head. It was a bizarre feeling that made the hairs on his neck and arms rise as if he were touching a grotesque mold on the one hand while fondling some sacred but forbidden object on the other. It occurred to him that he had never touched Katie Morgan before, except in his illicit dream.

He continued his indiscretion now, stroking her wispy scalp lock and pressing each stapled indentation. Little baby bites. He studied her mouth, barely parted, showing neither grief nor pain nor solace, only fatigue. He recalled that Indian summer day at Walker Park and saw her again in white shorts and a M*A*S*H T-shirt, the afternoon sunlight glittering on her blond curls as she swung little Linda by her arms. Then he did something a bit wicked. He mentally raised Katie from the bed and put Roger in her place: the dead husband, the grieving widow. Briefly he considered their life together, what might have been. Then he saw beautiful Stella withering away in the wooden box like a time-lapse video. Their daughter Cassie was next, followed by his mother and father, his grandparents. Then aunts, uncles, cousins, friends, one by one each of them taking their turn inside the terrible box. He saw himself: petty, pouty, shriveled, small.

He dropped to one knee, his hands trembling as he placed them back on Katie's naked head. He caressed it now, softly, tenderly, like a lover. Then—checking again—he leaned over as if to kiss her goodbye, goodnight. Instead, he fished into his pocket for the key chain with the tiny metal vial of consecrated oil. He unscrewed the cap and poured two drops on her crown, rubbing them gently into her fuzzy scalp. Then he laid his fingertips on her head, and he blessed her with death.

PREMONITIONS

Because for you, Mom—Mother—each time it was like reliving a nightmare, a brief descent to hell and back that always left you mute and lifeless for the rest of the day. Yet, you persisted anyway, even when I (in my youthful belligerence) rolled my eyes and called you a hyper-paranoid broken record. You see, for me it was your excuse to keep me tethered and tending the home fires in my father's premature (and permanent) departure: midmorning, your urgent hands clearing the breakfast dishes as Dave—"Little Davey"—hollered on his way out the back door: "Goodbye, Mom! I'm going out to play with the angels!" A maternal sigh. Angels. You bet. Cute kid. Your firstborn son bounding out into the luscious world on a cloudless summer day, the sun preening above the hills, the garden in full bloom: corn stalks, cherry tomatoes, melons the size of basketballs. I was still in diapers, locked in a highchair, destroying pancakes with my fingers like a mini Godzilla. It wasn't a minute (you said) before we heard the shriek of tires and the terrible clunk like a crate dropped from a tall building.

After that you slept on pins and needles. Calling me at school, scout camp, the Mission Training Center. Calling me at odd hours on the coast: "Jimmy? You mustn't go on that fishing trip down there to Ensenada. I had a dream …"

"You and Martin Luther King—"

"Jimmy, this is serious. You were down to the beach and the waves reached out all of a sudden and pulled you under and wouldn't let you go. I saw Lucifer's face laughing in the water; his arms and legs were like two black snakes reaching and pulling you down, and his terrible teeth were just laughing and laughing. You were underwater, spinning round and round like you were trapped

215

inside a washing machine. Calling for me, Jimmy, you were calling: 'Momma! Momma! Momma!' Just like that."

I told you that I didn't believe in those things, that we all have an appointed time. I even cited scriptures to prove it: II Kings 20:1; Job 7:1; Isaiah 38:5; I Corinthians 4:9; Alma 12:27. And the slam dunk, Doctrine and Covenants 42:48: *He that hath faith in me, and is not appointed unto death, shall be healed ...*"

"When your bell rings, you get off the trolley—no sense fretting about it."

But I was all false bravado, cancelling trips, changing dates, always coloring between the lines. Until the day I didn't.

"Jimmy? Jimmy, you just can't marry that girl."

"Mom, it's two in the morning."

"I have a bad feeling about her. I just do."

"Now you're telling me this? We've already sent out the announcements."

"It's never too late."

"Well, this time it is."

"Don't say I didn't try to—"

"I know, Mom. You always try. A little too hard sometimes, I think."

⸻

So, here's my question, Mother: where were you four months ago with your doom-and-gloom prophecies as I led the twins— your grandchildren, *our* posterity—up the south face of Bear Mountain? A perfect summer day: wildflowers everywhere, pot-bellied marmots playing hide-and-seek in the lichen-crusted granite, the aspens shaking their leaves like cheerleaders. Halfway across the wooden footbridge, Melanie stopped.

"What's that sound?" she asked. "It's like a jet taking off, but it never stops."

I smiled. "You'll see."

We zigzagged up the mountain for an hour. When the trail turned to talus, as loose and shifty as ball bearings, I gripped their wrists—Tanner in front, Melanie behind—and nursed them along the vertical cliff. The trail was wide enough for two, but I wasn't taking any chances.

In another fifteen minutes, we were high enough to see it.

"Look down there," I said, directing their eyes to the long column of white water plunging down into the granite canyon.

"That's so awesome!" Tanner said.

Melanie watched in silence, a smile simmering on her lips.

"Hey, Daddy, if I fell …" A pause. That pixie look of hers, part wonder, part mischief. Definitely the daredevil of the two, my little warrior girl in the making. "I haven't been baptized yet," she said.

"No, you haven't," I said, wondering what peculiar direction the wheels in her head were spinning. "Three more months to be exact."

"So, if I fell, I'd go straight to the Celestial Kingdom, wouldn't I?"

My turn to pause. "Well, yes—yes, you would, but—"

"Tanner too, huh?"

"Yes, Tanner too, but that's not going to happen now, is it, Mel?" My human handcuffs tightened on their wrists.

"Dad, not so hard," Tanner said. Melanie giggled.

We turned back after that, and as we picked our way down the trail, I suffered a dose of your disease, the agony of expectation all those sleepless nights, the obstinate *why* behind the obsessive head-gear and hyper-alerts at every intersection. A quarter mile from the trailhead, I looked down and saw our red SUV shining like a giant ruby in the parking lot, and I finally breathed easy, or easier: home free—although I suppose you never truly are.

As we recrossed the bridge, the roar of the waterfall grew louder, and Melanie begged for a closer look. "Please, Daddy? Pleeeeeez!" You can't keep them on a leash forever. You can't carry them in your hip pocket until they're big enough to carry you.

We veered off through the wildflowers, towards the thunder of falling water.

"Stay away from the ledge," I warned. "Hold my hand."

We stood on a long, flat rock, mesmerized as we watched the river of molten glass roll over the ledge, instantly transforming into a raging white monster that thundered down into a bottomless cauldron of mist and froth.

Melanie tugged my arm. Could she take her shoes off and stick her feet in, just for a second, Daddy? Just one second? Please oh please oh pleeeeez?

Was that pounding in my heart the Holy Spirit warning me away or the Cowardly Lion gene that had nagged me all my life? The one that I didn't want to pass on to my kids?

You always know so much better after the fact.

As I turned to secure Tanner, his eyes bulged like baseballs. I swung around just in time to see his sister's face, all mouth, as big as a manhole, as the water reached up with pure white hands and pulled her over the edge and down.

I know what you're thinking, Mother: what about Tanner, what if he'd slipped?

For a split second, I too sinned: the girl or the boy?

But you can't think about that. You can't think about anything—there's no time for debate; no time to flip a coin. So, you do what any good parent would do—what *you* would have done. You turn to the boy and shout in your most commanding, threatening voice: "Stay there! Don't move!" Then, gently, pleadingly: "Don't move." And then you leap, leaving the other behind, dumbfounded and trusting and hopefully not too courageously stupid to follow. You leap, screaming above the thunder. And during the long, swift fall you pray for multiple miracles: a soft landing, a quick comeuppance, a piece of beach, air, flesh, her little hand somehow finding yours in the white chaos. You beg. You make absurd promises you know you can't keep and offer things you know you'll regret. You bargain: another time, another place; just not here, not now, not her. Anyone, anything, but her. Or him. All this in a seemingly never-ending instant that abruptly ends with a crash you cannot hear because everything around you is perpetually crashing: buildings, cities, skyscrapers of water endlessly crumbling—and one moment you're free-falling in the thick of it, and the next you're not. You feel the impact, a full-body sledgehammer smashing you to smithereens, but the adrenal juices dismiss it for the moment, even as you realize you're still plunging, even as the enraged waters try to rip your limbs from their sockets.

And then you're thrashing in the soup. Fighting in the direction you think is up while the water bullies you under, stuffing you down, down, down. Then, as if it is bored with this repetitive action, or just for the morbid hell of it, because you're flimsy and mortal and *it* is so much greater, grander, and mightier than you can ever possibly hope to fathom, it scoops you up like a kitten and hurls you against the rocks. Two, three, a dozen times until it's bored with that too. Bored with you. Or so you hope and pray. But as it slaps and pounds you with such virulent anger, you realize that you're no mere plaything. There's a message in its madness: how dare you trespass on this sacred place! How dare you challenge this glorious edifice of rock and falling water crafted by God's hands to please the eye and inspire awe and wonder and fear—not boastful conquest, not human sport. How dare you! How dare you defy physics, geology, theology, and plain common sense! How dare you defy inevitability! You, with your petty, puny human ambitions and ideals.

Air, oxygen—gold at the moment. A gulp, a bite of it, then fighting again. Thrashing. The water wrestles you back under, pinning you down until your strength is sapped, your arms and legs are feckless noodles. But you refuse to submit, because you have one thought only: your daughter, your little baby girl, is somersaulting somewhere inside the bowels of that canyon, and you don't care how big, magnificent, powerful, angry, or offended it is, you're not quitting, not surrendering, not vacating, not drowning until you find her. Save her. You're not.

Air. Oxygen. Again. And suddenly the current is mellowing, the mighty hands relenting like Jacob's angel at first light. You're floating almost peacefully through lofty corridors of granite, the tough, craggy faces of the patriarchs glaring down at you less grimly and indignantly, with a trace of pity perhaps, and respect. Maybe even homage. And in the deeper stillness, reverence.

I didn't find her, Mother, but she found me: bones bashed, body broken, face-down in the sand. Unscathed, she found me. Miraculously unblemished, she held my head in her little hands. A miracle. A gift.

And so, I sit here, strapped in this mechanical chair, typing with my teeth, asking myself the obvious: would I do it again—initiate this ruthless exchange of hostages? For this costly outcome? Yes. Of course. A hundred times. A thousand. Yes.

GOODLY PARENTS

The missionaries call at 7:00 p.m. to see if I can join them for a home visit at 8:00.

"We know it's real short notice," Elder Pulsipher says, "but we could really use the help."

Periodically the missionaries call me if they need an older adult male to act as unofficial chaperone when they're teaching a single adult female. Other times I think they just want extra company or someone who can update them on BYU's chances to make it to a respectable bowl game. Or maybe they want to expose their investigators to the extremes of church membership, i.e., my scruffy, graybeard look versus their clean-shaven youth. Or maybe they just feel sorry for me.

On my end, I enjoy going with the missionaries because it gets me out of the house while doing some good in the world. And I like being around young people, especially the missionaries with their bright-eyed, faith-in-every-footstep optimism. Somehow, I always feel better after a night out with the elders, especially now. But I'm also giving a little payback: I never served a full-time mission in my youth. I was too busy playing hippie at a commune in northern California.

We meet at the church at 7:55 and squeeze into my Toyota Tercel, a 1983 model that's valiantly chugging towards the half-million-mile mark. If the missionaries were disappointed the first time they saw my vehicle, they disguised it well. Brother Miles, the retired orthopedic surgeon, can chauffeur them around in his black BMW with moonroof and heated leather seats. My Tercel has push-down locks, roll-up windows, and a wire hanger for a radio antenna. I should probably upgrade, but I've got a lot of memories in that old clunker, mostly good ones.

"I love this car!" Elder Thompson says.

"I'm getting antique vehicle plates," I say. It's supposed to be a joke.

"Cool!" Elder Thompson says.

"Yeah, cool!" Elder Pulsipher seconds.

I'm wearing my black suit and white shirt to match the missionaries, but any other resemblance stops there. Elder Pulsipher from Bountiful, Utah, looks like a lanky Harry Potter clone: rosy-cheeks, choirboy bangs, and wire-rim glasses. Huskier and hairier, Elder Thompson is a ruddy Esau with a mischievous twinkle in his eyes. His oblong jaw could slay a thousand Philistines.

We drive to a hodgepodge neighborhood that looks like the capital city of yard sales. Elder Thompson directs me to park in a gravel driveway fronting a mobile home with plastic flowers sprouting out of rusty coffee cans. As we mount the rickety steps to the porch, I notice a young man with a bushy black beard staring at us through a gap in the curtain. He takes a long drag on his cigarette and looks away.

The front door opens a crack and a cloud of blue-gray smoke floats out to greet us, followed by an angular face sporting a little billy-goat beard.

Elder Pulsipher's blue eyes light up. "Can we share a message," he asks in a schoolboy falsetto.

The young man sizes us up as if he's contemplating a drug deal. "Sure," he shrugs, and the door swings open to his living room, a cramped rectangle with a sagging sofa on one side facing an old TV monitor the size of a bank vault on the other. Presently, men in military uniforms are obliterating each other on the screen while the black-bearded man calmly works his double joysticks. Smoke hangs from the ceiling like cobwebs in a haunted attic.

A German shepherd enters and begins barking, mainly at me because I'm the stranger in the house: the missionaries have been here before. The man with the billy-goat beard tells the dog to shut the hell up, and it does. Elders Pulsipher and Thompson sit on the sofa near the man with the billy-goat beard; I take the padded chair close to the door. The man with the black beard crushes the remains of his cigarette in an ash tray fashioned out of the bottom of a beer can. He nods at us and then resumes his virtual slaughter.

Rock music is blasting from the adjacent kitchen. I don't recognize the tune and can't understand the lyrics, which is probably a good thing. The German shepherd starts up again and the man with the billy-goat beard tells it to shut up or he's going to kill it and he's not joking this time. He means it. Really means it. He introduces himself and says his name is Marcus, but we can call him Mark.

"Where's Connie?" Elder Pulsipher asks.

"She's laid out," Marcus says. "She's on her face."

A three-year-old with dark hair and button eyes toddles up to me and begins stroking my necktie as if it's a pet. I smile at him but don't offer my hand. A yellow slug of snot drips from his nose, which I'm sure has been a playground for his curious little fingers.

Marcus hastily clears the remains of dinner—paper plates, plastic cups, and utensils—from the badly scarred coffee table. He leaves behind three packs of Chesterfields and the makeshift ash tray overflowing with cigarette butts and ashes, some of which have spilled onto the carpet, joining scraps of paper, glitter, pieces of string, nuggets of dog food, and the grisly remains of a stuffed animal.

Elder Thompson asks Marcus if he'd like to watch a DVD about the life of Christ.

"It's cool," Marcus says as the dog settles at his feet.

The black-bearded man sighs wearily, sets aside his joysticks, and saunters into the kitchen. A six-year-old boy in white briefs and a T-shirt is sneaking down the unlit hallway. He stops at the edge of darkness, mentally debating his next move, then eases his big toe out into the light. Marcus throws a finger at him and barks: "You're grounded! Go to bed!" The boy vanishes like an aborted magic trick.

Marcus turns to the three-year-old, sitting quietly in the corner. "You, too! Now!" The younger boy scampers down the hall and out of sight.

Music with lyrics so loud and overtly foul that even I can understand them floods into the living room, trailed by a young male voice (the black-bearded man?): "I'm going to freaking rape you!"

Elder Thompson asks if maybe we could shut the door

Marcus reaches over and gives the slab of wood hanging crookedly in the door frame a gentle shove.

Elder Thompson asks if we can have a word of prayer. Marcus says sure and points his billy-goat beard at me. I close my eyes and bow my head. In my mind, I remind God that we are on his errand, doing his bidding in this home where we can barely breathe due to the thickness of the smoke. Out loud, I thank him for Marcus's hospitality. I bless this home and this family and ask God's spirit to be with us tonight. I add a silent postscript to please protect us from the deadly carcinogens in the air.

Elder Pulsipher presses the play button, and the DVD begins with a midnight storm at sea. As his disciples desperately cling to the gunwales, Jesus calmly lifts his hand: "Peace, be still," he says, and the sea turns from roiling mountains to horizontal glass.

Unfortunately, the Savior's words don't penetrate the household.

"I said go to bed!" Marcus shouts. The three-year-old has reappeared. From the kitchen, the repetitive thuds of a bass guitar seem to be battering down the door. Marcus tells the three-year-old to shut up, although I don't remember the boy saying anything. Marcus grabs the boy by the scruff of his neck and hauls him across the room.

Jesus is healing a blind man.

"You sit down and shut up!" Marcus says as he deposits the boy on the floor in the corner.

A plus-sized woman in a white T-shirt and black gym shorts enters from the kitchen carrying a 48-ounce cup of Polar Pop and a paper plate heaped with fried chicken and rice. Her thighs wobble magnificently as she promenades across the room and plops down on the sofa chair. A large butterfly is tattooed on her left calf.

"How are you guys tonight?" she asks cheerfully, then turns to me, the newbie: "I'm Connie."

"Nice to meet you," I say. "I'm Brother Canfield." I start to stand, but she waves me off. "No, don't get up."

Jesus is drawing with his finger in the dirt, contemplating how he will outwit his critics and rescue the adulterous woman from a church-sanctioned stoning. "He who is without sin among you," he says, "let him first cast a stone at her." The crowd disappears. Jesus looks up. "Woman, where are thine accusers?"

My eyes are tearing up but not from the story. I inhale solely through my nose, hoping to filter out some of the airborne toxins before they can reach my lungs.

The six-year-old peeks around the corner.

"I said *go* to bed!" Marcus thunders. "You are *so* in trouble!"

A lithe young woman in spandex shorts and a T-shirt sashays in from the kitchen, swiveling her hula hips. A crystal stud sparkles in her nose. Two purple streaks run the length of her jet-black hair like competition stripes. She casts me a "come hither" look, more sarcastic than wily, grabs a pack of Chesterfields, and disappears back into the kitchen.

Jesus is telling the corpse of Lazarus to arise and walk. It's a gentle, loving mandate. Lazarus opens his eyes and obliges. Even the murmuring Pharisees are impressed.

"I said shut up!" Marcus hollers. He grabs the three-year-old by the neck again and drags him down the hall and into the bedroom. "Stay there!" he shouts.

Connie intercepts Marcus on his return. "My Love, can you get me some water?"

"Sure thing," he says and detours into the kitchen.

Connie tells us she works at the Center for Disabilities. "I've been spit on, kicked, thrown down the stairs, sexually assaulted ..."

Re-entering, Marcus gives her a bug-eyed look.

"She's talking about her job," I say.

Marcus nods, but he's empty-handed.

"I asked you to get me some water," Connie says.

Marcus's head droops; he returns to the kitchen.

Jesus is on hands and knees sweating blood in Gethsemane.

We hear a crash in the kitchen, followed by the sound of millions of tiny hard somethings scattering across the floor.

"Is that jasmine rice?" Connie yells. "I'll put my foot up your butt! If that's jasmine rice, you'd better get the lubricant, cause I'm going to put my foot up your butt!"

Jesus is hanging on the cross asking God to forgive them, for they know not what they do.

Another crash in the kitchen.

"Get that lubricant!" Connie yells.

Jesus is approaching Mary in the garden. "Touch me not," he says.

The screen fades to black. *John 3:16* appears, followed by *For God So Loved the World …*

Marcus is back. "They shoulda done the whole thing," he says. "All the way to verse twenty-one. That's the best part."

"Well, what did you think?" Elder Pulsipher asks.

Marcus nods. Connie slurps her Polar Pop. "Good," she says.

Elder Thompson turns to me. "Brother Canfield, can you tell us what you love about the gospel of Jesus Christ?"

I'm caught off guard. I should have a short, simple answer in my hip pocket, but I don't. Such an epic question with so many possibilities: life, death, the hereafter. Mentally I grasp for the profound before settling for the commonplace: "Well, I think the great message of the gospel of Jesus Christ is … it's hope." I'm disappointed with myself. Six decades in the church and this is the best I can do? Connie and Marcus are unimpressed as well. I try again: "We can change," I say. "We can be spiritually reborn. We can be a totally different person from who we are now or who we used to be."

Connie takes a long, loud swig of her Polar Pop. "What if you like yourself the way you are?"

The missionaries turn to me, waiting for pearls of wisdom.

"Well, everyone can use a little improvement," I say.

"I think we're doing all right," Marcus says, patting his wife's thigh. "Don't you?"

Connie takes another gulp of Polar Pop and nods. "I think so. Yes."

In my mind, I'm thinking, "Are you freaking serious? Look around here, folks! Get real! Get a clue!" Instead, I share a "Good, Better, and Best" analogy to illustrate the need for continuous improvement, but it doesn't register.

Elder Thompson wants to wrap things up. "Would it be all right if we come back?" he asks.

Marcus strokes his billy-goat beard. Connie says, "Sure."

"Can we have a prayer before we go?" Elder Pulsipher asks.

Connie says yes. She says she'll say it. This surprises me, although it shouldn't.

"Heavenly Father," she says, "we thank thee for this day. We thank thee for our families and our friends and for all the beautiful things in the world. We thank thee for the missionaries and their friend who came to teach us tonight. We say these things in Jesus' name. Amen."

It's short; it's sincere. We shake hands with Marcus and Connie. The dog looks up at me with opium eyes.

We step out into the chilly autumn night and squeeze back into my Tercel—Elder Thompson in the passenger seat up front and Elder Pulsipher in the back. I pop open a mini bottle of hand sanitizer and squeeze a few drops into my palms, rubbing them together briskly. "There's a nasty flu bug going around," I say, offering the bottle to the missionaries. Elder Thompson squirts a few drops into his hand, then passes the bottle to Elder Pulsipher who does the same.

As we drive back to the church, I ask about the family dynamics.

"Who were those other three or four or however many there were in the kitchen?"

"We don't know," Elder Pulsipher says.

"Are they visitors? Do they live there?"

"Different people every time," Elder Thompson says.

I nod.

"Would you believe we've been working with them—well, missionaries have—for a year and a half?" Elder Thompson says.

"Yes, I can believe that," I say.

I twist my head to the side, chin to my lapel, and inhale. "So, what do you guys do to get the cigarette smell out of your clothes?"

They laugh and shout in unison: "Febreze!"

We arrive back at the church and the missionaries thank me for joining them.

"Any time," I say, although I'm tempted to add a qualifier: unless it's Marcus and Connie's place. Nothing against them personally, but in addition to the tobacco stench, the visit has left me with a disturbing aftertaste, a coin toss between dark comedy and mild depression.

I exit the highway a few miles early and take the long route home, rattling along dirt roads that twist through tight corridors of Gambel oak and ponderosa pines. I drive slowly, ostensibly so I can hit my brakes if any wildlife dart across the road. In reality, I'm in no hurry to get home. At the bottom of my driveway, I pause to remove a handful of letters from the mailbox; then I gun the engine to the top of a long hill where four cow elk are munching on the manzanita bushes outside my front door. They glare at me as if I'm an unwelcome guest. I smile and wave: "Good evening, ladies!" Shannon always loved the elk, even when they treated her summer garden like their personal salad bar.

I close the garage and enter through the kitchen. It's not quite cold enough to light the pellet stove, which is a shame: live flames tend to shrink the vaulted great room, turning it into an intimate little cave. It's looking especially large tonight, far more house than I can handle.

I switch on the kitchen light and sift through the mail: a water bill, three ads robo-stamped *Current Resident,* a greeting-card-sized envelope, and a flyer asking me to consider donating a Thanksgiving turkey to St. Vincent de Paul Food Bank. The flyer makes me smile. When our kids were growing up, every Thanksgiving morning Shannon would roust us from our beds at 5:30 to drive downtown in the dark to help prepare and serve lunch at the soup kitchen. Complaints were dismissed with a cavalier wave of her hand: "Let's go! Hubba hubba! We're all in this goulash together!" If we resisted further, she'd threaten us with cosmic justice: "Come on! These people need a good hot meal! Someday you might need one too!" After our youngest left for college, Shannon and I had continued our Thanksgiving tradition until our big move a year ago. There's no soup kitchen in our mountain town, but I'll do the next best thing. I scribble myself a reminder on the wall calendar: *Turkey—St. Vincent's.*

Next, I open the card-sized envelope, surprised to find Christmas greetings this early in the season. The card features a color photo of my cousin Vangie's burgeoning clan: she and her husband, Bob, dead center, with three sons and their spouses on the left and two daughters and their husbands on the right, and an army of grandchildren filling in the white space. Everyone is color-coordinated in blue jeans and white shirts or blouses. And everyone is smiling, even the newborns.

Shannon would always tape the cards to the fridge, creating

a jubilant holiday collage. She would usually make a joke first—"Looks like Santa gave Vangie a new pair of boobs"—but ultimately she would do the right thing; so I follow suit. I tape my cousin's card to the stainless-steel panel, at eye level, so that I will see those cheerful legions every time I raid the fridge.

Also tucked inside the envelope is Vangie's annual Christmas letter in which she enumerates the many blessings God has showered upon her progeny: how many have married in the temple; how many are serving missions; how many are doctors, lawyers, senators; which ones have cured cancer or received the Nobel Peace Prize. "The Annual Brag Sheet," Shannon used to call it. I'm sure my cousin didn't intend any harm when in one of her holiday missives she wrote: *It's really true. If we just teach our children correct principles and obey the commandments, God will take care of the rest. Bob and I are certainly enjoying the fruits of our labors …*

After reading that, Shannon plunged into a DEFCON-2 depression for a month.

In this year's edition, Vangie explains that she and Bob are leaving on a cruise around the world, so she wants to get her Christmas cards out early: *lest we be posting from Manila or Sri Lanka!*

I should be happy for my cousin. I should take the high road and send her a congratulatory Jackie Lawson e-card or at least a token text message: *Awesome! Kudos to you and Bob! Bon voyage!* Minimally, I should keep my big mouth shut. Instead, I slap the letter face down on the granite countertop and growl: "Vangie, get your head out of your armpit for once in your life."

Thou shalt not envy. Another strike against me.

I still stink of smoke, and good old Febreze will only mask the symptoms. I want that stench gone, now more than ever.

I Google *how to remove cigarette smell from clothing* and follow the instructions. First, I remove my Sunday shoes and socks and then my black suit coat and pants, careful to keep them free from other fabrics. I leave my priesthood garments on for now.

Next, I run a blow-dryer over the suit coat and pants, brushing them with a damp cloth as I go. Then I put them on separate hangers and take them outside on the deck to air out. It's a gorgeous night: cool, still, and silent. I can see three lights shining in the dark forest like fallen little stars: my closest neighbors to date. Shannon and I retired, moved to the mountains, built our dream house, and sat out here on New Year's Eve watching our first big snowstorm. She clapped her hands like a gleeful little girl. "Snow!" she exclaimed as if she were from another planet or downtown San Diego. "The angels are having the mother of all pillow fights!" At midnight we heard fireworks popping over the hill, beyond the woods. We kissed, then went inside and made love like two panda bears.

Two weeks later, Shannon went in for a routine checkup and came out with a death sentence. Dr. Dalrymple gave her six to nine months; she made it five.

I go inside and remove my garments, which will join my shirt and socks in the washer tomorrow. Then I take a shower, lathering up from head to toe, scrubbing hard, shampooing my hair twice. I put on fresh garments, a T-shirt, and sweatpants, but the phantom smell of cigarettes still lingers.

It's only 9:30 and I'm not really tired, so I plop down on the sofa and switch on the TV. I've been watching the *Mad Men* saga on Netflix, and I'm halfway through season five. Macho advertising ace Don Draper is staring out the window of his Madison Avenue office as he lights a cigarette, twin plumes of blue smoke intertwining like lovers in the air. I'm wondering how he and his chain-smoking associates remove the cigarette stench from *their* crisp white shirts and pinstriped suits. Most likely they're oblivious to the smell. I know I didn't notice it as a boy growing up in the only Mormon household in our neighborhood. Back then, schoolteachers used to smoke during playground duty, and housewives habitually lit up while browsing the aisles of Gelson's Market. The fragrance of slow-burning tobacco was as commonplace at high school football games as the aroma of popcorn and hot dogs. It was a smell so ubiquitous that I didn't notice it even when I did. It defined every home I entered except my own.

Don Draper is reclining on his office sofa, trying to gather inspiration for his next big pitch, the smoking cigarette in one hand, a glass of scotch within easy reach of the other. Watching him, I think of my father, Don Draper's moral opposite. Five mornings a week he left our home in the San Fernando Valley and drove over the hill to conduct business in the dark heart of Los Angeles. The smell of second-hand smoke must have routinely contaminated his suits and white shirts, although I can't remember it ever invading our home. I wonder now how he managed that in a Febreze-free, smoker's paradise like L.A. As a boy, I'd never appreciated how adroitly he had tight-roped between those two parallel worlds, the family man/Mormon bishop vs. the cut-throat corporate executive. In spite of his tidy Sunday sermons, my day-to-day life was muddled by ambiguity.

I remember him barging through the front door at 10:45 every Tuesday night, still wired after a full slate of bishop's interviews with quarreling spouses, lonely widows, jobless fathers, and recalcitrant teenagers. My mother would already be in bed, so he would plant a chair in front of the TV to catch the last fifteen minutes of roller derby, live from the Olympic Auditorium in downtown L.A. First, though, he would grab a half-gallon carton of Ralph's discount ice cream from the freezer so he could devour large spoonfuls while cheering on Terri Lynch and Big Danny Riley of the home-team Thunderbirds and hissing at Shirley Hardman and some bearded villain from the Texas Outlaws. I think this was his way of de-stressing after a full day at the office and a long night at church.

If I was up late doing homework, or pretending to do homework, I would pull up a chair and watch with him. It was an unusual mode of father–son bonding, but I was his second-born of seven and my mother's child, so I cherished those precious morsels.

One Tuesday night when I was eight, my father returned home a bit earlier than usual. Instead of bee-lining to the TV with a bucket of ice cream, he tiptoed down to the master bedroom. My mother had been sequestering herself since midmorning when she got word that our neighbor, Lorraine Goldman, had been killed in a car accident. While it was reasonable to assume that Mrs. Goldman's death had triggered my mother's latest episode—that's what my father called them, "episodes"—I could never be sure because they often seemed so arbitrary. One moment she would be flitting around the kitchen humming a Broadway tune, and the next, for no apparent reason, the joy would drain from her face and she would trudge into her bedroom and lock the door, sometimes for several days.

Concerned, but also curious, I crept down the hall and leaned close enough to the door to hear my mother's garbled voice.

"Why Lorraine?" she sobbed. "Why couldn't it have been me?"

At first, I thought she was nobly projecting herself in place of our late neighbor. Then, through another burst of tears, she wailed angrily: "Why did *she* get to go? Why not me? Why?"

I waited hopefully for my father's response—although I'm not sure what I was hoping for—but heard nothing. I'm not saying he was silent; I just didn't hear anything except my mother's gasping grief, which frightened me almost as much as what happened next.

The door opened abruptly. My father glared down at me like an angry bear. Even though his baritone voice was soft and modulated, to me it sounded like a bomb exploding: "What are you doing?"

My heart jammed halfway up my throat. "I-I-I just wanted to t-t-tell you ... r-r-roller derby's on."

His eyes burned like little blue torches. Over his shoulder I could see my mother in her terrycloth bathrobe, partly open in front, her eyes red and ravaged. She pulled the flaps shut and turned her back to me, embarrassed and ashamed.

"Well, we'd better go watch then," he said and stepped out into the hall, pulling the door shut behind him.

My father followed me into the family room where I had set a folding chair in front of the TV for him.

"Where's yours?" he said.

I smiled, flattered by the invitation, and brought in another chair. "Want some ice cream?"

"Rocky road if there's any left," he said. "Get yourself a bowl too."

I returned with a bowl of ice cream for me and handed the carton—about half-full—to him.

"That's the ticket," he said joylessly.

We watched the last five minutes of roller derby which culminated in a bench-clearing brawl between the Thunderbirds and the Outlaws. Then my father switched the channel to the NBC late night news.

"Do you want to play some chess?" he asked.

This took me by surprise. It was 11:00 p.m. on a school night.

"Sure!" I said, excited but nervous too. I was not a good chess player like my older brother, and my father was bound to be disappointed.

The first three games he pulled his punches but still won handily: he could only do so much to compensate for my lack of expertise. In game four, however, he got sloppy and distracted. The news had long since ended and *The Tonight Show* host Johnny Carson was trading jabs with one of his guests as I slid my queen across the board and said triumphantly, "Checkmate!"

My father looked up as if he had just awakened from a dream: "Well done, Jason."

I started feeling more confident, even a little chummy. We were two guys playing chess late into the night. Emboldened, I asked, "So, how's Mom doing? Is she going to be okay?"

My father stared at the board, contemplating his next move which, I realize now, had nothing to do with chess. After a minute of stony silence, he said, "If you want to be a good chess player, Jason, you need to concentrate."

He angled his bishop between two of my pawns, removed my unsuspecting knight, and stared at me, long and hard, until I tipped my king on its side. Johnny Carson was signing off for the night which meant it was 1:00 a.m.

"Well, you'd better get to bed," my father said. He didn't look one bit tired.

I was heading down the hall when he called me back: "Jason?"

"Yes, sir?"

"Are we going to make it?"

I nodded vigorously. "Of course!" I said, then recited a favorite family aphorism: "We're Can-do fields, not Can-don't fields."

He gave me a thumbs up. "That's the ticket!" he said with considerably more gusto.

───※───

At my mother's funeral, they said she was in a better place now and that someday "we" would all be joyfully reunited. They didn't say a word about her crazy twin sister who randomly showed up and locked my mother in the attic while she moped around hanging sackcloth throughout our home. Instead, they talked about a kind, generous, fun-loving woman who delivered hot meals to the hungry and quirky pep talks to the dejected. They talked about her love of Renaissance art, the Brontë sisters, and MGM musicals. And they talked a lot about how much she loved to serve—her husband, her children, the church, her friends, neighbors, everybody. Love love love. Serve serve serve. But throughout that hour-and-a-half flurry of words, my twelve-year-old brain fixated on a single incident three years earlier.

I was finishing up third grade, a certified troublemaker at school. According to Mr. Margetts, I was: hot-tempered, belligerent, unable to channel my emotions in a constructive way. In other words, I fought a lot. My father's solution was "the boot or the belt" (he always gave us a choice), but my mother convinced him that a soft touch might be more effective. So, she took me out for ice cream, just the two of us—a big deal in our family of six and soon-to-be seven children. As I licked my single scoop of chocolate chip, she asked me why I was so angry. It was the first time anyone had ever asked me that so directly and lovingly, so I told her about the teasing.

"What do they tease you about?"

"My clothes. My haircut. Everything. Church."

"Church?"

"When I told Jeff Levy I was Mormon, he laughed and said I was a *moron*. He yelled it and everybody laughed."

She smiled, smoothing her hand over my butched head. "It's hard to be different, isn't it?"

I started sniffling. "Y-y-y-y-yes." Now I was angry. I was supposed to be tough, and tough guys didn't sniffle.

"It takes courage," she said. "You have to be strong." She was appealing to the wannabe warrior in me. She had a plan—she always did. She handed me a small, hand-made chart showing each day of the week. She said that if I had a good day, she'd draw a smiley face in the square; if I had a bad day, she'd draw a frowny face. If I got all smiley faces for the week, she'd buy me an ice cream. She put her hand on my forearm. "This is our little secret, okay?"

I was four days into the experiment with all smiley faces when Jeff Levy made a crack about my new Fed-Mart sneakers: "Hey, look! Canfield finally got his care package!" We were waiting in line outside our classroom for the morning bell to ring, and Jeff got them all laughing and chanting: "Care package! Care package! Care package!"

That's all it took. I reared back like John Wayne in a saloon fight and rammed my fist into Jeff's face just as Mr. Margetts stepped outside to welcome us. Jeff's nose was gushing blood like Old Faithful as they hauled me off to the principal's office.

I spent the morning sitting outside Mr. Hoffman's door, awaiting my punishment. Shortly before noon, my mother entered the main office holding a small paper bag. She was as surprised to see me as I was shocked to see her. She was wearing a billowy muumuu to accommodate her seventh pregnancy. She didn't wear sleek stretch pants like the other moms, and the neighborhood kids mocked her behind my back.

Her initial reaction was joy but that quickly shifted to maternal worry as she rushed over and sat beside me.

"What's the matter?" she asked. "Are you sick?" She placed a hand on my forehead, but I flicked it away: I didn't want her sympathy; I didn't want her concern. And I certainly didn't want her love. Not now. I didn't deserve it. She looked hurt and surprised. "What's wrong?"

A door opened and Mr. Hoffman appeared, a stocky martinet with a crew cut and a combat general's voice. My mother put two and two together. Unanesthetized amputation would have hurt far less than the look of disappointment on her face. "Oh, Jason," she whispered, and that was my first brush with true heartbreak. I looked at the paper bag in her hand and remembered that I'd forgotten my lunch that morning.

After Mr. Hoffman sentenced me to two weeks of detention, I was excused to go to lunch. The lower grades had already eaten, so I was obliged to dine in the second shift with the older kids. I sat alone at a random table that soon became the gathering place of a chatty pack of girls.

Usually, my sack lunch consisted of a peanut butter sandwich and an apple or a small box of raisins. We weren't poor—we never went without food or clothing or anything like that—but we were a no-frills family: it was the trade-off my parents had made for a nice home in the foothills. When I opened the paper bag, I was surprised to find a Hostess Snoball inside—a kind of chocolate cupcake covered with a thick, coconut-flavored pelt. My mother must have purchased this special treat on the sly en route to school, no doubt at the expense of her weekly budget. The girl sitting across from me was a sixth grader, but to my young eyes she looked like a full-grown woman. She pointed at my Hostess Snoball and sighed: "Oh, you lucky puppy!" I smiled, but I'd never felt so miserable or so angry.

A few months after my mother's funeral, my father took me to the Olympic Auditorium to watch the L.A. Thunderbirds in person. It was a noisy venue with the crowded pack of skaters cursing and throwing elbows as they thundered around the wooden track. But even louder was the crowd—tattooed white men in black leather and women with cotton-candy hair and bare midriffs; Black men rattling chains and Hispanic women swearing in Spanish; all of them stomping their feet and screaming like animals as peanuts and flattened popcorn boxes sailed across the auditorium. No white shirts and pinstripes here, but lots of smoke. My eyes wept most of the night.

My father sat there like a wax effigy, lips straight, blue eyes empty. Gone were his vigorous thigh slaps and cathartic cries when Miss Lynch delivered an elbow to Miss Hardman's throat, sending her somersaulting over the guardrail.

Afterwards, my father negotiated the midnight traffic in silence. I finally asked him how he liked the game. I didn't know what else to call it.

"Jason," he sighed. "All I could do was look around at all those people wondering why Heavenly Father took your mother instead of half a dozen of them."

Maybe I was simply too young to catch the full nuance of "those people." I cupped my hands in my lap, a bit too self-righteously in retrospect, and remarked, "Weren't we there, too?"

My father's face hardened, but only for a moment. "Yes, we were," he conceded, retraining his eyes on the orderly procession of speeding lights that was the L.A. freeway at night. "And you'd best remember that any time you start getting on your high horse."

Five years later, I left home after another midnight shouting match with my father. I was a senior in high school, and our relationship had deteriorated to the point where if he told me to turn right, I'd turn left even if it meant leaping off a thousand-foot cliff into a pool of mako sharks. We argued about everything: curfews, car privileges, sports, politics, religion, the Vietnam War.

"You don't think it's important to defend your country?"

"I wouldn't be defending my country. I'd be defending a steady cash cow for Standard Oil."

"Maybe you should run off to Canada like those other cowards."

"Beats coming home in a body bag with a thank-you card from Tricky Dick Nixon!"

"Don't you talk that way in my house!"

"That's right—*your* house! Not mine!"

He finally gave me an ultimatum: *if you don't want to abide by my rules, there's the door!* I could hear my stepmother celebrating in the other room. In her mind, I was Korihor, perverting the fragile minds of my younger siblings. That night, I stuffed my essentials into a duffel bag. I didn't leave a note. I didn't say thank you. I didn't say goodbye.

⸙

I push the stop button on the remote, realizing that I've long since lost the thread of this episode. Apparently, Don Draper's heading out for another afternoon liaison with his neighbor's wife. Even though he knows better, he has a ready-made excuse: Don Draper was not raised by goodly parents; he grew up in a brothel without a father. Don Draper didn't go to Sunday school. He didn't have Family Home Evening or early morning seminary or daily scripture study. And all of that should matter—it should matter a lot.

When Shannon got really down on herself—on life, on us—I'd remind her that God's spirit children existed for eons before entering our homes. They come with their own personalities and proclivities, and, sure, we can teach and nurture them, but in the end, they make choices. Adam and Eve birthed the world's first murderer; Jacob's family was a dysfunctional mess, the root of all contemporary soap operas. If your kids are all lockstep following the program, God's probably lobbing you softballs. Even Father Lehi sired a couple of stinkers.

"Are you saying our kids are stinkers?"

And then I'd have to back-pedal, tap dance, grovel. "No, no, that's not what I meant. What I meant was …"

Humor didn't help. Humor at those moments blew up in my face like a cartoon cigar: "Hey, two out of three ain't bad—we're batting .667, about on par with the Almighty."

Shannon would remind me that we were actually batting only .333 and, by some scorecards, we were a big fat zero. Then she would say one word—Sheila—and the conversation would end.

If they'd found her shattered, face down at the foot of El Capitán, a victim of hubris and a faulty climbing harness, or crushed behind an airbag after a meth head barreled through a red light and T-boned her sedan, or ravaged piecemeal by some insidious disease, it would have at least made some sense in the eternal scheme of things and brought us some degree of consolation. But the police kicked in the door to her apartment and found her spread across her bed like a false fugitive mistakenly gunned down—the weapon, two little plastic bottles of Unisom on her nightstand. Thirty-two tablets per bottle. Empty. Taking no chances, she'd swallowed them all. No note. No explanation. No thank you. No goodbye. An honors student on a tennis scholarship. Our baby girl who never strayed. How could we have missed the signs? You mean like her 4.0 GPA? Her volunteer work at Habitat for Humanity? Or maybe it was the way she'd put a consoling arm around her opponents after she demolished them on the tennis court? Signs. How do you talk your way around that as a parent? How do you not question and second-guess everything you ever did or said, or meant to do or say but didn't to that child? How the hell do you put that in your annual Christmas letter?

Or this.

A week after returning from his two-year mission to Guatemala,

Damien poked his head inside my office where I was putting the finishing touches on a proposal.

"Dad? Got a minute?"

Of course, I had a minute! I had an hour! I had whatever amount of time he needed! There stood my beloved son, and I was so proud I could hardly contain it. Baptism, priesthood, Eagle Scout, mission. Unlike his wayward father, he'd checked off all the boxes with more to come: temple marriage, medical school, kids, career … He looked a bit disoriented, but that wasn't unusual for missionaries reacclimating to civilian life.

"It's a tough adjustment, isn't it?" I said. "You take off that little black badge and your whole world changes."

He gazed down at the hardwood floor. At that moment he looked so young and vulnerable, as if his adolescent freckles and awkwardness had magically returned.

"What's up?" I asked.

Then my son proceeded to ruin my day and my life—*our* life. He didn't mince words, I'll give him that.

"Dad," he said. "I'm gay."

I laughed. It was so absurd—so totally off my radar screen—that I didn't know what else to do. He may as well have said, "Dad, I'm a snow leopard" or "Dad, I'm an alien from the planet Moogooboo."

He closed his eyes and clenched his fists at his side, bracing himself. Calmly, he repeated, "Dad, I'm gay."

We all have an absolute low point as parents, and this would be mine. My voice rose. "No, you're not! I don't know where you got this cockeyed idea or what crazy books you've been reading or who you've been talking to, but you are not gay! Do you understand?" I was yelling, but he stood his ground, taking it like a good martyr. Louder: "Do you understand?"

Those sugar-blue eyes that had stared down into the congregation at his missionary farewell as he'd publicly thanked us—Mom, Dad—for everything we'd done for him, the example we'd set, the lives we'd lived, the service we'd rendered, la-de-da-de-da—those beautiful eyes teared up as he bowed his head and whispered, "Yes, Dad, I understand."

"Good!" I said. As he slouched away, I yelled after him; I roared:

"You are *not* fucking gay!" And then grabbed the stapler off my desk and hurled it against the wall, taking a big angry bite out of the drywall.

He was gone the next morning. I got to explain the whole mess to Shannon, who was appalled—not by Damien's revelation but by my reaction to it.

"Seriously? I've known that since he was fifteen."

"Why didn't you tell me?"

"Because I knew you'd act like this!"

"This? What's *this*?"

"Like a horse's ass!"

It took me two years before I finally swallowed enough of my anger and pride to call him. But the damage was done. He'd found another home and another father and mother in another state, a Lutheran couple who loved their boy and my son more than my precious image of him. We all make choices. The eternal fail-safe.

The day Shannon got her diagnosis, I made the mistake of trying to give her a pep talk. "Hey, we're going to beat this thing—"

She glared at me, her eyes screaming: Knock it off! You heard what Dr. Dalrymple said. Nobody beats pancreatic cancer.

I lowered my head and she drove the rest of the way home in silence. We'd taken her car that day, the Honda SUV. After pulling into the garage, I started to get out of the car, but she remained in her seat, staring at the windshield: "I'm pissed, Jason! I'm really really really pissed! We worked our whole lives to get to this point."

She turned to me, but very briefly. Tear tracks stained her cheeks. She was still wearing her seat belt.

"I'm not going to be one of those brave, self-sacrificing Molly Mormons that drag themselves into the temple on hands and knees to squeeze in one last endowment session before they croak. I'm not doing that shit, Jason!" She punched her fist against the dash four times. "None-of-that-shit!"

And then she did. All of it and more. Went to church. Put on the happy face and smiled at everyone. Gave Relief Society lessons. Never missed a birthday card for her ministering families. Cranked out temple names like they were lottery tickets. And at her last fast and testimony meeting, she sat next to the pulpit in a wheelchair holding a microphone in one hand while plucking Kleenex from the box with the other as she testified of God's unwavering love and how these past few months she'd felt the Spirit more powerfully than ever before. "Every cliché in the book," she said later, laughing. "I can't believe it! What did you put in my fruit juice?"

In return, God called her home quickly. We thought we'd have a few more months. Nikki was overseas tying up some loose ends so she could take extended leave to help me nurse Shannon to the finish line. She wept on the phone, berating herself mercilessly, and then caught the next flight out of Tokyo.

Damien was the first to arrive and stayed for a month, cooking me gourmet meals and chasing the dreadful loneliness from my house. We talked in ways we never had, sharing confidences and confessions. To counterbalance the bad news, he'd brought good tidings: he and Hugh were expecting in April, providing that their in vitro surrogate didn't back out at the last minute. I was skeptical until Damien told me the surrogate was Hugh's sister. Then I laughed. Damien's sperm and Hugh's sister's eggs! What a creative way to keep the DNA in the family! More important, my boy was going to be a dad, and I was going to be a grandfather. There's a good chance they'll have twins. Or triplets. My first and (probably) only grandchildren since Nikki remains a proud and independent bachelorette. She half-laughs when she claims she's discovered the true secret to happiness: no husband, no kids.

⌇⸻

I won't be able to sleep tonight, I know that. It's 10:30 and I'm still revved up. I'd call Nikki or Damien, but it's 1:30 on the east coast. I don't know what else to do, so I dial the missionaries. Elder Pulsipher answers.

"Is everything all right?" he asks. He sounds surprised and concerned. There's a long silence, and he finally fills it. "Can we help you with anything, Brother Canfield?"

"Thanks for inviting me tonight," I say.

"We'll do it again sometime," Elder Pulsipher says.

"Yes, I'd like that."

"Well, you have a good night."

"Elder, have you got any Febreze?"

"I think so. Do you need some?"

"No, I'm trying a little different approach. I read about it online."

"Well, let us know how that goes."

"I will," I say. "I'll let you know."

"Okay. Good. Well, you have a good night."

The conversation has already ended three times, and I don't want to sound desperate. I don't want to sound needy. I'm not like this usually. But tonight, mild depression has won the coin toss. Marcus and Connie don't seem like such a slapstick sitcom anymore, or like two more screaming faces at the Olympic Auditorium.

"When are you going to visit that family again?" I ask.

"I don't know. Probably next week maybe."

"Don't give up on them."

Elder Pulsipher laughs. "Oh, don't worry. We won't." He says this a little too casually, too easily.

"You need to keep teaching them," I say.

Elder Pulsipher's voice grows lower and more solemn, like he means business. "We will, Brother Canfield."

"Good," I say. "Call me again. Please. Next time you go see them."

"We will, Brother Canfield. You're sure you're okay?"

"I'm fine. We're all in this goulash together, you know."

I hear silence, followed by a laugh. Then: "Yes, I guess we are."

CONFESSION

I'm not making excuses, Bishop, I'm really not. What I did, it's inexcusable. Reprehensible. I broke sacred vows. I totally crossed the line, and I'm sorry for that. All that stuff. But the thing I honest-to-gosh don't get is why my husband's so hot and bothered about it unless it maybe bruised his big fat little ego. Yes, I told him. A week ago. At first he went all Incredible Hulk on me—eyes bulging, face bloating. From there it was the Grim Weeper: "How could you have done this to me? To *us!*" Meanwhile, I'm wondering who's this wonderful fairy tale *us* he's talking about?

No, of course not. That's why I'm here. I'm willing to do whatever to make things right, but I'm a little new to this. You know the parable about the workers in the vineyard? I showed up with the sundown shift, an hour before quitting time. Okay, so maybe not quite that late. Twenty years ago, next July. The second happiest day of my life except for the fact poor Elder Duncan couldn't quite get me all the way underwater. My toe popped up the first time, my elbow the second, and my hair came loose and surfaced on the third. By the fourth try I was seriously reconsidering, but it all worked out. In the end, it all worked out.

So, no, I've never done this before. I guess I never had to until now. Courage? I don't know if it takes courage as much as desperation. And guilt. Lots of guilt. I want to make things right between me and the Lord. George? Well, yes, him too, but we'll get to that. No, this is the second tour for both of us. He lost his to cancer and mine took a permanent French leave—good riddance to bad decisions! What can I say? The young and the restless and the dumb! I fell in love with Johnny Dangerous my senior year of high school.

So where should I begin? Because in my opinion, it's not so

much the incident itself as all the stuff leading up to it. It's more like this state of mind that developed over time. And it wasn't so much what he said but what he didn't say. Like whenever he saw me stepping out of the shower or squeezing into a dress or a swimsuit, heaven forbid. "Are you really wearing *that*?" Or: "Hey, when did you graduate to super-size?" Or: "Hey, do you want me to stamp 'Frigidaire' on your hindquarters now or after you dry off?" No, he didn't actually *say* that, but I could see it in his eyes; I could hear it in his voice even when he was saying something else.

The thing is, I know I don't look all that bad, especially for my age, if that's a factor. I know I'm not twenty-something smooth. I've got a few more lumps and bumps—I get that. But dressed up in a pencil skirt and heels I'm good enough to get a second look. Maybe a third if it's not a close-up. I look nice. I think I even look, well, desirable. Is that bad, Bishop? Is it a sin to want to be wanted? Because that's the thing, I think, for women at least—maybe it's the same for men too—but once you stop feeling desirable, you're old. Well, of course it's just a state of mind, but it's *my* mind and *my* body too. Throw the spirit in there and you've got the whole trifecta. No, but that's the whole point: it's not just physical, but that's part of it. Not all, but part. For women, probably a bigger part than men. No offense, Bishop, but I've seen Humpty Dumpties in Speedos and sunglasses parading around the beach like they owned every girl on it. Not pretty. Certainly not eye candy if you catch my drift. Women are more discerning, I think. I mean, I get the whole love-me-as-I-am-all-300-pounds-of-it movement. I do. And maybe the whole plus-sized revolution is a good thing. My generation burned the bra; today's kids are junking bathroom scales and tape measures. Sweet freedom!

My point is, I know I'm no spring chicken, but I'm not on life support either. I'm not quite ready for mummification. So, it's the little digs, the unspoken insults, the *attitude*, Bishop, the attitude. I mean, how would you feel if you put your arm around your wife and she twisted away like she's breaking out of jail? Oh, he'll hold my hand in sacrament meeting and take me by the arm and open the car door and do all that chivalrous Sir Walter Raleigh stuff in public. But safe at home, I'm invisible. I'm the chef—more like the short-order cook. I'm the laundry lady. I'm another paycheck, although not the big one, but still … I get shrugged and shunned and turned away from so often I start believing the rumors in his eyes: I'm fat. I'm ugly. The Colossus of Kern County. Excuse me? Specifics? Sure, here's specific. It's a Friday night, we've just finished a nice dinner, and I sit down next to him on the sofa with a blanket for two. I've got scented candles burning, and a DVD on the screen. No, Bishop, it wasn't *Beaches*. Give me a little credit here. But it wasn't *Terminator 3* either. It was a nice little rom-com. Anyway, I spread the blanket over our laps and he doesn't scream "Fire!" and head for the exit, so I'm thinking, well, that's progress. It's a step in the right direction, anyway. I get braver; I put my hand on his thigh and start to rub a little, trying to generate some electricity, if you know what I mean. I'm sorry. Am I getting too graphic? Too much information? No, I didn't think so. You've heard it all, right? Broken marriages, runaway kids, sex, drugs, the works.

Anyway, George isn't reacting, but he's not giving me a double stiff-arm either; another victory. I get a little more daring, venture a bit higher up the thigh. He throws the blanket aside and says, "I need a drink!" and he's off to the kitchen. "A drink?" I say. I'm wondering if maybe he's having problems in the you-know-what department. They've got plenty of remedies now—pills, shots, all kinds of little inflation tricks. Maybe, but how would I know? It's been so long—look, if that's it, fine! Fine! He should just tell me. Because instead of thinking, what's wrong with *him*, I'm thinking what's wrong with *me*?

Anyway, he gets his drink and goes off to bed while I go into the bathroom and have a little moment of truth with the mirror. I take a cold, hard look at the little saddlebags under my eyes and the extra chin growing on my throat and confess the obvious: I couldn't turn on a light bulb.

So just when I'm about to emotionally retire to the elephant's graveyard, the first day of school some new kid shows up. I say kid, but he's thirty-five, give or take, no tats, no nose rings, clean-cut and sleek-cheeked. He looks like a returned missionary minus the baby fat and the little black badge. He's in the teacher's lounge and he's totally flirting with me and I don't even know it—that's what

Barbara Mason the P.E. teacher tells me later. "It was so totally obvious," she says. He's waiting to use the microwave to heat up his little Tupperware of leftovers and so am I, and he motions me forward: "Youth before experience," he says. It just happens to be my birthday, the dreaded Six-O, and I don't want people making a big deal out of it with black balloons and Styrofoam headstones on my door, but they do anyway. "Congrats on number twenty-nine!" he says. "Oh, right," I say. "Tell it to the Man on the Moon!" It's such a flagrant line, but I'm loving every syllable of it. When I mention I've got four kids and six grandkids, he says, "Did you get married when you were ten?"

I wave him off, but I'm blushing—like totally blushing, according to Barbara. "Oh, you so totally were," she says.

He's a nice kid, a nice man. Like me, he teaches fifth grade and his classroom's just across the hall, so we share kids for compartmentalized teaching: I do English and social studies, he does science and math. There are joint field trips, joint planning sessions, open houses, evening events, and after-school stuff. My husband doesn't move a molecule over these extended hours and excursions. Never protests, never laments the lack of my company. Shrug. Yawn. Bite. Gulp. Swallow. Belch. Pass the remote.

One night, after the science fair, everyone pitches in with cleanup—many hands make light work, as the saying goes—and before I know it the gym's vacant, the lights are off, the doors are locked, and it's just the two of us, although we don't know that yet. I'm tidying up in the supply closet and he's just cut the light in the hall. "Diane?" he calls. "Everything all right?"

"In here," I say, and he enters the walk-in closet where I'm standing on top of a stool trying to stack some jars on the upper shelf.

"Hey, that's dangerous," he says.

I turn and smile and say, "I'm fine." But there's something odd in his expression. I'm wearing a skirt and hose and a nice satin top with horizontal stripes that are supposed to visually aggrandize the bust, as if I need aggrandizement. And suddenly I'm wondering if I dressed this way on purpose. But who am I kidding? Lying to yourself is like lying to God: you can't. I know; *he* knows. Sorry. I guess I'm getting off track again.

"Is something wrong?" I ask, and he smiles like a little kid caught in the act.

"What?" I ask.

"I don't want you to take this the wrong way, but ..." And he stops, and it's like he's mulling it over whether or not he's going to commit and maybe make a fool of himself, and the whole time I'm thinking, *say it, you fool; say it say it say it!* And then he does: "You have the most beautiful calves. Like a dancer's."

Now I'm blushing as I step down off the stool and I almost stumble, and then I do, and he catches me like Superman snatching Lois Lane out of the sky. Or like a groom carrying his bride across the threshold. I smile awkwardly. Then I'm babbling like I'm back in middle school. There's that initial moment of contact where you can either break free and flee like Joseph from Potiphar's wife or you can summon Bathsheba to your bedchamber. And I know this should all stop right here and now, and yet I'm also thinking this train may never pass through this old ghost town again. Then I've got the two puppets, Punch and Judy, arguing in my head: yes no yes no yes no; stay go stay go stay go. But he doesn't let me decide. He looks at my eyes like no one else has looked for longer than I can remember; not like one of my puppy-eyed students or my polite friends for dinner or Brother This or Sister That at church, or least of all my husband, wondering why leftovers again? Not since the day I knelt at the altar in the L.A. Temple thinking, yes, this is the man I want to walk that timeless, endless path through the eternities with—drunk, Bishop, love-sick drunk with that deep, aromatic mix of love and desire that was going to fuel us through all obstacles—fires, storms, ravages of any brand. And still might have, with just a little work and forgiveness and, oh my gosh, maybe an ounce of imagination. But now, in retrospect, the biggest surprise wasn't that it cooled but how quickly. Overnight, it seemed.

I know, I know, but Junior's not through. In fact, he's just warming up. "And your eyes," he whispers. "The most beautifu—"

The rest I'll leave to your imagination. Let's just say it wasn't like in the movies where I leap into his arms and he slams me against the wall and drills me right there in the hotel lobby, fast and furious, in full view of a thousand security cameras. Not at my age.

First, I question the physics of that particular posture. This was soft, slow, gentle—the old-fashioned way. It was delicate and lingering; starting high and working low—not working, but delighting, so you can actually feel it seeping deep into your blood and bones. A slow freefall, and then suddenly he pulls the rip cord! Whoa! Then another fall and—whoa! And another! Whoa! And again!

And the whole thing, it was ... ecstatic. Yes, ecstatic! Even when the angry little voice in the back seat was screaming, "Stop! Stop! You mustn't do this! You're violating covenants! You're throwing away your eternal inheritance! You are so totally blowing it!" And yet the other voice kept countering: Inheritance with who? Time and all eternity with Mr. Frump? Elmer Fudd in slippers and a bathrobe? Every scripture and verse from every Sunday school lesson since my baptism was pounding on my head trying to get in: didn't hear it; didn't feel it; didn't care. The voice I heard was the silence of my husband; the voice I heard was no and not now and I don't have time and I've got a meeting; the voice I heard was this young man breathlessly celebrating every pre-plowed inch of me, furrowed or fallow. And when I fell into his arms it was like the tolling of cathedral bells. Eternal bells. From the high Alps to the deep deserts. We clung to each other afterwards, the two of us alone on the floor of the walk-in closet, both of us knowing (and me saying over and over) that this would not (must not) ever happen again, yet lingering together for as long as we possibly could—or as long as my bladder allowed, which turned out to be about fifteen minutes.

No, no. Absolutely not. Not an excuse, Bishop, just an explanation. It's my fault, I totally get that. But don't you think there's at least a little bit of blame to share? Can I speak bluntly? Yes, I suppose I already have been. But do I have to shoulder all the blame for this while he walks away with a halo over his head? The poor, long-suffering, cuckolded husband diligently going about his church business while I'm tramping around the barnyard? Is that how it goes down? What about equally yoked, as they say, in the honeymoon suite or in the outhouse; equally yoked? Because it's a lonely life, Bishop. It's a lonely life, and we try our best to fill it with other things: kids, church, work, grandkids. Yes! Yes! Exactly!

All the while trying to forget this other void that's supposed to be the heart of our eternal happiness. Excuse me? Or relegating it to prohibition? Wow! Interesting take, Bishop. Really interesting take. No, I had no idea. You two look so—so perfect together! I'm so sorry to hear that. Yes, that must be really hard. I can only imagine. I mean, at least I've got my book club.

LOST AND FOUND

Over the years he had tried all kinds of tricks to outfox it. He had eaten humble pie by candlelight in the dark privacy of his hovel while reading the Nativity story from Luke. He had tried to lose himself in anonymous acts of service in the village. Once, in a fit of self-spite, he had driven a hundred miles into Gallup and gotten roaring drunk. Another time he had gone all the way to Flagstaff to sit through midnight mass at St. Mary's Church—as a novelty and a diversion more so than religious devotion: he had his own church. Sort of.

Tonight he was going to drive to the top of the mesa in a snowstorm to rescue a beautiful young woman in distress.

Actually, he did not know if she was beautiful. Nor did he know if she was truly in distress. Her foster mother in Phoenix seemed to think so. Her voice, scratched to obscurity by the crackling static, was controlled hysteria on the phone. "Well, we'd do just about anything to get her back." A telling pause. "Well, just about. I mean, we really want her back. Especially under the circumstances."

Her name was Loretta Yellowhair and she had been missing from the Indian Placement Program since August. It was a mystery. No one knew where she had gone, not even her natural parents—or if they did, they weren't talking. But a week ago the Placement caseworker had heard a rumor ...

"I guess what happened is that last winter was really hard on the family. A lot of sheep didn't make it. Loretta's mother got real desperate and borrowed a thousand dollars from some old fellow with the promise he could marry Loretta in exchange."

Another voice, Brother Myers's, interrupted on another line:

"Yeah, if you could, we'd like you to intercept the old coot's pass, so to speak!"

Tom winced at the reference to old coot.

"Brother Giles—the caseworker?—well, he says Loretta can go back on Placement and finish up her senior year," Sister Myers explained, "but she's got to be in Phoenix by Tuesday morning for an interview, absolutely positively."

"Tuesday?" Tom said. "What's so sacred about Tuesday?"

Sister Myers chuckled, almost intimately. "Monday's Christmas, silly!"

"What's so sacred about Christmas?" Tom quipped. And he laughed. Once.

Sister Myers was silent.

"Sorry," Tom said, wondering who had given her his name and number. The missionaries maybe. Or the idiot caseworker. At moments like this he almost wished the Tribe hadn't put in phone lines a year ago. Electricity, yes. Running water, great. Telephones? They reduced his insularity. He could feel the outside world creeping in, tightening its noose.

Tom clasped his hand over the receiver and looked at his cat, an ornery old Siamese-and-something curled up on the rumpled bedspread that drooped to the warped floorboards beneath his metal-frame bed.

"What do you say, Nashdoi? You up for a little adventure tonight?"

The animal didn't stir. Beside the bed was an old chest of drawers. A single lightbulb burned in the cramped kitchen where a pine sprig in a glass jar served as Tom's token tribute to the holidays. Normally his quarters seemed warm and cozy, but tonight they felt dark and claustrophobic. Grim.

"I just hate to see it happen," Sister Myers said. "She's just such a wonderful girl—bright, gifted, a valiant testimony. I know it's Christmas Eve, but …"

Tom unclasped the receiver and whispered into it, tentatively, so as not to arouse false hope, "Sister Myers, I'll do my best!"

"Oh, thank you, Bishop! We really do appreciate this!"

Tom winced again. He wasn't really a bishop but a branch president by default: he was the only ordained elder in the area. But he had retired from truly active duty years ago—he thought he'd made that clear.

He fed a couple sticks of juniper into the woodstove, turned the vents down low, and put on his Marlboro Country coat—suede with a sheepskin collar. He was tempted to bring Nashdoi along for company, but he didn't have the heart to awaken him from such a deep, exclusive sleep. He was a little jealous, really.

Snow was falling lightly but steadily as his battered blue pickup rumbled past the trading post, a big stone box locked up for the night. The village was abandoned—a ghost town. Winter had pronounced it dead and tossed a white sheet over it. A pregnant mutt, her swollen teats dragging along the snow, plodded towards the rock schoolhouse where Tom earned his daily bread. About the only joyful thing in sight was the play of the snow in the lone security light. The dainty flakes were twisting and tumbling like gleeful little gymnasts. But even here he saw a tragic element in that they could just as easily be butterflies trapped inside a jar of light, trying desperately to break out. He could almost hear their wings beating frantically against the glass. Or was that his heart, rap-tap-tapping, or his truck thumping across the cattle guard?

Or his heater? He flicked the switch and the little fan rattled like dice in a cup, spewing out lukewarm arm. Up ahead he could see Hosteen's old hogan, a dark face with a white helmet. Two years ago he would have asked Hosteen to join him. The old man had just the right touch of craziness for a wild goose chase like this—and it would be a wild goose chase, Mission Double-Impossible, Tom knew that. So why was he going? Well, boredom was a factor (what else was on his agenda tonight besides huddling by his wood stove feeling sorry for himself?). And duty (she was a lost lamb; it was his job to find her). And, yes, there was curiosity, too: who was this young beauty who commanded a bride price of a thousand dollars, a phenomenal fifty sheep in Navajo currency? He wanted to know.

Tom smiled, recalling the way the old man's eyes used to peer out from under the flat brim of his black felt hat, the dark little orbs floating behind his Coke-bottle lenses like little fish in formaldehyde. A fringe of silver whiskers dripped from his gaunt jaw like pieces of clipped fishing line, and calluses doubled the size of his gnarled little hands. Tom had first met him twenty-five years ago while making home visits with the missionaries. Hosteen was limping out of his outhouse on skinny bowlegs, zipping up his fly. One look at the missionaries in their dark suits and white shirts and he had quipped: "What are you folks doing, selling life insurance?" Tom had liked him instantly. Later, when the missionaries asked the standard question—"Is there anything we can do for you, Brother Benally?"—the wrinkled corners of the old man's mouth had twisted sardonically. He'd led the threesome back behind his hogan and pointed to a huge mound of piñon and juniper. "You folks can cut all that up for me. About this size," he'd said, spreading his hands shoulder width. "Better hurry, though. Sun's going fast." Hosteen used to say he didn't exactly believe in the old ways–or in the new ways either. "I'm just a horse-teen of a different color," he would chuckle, punning on his Navajo name.

Tom tried not to think about Hosteen; it still saddened him. Somehow that too had been his fault. He turned his thoughts elsewhere—Sister Myers. He could still hear her voice crackling in his ear. "Well, they think she might be up to the mesa."

The mesa! Swell! Talk about a needle in a haystack!

"Or they say she might be staying with Louise Yazzie's brother-in-law. Do you know Louise?"

A needle in three haystacks.

Driving the desolate reservation roads on a winter night, Tom could go for miles—light years—without seeing anything but the infinite swirl of snowflakes. He was an astronaut hurtling solo through outer space, and the feeling could be terrifying or exhilarating, depending upon his particular state of mind. At that moment he felt neither terrified nor exhilarated, only a general desolation that seemed to always intensify about this time of year. The simple truth was he really didn't much care what transpired tonight. He just wanted to get it over with—"it" being this night. His front tire plunged into a pothole, rattling the truck and sending a shaft of pain into his lower back. Several years ago he had injured it falling off a horse, and now every little bounce or vibration was a voodoo pin in his fifth lumbar. Great, he thought. Swell. I'll be a pin cushion by midnight.

The pickup crawled past the little trailer where for one hour every Sunday morning Tom went through the holy motions on behalf of old Sister Watchman and a few other faithfuls of the Bitterwater Branch of the Mormon Church. Sister Watchman, who had no eyes to see but could weave an intricate rug of many colors, could also read the desperate scribble on his heart: "I feel sad for you, Man-Without-Woman. You feed all these others; who will feed you?"

"My Heavenly Father," he used to say, but each time with a little less conviction.

Straight ahead, a giant boulder was sitting comically atop a skinny spire, like a giant head with a pencil neck. Striped with snow, it was a weird giraffe-zebra hybrid straight out of Dr. Seuss. In the background, the mesa rose up like a great white wall. In the fuzzy snowfall, it appeared to be wavering ethereally, as if any moment it might swell up and crash down upon him like a tsunami, or simply vanish altogether like a mirage.

Tom wondered about Loretta Yellowhair. Who was this young Navajo woman in distress? "Yellowhair" would be a misnomer. Black hair, dark eyes. He tried to visualize her in his mind, but she remained as fuzzy and obscure as the falling snow.

"Distress" might be a misnomer as well. His personal feelings about the Indian Placement Program had always been ambivalent. The dark view held that Navajo children were being taken from their natural families so they could be transformed into white and delightsome little Mormons. The "inspired" view said it gave them a shot at a "real" education. Tom had seen both sides of the coin. Placement was a ticket out, but to where? Anything to spare them the B.I.A. boarding schools. Every year when his handful of little sixth graders graduated, he felt an overwhelming sadness, as if he were sending them off to war. Half the girls would end up pregnant; half the boys would come back little drunkards and dopers. Placement? Stealing their culture? There were six sides to that story. Ask Celeste Bighorse.

Tom had always been lenient on Placement interviews. If a kid had a shot, he wasn't going to nix it on a minor technicality.

"What church is this?"

A look of stupor. "Uh ... Catholic?"

"Close enough."

The snow was falling so thickly now he seemed to be submerged in it. The pickup struggled along like a submarine in rough waters. His thoughts drifted back to the little chapel he had passed a few miles back. A week ago, Sunday, opening his official church mail, he was shocked to see his mug shot, albeit a very outdated one, on the missing persons bulletin. By some computer glitch, perhaps the simple inversion of two digits in his membership record number, church headquarters had failed to link one of their anointed local leaders with the black-and-white countenance on the bulletin. It had been sobering to see his face amidst the other lost sheep: teenage runaways with pimpled cheeks and hair in their eyes, a watermelon-shaped man who could have been his father, a jolly white-haired woman who reminded him of Mrs. Claus. Tom had always felt depressed when perusing these monthly alerts. Each face was a tragedy in miniature, a despairing tale of loss. He pictured heartbroken parents grieving for their prodigal sons, grown-up children searching desperately for crippled mothers and fathers on the run. Sometimes, studying the photographs, he would invent stories of his own—whole sagas and family histories. And sometimes in the process he would mentally rewrite his own. He sometimes wondered who, if anyone, might be searching for him.

He had noticed a crucial difference between his mug shot and the others. They were accompanied by a brief physical description (height, weight, eye color, hair color, distinguishing features), the location where the individual had last been seen, his or her hometown, and a contact person to call. His read, simply: Thomas David Barlow. That was all. No contact person; no phone number.

Tom had recognized his high school graduation picture. The blond ponytail was gone now, and the cocky grin. His chiseled cheeks were padded, tanned, and leathery, and his jaws were beginning to sag in the sad-sack manner of Dick Nixon. Mentally he had updated his description: 5'10", 205 pounds, built like an over-the-hill linebacker. Hair (the surviving patches on top) like sun-singed grass. Hazel eyes—vacant. Twin flashlights with dead batteries.

His hands had trembled while handling the sheet of paper, as if ghosts or spirits had been captured on the page. On the one hand, it had been like reading his own obituary. On the other, it meant that someone, somewhere, was still looking for him. But who? His mother and father had gone AWOL before he could even walk; he had no brothers or sisters, no real family to speak of ... His father-in-law, maybe? Tom had laughed. Fat chance of that. "You're a very intelligent young man, Tom; you're very smart. But you've got no heart. You're a taker, not a giver." That was the last thing Bishop Tyler (the *real* bishop) had said to him two days before Tom had eloped with his only daughter. She had liked him because he was a California oddball who was going to set the world on fire, although he wasn't quite sure how. She had liked him because her father hadn't. The bishop had mapped out his daughter's life a little too perfectly: temple marriage, kids, grandkids, death. Sorry, that wasn't Kathy. Of course, Tom had had to be baptized and join the fold. Kathy was saucy and spicy and radical for her little Utah town, but she was still Mormon. "I want you forever," she had whispered during a pre-erotic moment, "not just the here and now. Don't you want me forever too?" Sweet persuasion. Failing that: "Look, I'm not a one-life stand!" So he had played the game until it had become almost real to him.

He had promised her the sky, but instead had given her Bitter-water, Arizona.

He switched on the radio; it spit and crackled. He should have had it fixed back in October. He fiddled with the knob, searching for a voice, any voice, but found nothing but fuzz and static, an audio version of the falling snow. He noted the permanent film of dust on the dash, and the ever-widening cracks across the faded blue vinyl: they were tragic mouths, gaping wounds, sarcastic smiles aimed at him.

He tried to keep his eyes and thoughts on the road, but they kept drifting to Christmases past. One year—he was seven or eight, he forgot exactly—he was living with Aunt Margie in Del Mar and decided to play a joke on his cousins. He made them all joke gifts. They were poems: "Roses are red / Violets are blue / Christmas is dumb / And so are you!" Stupid little ditties. Christmas Eve he placed them under the tree. But when he got in bed, something funny happened. Maybe it was the carolers outside. Or maybe Uncle Max had spiked the eggnog again. Tom wasn't sure. He just felt weird about it. So he sneaked out and took back all the joke gifts, and he trashed them.

Except he didn't get them all. He thought he had, but he missed Sherry's. She wasn't mentally disabled—not clinically—but she was … well, she was slow. Her present was buried at the bottom of the pile, and before Tom could stop her, she'd unwrapped it. She started jumping up and down, shouting, "A present from Tommy! A present from Tommy!" She gave it to her mother to read because she couldn't. Aunt Margie smiled at first, and then her face turned to steel. She gave Tom a nasty look but smiled at Sherry. Then she read: "Roses are red / Violets are merry / Christmas is here / And I love Sherry!" Tom had never seen his cousin so happy. She threw her arms around him and danced and danced. He couldn't look at his aunt. He couldn't look at anyone after that. He just stood there feeling like absolute dirt.

It was the story of his life: big plans, big screw ups.

Tom put his hand over the heater vent: still lukewarm. He should have had *that* fixed, too. He could feel the cold creeping into his toes, slowly taking over. The steering wheel was turning to ice; his hands were stiffening. Why hadn't he brought his gloves? He always brought gloves—always! He gripped the steering wheel in anger and stamped the accelerator to the floor. The truck lurched forward and hit a slushy spot, shimmying several yards before the tires regripped the road. More Christmases came to mind. This time he was nine, living with his Aunt Winnie (they were never blood relations, but he liked to call them "aunt," "uncle," "cousin," if they allowed it). For Christmas she had given him a little pet hamster. He loved it because it was small and soft and furry and warm and absolutely his. Two days later he woke up and it was dead. He hadn't even named it yet. Charlie. Furry. Toby. He was still trying to decide. It was his fault. He wasn't sure why, but it was. It was the first thing he had ever really truly loved, and he'd killed it.

That night he had a dream. There was a noise, a rattling in the plastic bucket under the bathroom sink. He reached in, thinking it was Hamster. He grabbed—and screamed! Not Hamster, but a giant rat leaped onto his collarbone and bit him in the neck. Like a vampire.

Tom shut his eyes a painful moment, trying to clear the white fog in front of him. He tried to think of other things: the missing persons bulletin. He had been tempted to call church headquarters to see if he could find out who had placed him on the bulletin, but ... why borrow trouble? No news was good news.

A third of the way up the mesa, in the proverbial middle-of-nowhere, he saw off to his right a tiny nest of colored lights, like a multicolored constellation. You just can't escape it, he thought, not even out here. Then he felt ashamed of his feelings as he turned down a side road and made a silent confession: he didn't like Christmas. Every year, privately, he wished he could drop a black cloth over it. In his head he knew better: Christmas. The birth of Christ—Lord, Savior and Redeemer of the World. The Prince of Peace. But he couldn't feel the occasion, couldn't feel the music or the good cheer. He wasn't a Scrooge about it; he always put on a happy face and taught his students some carols and encouraged them to decorate their little classroom tree. But he was always glad when it was finally over—yet saddened too.

The pickup squirmed and squiggled down the mushy side road leading to Louise Yazzie's shack. The snow had graciously covered the splintered dwelling with a fresh white coat. Chicken wire covered the lone window. A slender little woman with beautiful almond eyes answered the door. A few threads of gray lined her shiny black hair, which was tied in a traditional Navajo bun.

"*Ya'at'eeh, shimayazhi,*" Tom said, offering his hand. Hello, my auntie. They touched palms, Navajo-style. "I'm looking for Loretta Yellowhair. Do you know where I can find her?"

Louise's lithe frame blocked the narrow doorway. Two little girls poked their black-braided heads around either side of her pleated skirt and giggled.

"No," she said. Short and bittersweet. Although Tom had visited Louise on several occasions, she always treated him like a total stranger. Why did he always have to play these stupid games? He wearied of them. He wearied of frantic foster parents. He wearied of everything. But he knew the rules. Fight fire with fire, ice with ice. He waited, stubbornly.

"She's up on the mesa, I think," Louise said. "I don't think you can get up there tonight."

"I need to talk to her about Placement," Tom said coolly.

Placement! It was like saying *abracadabra*! Suddenly Louise became cooperative.

"Yes, I think she wants to go on the Placement. I think she's at my brother's house. I'll tell him you came by."

"I need to talk to Loretta tonight," Tom said. "I need to interview her. She has to be in Phoenix by Tuesday."

"Tuesday?"

"Yes, Tuesday."

"I can go up there and tell her, I guess."

"Maybe I could follow you over … since I need to interview her."

Louise didn't like that idea. Tom posed what he knew would be a more agreeable option. "Or I could just drive there myself—if you can tell me where to go."

"Okay," she said, "why don't you just drive over there yourself? It's Sam Bizaholoni. Just follow the road. You'll see a trailer. There's a camper shell out front."

"Okay, I'll try there. I'll drive to the top of the mesa if I have to."

"Well, she might be on the mesa. Or she might be in Sheep Springs, at her mother's. Last weekend she went to Sheep Springs. Her mother lives there."

A needle in six haystacks.

"Thank you," Tom said. "*Ahehee.*"

"*Aoo',*" she said. And then she reminded him of what night it was. "*Ya'at'eeh Keshmish!*"

Tom flushed, embarrassed. Of course. "Merry Christmas to you, too."

He continued up the mesa, the pickup crawling stubbornly through the mud-and-snow mix. The sky continued falling, swiftly and steadily. The road before him was paved perfectly white; behind, it was a black-and-white smear, like a child's chocolate fingerpainting, or the tracks of a drunken skier. Scrub pines hunkered on the rock ledges like Cro-Magnon hunters in polar bear skins. Lying in wait, it seemed.

Again, he tried to visualize Loretta Yellowhair. Instead he saw the ghost of Celeste Bighorse: small, slender, doe-eyed. A heartbreaking, dimpled little smile. Glossy cheeks, glossy black hair in a ponytail that dropped past her waist like a long velvet cord. She must have had a crush on him from the very beginning, because she would always stay after class, just sit there with her mahogany hands clasped on her wooden desk until he would finally ask, "Celeste, would you like to erase the blackboard?" And she would dip her chin shyly and smile—those sweet little dimples! Kathy's smile in miniature. And she had a gift—she could draw horses that leaped right off the page. Every day after school he would help her with her sketches.

She liked it; she liked him. Then one day he told her she had a great future if … No. Not that. Something terrible had been misconstrued, hopelessly lost in translation. He had never ever ever … except for maybe an encouraging hand on her shoulder. No! No! Her *shoulder*, just her shoulder. Like this—see? Just like this. But she was an early bloomer, a sixth grader with incipient breasts, and he was—well, he was white, and he was alone. And no white man chose to live alone out there. No normal white man. There was talk. Celeste was having bad dreams, her mother said. And she was a big intimidating woman who wore sunglasses and stretch pants and had her hair permed in Albuquerque. "You *bilagaanas* think you can come out here and get away with anything!" She went to a crystal gazer who intimated Tom, then took Celeste out of school for two weeks to have a *yeibichei* ceremony performed over her. Hosteen said Gladys Bighorse had a bug up her rear end, but it was only the protests of Sister Watchman that had saved his job. After that he had always walked on eggshells, careful to avoid even the appearance of idiosyncrasy. He had kept a safe, professional distance from everyone—students, teachers, men, women, missionaries. It was a lonely life. Safe, but lonely.

Celeste graduated from the elementary school that June. She was supposed to go on Placement, but after the incident her mother had withdrawn her application. So little Celeste had left for the boarding school in August, young, pretty, talented. Three years later she had returned for summer break a mini mom.

Tom found the trailer with the camper shell in front. He left the truck running. No colored lights here: the power lines stopped at Louise Yazzie's place. A paunchy man with oily black hair met him at the door.

"Are you Sam Bizaholoni?"

He eyed Tom suspiciously. "Why?"

"I'm looking for Loretta Yellowhair. She wants to go on Placement. Louise said you might know where she is."

His face scrunched up like a sponge. "Louise?"

"Your sister. Do you have a sister named Louise?"

He smiled. Tom counted three teeth in his impoverished mouth. "She's not here," he said, shaking his head. He was barefoot in baggy pajama-like pants. Tom relished the heat wafting out from the woodstove. He could hear children laughing and a woman's voice. She was singing "Jingle Bells" in Navajo. Tom thought it should make him feel happy, but instead it was a rusty nail scratching more sad graffiti on his heart. He heard phantom voices, phantom laughter. "She's not here," Sam said. "I think she's on the mesa."

"Or in Sheep Springs, maybe?" Tom muttered under his breath.

"What?" He was clever, playing the dumb Indian. "Did you say Sheep Springs? No, I don't think she's in Sheep Springs." He chuckled indulgently. "No, she's up on the mesa." Sam poked his head outside. "Brrrr! Wouldn't go up there tonight. Nas-teee!"

"Can you tell me where to go? It's important. I need to interview her for Placement."

The magic word again! Tonight it seemed to hold more hope, more promise even than the word "Christmas."

"Sure!" he said, flashing his three-fanged smile. "Just follow the road. You go past the cattle guard, the third cattle guard, I think. There's a great big rock; it looks like a whale, kinda." Then he laughed in that inimitable way of the Navajo. "You can't miss it!"

"Thanks. *Ahehee.*"

"*Aoo',*" he said. "*Ya'at'eeh Keshmish!*"

Tom had to smile. Sam reminded him a little of Hosteen, that same wry humor. But then he was overcome by an old despair. It was not Christmas this time, but close enough. Winter. White. Cold. Icicles hanging like six-foot fangs. He had made a rare trip into Farmington to buy supplies. He still wondered what spirit had prompted him to check into a Motel 6, and for not just one night but two? When he returned late Saturday evening, they said the old man was *ádin*—it didn't mean "dead" exactly, but gone, not existing. He had died in his sleep, and *chindi*—his ghost spirit—had claimed the hogan, forcing his brittle old wife and two daughters to vacate. The only white man in the village, Tom routinely prepared and buried their dead; the Navajo wanted no contact with *chindi*. In his absence, though, they might have simply burned the hogan down— they had done that before. Instead, they had wisely waited three days for his return so he could remove his friend's body and prepare it for proper burial, meaning a "proper Christian burial." They had realized that he too had lines that couldn't be crossed, although Tom had always tried to respect their beliefs and traditions. "We know you don't believe," Hosteen had once said, "but at least you try and understand. You don't laugh behind your sleeve like the others." Tom had wondered what Hosteen had really meant by that, "the others?"

Although in his head Tom knew better, something still whispered that it had been partly his fault; that if he had not gone to town that day and stayed so long, Hosteen would still be alive. He also knew his logic made as little sense as their fear of Hosteen's ghost, but ... one man's superstitions were another man's religion. He had learned that much.

Tom was glad to get out of the blowing cold and back into the lukewarm cab. His feet were numb from just that short stint outside. Ice had crusted on the windshield, infringing on the easy sweep of the wiper blades and cataracting all but two hemispheres on the glass. He glared at the eternal snow. *This is crazy; this is stupid. Why am I doing it?*

For Loretta, he thought, or tried to convince himself. For God. *Inasmuch as ye have done it unto the least of these ... Okay, for me, then. Me. And how so me?*

The tires spun and the rear end wriggled as the truck struggled up the slick road. Although he couldn't see beyond the hood, he could feel the road growing steeper and narrower. The snowfall thickened; it was pouring down like sugar through a giant sifter. Far to the right he saw a tiny light shining in the white commotion. It was a dark-horse chance, but he decided to take it: anything beat driving to the top tonight.

He left his truck parked in the road, the emergency flashers spitting blood onto the snow, and plodded several hundred yards until arriving at a homestead: a couple of shacks, a hogan, a corral, an outhouse. Padded with snow, they looked artificial, like stage props or pieces in a diorama. He wondered what he must look like, laden with snow—a ghost maybe, or the Abominable Snowman.

As he headed for the lighted hogan, three mutts sprang out from under a plywood lean-to, snarling and barking. He cooled them off with a couple snowballs. A stocky woman answered the door, remarkably indifferent, Tom thought, as if this were nothing out of the ordinary, a white man appearing at her door in a blizzard on Christmas Eve. She looked about forty-five. A green velveteen blouse covered her broad shoulders and torso, and a pleated skirt dropped to the middle of her pillar-like calves. She had big, bulgy cheeks, as if she were hoarding walnuts in them, and the part down the middle of her gray-streaked hair appeared to be widening, as if from some peculiar erosion. "*Woshdee*," she said at length, and he stepped inside, ducking his head a bit.

It was a large hogan with a dirt floor. The smell of fried potatoes and mutton tortured his empty belly. Instinctively he gravitated towards the woodstove whose sweet heat seemed to reach out and grip his frostbitten parts, pinching them painfully, wonderfully. The stovepipe soared through the square smoke hole in the ceiling like a fat periscope. He noted the coats and cowboy hats hanging on nails along the north wall. A Mexican felt painting featuring wild stallions on the run, family photographs, and certificates of school achievement covered the other walls. Three youngsters were cuddled together like bear cubs on sheepskins beside a small piñon tree, laced with strings of popcorn. Little wrapped gifts were piled around the wooden stand, and the ochre hand of a sleeping boy rested upon one of them as if he were prematurely claiming it. The tinfoil star on top of the tree reflected the stingy light from the kerosene lamp on a wooden table where a skinny old woman was kneading a mound of dough. An old fellow with a face as deeply seamed as a cassava melon sat cross-legged nearby the children, keeping vigil. He wore a black felt hat with a flat brim and a silver band, reminiscent of Hosteen's. A young mother in T-shirt and blue jeans was casually breastfeeding her baby. On the other side of the hogan sat two middle-aged men, one big and round, the other austerely cut, with the high, chiseled cheekbones of a warrior. He was wearing a red headband around his silver hair, and his dark eyes were fixed on Tom like bullets waiting to be fired. Tom wondered if this was the old coot to whom Loretta had been promised. If so, he looked quite formidable: a Navajo Clint Eastwood.

The heat was suffocating. Tom quickly regained the feeling in his hands and feet. As much as he wanted to doff his suede coat, he didn't want to send the wrong message. This would be a short visit.

The matron spoke first, surprising him. "She's out there," she said, motioning towards the door. Tom was confused. She? Loretta?

"Last night," she explained, "in my sleep, a man in white came and took her away. He said don't worry. She'll be all right. He said she's coming with me. That's how come I knew you were coming."

Tom felt a tingling warmth. He looked at his sleeve: most of the snow coating him had either melted or dropped to the floor, but it had made the point. This was going to be easier than he had thought.

"I need to see Loretta," he said. "Loretta Yellowhair."

"Loretta?" Now the matron looked confused. Tom wasn't sure how to interpret her colossal disappointment.

"Are you her aunt?"

She shook her head. "Loretta's not here. She's on the mesa."

"On the mesa?"

She nodded solemnly. "*Aoo'*."

Tom gazed up through the smoke hole at the wild flurry of snowflakes. They were insects flying too close to a fire, or falling stars melting by myriads. They wanted in, it seemed, but the instant they came too close to the invisible heat—poof! Oblivion. They were the opposite of those white butterflies caught inside the cone of light. Or were they brothers? Cousins maybe? Tom looked at the sleeping children by the tree and thought that maybe he wanted to sit down. Maybe he wanted to stay awhile. He didn't want to leave, he knew that.

"*Ahehee*," he said, and he could feel their eyes upon him as he trudged back into the snow.

An hour later he curved around the great whale-shaped rock only to find himself facing a meadow of knee-deep snow. He pushed in the clutch and jerked the stick into reverse. The gears whined as the truck struggled backwards fifty feet. He shoved the stick forward and bore down on the accelerator, gathering speed down the plowed stretch until the headlights slammed into the snowbank. It was like ramming into a tackling dummy: the snow gave a bit but then held firm. Smoke rose from the extinguished headlights. He backed up and took another running start. Again, the snowbank relented a few feet and then held fast. He tried again, gunning the engine full throttle. The snow gave a little more, but not much. This time he did not back up. He pressed the accelerator to the floor. Pinwheels of mud and ice flew past the side windows, black-and-white blurs, as the headlights burrowed deeper and deeper into the snow. He could smell the transmission cooking.

"Damn!" He slammed the cab door and checked in back: no shovel. He must have forgotten to put it back after clearing his walkway. "Dammit to hell!" He knew he shouldn't swear, but right now he didn't care. He didn't care about anything except getting his damn truck out of the damn muck. He glared at the falling snow as if some invisible nemesis were hiding behind it, or within it. He felt like yelling at it, challenging: Come out and show yourself! Come out and fight me face to face! He threw himself on his knees by the front tires and began scooping out the snow with his bare hands—madly, angrily. The cold nibbled piranha-like through his fingers and his legs from the knees down. At first he was too angry to feel any pain, but after a while, each time he plunged his hands into the mud it was like sticking them in a fire, or into the jaws of a wolf to be briefly masticated. He buried them over and over, until they were gone, and it was just his arms, sticks with floppy pads on the ends, which he kept stabbing into the snow, muttering and cursing until tears leaked from his eyes—tears of anger and frustration and a pain that cut much deeper than this simple calculable cold; an anger and frustration that had nothing to do with his impossible quest to find Loretta Yellowhair.

He dug; he scooped; he swore—angrily, fanatically. Insanely.

The snow kept falling, relentlessly, invidiously, like a great white plague, like locusts attacking his precious crops. He stood up and waved his arms wildly to chase them away. He felt utterly helpless, like a blindfolded kid trying to break the piñata but his older brother keeps yanking it impossibly out of reach. Turning full circle, he saw nothing but the white madness. Distress? Who was in distress? That seventeen-year-old kid? Distress! He could tell you all about it! He wondered bitterly if anyone was braving the storm to visit *him* tonight? He whirled around and roared at the omnipresent snow: "Where the hell's *my* shepherd? Who the hell's going to rescue *me*?" So this was his reward! This was his fate, his destiny! His stinking, rotten, lousy, miserable thanks! "Your vessel, your lonely, solitary vessel, and what do I get? Shat on, spat on! Well, to hell with them! To hell with you!"

Then he repented. Sort of. He thought the real Jesus would understand his momentary craziness under duress. The real Jesus would accept his intentional lack of Christmas fanfare. The real Jesus wouldn't be dumb enough to be born in the dead of winter, either. In a stable, yes. In rags, sure. Winter? Never. The real Jesus would know better. He'd understand about Hosteen and Kathy and Celeste Bighorse and the missing persons bulletin and Loretta Yellowhair and all the rest. Didn't care about colored lights and tinsel. Wasn't sitting by a fireplace opening gifts and getting fat on rice pudding. The real Jesus was probably slouching on a snowy street corner waiting (wondering? hoping?) for some true-blue disciple to invite him in out of the cold. To heat him up a can of soup and make him a ham on rye. Wherein saw ye me a stranger? Naked and clothed me? Hungry and fed me? Wherein? Where out? Where?

He tried to reassure himself. The time his appendix ruptured and Hosteen drove him to the hospital in Gallup. According to the nurse, the old man had sat by his bed all night in ICU singing ceremonial healing chants. Later Hosteen had brought him a Louis L'Amour paperback—Tom hated Louis L'Amour, but the thought—the thought! When he asked about the healing chants, the corners of the old man's mouth curled in a familiar way: "Hell, I was just singing a bunch of old squaw dance songs—just a lot of Indian mumbo jumbo. It's the only way they let me stay in that crazy place with you all night."

Hosteen! Five years later he was dead. *Ádin*. Removing his body from the hogan, Tom had been startled by its lightness. Hosteen was tiny anyway, but minus his spirit it was like lifting a large piece of balsa wood. Carefully, lovingly, Tom had prepared the corpse for burial, wrestling the purple tunic of velveteen over his stiff little doll-like body, the silver concho belt around his narrow waist. At one point, Tom's fingers had searched the old man's face, reading the deep corrugations there. Each wrinkle was a lifeline, an arroyo, a timeless impression in the land Hosteen and his forefathers had claimed by blood and birthright. At that moment, Tom had never felt so lonely and displaced, so totally outside the pale. He had wept, and through his tears he had watched the old man's face grow smooth and soft, youthful, but thin as air—like a full-color shadow or a reflection on water. Tom thought if he had pressed down, his hand would have punched right through it. Instead, he held up his own palm like a hand mirror only to see his face in similar form: soft, smooth, youthful—a shadow. He made a fist, and it had all disappeared.

Later, as he was delivering the eulogy in English, a small miracle had occurred. Halfway through, he noticed that everyone was glaring at him in collective disbelief, several heads nodding, others shaking. He glanced at his interpreter, Sister Watchman's son. What? What? Had he stuck his big fat foot in his *bilagaana* mouth again? Had he violated some unpardonable Navajo taboo? No, Herbert's expression said, his gritty little smile shining beneath his black mustache. Just keep on talking. You don't need me today.

Tom had gazed down at the crowd of wrinkled faces, head-banded and cowboy-hatted men, silver-haired women, packed in rows of folding chairs beneath the red and white-striped revival tent, all nodding, nodding, nodding. Later he would not remember any of it, only that it was like a beautiful gold scroll rolling out of his head, and all he'd had to do was read it. He couldn't recall any of the symbols—they were runes, hieroglyphics, hapless kid scribble—yet at the time they had made perfect sense to him, to them.

Tom glared at the falling sky as if it were attacking him personally. His teeth were chattering and his shoulders shaking. What was he trying to prove? What was he doing here? Boredom, duty, curiosity. No no no! He clenched his teeth and plunged his frozen paws deeper into the icy mud.

Then a thought: Sticks! Branches! He got up and staggered through the knee-deep snow, flailing his arms like a blind man on the run, until he smacked into a dead piñon tree whose brittle branches he began attacking with kung fu kicks and karate chops. Using his numb arms like giant tweezers, he carried the broken branches to his truck and laid them in two narrow trails behind his rear tires. But when he looked back, he saw the snow was smothering the sticks faster than he could spread them.

He crawled back into the cab. Most of the interior heat had dissipated, but it was a relief just to get out of the blowing cold. He could feel the voodoo pins piercing him all over. He closed his eyes and whispered: "Dear God, please get me unstuck." But it had been so long since he had prayed sincerely, beyond the Sunday rote to appease his little flock, that he now felt ashamed for waiting until his moment of despair to finally cry out. Or was he admitting something else? Confessing even more: not just that I don't like; I hate. Who? What? Wherein? Where out?

He tried to turn on the ignition, but his hands were gone. It was like trying to thread a needle wearing boxing gloves. He swore, he laughed, and then he stuffed his hands down his pants, between his legs, and waited as his body warmth slowly carved out of the two cold clods fingers, knuckles, creases, veins. He tried again. The starter whirred, the engine grabbed, the wheels churned, and he went nowhere.

"Dammit all!" He slammed the door again. His whole frame was shaking now, and for the first time he thought he might be in genuine danger. He thought he ought to start a fire, but he had no matches, no lighter. And even if he did—how, with these worthless hands? Idiot! Stooge! Moron! Had he set himself up for this or what? He knew better—he knew! Suppose he couldn't get out now and the snow kept falling? He looked around to get his bearings and saw nothing but a white blur. His truck was gone; its tracks were covered. He was next. He imagined the snow building, rising like flood waters: it was at his knees, his waist, his chest, his neck. He was under. Buried. Gone. *Ádin.* He imagined his body stiff at attention, like an arctic sentry, frozen on duty. Who would know until the spring thaw? And who would care? Nashdoi maybe? Would his cat even notice, as long as someone—anyone—filled his plastic bowl with table scraps? And who would feed old Nashdoi? Who would come looking? Sister Watchman perhaps?

He wondered about his spirit passing through the veil. His mother and father had disclaimed him in life, would they do likewise in death? How would Kathy receive him? With open, loving arms? Had he fought the good fight? Or would she turn her head in shame, embarrassed by the way he had squandered his life, his whole damn life, among these people? Oh, he had married them and buried them, had taught their children to read and write, had wiped their runny little noses on cold winter mornings. But would she embrace him for that, or merely out of marital duty? Or deny him altogether? Would she too condemn him for Celeste Bighorse? Or had she died for his sins? Then where was the real Man in White? Where was the real Jesus? Or was he the white veil with a zillion fluttering parts, waiting to smack or lovingly smother you?

Then another possibility came to mind: suppose the Mormons were wrong, the Navajos right? Suppose the hereafter was a nebulous netherworld, an eternity of falling snow?

Tom calmly sat down and waited as the cold consumed him cell by cell. It had taken his legs and belly, and it was moving into his chest now. Soon it was a blanket covering him with motherly warmth. He lay back, closed his eyes, and succumbed at last to the Christmas memory he had been trying to evade all night: their first Christmas Eve together as man and wife, their first on the rez. They were still strangers in the village. She was eight-months pregnant, very vulnerable, atypically weepy. Sitting in their dark little kitchen staring glumly at the scrub pine he had cut down and which she had dressed with her construction paper decorations, he did something very stupid. He made a little joke: "How about some eggnog?" And right there her spirit snapped. He thought he could actually hear it.

"Eggnog? *Eggnog?* Very funny! What eggnog? What anything in this lousy rotten hellhole? Drunks and dead dogs, that's all you ever see. Eggnog? All anyone ever wants around here is a big fat handout! They come to church for handouts, they come to the school for handouts! If they're so broke, how come everyone's driving a new pickup? *We* can't even afford a tune-up for our lousy rotten VW Rabbit! And these people act like you owe it to them. They look at you with their hatchet faces: gimme gimme gimme gimme. I'm sick of it, Tom! I'm fed up! Every time it rains or snows, this place turns into a mud swamp. And if it's not the rain, it's the damn wind blowing so thick you can't see your nose in front of your face. I hate it, Tom! The water's orange. God knows what creepy critters inhabit that stuff. And this lousy, rotten trailer. We freeze all winter, fry all summer. I'm sick of it. There's no one—absolutely no one—here for me to even talk to. You go to work, sure, to your little rock schoolhouse where you're treated like the Great White God, but I'm stuck here in this tin can. Stuck! No telephone, no TV. I carry water in a bucket. I practically cook over an open fire. I hate it! I'm not a damned pioneer. I said whither thou goest, but this is the end of the road for me! I mean it, Tom. This is it! My father was right: you're a loser and you'll always be a loser! Misery's your middle name!"

Later she apologized: "This volleyball in my belly. It does weird things to you. It really messes up your mind." But when he told her to forget it, he understood, she unleashed again: "How could *you* understand? You had nothing to lose; I had everything!" And then fled into the bedroom and slammed the door: "Merry Christmas!"

It was close to midnight when he was awakened by a knock. He had fallen asleep on their ragged couch. It was Rose Tsinijinnie, the school secretary. A tall, slender cowgirl, she was out of breath. "Come to the school," she panted. "Hurry!" And ran off.

Tom put on his snow boots and coat and trudged over to the rock schoolhouse. Rose met him at the door. "Where's your wife?"

"My wife? You didn't say anything about—"

"Go get your wife!" she ordered. Then laughed in that delightful way of Navajo women. "Go get your wife or we'll have to find you one!"

271

He trudged back to the trailer and begged her to come.

"I was almost asleep."

"We can't say no. You know how they are."

Grumbling, she threw on a maternity smock, boots, and a coat. "I feel like an Eskimo," she muttered.

"A very beautiful one," he said.

"Don't placate me."

"Okay, ugly as an Eskimo. Fat as an Eskimo. Ornery as an Eskimo. Snotty as an—"

"All right, all right. I get the picture."

When they arrived at the schoolhouse, the lights were out, and Rose was gone.

"Swell," Kathy muttered.

They were wet, cold, and the snow was falling. As they turned back towards the trailer, Rose appeared around the corner, waving them to the side door. "Hey! Psst! Come on!"

When they stepped inside, the lights came on. And the most incredible thing: the whole community was there—parents, students, babies in cradleboards, grandpas in cowboy hats, grandmas in pleated skirts. Two-hundred-plus crammed into that little room, and they were all smiling while the children sang "We Wish You a Merry Christmas," which Tom had taught them the week before in school. There was a pine tree in the corner with presents piled up underneath—baby clothes, boxes of disposable diapers, Navajo rugs, turquoise jewelry, a cradleboard of varnished cedarwood. He and Kathy stood there, stunned, silent, weeping.

Afterwards they trudged through the mud and snow back to their dingy little trailer with the foot-long cockroaches and the scrawny little Christmas tree, and they made the wildest, wickedest love they ever had. Tom remembered lying in bed afterwards, listening to the snow, like gentle fingers tapping on the glass. Her head was on his shoulder and she was stroking his chest as she whispered, "I'm so happy!" And at that moment so was he. It was the first time she had ever really said that. She had said "I love you" often enough, but never that. For the first time he really honestly truly thought they were going to make it.

A week later as they were driving home from a New Year's Day shopping spree in Gallup, he fell asleep at the wheel. When the VW Rabbit veered onto the shoulder, jerking him awake, he overcompensated, and the little car hit the gravelly shoulder and became a flying missile. And that was it: two in one blow. Why he had survived and not her still angered and puzzled him. Maybe God leaves behind the one with the roughest edges. (But he could hear her counter from the other side: "Don't placate me!") Besides, he knew better: he was doing penance.

Hosteen used to tell him it was bad luck to speak about dying or the dead: to even think the act would increase its likelihood of happening. Tom always wondered if there wasn't some truth to that, or if Kathy had just had a premonition. A month or so before, she had instructed him—no, ordered him was more accurate: "If anything ever happens to me, I want you to remarry!"

"But who would ever be stupid enough to marry the likes of me?" he had protested.

"I don't know. But look hard. You'll find some sweet little sucker. But just make sure you do! I don't want a horny husband meeting me on the other side of the veil! Understand, rubber band?"

He'd had no intention of staying. In fact, his plan was to leave immediately. Just go. But where? To whom? One year ran into two, two to three, and before he knew it, he was stuck there, stuck up to his axles. He was like the snowflakes swirling around in the cone of light: white butterflies trapped in glass.

He jackknifed to attention, brushing the snow from his body as if it were white vermin. The snow had stopped, and the skies had cleared, the stars twinkling like tiny ornaments. Moonlit, the snowscape glowed with a weird fluorescence. It was a glittering wasteland, cold, clean, beautifully barren. Radioactive. Out of this world. Tom closed his eyes and took a deep, cleansing breath. He saw a light shining at the foot of the white cliffs far ahead. As he trudged towards it, the snow started up again. The sky was perfectly clear, but flakes were falling, as if the whole Milky Way were fluttering down. Soon he was the man in white again. Hands, feet, legs, head. His body was numb, but his heart was on fire. He trudged: left foot, right foot, left foot.

It was a homestead almost identical to the one he had stopped at down the road—the corral, the outhouse, the shacks, the hogan. Three pair of eyes glowed orange underneath a plywood lean-to. The same matron answered the door. Clint Eastwood was there too, glaring at him, but sadly this time, as if his bullet eyes had prematurely misfired. The old woman was still kneading her dough, and her black-hatted mate was keeping watch over the children sleeping by the tree. The young mother turned away abruptly and pressed the swaddled infant against her chest.

This time the matron spoke sternly to him. "She's in *there*!" she said, and her finger steered his eye across the corral towards a little hogan on a hill. "This morning, we dug a hole for you. There's a pick and shovel too. Last night, in my sleep, a man in white came …"

And then he understood.

She belonged to the Salt Clan and was born in the year the cottonwoods greened early, which made her a little over 90 but under 100, and that was all he would know, all they would tell him. But as he trekked across the white field towards the hogan on the hill, all the rest would become perfectly clear. And he would wonder, since the year the cottonwoods had greened early, how many hundreds of sheep had she shorn, how many thousands of pieces of fry bread had she made, how many rugs had she woven, how many winters, snows, how many Christmases had passed? He tried to picture her in his mind. Instead, he saw the dimpled smile of Celeste Bighorse. He looked back only once, surprised to see the others watching on the far side of the corral: the bell-shaped matron, a young woman in a screaming-yellow windbreaker, and the sketchy silhouette of the old man as he touched his forefinger to the brim of his black felt hat, and with that simple gesture thanked him across the white eternities of the omnipresent snow.